ALSO BY SHILOH WALKER

SECRETS & SHADOWS SERIES

Deeper Than Need

Sweeter Than Sin

Darker Than Desire

SECRETS & SHADOWS E-NOVELLAS

Burn For Me

Break For Me

Long For Me

AVAILABLE BY ST. MARTIN'S PAPERBACKS

HEADED FOR TROUBLE

SHILOH WALKER

St. Martin's Paperbacks

This is a work of fiction. All of the characters, organizations, and events portrayed in this novel are either products of the author's imagination or are used fictitiously.

HEADED FOR TROUBLE

Copyright © 2016 by Shiloh Walker.
Excerpt from *The Trouble with Temptation* copyright © 2016 by Shiloh Walker.

For information address St. Martin's Press, 175 Fifth Avenue, New York, NY 10010.

ISBN: 978-1-250-06794-4

Printed in the United States of America

St. Martin's Paperbacks edition / January 2016

St. Martin's Paperbacks are published by St. Martin's Press, 175 Fifth Avenue, New York, NY 10010.

10 9 8 7 6 5 4 3 2 1

Dedicated, as always, with love to my family . . .
thank God for you. I love you all so much.

With lots of love to my readers out there.
You all are amazing.

A huge thank you to my editorial team at St. Martin's . . .
thanks for putting up with me.

ACKNOWLEDGMENTS

I spent a week in Scotland in 2014, not long after reading the story of Captain Kidd, so I guess I should acknowledge that amazing country, because the McKays came to me not long after my trip there and I'm not sure they'd be who they are without that trip. I found so much inspiration there . . . and I think I left a piece of my soul.

I need to say a special thank you to my son, C, for his help in selecting ultracool cars for the McKay clan. They do like their toys and not just any toy would do.

CHAPTER ONE

It had been on a Friday night when trouble blew out of town. To be precise, 9:14 P.M., the summer night air hot and hazy—once of the hottest summers to hit the area in a while, and the small Mississippi town of McKay's Treasure had seen more than its share of hot summers.

The entire town had seemed to hold its breath, waiting for a storm that had hovered and hovered.

The storm never came, and here, almost ten years later, trouble blew back into town in almost the same fashion she'd left.

It was 9:14 exactly when Neve McKay drove past the sign that read WELCOME TO McKAY'S TREASURE—AT THE HEART OF IT ALL.

It was hot and humid, and the night air was still, the promise of a thunderstorm hovering in the air.

She'd left driving a murder-red Koenigsegg—a sweet little car that her brother had bought her in exchange for good behavior, and to get her to stop pestering him to let her drive *his* car. The McKays were well known for liking their toys.

She came back driving a junker of indeterminate color, although the passenger door was white—clearly something that had come from another car, same make.

She still drove like a bat out of hell, though.

Neve McKay pulled her car up in front of the bar and shoved it into park. She climbed out, eyeing the place that had been called Treasure Island for as long as she'd been alive.

It had been an eyesore for that entire time.

Not so much now.

Somebody came out—no, several somebodies—but not in a cloud of smoke, something that Neve had always associated with the bar.

Eyes narrowed, she rocked back on the worn heels of her boots. She wore faded jeans that fit like a glove and a T-shirt that was worn thin in some places. The only thing she carried with her was a backpack that had seen better days.

Studying the building in front of her, she compared it to the memories she had from ten years ago. They didn't fit. Her eyes landed on the neon sign in the window. GUINNESS.

Well, the place had booze.

That was all that mattered.

She'd been craving a drink for the past three days, but she hadn't given in to the urge, had barely even allowed herself to sleep, for fear of dulling her senses. Getting caught off guard was one thing that absolutely would *not* happen.

Now that she was here, now that she was home, one of the bands around her chest eased.

Maybe there were another two or three—dozen— that kept her from breathing as deeply as she'd like. But despite the nerves she had about seeing her brother and sister for the first time in forever, she breathed easier.

Tipping her head back, she breathed in the air. She caught the scent of food that came from the nearby restaurants, but under that, it was the river she smelled, the lush green that grew around it.

Home.

Her throat clogged from the memories, and she blew out a breath. She'd let herself get all sentimental and stupid later. For now, though, she was going to have herself that damn beer and figure out her next step—decide if she was going to call her brother and sister right away, or wait until tomorrow.

Some frisson of nerves twisted inside her at the thought of trying to deal with the rift she'd caused in her family, but she'd deal with that when the time came. All of that was for later.

Tonight?

"Just a drink," she told herself.

And with that in mind, she started toward the door.

She had to take a minute to acclimate herself once she ducked inside.

The few glimpses she'd had inside the dive that had been Treasure Island didn't match up with what was before her now. The servers wore kilts, shorter lengths for the girls—although nothing that would make their mothers hide their eyes if they bent over—while the guys had a similar style that hit the knee.

She smirked, amused. So they were going for a Scottish theme? And still using the name Treasure Island? *Oooookkayyy.*

To each their own, she mused, as she wound her way through the crowd, ducking her head when somebody looked at her too long, averting her face when a person looked familiar.

She had to avert her face a *lot.*

Treasure wasn't a big town—the population at the last census was just under nine thousand. Her graduating class hadn't even topped two hundred. Just in the short walk from the door to the bar, she'd heard several familiar names and spotted people she hadn't seen in years.

But she hadn't seen the people who counted the most, and that was all that mattered.

As long as she could brace herself before she had to see them, then everything would be just fine and dandy.

Spying an empty seat, she slid onto it and looked up at the bar. She put her backpack on the little hook in front of her and shifted to keep it between her legs. She'd had people try to relieve her of her belongings more than once.

Breathing out a sigh of relief, she let herself relax. Now . . . for that drink—

"Well, 'allo. What can I get you?"

At the sound of that voice, a shiver raced down her spine, and a punch of heat—something she hadn't felt in far too long—spread through her, warming her from head to toe.

Ian Campbell had left Scotland for a couple of small reasons, and one rather big one. The small reasons were varied—he liked to try new things, he'd always wanted to run his own pub, and he'd never been one to turn down a chance at an adventure. Living in America for a time could definitely be that.

The rather big reason was simple.

Money.

He'd been offered a fat sum to come across the pond and run this pub, and if all went well, then he could even buy it. It had been a hard choice to make, he wouldn't lie.

More than once—once a week even—he wondered if he'd done the right thing, and considered going home. He could. He'd have to start over, but he wasn't afraid of hard work and he wasn't afraid to start over, either. He'd had to do that more than once in his life, that was certain.

But then he'd crawl out of bed, get himself a cup of coffee—or better yet, three. Ian Campbell wasn't a pleasant man without his first cup of coffee in the morning. Once he was awake, he'd go to his balcony and stare out over the river.

This place was thousands of miles from Braemar, the small village in Scotland where he'd lived for the first thirteen years of his life and just as different from the house where he'd lived after his mother died and he moved to Aviemore to live with his grandparents. He'd lived there from the time he was thirteen until he was eighteen, in a house where raised voices and flying fists had him desperate to leave, and even more desperate never to return.

Nobody here looked at him and whispered as he walked past.

True, it had been a long time since people had done that back home.

But he didn't see the looks in their eyes, and if he lifted a pint at the end of the day, he didn't have to wonder what they might think.

A clean slate, that was what he had here, and he couldn't help but appreciate it.

Perhaps he didn't like the heat that hit you like a sweaty fist for too much of the year, but any circumstance would have its drawbacks now, wouldn't it?

And . . . there were the benefits.

He found himself studying one now and felt a stir of interest he hadn't felt in more time than he cared to think about.

She stood in the doorway, oddly apart from everybody else even as she studied his pub, eyes moving to linger on a group here, then there. After a couple of moments she moved away, and he found himself tracking her progress.

Don't be here to meet somebody, he thought, and immediately, he wanted to kick himself. What did it matter if she was?

He told himself it didn't and glanced up as Gary Harnett settled down and ordered his usual. Ian started to build the Guinness as they chatted, but the entire time he watched her from the corner of his eye.

She moved like a dancer, with effortless grace and easy elegance. He could imagine those legs, long and slim, wrapped around his waist, could picture that torso, just as long and slim, bent back as he leaned over to press his mouth to pale, soft skin.

Gary said, "They say it's going to break a hundred again tomorrow."

"Imagine it will," Ian murmured, the easy chatter second nature, while in his mind, he continued to mentally undress the redhead.

She slid onto a vacant stool tucked up against the wall just as he finished Gary's Guinness, and Ian took a moment to appreciate the fact that he had a heavy, solid bar between the two of them, because, thanks to his wandering mind, his bloody cock was hard as iron and pulsing.

She looked at him then, her mouth unsmiling, but wide and soft and lush.

Fuck me.

He rested his hands on the bar and smiled. *You've a job to do, so do it.*

He opened his mouth.

You're the sexiest fucking thing I've seen in ages— maybe forever. He could feel those words hovering on the tip of his tongue.

Biting them back, he fell back on the job he'd been doing for ages.

"Well, 'allo. What can I get you?"

A faint smile flirted around her lips, and a hot ball

of lust twisted inside, settling down low in his balls. Mad. He'd gone mad—that's all there was to it.

She nodded toward the Guinness he'd just finished and said, "I'll have one of those."

He nodded. Self-preservation told him to move his arse and get to work.

He told self-preservation to get fucked as he got to work on her Guinness. As he did, four more orders came in, and he filled three of them before her Guinness was ready. By the time he had another minute to breathe, she had folded her hands around her glass and was studying everything around her, almost mesmerized.

"Visiting?"

She blinked, a startled look in her eyes. Her gaze slid away. "Depends on your point of view." Then she flashed him a wide smile.

It was disarming, that smile, bright and wicked, the kind of smile a temptress would give a saint to lure him into all manner of sins.

Ian was many things—a saint had never been one of them. As she propped her elbows on the bar, he found himself easing closer. "I'm here for . . . personal things, but that's for later," she said, lifting her shoulder in a shrug. "Tonight . . . ? Tonight I'm just trying to not think."

I can help you with that.

The words popped into his brain and they almost escaped his lips.

He managed to keep them trapped inside, but one thing he couldn't do was keep his eyes off that mouth.

She noticed, too. He could tell by the hitch in her breathing, the way her pulse slammed against the fragile wall of her throat. Curious, he reached out and pressed a finger against it.

He could very well be doing the stupidest thing he'd ever done.

Her lids drooped and her head slumped, angling slightly to the side. He skimmed his finger down lower, tracing the elegant line of her collarbone. "I've had days like that," he said softly. "Days where the last place I want to be is inside my own head."

He lowered his hand.

She lifted her head and met his gaze dead-on.

He started to turn away.

"How late do you work?"

Neve couldn't have been more appalled with herself if she'd climbed up on the bar and stripped herself naked.

Blood rushed up to scald her cheeks, and she was already trying to mentally calculate how much her drink would be. She had a twenty dollar bill tucked inside her pocket. She'd just leave the whole thing—

His hand closed over hers, and then he bent over the bar.

He was big.

She'd already noticed that.

Big and almost brutally beautiful. If she had guessed right, he was close to six five, and his shoulders strained the snug fit of his T-shirt. His hair was dark, possibly black, but it was hard to tell in the dim light of the pub. His eyes were arresting—a pale, lovely gray that reminded her of the mists that slid around the ground, winding through trees, clinging to the river of a morning.

They gleamed against the warm gold of his skin and seemed to glow now. Then there was the beard.

Neve had never been attracted to a man with a beard. At least not until that very moment.

But this man with his short beard and that beautiful

mouth—she suspected he could make her go for just about anything.

That beautiful mouth, framed by his dark beard, parted on his harsh intake of breath.

Her heart knocked hard against her ribs.

She had to drag her gaze away, but as she went to fumble the cash out of her pocket, his hand slid up her arm, leaving a hot, burning trail. "Another thirty minutes . . . if you're up to waiting for me."

Say no.

Get up.

Walk away.

Do something!

The logical part of her mind screamed at her.

Instead, she found herself meeting his gaze once more. As he turned away, she reached for her drink and downed a healthy swallow. Maybe it was for courage.

Or maybe it was to cool the suddenly blistering heat that had washed over her.

She'd done gone and lost her mind, Neve was sure of it.

Ian had been propositioned before.

It had even happened here.

But what had happened between him and the sleek, sexy redhead was something that defied definition. The final thirty minutes passed by in a crawl, and when he was done, he had to make himself *walk* with her through the pub, not drag her. Leading her through the crowd, he paused by the office to collect his keys.

A few people slid her curious glances, but her gaze moved away. Her sleek hair fell to shield her face. That just made him think about fisting his hands in it, then covering her mouth with hot, hungry kisses until she moaned and opened for him—opened for him in every way imaginable.

The noise of the pub muted as he shut the back door, and he looked down at her, half expecting her to take off, to disappear into the night like the fantasy he thought she must be.

Her gaze came back to his, and a groan started deep inside his chest as she licked her lips.

He couldn't stop himself from reaching for her, and she didn't seem inclined to stop him, either. No, she actually reached for him, and he half turned, putting her back against the wall as he reached up to frame her face. It wasn't a good fit, and he caught the straps of her backpack and tried to push it off her shoulders. She let him take it off, but kept it hanging from the other arm.

Good enough for him.

Now, staring down at her, it hit him—the punch of lust unlike anything he'd felt in a long while. Maybe ever.

The first brush of their mouths created a connection that hit straight through him.

Ian shuddered and lifted his head, stared down at her.

She blinked, a dazed look in her eyes.

He had to do that again.

Reaching up, he cupped her cheek in his hand and angled her head back, lowering his mouth back to hers.

Slower this time, because he wasn't quite sure he'd felt what he'd felt.

Wasn't quite sure it was possible for such a brief kiss to ripple all the way through him, like a rock thrown into a pond.

Her mouth parted and he groaned against her lips, wrapping his forearm around her waist, pulling her closer. The bloody bag got in the way again, bumping against him. She curled one arm around his neck and pressed even closer, until he felt every last delicate curve, the slight swells of her breasts, the long lines of her torso, her thighs—

A burst of laughter echoed close by—too close.

Snarling, he tore his mouth away, heart pounding.

Staring into wide, hazy green eyes, he sucked in a desperate breath of air.

She licked her lips again, a soft hum in her throat, and he swore. "Don't," he warned, dipping his head and biting her lower lip. "Don't go doin' that or I'm going to lose it right here."

The laughter came again, even closer, and he looked around. Grabbing her hand, he started to walk.

It wasn't thirty seconds before he had the wooden gate shut behind him. The small garden was something he'd snorted at when he'd been given the apartment, but he'd come to appreciate it, and never more than in that moment.

Flipping the latch, he turned and pushed her gently back against the gate. He caught the bag she still carried and tugged it free. "My flat. You can let this go for a bit, love."

She still held on, then reluctantly uncurled her fingers from it.

He put the backpack on the stones next to them and then reached up, hooking his hands over the top of the gate, caging her in. "If I was one to believe in such things, I'd swear you'd gone and bewitched me."

She laughed, the sound shaky. "Ain't that just like a man . . . blaming the woman?"

"Oh . . ." He moved a hand from the fence, trailing it down the sensitive inner skin of her arm, watching as she shivered. "I'm not blaming you, love. I'm *thanking* you. You're already turning my brain into jelly, and I haven't done much more than kiss you."

He touched his lips to her neck. "I want to do much, much more—wanted it even when I saw you standing in the door of me pub."

That accent of his was going to do her in. Neve had always had a thing for Scots—with a name like McKay and the history her family had, who could blame her? His brogue, though, was pure sin.

She reached out, skimming her hands down the snug cotton of his shirt.

It fit like a second skin, right down to the waistband of the kilt he wore. It wasn't the same style as the ones everybody else had worn—it was a simple, utilitarian khaki. But the T-shirt had the logo of the pub on it, including the tartan that matched the kilts the servers had worn.

"I've been to Scotland," she murmured, turning her head to meet his eyes. "Do you know . . . I can count on one hand how many times I saw a man wearing a kilt while I was there."

A grin split his face. "Is that a fact?" He leaned in and nuzzled her neck.

It sent shivers of sensation running through her. She angled her head, whimpering in satisfaction when he followed her cue and raked his teeth down her skin.

"It's a fact," she agreed. Her breaths sounded ragged even to her own ears. "Since none of them looked as good in one as you do, I've decided not to smirk over the fact that you're wearing one in a pub called Treasure Island."

He laughed, the sound low and husky. "It's a terrible name for a pub, Scottish or no. And I'll thank you for not laughing." He caught her earlobe, bit lightly. "I don't think my pride could handle it."

He rocked against her as he said it, and a wave of want swamped her.

His *pride* throbbed against her. She had to wonder if *she* could handle it.

He slid a hand down her side, toyed with the hem of her shirt. "Since we're in a sharing mood, can I tell that when I first saw you, I thought you had to be the sexiest fucking woman I've seen in a long while—maybe ever?" he murmured as he slid his hand under the hem of her shirt.

Neve barely heard him.

The feel of his palm, rough and strong, sent a shiver through her. She dug her nails into his skin and arched against him.

A harsh noise ripped out of him, and he slid his hand lower, caught her hip, tugged her tighter.

When he rocked against her, hard and fast, the hunger stabbed into her. She curled a leg around his hip and he swore, boosted her up. The wood of the gate scraped against her back. She didn't care.

Everything centered on the fact that he was now rocking against her, and the worn fabric of her jeans, the silk of her panties, and the material of his kilt seemed a terrible annoyance.

Sensation slammed into her.

She gasped as her muscles clenched, the need drawing tighter and tighter—

And then it stopped.

Her feet settled on the ground and she slammed out a hand to steady herself.

He was talking and the words made no sense.

None at all.

Her eyes were blind.

Ian clasped her skull in his hands and sucked in oxygen. He felt like he'd run a bloody race.

His cock pulsed, and what he wanted more than anything was to strip her jeans down and drive into her.

He'd almost done it, too.

"Fuck, do you have a bloody condom?" he asked again, rasping the words out. He was so hard he hurt with it, and if he didn't get inside her . . .

She moaned again, rolling her hips against him.

The feverish sound had him kissing her again. That taste—he didn't think he'd ever have enough. Did addiction happen that fast?

Trailing a hand down the middle of her torso, he freed the button of her snug jeans, slid his hand inside, passed the barrier of panties almost as silky soft as her skin. "Tell me you have a condom," he demanded against her mouth as he slid his fingers through curls already wet.

He trailed his finger around the firm bud of her clit. She gasped.

"Please . . ."

The broken moan set his balls to burning and he thought he'd die if he didn't get inside her, and soon.

But . . .

Well, the sound of her whimpering under his touch was the sweetest kind of music.

He stroked her again, following the cues of her body until he found the right rhythm.

She rose to meet him, her head turning toward him. He caught her mouth just as he pushed one finger inside her. She jerked—

And he felt his own cock jerk, felt the first few drops of precum seeping through when she climaxed, hard and fast. Just like that.

Snarling, he pumped his fingers faster, his movements constrained by the jeans still snug around her hips, but she whimpered and rocked, riding the climax, riding *him*—

Just not the way he bloody wanted.

"That's it," he growled against her mouth. "Ride me . . . that's it . . ."

She whimpered, the sound broken now, almost stunned.

He eased her down, slowly, because when he took her back up the next time, she was going to be wrapped around his dick.

Slowly, he withdrew his hand.

Feeling her eyes on him, he lifted his hand to his lips and licked his fingers.

She blushed, staring at his hand as if mesmerized.

"Ah . . ." She blinked and looked around.

He cut off the question with a hard kiss. "Tell me you have a condom with you."

Shit.

Neve blinked up at him. "Um . . . no?"

He squinted at her, as if the word made no sense.

Then he backed it up.

"What d' you mean . . . *no*?" he asked, dumbfounded.

"Just that. *No*." Her fingers hurt. The reason why became apparent. She was practically trying to imprint them on the ridged track that made up the sexy Scot's torso. Uncurling them, she looked around. Embarrassment would probably settle in later. But for now, all she wanted was a damn condom.

Blushing furiously, she stared at him. "I don't typically pick guys up in bars. I never really have a need to carry condoms around so I don't have them."

She didn't carry a purse anymore. She had her cash and credit cards with her, along with her cell phone. There was pepper spray on a quick release hook on her belt, and her passport was tucked in a concealed flap inside her backpack.

There were definitely no condoms.

As he continued to gape at her, she had to try not to sulk. "What about *you*? You're the damn guy. Don't you have anything?"

He opened his mouth, then shut it.

"I don't carry them because I don't often have a need of them," he said, looking put out. "But why does logic have to play into this?"

It took a moment for his words to make sense. She was so busy staring at his mouth and remembering how his beard had felt as he kissed her that she didn't care what he was saying.

"If you keep staring at me like that, I'm going to go mad."

She didn't even have time to breathe before his mouth crushed hers and she was trapped between him and the gate, his hard, heavy body driving into hers, the rhythm unmistakable. His tongue sought out hers, echoing the rhythm of his hips, and she reached out, closing her hands around the hard, round curve of his ass.

Thirty seconds later, he had her wrists in his hands.

No—

"Enough," he muttered, letting go without noticing anything was wrong. He sucked in a harsh gulp of air. "We're leaving. I'll go across the bloody square, buy a box of condoms. My flat is just up those stairs—we can be back here in five minutes."

His gaze came to hers and Neve's knees went weak as he added, "I'll be inside you within six."

She blew out a slow, careful breath, surprised she didn't just melt into a puddle of useless female flesh right there. Swallowing, she nodded and eased away from the gate. She grabbed her backpack and swung it back into place. "What are we waiting for?" she asked, her voice steady.

It was surprising, she thought, a few short minutes later, how things could go so very wrong, so very fast.

She'd been leaning in the shadows near the mostly vacant building next to the pub.

Back when she'd left, it had been a hardware store—Steve's Supplies and Lumber, she remembered.

Steve hadn't gone out of business. Nope. He'd expanded and relocated, across the street.

The building behind her was being fixed up for something else, and while some part of her was curious, it was a detached part.

She was mostly anxious, and filled with a blinding, blistering need.

Or rather, she *had* been.

Now she was just blistering.

"I *knew* it was you."

"Go away, Joel," she warned, irritation and disgust twining together and spilling up her spine as the boy who'd made her senior year hellish horned in on her personal space. She needed him gone—and now.

One night. She fought the urge to shoot the heavens a look and scream. *Can't you cut me just a little slack? I've been trying, haven't I?*

But God didn't do bargains. She'd figured that out a long time ago.

She was pretty sure He didn't care what she wanted anyway.

Joel reached out and she knocked his hand aside. He whistled under his breath. "You went and got nasty, Neve." Then he winked. "Always knew you had it in you."

He came in so close she could smell the garlic he'd eaten with his dinner—and the fact that he'd doused himself with some nasty male body spray. "Come on.

Why don't we go get"—he slid a finger down her upper arm—"reacquainted . . . ?"

She eased away, moving so that he no longer had her trapped between the building and his body. "Joel," she said quietly, giving him her best smile. It was a smile hundreds of thousands of people had seen. It was also a smile that would have warned anybody who knew her. The fact that she'd dropped her backpack would have been the second warning.

Joel knew her, but he'd always been an idiot.

"Did you forget what I told you I'd do . . ." She dropped her voice as he came in closer and flicked a strand of her hair.

She struck, spinning and grabbing hold at the same time. She used his body weight and her momentum against him. It took seconds, only seconds, to put him on the ground and he landed hard. She drove her boot down into his gut.

While he gagged and rolled onto his side, she finished, ". . . if you ever touched me again?"

"Oi!"

The deep bellow came from halfway across the street.

She looked up and saw the sexy Scot bearing down on her.

But now, so were several others.

The sight of one of them made her smile, even as the uniform had her blinking.

But all the others just made her want to curl in on herself.

Joel shot out a hand and she moved out of his reach and retrieved her pack.

"You . . . fucking . . . bitch," he gasped out.

"Well, well, well . . ."

At the sound of that voice, she closed her eyes.

CHAPTER TWO

The very last thing Gideon Marshall expected when he woke up this morning was to discover that trouble had come rolling back into town. But, unlike most people, the discovery left him more than a little delighted.

It had been a bitch of a day. He was pulling a double—*and* handling patrol on a Friday night—something the chief of police really should be able to dump off onto somebody else.

But his police department had a whopping ten cops on the payroll and it was down to seven currently. One of his officers had a very justifiable reason for not being here—she was pregnant, and on Monday, the baby had decided she'd just make an early appearance.

Another officer was on vacation.

What really killed him was the third—Beau Crawford had chicken pox.

Who in the hell caught chicken pox at thirty-six?

Gideon didn't know. But he didn't ask anything of his officers that he wasn't willing to do himself, and since they were scrambling to keep the shifts covered, he was pulling his fair share of doubles, too.

But heaven help the next person to ask for a day off between now and the time Beau recovered from his bout with chicken pox and Tommy got back from his fun and sun down in Jamaica.

Gideon had been this close to losing his mind, and when the call came in about the "drunken reckless hoyden" who'd parked in front of the "den of sin" down on the square, he'd already been gritting his teeth.

Now, though, he suspected he knew who the "hoyden" was.

With the exception of the eldest, the McKays drove like demons, and the piece of shit in front of the pub was from out of state. It didn't fit Neve at all, but he knew better than to expect anything *expected* from her.

The aggravation of the day melted at the sight of her, and he found himself smiling even as he prepared himself to restrain her.

And he just might have to—there was an ugly history between her and Joel Fletcher, and while there might be a version that most of Treasure believed, he'd always thought Neve had more sense than to get involved with that dickhead.

Her warning to him only solidified what he'd always suspected.

"Did you forget what I told you I'd do if you ever touched me again?"

"Well, well, well . . ."

Neve cut a look his way and the grin that lit her face had him flashing one of his own. He'd always had a soft spot for Neve, a hellion of the highest order and the youngest child of the McKay clan.

"Looks like Trouble is back in town," he said, ignoring Joel as he rolled to his hands and knees.

Neve rolled her eyes and hooked her thumbs in the front pockets of her jeans. "Am I going crazy or did somebody *else* go crazy . . . cuz it looks like there's a badge on you, Gideon."

"Well . . . someone had to take the job after old Crenshaw decided he'd retire." He tapped his badge idly, aware of the crowd gathering around them, equally aware of Joel as he climbed unsteadily to his feet, a sneer on his lips.

"Damn . . . bitch," he wheezed.

Ian Campbell, the bartender, manager, and possible future owner of Treasure Island, moved closer to Joel, his lips peeled back from his teeth. "Easy, Campbell," Gideon said. "I don't think Joel is going to do any damage at this point."

One big hand curled into a fist at Campbell's side, but he gave a short, terse nod. Turning his head toward Neve, he went to say something.

Joel chose that moment to speak. "I want that fucking cunt arrested, Chief! She assaulted me."

Ian snarled.

Gideon moved between them, slapping a hand against Ian's chest even as he said, "Fletcher, you're either stupid or you think I am. I saw the whole damn thing. If Neve hadn't taken matters into her own hands, the two of us would probably be having another . . . discussion. Our discussions usually don't end well now, do they?"

More often than not, they ended with Joel Fletcher's sorry ass in lockup for the night.

Fletcher looked at him and his small, ugly eyes narrowed down to slits.

Gideon just smiled at him and then shifted his attention back to Neve.

"Neve . . ." Ian said the name slowly.

Gideon glanced at him, saw the odd look he focused on her.

She had her arms crossed over her chest, chin angled up, one brow cocked. It was her *princess of the castle* look.

"Neve, I take it you just got back." Gideon recognized that haughty look all too well.

"Ah . . . mostly," she said, the look falling away as she grimaced. "Yeah."

Gideon nodded. "Ian runs the pub now. Ian Campbell, this is Neve. Neve McKay. Brannon's baby sister."

She was still trying to figure it out an hour later.

Gideon insisted on hauling her suitcase into his spare room—that was after he'd spent forty minutes trying to convince her to call her brother and sister. Once he realized it wasn't going to happen, he refused to let her stay at the single inn the town boasted. There was a nondescript motel near the hospital, but that wasn't acceptable, either.

So she was with Gideon.

She *should* be trying to wrap her mind around the fact that her brother and sister probably already knew she was in town. Somebody would have called them. As soon as she was recognized, they would have called. She knew that.

But was she worrying about that? Nope. She was trying to figure out why Ian Campbell, the very mouth-watering Ian Campbell who had brought her to one very earth-shattering climax, had heard her name and gone stiff as a board and rigidly formal.

It wasn't like her name hadn't affected people before.

Brannon had chased off more than a few boyfriends. And some guys had tried to hook up with her just because she *was* a McKay. Then there had been that brief starstruck time in New York City. It hadn't lasted long, not long at all, but for a short period of time there, her name had garnered looks of envy and awe—and it had been because of *her*. Not the McKay name, but because of Neve. Granted, it had more to do with her body and the glitz and glamour that had been piled on, but it was *Neve* who'd caught their attention.

That time had faded all too soon, and then she'd learned just how quickly things could change.

She definitely wasn't a stranger to having people respond to her name. But something about Ian's reaction had been . . . different

"Are you sure you don't want to go home? Moira is going to be desperate to see you—she's bound to know you're here by now."

Instead of answering right away, Neve moved to the large window facing out over the river. She dumped her backpack on the chair nearby and focused on the view.

It was dark now, but Gideon had a few lights placed around the backyard here and there and she could see their glow reflecting off the river. "I think I like your place."

"Thanks. I know I like it," he said dryly. "And you didn't answer me."

She tossed him a scowl over her shoulder. "I already answered that question—like five times over. I'm not ready to see them. Not yet. I needed tonight to get ready."

The floorboards squeaked under his boots and she saw his reflection in the window as he moved closer. When he reached up to wrap a friendly arm around her shoulders, she leaned against him, fighting the sniffles that suddenly seemed to clog her throat, as he said, "They're your family. You shouldn't need to brace yourself for that."

"You weren't here those last couple of years, Gideon. It wasn't . . . fun."

He rubbed her shoulder, the gesture familiar. He'd been like another brother to her—the more understanding brother who didn't mind if she clung to him a little too hard, the one who seemed to know that sometimes she needed that extra hug. Brannon had never cared. Moira had always been too busy.

That's not fair, she told herself.

It wasn't like life had been kind, punching them in the face the way it had.

"Fun or not, they love you. They've missed you."

She snorted. "Yeah, right."

"Hey, you haven't been home in ten years—did you think they'd just forgotten you existed?"

In the window's reflection, she looked at the back-pack she'd thrown on the bed, thought of what it held. It lay there, battered and innocuous. Almost everything she treasured was inside. "I don't know," she said, her throat tight. "Sometimes."

"Yeah, well, they didn't." He hugged her, a little tighter this time, his voice brusque. "I know for a fact that they didn't. Neither did I. It's about damn time you came home, Trouble."

She turned her face into his chest and hugged him. He hugged her back, and for those few moments, she let herself pretend the past ten, twelve, fourteen years hadn't happened.

Did you think they'd just forgotten . . . ?

At the sound of the door opening, Moira McKay rushed out of the family room and into the foyer, her heart jumping up into her throat.

Brannon McKay, younger than her by five years, towered over her by a foot and his hair was wild—either he'd been speeding around with the top of his car down or he'd been shoving his hands through his hair half the day. Possibly both.

His eyes connected with hers. "Is she here?"

Moira's heart, trembling in anticipation, seemed to freeze in mid-beat. Shoulders slumping, she closed her eyes. "No." With a wry smile, she looked at him. "I was kind of hoping it was . . ." She lifted her shoulders and then turned back toward the family room, heading for the fat, overstuffed chair. It was old and faded and probably should have been replaced five years earlier.

She couldn't stand the idea of parting with it.

Curling up in it, she drew her knees to her chest and watched as Brannon threw himself down on the couch. "Who called you?" she asked.

"Who didn't?" He jerked a shoulder in a shrug. "I've had"—he pulled out his phone, mouth twitching in a sardonic echo of a smile—"fourteen calls in since about nine forty-five. The first was from Shayla Hardee. The next one was twenty minutes later, from Cy Magnusson, and the list just goes on."

He threw the phone down on the table in front of him with barely controlled violence.

"Not a damn call from Neve, though."

Moira didn't say anything.

She'd been listening to the phone here at the house. Listening to her cell, watching her e-mail—no call, no e-mail, no text. Not a damn thing. She'd even checked her damn spam folder to make sure her baby sister hadn't shot her a message that might have gotten caught in the Internet version of the junk drawer.

"It's like she's forgotten we even exist," Moira said, her throat tight.

"She hasn't forgotten—"

"Oh, please." Cutting Brannon off, Moira shot up from the chair. Unable to be still another moment, she started to pace. "What would you call it? She storms out of town after a tantrum ten years ago and other than a few cards here and there at the beginning, a couple of phone calls . . . that's . . . it." Her voice went husky. Stopping in front of the windows facing out over the landscaped backyard, she murmured, "That's it. It's like that one fight undoes everything. We mattered that much."

A taut silence passed, and then Brannon said, "We could have reached out at any time ourselves, Moira."

"We've *tried*." Turning to face him, she lifted her hand, as though the answer to all the problems, all the mistakes she'd made, all the misery hung in the air and all she had to do was just *find* it. Then, slowly, she curled her hand into a fist and lowered it. "We tried. I called her, tried to get her to come to the wedding. You wrote her . . . went to New York to meet her after one of her shows."

Brannon laughed derisively. "We can't blame her for that. How the hell was I supposed to know she'd gotten that big?"

"If she'd answered her damn phone, then she would have known you were coming, and that wouldn't have been an issue."

Instead of answering right away, Brannon was quiet, staring at absolutely nothing.

It was a habit he had that drove her nuts. He'd take his time to think through just about everything, and by the time he responded to the simplest thing she was ready to shake him.

Finally, he looked up at her. "We'd told her that she couldn't do it on her own, that she didn't know how to survive away from us. We hit her where it hurt the most, right at her pride. And . . ." He blew out a breath and stood up. "Fuck, Moira. You laughed when she said she wanted to go to NYU instead of Ole Miss. You looked like you'd have a heart attack when she said she wanted to be a model. With everything she said she wanted, neither of us listened. Is it any wonder she was so upset when she left?"

* * *

"Well."

At the sound of that voice, smooth as molasses but still somehow sharp with a rebuke, both of them looked up. Brannon was already on his feet, hands behind his back. "Miss Ella Sue," he said.

"Don't you Miss Ella Sue me," she said, pursing her lips at him for a long moment. Her eyes, nearly black in the dark oval of her face, narrowed as she studied him and then shifted to look at Moira. Ella Sue Pendleton had been the with the family for nearly forty years, first as a cook and and then as the housekeeper. They both adored and feared her, even now. When their parents had died eighteen years ago, it had been Ella Sue who had stood between them and the wolves while they grieved, and when the state came knocking to determine if the *needs of the minor children were being met*, they'd had to deal with Ella Sue each time. She'd somehow managed to inspire the same measure of awe and fear in every single caseworker who ever came through the door.

Brannon and Moira had been dealing with her disappointment in them for ten years.

She'd never said it, but they'd both sensed it.

"She's not here," Brannon said, feeling like he'd brought home a *D* on his chemistry test again—and he wasn't even in school anymore, damn it.

Ella Sue arched a smooth brow and made a soft *hmmmm* under her breath. "I'd imagine not. If one of my babies had decided to come home to visit and the other two didn't call me, I'd be very put out. But you two know that."

It wasn't a question.

But both Brannon and Moira responded, "Yes, Ella Sue."

She moved with the grace of a woman twenty years

her junior, coming inside to sit in a wingback chair that angled away from the fireplace. "I do believe I've been waiting ten years to hear those words from you, Brannon."

Blood rushed up to stain his cheeks red. "Ah . . . *yes, Ella Sue*?"

"Smart-ass boy." She shook her head, but a smile tugged at her lips. "No. I meant about your baby sister, and you know it." She looked away and her shoulders slumped. "We fucked her up right and proper, we did."

Brannon rubbed at his ear. "Ah . . . we?"

"Yes, Brannon." She looked at him. "*We*. As in you"— she jabbed a finger at him, then at Moira—"you . . . and me."

She smoothed down the long black skirt she wore, staring at the plain material, but her eyes saw something else.

"*I* should have done better by her."

"Ella Sue," Moira said, her voice soft. "She was my respon—"

"Don't you hand me lines about responsibility," Ella Sue interrupted, her voice flat. "You know I loved y'all as if you were my own—and I *should* have done better by her. She'd lost her parents at such an early age. You were only eighteen, in your first year of college, Moira. Hardly more than a child yourself, dealing with school . . . you weren't ready to become a parent to that girl overnight. Brannon certainly wasn't. She *needed* a mother. She needed *me* to be that." Her voice softened as she looked away again. "I thought if she just had me there to love her, it would be enough. But she needed so much more."

Silence fell.

Taut moments ticked by.

Abruptly, Brannon stood, the motion rough, restrained

violence in every move. "What she needed was to stop being a spoiled brat," he said, his voice flat. "She thought she should have everything her way, never have to be told no. She thought she could get away with murder, do anything she wanted and never have to suffer the consequences. I'm sorry, Ella Sue. I know she had it harder than we did and, yeah, I regret how things were that last day, but I'm not getting on board with this *poor Neve* party train."

He started to the door.

"When was the last time you were around to tell her no?"

Ella Sue's question stopped him.

He turned to look at her, a response automatically rising to his lips, but the words wouldn't come together. He stopped and glanced at Moira.

"I asked you, Brannon," Ella Sue said, her voice firm. "You were gone to school those last few years. I'm not telling you that you shouldn't have gone—you had yourself to see to and you were *not* responsible for parenting that girl. But when you did come home . . ." Her words trailed off and a heavy sigh escaped her. "You didn't have time for her. She was too much trouble, too annoying, too loud. You brushed her aside more often than not."

Brannon didn't like the hollow, empty feeling that settled in the pit of his gut. Uncertain how to deal with it, he turned his back, staring around the house, at the familiar paintings on the wall, at the wide staircase with its hand-carved railings, and at the way the glass from the custom chandelier cast a gentle golden glow on everything.

"When you did have time for her, did you ever listen? When she asked for things, did you ever tell her *no*?"

When he didn't answer, Ella Sue looked at Moira.

Moira's dark green eyes glittered. "I did my best. I was juggling my duties with the board, trying to figure out how to fill Dad's shoes, and I barely managed to finish school. I did my *best*." She looked at Brannon and added, "We both did."

But her voice didn't sound so sure.

"I know you did," Ella Sue said quietly. "And I told you to let me help. I was the one who was here when she got home from school, the one she asked if she could go with friends. I *rarely* told her no. Rarely gave her any limits. I made more than a few mistakes. I acknowledge that. If she got in trouble, well . . ." Ella Sue shrugged now. "She'd had a rough time of it. I could understand why she acted out. I'd talk and talk and talk . . . but I never could *see*. Our *best* should have included a little more parenting—spending more time with her, and not just . . . giving in."

Now Moira's eyes fell away.

Ella Sue rose, her quiet sigh echoing around the room.

"Children learn limits because the adults around them *set* the limits. We never gave her limits." She moved to the doorway, pausing just once to look back. "You let me know if she comes by when I'm not working."

"I told you I'd find you . . ."

A hand pressed over her mouth and Neve tried to scream. The knee digging into her stomach prevented that, though, and she swung, tried to hit him. She knew who it was. He'd found her.

Again.

She had to get him off her.

Had to get away, call for help, something, anything—

Swiping out a hand, she scrambled for the thin metal baton she'd taken to keeping in the bed with her. But it was—

"Looking for this . . . ?"

Wait . . .

She sucked in a breath. Something was wrapped around her throat. Something silk and smooth and even though she hadn't known what it was at the time, she could see it now. The green scarf. That lovely green scarf he'd given her—he'd use it to kill her now.

You're dreaming, a calm voice at the back of her mind said.

The rest of her mind dissolved into panic.

It didn't matter that she'd had this dream a hundred times—more.

It didn't matter that, in reality, she'd gotten free. That she'd managed to scream and grab the glass on the bed-side table.

All that mattered was the air dwindling away in her lungs, and his ugly, vicious voice.

Scream, you little cunt—

Neve jerked upright.

Sweat bloomed on her skin, sticky and cold.

And in her hand was the solid, five-inch-long piece of metal she'd started sleeping with more than a year ago.

After he'd gotten in.

He'd been gone by the time the police had arrived. The only sign that anything had happened at all were the broken shards from the glass she'd slammed against his head, and the water that had spilled over them both.

They hadn't believed her, were convinced she was having nightmares and panicking, because of the news she'd gotten.

Who *wouldn't* have nightmares over that?

But they'd only done a sketchy investigation—and they'd been wrong.

She'd seen him two days later at the teahouse in Dingle, and the side of his nearly bald scalp had a long laceration. She'd hit him there, with the glass.

And he'd stroked it as he smiled at her. Then, as she went to rush out, he'd lifted something from the table.

Her green silk scarf. The one she'd left behind when she fled from him.

Rising from the bed, she moved to the window and brushed back the curtains, staring out into the pale, pearly gray of the coming dawn.

Was he out there yet?

Had he followed her this far?

You're mine, Neve. Wherever you go, wherever you run, I'll find you. I'll always find you.

"I'll find you."

He stood in front of a window, staring out over the twinkling lights of the city, fingering the green silk scarf with absentminded familiarity. He could remember when he'd given it to her. The green was almost the same shade as her eyes, and he'd made love to her wearing nothing but that scarf.

It had been their first time. She'd tried not to cry and he'd loved it, loved knowing no other man had touched her.

Every time she wore the scarf after that night, he remembered how her breaths had hitched, the soft sobs.

He remembered. All of it.

It was nearly midnight. There was still traffic on the road but the noise was muted. He took little notice of it.

She'd had friends here.

He'd hoped to find Neve here, but the investigator had called only hours ago, claiming he'd picked up her trail in Memphis. A report that she'd been seen in a women's shelter.

His lip curled at the thought of it.

He wanted to believe it was false, but he'd found her at one himself in New York, months earlier.

Absently, he reached up and rubbed the scar behind his ear. Yet one more thing she'd pay for.

She had done the one thing he'd told her to never do—she'd run from him.

Again.

She'd run from him. Worse, she'd *humiliated* him.

But he was getting closer.

Memphis. He could be there in hours. He'd get a night's rest and then move on in the morning. Memories of the green silk twining around her neck, memories of her dark red hair fisted around his hands. Her skin, soft and pale. She never freckled. Whether it was because she slathered her skin with sunscreen or she just had good genes he didn't know, but he had always loved that delicate skin, unmarred by a blemish, a freckle, even a scar. He'd loved the way he'd seen her eyes go wide when she realized he'd found her.

How she'd struggled to scream.

It had been almost as good as the way she'd moved against him . . . before.

Lids closed, he let the memory wash over him.

They'd have it again.

He'd find her. He'd take her back and make things as they should be.

After all, Neve McKay was his.

The McKays had been the driving force behind the small southern town of McKay's Treasure for more than a hundred and fifty years.

The current generation—Moira, Brannon, and Neve—were, in the eyes of some, a disappointment to the family name. Especially when it came to Neve—the townspeople were changing their minds about Brannon and Moira of late.

Personally, Gideon thought those people could kiss his ass. Half the time, those thoughts extended to Brannon and Moira.

Neve had grown up hearing people say of her, *She's nothing but trouble*—hence the nickname.

Neve simply gave them what they wanted. Trouble. That included her brother and sister.

Right now, as she slumped over a cup of coffee, her choppy red hair disheveled, she did the same thing when she caught sight of him in the doorway.

She gave him what he wanted.

A smile.

It wasn't the same smile, though. That hit him, right in the heart. He'd noticed it last night and had hoped it was just exhaustion, or maybe it had something to do with Joel, but no. The misery was still there, hiding just out of sight.

Neve was like the little sister he'd never had, and that wan, tired smile made him want to pull her against him, hug her tight. At the same time, it made him want to sit her down and demand she tell him what in the hell was going on.

The hug, he could do.

But demands weren't the way to handle Neve.

He'd figure it out, though.

Moving into the kitchen, he reached down and caught a lock of her hair—deep red and soft—and pulled. "You're sitting here drinking my coffee. I hope you made enough for me."

She gestured at the pot. "I made enough for five of us. I needed the caffeine."

"Excellent." He poured himself a cup and leaned against the counter to study her. "How did you sleep?"

"With my eyes closed." She gave him a sidelong smile. "This is excellent coffee, by the way. I was afraid you'd have nothing but instant or decaf on hand."

"Please." He took a sip and sighed with satisfaction. "I'm a cop, darlin'. You cut me and I'll bleed equal parts coffee and blood. Decaf shit just won't do the trick. As for instant"—he shrugged and looked away—"I spent too much time in my life over at Ferry growing up. I got hooked on the good stuff."

McKay's Ferry was the sprawling plantation that had been home to the McKay family for generations. Gideon never would have left that place if he'd had anything to say about it. There had been a time when he and Moira had been inseparable. And if he'd had anything to say about *that*, well, that wouldn't have ever changed, either.

"Well. That answers that," Neve said softly.

He looked back to see her watching him with knowing eyes.

When he said nothing, she smiled. "I always wondered if you ever did the smart thing and fell in love with somebody else, but I guess not. You'll never love anybody but Moira, will you?"

He didn't say anything. But as their gazes locked and held, Gideon knew he didn't have to. She wouldn't tell anybody. Neither would he.

Their secret.

After a moment, he turned away. He grabbed a banana from the basket. "I'm not much on breakfast or anything, but there's bread for toast. Bananas."

"I had one—a banana that is. I never eat a lot in the morning."

"I noticed," he said, shooting her a dark look over his shoulder. "You don't look like you eat much *period*, Neve."

"Don't," she said, shaking her head. "I eat enough. I

just . . . don't have much of an appetite. I make sure to eat what I need to, okay?"

Something in her eyes there, he mused. Because he saw it, and recognized her need for privacy, he let it go. If she said she was taking care of herself, he'd believe her. "You ready to go see them?"

"Nope." She shrugged. "But I'll do it anyway. Figure they're at Ferry or already out doing . . . whatever?"

He peeled the banana. "Now what makes you think I know what's going on with your family, Neve?"

She just lifted a brow at him.

He took a bite of the banana and chewed, swallowed it. Just on principle. Then he shrugged. "Brannon might be at the pub—he's the one who bought it a few years ago, fixed it up. He gets bored easy. He's been buying some of the older places, fixing them up. If the current tenant wants to stay on, he'll offer to be a partner or even just fund the renovations for a cut of the profit. If he's not at the pub—or out looking for *you*—try the empty space next to the pub. He bought that off Steve Fuller, you might have seen the new place." He grimaced and rolled his eyes. "The plan for that? Get this—some frou-frou winery."

Neve widened her eyes. "A winery? *Here?*"

"Yep. Actually, that's just going to be the storefront. The winery is the old Mulligan farm. He's been working on this project for five, six years now." He paused, the surprise on her face surprising *him*. "You . . . haven't been talking to them at all, have you?"

She just looked away.

He did, too. He'd known the rift was there. Brannon had been brusque and tight-lipped about it, but he'd assumed they'd had *some* contact, even minimal.

But there was nothing.

"What about Moira?" she asked quietly.

Son of a bitch. Jaw locked, Gideon stared at his shoes. He didn't want to say a damn thing now. *Why the* fuck *didn't either of you try to talk to her?* he wondered, thinking of Brannon and Moira.

But then again, he supposed he could ask Neve the same thing.

Looking up at her, he said softly, "Why haven't you called, Neve? Why haven't you come home before now?"

The taut, heavy silence seemed brittle. If it had shattered and fallen down around them like broken glass, he wouldn't have been surprised.

When she finally turned her head to look at him, the bruised, stark expression on her face hit him square in the chest. "I tried," she said flatly. Then she got up. "I'll track her down. Thanks for letting me crash here, Gideon."

He caught her arm before she left the room. *You tried?*

He wanted to ask what in the hell that meant.

But this was between her and her siblings. If nothing else, he had to respect that—and be there for her. She was going to need a friend.

Tugging her up against him, he hugged her close.

She stood there, stiff as a board and unyielding for the longest time, then finally, she relaxed.

"There's a museum going up," he said softly.

You haven't been talking to them at all . . .

She'd called home. Several times.

She'd written. Often.

The letters came back or just went unanswered. Once she'd come back to the United States, more often than not they were sent back with a snide little *Return to Sender* note scrawled across the envelope. She had to wonder how many times she'd written from Scotland, waiting for a response to a letter that hadn't even been read.

She'd tried not to let it hurt. It wasn't like she'd left under the best of circumstances, but the past few years, she'd needed her brother and her sister. She'd needed them so badly, it had hurt.

They weren't there.

Now, when she had no place she *could* go—no. She cut that thought off. There were places she could go. If she absolutely had to, she could get money—there was plenty of that—and hide herself away, hire bodyguards, whatever she had to do.

But she didn't *want* to do that.

She wanted to be here.

Wanted to be home.

Neve was a lot of things, but she'd never been a coward.

Gideon squeezed her gently and sighed. She braced herself for more questions, but instead he said quietly, "There's a museum going up."

A museum . . . ?

"What kind of museum?" she asked, unaware that her voice was shaking.

Gideon sighed and leaned back, brushing her hair from her face.

The familiarity of that gesture made her heart squeeze. "It's down near the dock. Your family . . . well, your sister is behind it. It's going to have exhibits on riverboating, the history of the area, and that sort of thing, but the main focus is your family . . . about Patrick."

"Patrick." She smiled a little, and despite the raw, aching wound that had taken the place of her heart over the past couple of years, she discovered a curious warmth spreading through her. "Patrick . . . and Madeline, I'd imagine. Jonathon, the Steeles. All of McKay's Treasure. This whole town is the story of them."

"You said it in a nutshell." Gideon looked like he wanted to say more, and then he just shook his head. "Go. You should go. See it. It's almost done."

There were things unspoken in the way he studied her—and she heard every last one.

But she just nodded. "Yeah. I think I'll do just that."

Maybe seeing the museum might help ease the ache inside her. She had always been fascinated by the history of her ancestors: the riverboat captain and his lovely lady who had made this place their home and how they'd made the settlement that would become McKay's Treasure. Later, as she learned more about the tragedy that would befall them, it had also broken her heart.

A museum—a *memorial*—to him, something that would tell the truth of it, the very idea made her smile. Leave it to Moira to come up with that kind of thing.

Moira . . . She paused in the door of the kitchen and looked back at him. "How did you manage it?"

He frowned.

"I know she divorced that schmuck she married, but how did you manage it? Staying here, being around her while she was married to somebody else, and you loving her the way you do?"

His pale blue eyes went blank and she wondered if he'd answer.

But after a moment, he just shrugged. "Whether I'm here or not, she would have been married. Whether I was home or somewhere else, I would have been miserable. I might as well be miserable at home rather than in a city I'd hate."

There was more to it.

But he didn't say anything else.

She nodded. Then, because it would have to be done, she blew out a breath. "Look, um . . . I've got problems. They're kind of bad. I need to talk to you about them. Sometime soon."

He shoved off the counter. As he came toward her, he reached into his pocket. Without a word, he held out a card.

She stared for a second and then took it.

"Call me," he said softly.

She nodded, then turned toward the hall. Once they were outside, he bent his head and looked at her. "Neve?"

"Yeah?"

"I missed you." He paused and then added, "So did they. Even if they are too stubborn at first to say so."

CHAPTER THREE

Torn between hunting down her brother—who would probably be the easier one to face— and her sister, in the end, Neve decided to bite the bullet and take on Moira.

If she bearded the lion—or the lioness, as it were— in her den, dealing with Brannon might come off as child's play.

Besides, she wasn't quite ready to face Ian Campbell of the sexy kilt and even sexier accent and wicked kisses yet. Especially after the sharp one-eighty he'd dealt her last night.

It wasn't hard to find the museum. McKay's Treasure had grown from the tiny speck, not even on the map, that it had been back in the 1800s when it had been settled by her many-times-great-grandfather, but it was still just a small Southern town, perched on the edge of the Mississippi. The strip of road that ran along the docks gave a pretty decent view of the river.

Ten years ago, there had been a bait-and-tackle store and a diner. That had been it.

Now there was also a coffee shop and a bistro, and the bait-and-tackle store looked like it had been expanded and fixed up. The diner definitely had, it's black and red fifties retro look was far more appealing than the crumbling facade it had boasted back when she'd been in high school. She remembered what Gideon had said about Brannon and his projects and she wondered if the diner was one of them.

The diner had the best burgers and the best chocolate shakes, but only the locals had known that.

Now it was crowded, with a little patio area for outside dining.

Her throat ached at some of the changes.

She studied the shops before heading on to the area that had to be the museum. It was the only place with any recent construction.

It was on the opposite side of the road, elevated to protect it for when—*when*, not *if*—the river flooded. The elevation was man-made, but cleverly so. Neve suspected that inside the building they'd find more ways to keep valuable exhibits protected. On higher floors or something.

Nothing about the place screamed *museum*, she had to say. If anything, it looked like . . . well, a home.

"Old Paddy would have liked that," Neve said quietly as she rubbed the heel of her hand over the ache that had taken up residence in her chest. There had been a few times, back when she was really, really young, before Mom and Dad had died, when Dad would let her sit in his lap while he read her some of the passages from one of Paddy's old journals. Paddy had written about home, his life in the Highlands and the home he'd left, then the one he wanted to build, and his Maddie.

For Patrick McKay, the man who had founded this town more than one-hundred-fifty years earlier, everything had been about home.

That was probably why she was here.

No. That *was* why she was here.

That was why she'd started moving back in this

direction nearly ten months ago, although she hadn't realized her destination at the time.

Instead of trying to stay a few steps ahead, she needed to draw her line in the sand.

But she needed to do it on her turf. On her *terms*.

And there was only one place in all the world where she'd do it.

Home.

No more running.

No more worrying that she'd be volunteering at a shelter and come outside to find him leaning against her car.

No more worrying that the knock on the door of her hotel might be him or that the delivery at the front desk wasn't some clothes she'd ordered to replace the ones she'd had to leave behind.

If he wasn't here yet, he would be soon.

He was too good at tracking her down, although she doubted there was much *tracking* going on now. Once she'd crossed the line into Mississippi, he'd have figured it out.

He'd last called two days ago, when she'd left Memphis. She hadn't answered, but that hadn't stopped him from sending her a text. No words, just a picture, and she'd been torn between rage and revulsion.

He still had those pictures. Or copies of them, stashed somewhere on a thumb drive or something, after all this time.

She'd hurled her phone on the ground, smashing it in a fit of misery, fear, and nausea.

She'd bought another phone, one of those cheap, pay-as-you-go phones, and she'd gone online in the truck stop, using her laptop to activate it. Now she had a phone with a number he didn't know.

For a while.

And she was home.

He'd show up here, she had no doubt of that, but this was *home*. She had family here. Roots.

But first . . . she had to figure out how in the hell to fix everything she'd fucked up.

"I'm sorry, ma'am, but the . . . oh, my goodness."

Neve smiled, feeling out of place, but she wouldn't let it show.

That was the trick, you never let it show, no matter what.

The woman who came bustling around the nearly finished counter was the closest thing she'd had to a mother for the majority of her life, and Neve found herself already battling tears. She braced herself for the hug that would smell of orange blossoms and too much perfume.

It did.

Sniffling, she wrapped her arms around Ella Sue's neck. "Hi, Mrs. Daltry."

"It's Mrs. Pendleton now. That no-account fool Billy ran off and I divorced him." Ella Sue leaned back and smiled. She was sixty if she was a day, but her face was unlined, smooth and warm, the color of coffee laced with just a touch of cream. She winked and added, "I married his accountant and we took over the business Billy thought he'd have to shut down. We'll be able to sell it in five years and move to Lake Tahoe, if we want."

Neve arched a brow. "You'd never leave Treasure."

"Of course not." Ella Sue lifted a hand, cupped Neve's face. "My baby looks worn out."

Neve covered Ella Sue's hand and pressed it to her cheek. "I've been driving the past few days. That would wear anybody out."

Ella Sue eyed her shrewdly and Neve suspected she wanted to say more, but chose not to. "I heard you were here last night . . . I hoped you'd show up at Ferry." Then she smiled. "But you're here now. You'll come home. I'm making your favorite for dinner and I've already had my Aneila ready your room."

Relief gripped Neve's heart. "You're still at the house."

"Of course I am." Ella Sue sniffed. "Like anybody else could handle the lot of you. I'll call Aneila, though, make sure she has everything ready for you."

"Oh, please—"

Ella Sue's eyes went steely. "Hush, now. And don't you dare give me any lip about not staying at the house."

"Of course." Neve wisely hushed. Now. Then she slid her hands into her pockets and wandered in a small circle around the wide, open space of the lobby as she waited for Ella Sue to finish.

Pausing by the black-and-white images—copies, she knew—of several generations of McKays, she smiled. Bits and pieces of family history to start the visitors off, leaving them with just enough questions to make them want to know more.

"Ella Sue—well, hello there. Can I help you?"

At the deep voice, brushed with the crisp tones of England, Neve turned.

Automatically, she pasted a smile on her face as she met a pair of velvety dark brown eyes. His eyes were seductive and rich, like melted chocolate, something a woman might want to gorge on. But Neve knew better. She'd never much liked Charles Hurst, not when he'd traveled with Moira a few years ago to meet her and not during their infrequent conversations since. The few times she *had* talked to Moira she'd also talked to this smug son of a bitch, and if she was being honest, she'd have to admit that she'd stopped trying to call as much once she knew she'd likely have to deal with him as well.

Charles inclined his head, studying her. Then he

smiled. "Neve. It's you. Don't you look . . . lovely." That faint pause was almost imperceptible but she picked up on it.

No. I look like hell. I would have thought better of you if you'd just left it alone or even called me on it. Instead of saying anything to that effect, she just lifted a brow and went back to studying the family images in front of her. "Hi, Charles."

"Here to see Moira, I assume."

"Yep." She crossed her arms over her chest. The air-conditioning had felt good at first, but now she was cold. The simple cotton top she'd pulled on didn't do much of anything to protect her from the cool air, and she had goose bumps breaking out all over. "Any idea where she is?"

"Of course."

She turned to look at Ella Sue.

The older woman was tucking away her phone. "Mr. Charles, I'll take her back. I've missed her so much. Besides, I'm sure you have so much work going on." She smiled.

That smile, friendly as it was, sparked something in Neve's mind. It was the smile Ella Sue had given the vultures who had started to circle after Devon and Sandra McKay—Neve's parents—had died in a car wreck years ago. It was the smile Ella Sue had used when cops would show up at the door, intent on questioning Neve. *Why, yes. I'll be happy to help you . . . but I'll do it my way.*

Charles remained at Neve's side. "Nonsense, Ella. It won't take but a minute."

Unaware of just what the issue was between them, but more than happy to get away from her former brother-in-law, Neve gave him a sunny smile and crossed over to Ella Sue. "Charles, I'm sure we'll have lots of time to chat. But I haven't seen Ella Sue in years and I've missed her."

A moment passed and then he nodded. "Of course. You can use your lunchtime, then. Just remember, Ella, you are working." He brushed a hand down the front of his suit and gave Neve a friendly smile. "Before you disappear, let me show you my office. You can swing by and say hello before you head out."

Yes, because I'm so determined to spend time with you. Biting back the sarcasm, Neve headed across the floor and followed him behind an opaque, flowing wall of colored, carved glass. It made her think of water, ever flowing. Ever changing.

The wall hid several doors, and he disappeared behind one that led down a long hallway. It ended in a set of stairs that went up, up, up, curving around until she found herself in an office that looked out over the lobby, with little windows that offered views down into other areas of the museum she hadn't yet seen.

"So. You're working here, huh?" she asked as he pushed open a door.

"Yes. I'm the director and I'll handle day-to-day operations once we're open. You might not realize how busy Moira is with the board and keeping McKay operating."

The barb was subtle, but oh so sharp.

When he smiled at her, she smiled back blandly. "Bless your heart, Charles . . . it's so kind of you to stay on even after things . . . didn't work out with you two."

A small smile curled his lips. "If I may . . ." He inclined his head and reached into his desk.

"Yes?" She tucked her hands into her pockets.

"Moira has a great deal on her mind right now."

Charles watched her, his expression flat, his eyes unreadable. "While . . . things didn't work out as either of us had hoped, I still care a great deal for her. She doesn't need any more stress piled on."

"She's always had a great deal on her mind." Neve shrugged. "It's a wonder she has enough room in her mind for the thoughts she likes to think. And *more stress* is practically her motto."

If he was amused by the comment, he didn't show it. All he did was continue to watch her and then after another thirty seconds ticked by, he pulled something out of the top drawer of his desk. "How much do you need?"

"Excuse me?"

"Let's not play games, Neve." He gestured to her, somehow managing to encompass her entire body, from her head to her feet. "You look like you found your clothes in a homeless shelter. You haven't slept well in weeks, and if you've had your hair cut in the past year, then you did it yourself. I always suspected that you'd fall, and fall hard. So. How much do you need?"

That was a hit, straight to her pride, and it did more to clear away the apathy, the misery, even the fear than anything else could have done. Placing one foot in front of the other, she moved to his desk with slow, easy strides. "So. You're willing to pay me to just leave . . . and not bother Moira, I assume? Just disappear right now?"

"You are quite the intelligent one. I thought as much." His gaze was cool and direct.

"I wonder, can you pay me enough?" She cocked her head, narrowing her eyes. "Let me think—considering that I own a third of the McKay family empire? Dynasty? Enterprise? What do you call it when your family owns a little of this, a little of that . . . you know. The bank in town, half the real estate, two of the restaurants . . . then there are the patents . . . well, the list goes on. Should I continue?"

Curling her lip at him, she finished by saying, "I don't need your money, *Charles*. Nice of you to worry about Moira, though."

She turned on her heel and strode to the door. Hearing him move behind her, she put more speed to her steps and hit the door just as his fingers brushed her arm.

She jerked her arm away. If he laid a hand on her, she'd lay the son of a bitch out flat.

She hit the steps and didn't stop until she saw Ella Sue's familiar face.

Moira looked the same.

Well, except for the blue silk scarf she'd tied around her hair, a darker shade of red than Neve's.

The blue gleamed against the soft waves. The blue, the dark red of her hair, and her pale complexion—the smooth, creamy skin—all of it had Neve pausing in the doorway for a second.

Even as she helped pry open a box, her skin glowing with sweat, her eyes gleaming, Moira McKay was beautiful.

In comparison, her kid sister felt awkward and gangly.

Out of place, like she'd often felt.

But that wasn't Moira's fault. Too often, Neve had done her best to *not* fit in. If she didn't fit in, then she stood out. If she stood out . . . well, they paid more attention.

"Moira."

Ella Sue's soft voice drifted through the air and Moira looked up.

Her gaze connected with Neve's.

For a second, just a second, something bright and

vivid lit Moira's dark blue eyes. But then it was gone and her expression smoothed over. A calm, easy smile settled into place as she put down the tools she'd been using on the box.

"Neve." Moira cocked her head. "I was hoping we'd see you today. I heard you got back last night."

There might have been the faintest bit of censure. Self-conscious, Neve shrugged. "I got in pretty late. I was tired. Stopped in town, ended up running into Gideon and I just crashed at his place."

Moira's features froze.

Completely froze.

Well, what do we have here . . . Neve wondered. Then she smiled, a little more naturally this time. "He's got a great place. The guest bedroom faces right out over the river. He must have shocked the hell out of some people when they pinned a badge on him."

Moira looked away, but not before Neve caught the way her shoulders sagged. "Oh, did he ever." She laughed softly. "Sometimes I still have a hard time believing it myself. Gideon Marshall, reformed bad boy . . . now the chief of police."

Moira's gaze came back to her, roaming over her, and Neve fought the urge to squirm as the concern in her sister's eyes grew.

A sigh ghosted from Moira and she turned to look at the man who'd been helping her wrestle with the box. "Max, can you give us a while? Take an early lunch if you want."

He nodded and smiled over at them before heading out of the room.

"I . . . you look busy. We can talk later," Neve said, resisting the urge to back away.

"Don't be silly." Moira frowned as she moved closer.

Neve stood seven inches taller, but she lacked the confidence, the ease with her own body that Moira had always had. "Neve, don't take this the wrong way, but you look like hell. I . . ."

She stopped and blew out a breath, and then, with a tiny shake of her head, pinned a hard look on Neve. "Have you been sick? *Are* you sick?"

Ten years ago, that would have pissed her off—the demand, the flat tone. Now, though, she heard the concern and it soothed something inside her, the hurt she hadn't been able to hide. "I'm not sick," Neve said quietly. She shrugged restlessly as she turned away to study the room around her. "I've had a rough few months. Okay, the past few years have kind of . . . sucked."

Now she turned and looked back at her sister. The ugliness of that final night lingered like a raw, gaping wound, but she shoved those memories aside for now. Swallowing, she said roughly, "I . . . I needed to come home."

"Honey."

A second later, she was wrapped in Moira's arms and it caught her off guard. "I'm sorry," she whispered.

"Hush." It was a command. Not a request, but a command. "Of course you came home—this is where you belong."

Brannon probably wouldn't be considered the most *sensitive* of souls, a fact he was well aware of.

He was, however, observant.

Observant enough to know when somebody was walking on eggshells. Particularly when that somebody was six feet five and had a predisposition toward the bold and brash, not the quiet and tentative.

After the seventh or eighth sidelong look from Ian,

he thumped the plans he'd been working on down and demanded, "Out with it."

Ian looked up from the schedule he'd been dealing with. "Out with what?"

"Don't give me that shit, Campbell. Something's chewing on your ass so just lay it on me and get it over with."

"My arse is fine, but thanks for the concern," Ian said. Then he straightened, hands braced on the bar. After a moment, he hooked a hand over his neck and rubbed at it. "There's this thing, though . . ."

Brannon hooked one boot on the rung of his stool and waited.

Ian blurted out, "I didn't know she was your sister."

Brannon scowled. Ian's accent got thicker when he was pissed or aggravated, but Brannon had known Ian for years—they'd gone to university together in London and had spent more than a few vacations with each other since. The thicker brogue, the *I dinnae—I didn't know*— and the mash-up of the entire sentence weren't what threw him off.

He just had no idea what Ian was talking about.

"Huh?"

Ian scrubbed his hands over his face. "Look, I thought she was just this pretty lady passin' through. Stopped in for a pint—more than a few people have been known to do that. And she's right beautiful, you can't say she isn't, and we were talking and if I'd known she was your sister . . ."

Ian's words started to run together, but it was probably Brannon's fault now.

Groaning, he buried his face in his hands. "Please tell me you didn't sleep with my sister."

"I didn't sleep with your sister."

Dropping his hands, Brannon stared at Ian. "Oh. Well, okay then. What the hell is the problem?"

"I . . ." Ian's face went bright red.

Brannon stared at him. He didn't think he'd ever seen Ian blush, not once in all the time he'd known him. "Ian, was my baby sister, Neve, in here last night?" he asked quietly.

"Aye." Ian shrugged. "She was."

Brannon reached out and gripped the bar, squeezing the mahogany as he tried to think. "Ian . . . did you sleep with Neve?"

"I already *told* you. *No*," Ian said. Then he looked away. "But . . ."

"Aw, fuck," Brannon muttered. "Damn it, Ian. You've got women in here flirting with your crazy ass all the time. Why did you have to put the moves on my sister?"

Then he stopped. "Or was she putting the moves on you?"

Ian saw the way Brannon's eyes narrowed, almost jumped on the chance to just be done with the conversation.

But what kind of man did that make him?

Not much of one, really, if he lied about his very willing participation in what had happened last night. Reaching for the bar towel, he wiped off his hands. He didn't need to, it wasn't like he'd gotten them dirty working on a schedule. But the distraction? That, he needed.

"You could say it was . . . mutual moving," he said, flicking Brannon a look from under his lashes.

"Mutual moving," Brannon said slowly. The red-headed man looked like he wanted to pick up one of the stools and thump Ian right over the skull with it. He decided maybe he could handle taking a swing from his friend. He didn't have a sister, but he wasn't sure he'd want his best friend putting his hands on her. Although, Neve . . . he cut the thought off. Because there wouldn't be any more putting hands on her, lovely as she was.

"If you're going to take a swing at me," Ian said, mind made up. "Let's get it done."

"What?"

"I said it clear enough. If you're going to take a swing at me, then just do it."

Brannon dropped back onto the stool. "I'm not breaking my hand on your hard skull, Campbell. If you want to go chasing after Neve, I can't stop you."

"I'm not." He turned back to the schedule.

The taut silence had him looking back up to find Brannon staring at him, hard.

"You're not," Brannon said, the words slow and flat.

"No." Ian shrugged. "She's your sister. If I'd known, I'd have not touched her in the first place."

Brannon shoved a hand through his hair, a hard sigh escaping. "Why? Because she's my sister? Look, Neve's a grown . . ." His words trailed off. "Hell. Twenty-eight. It's been years since I've even seen her and that was for all of one afternoon. But she's not a little kid. If she wants to hang out with you, then . . ."

"Brannon," Ian cut in softly. "You're my best friend— like a brother to me, and you know it. What's gone on between you and her has torn a hole in you, and *I* know that. Maybe she's here to mend it, maybe not." He shrugged and bent back over the schedule. "But . . . there's a hole. Her being here is either going to make it bigger or help it close up. I can't get involved without knowing."

He flicked Brannon one final look. "It's not what a friend does."

He just had to convince himself of that, because he'd

lain awake most of the night, remembering the taste of her . . . and the feel of her in his arms.

Most of all, the way everything in him had just seemed to . . . *know* her.

CHAPTER FOUR

"It all looks the same." Neve had always kicked ass when it came to acting, and she was pulling out all the stops as Aneila walked with her around the house.

Aneila had been all of ten when Neve had left. She was twenty now and she must have been training at her grandmother's knee, because somehow, she already had Neve sitting at the island, and the smells of whatever was cooking had her belly rumbling.

"You didn't think it would change much, did you?" Aneila asked as she plated up a sandwich.

Neve winced at the size of it. And when Aneila started to put together a salad, she said, "I'm really not that hungry . . ."

A steely look entered Aneila's eyes, one almost identical to Ella Sue's. "If Granny calls here and asks if you ate anything, do you really think I want to tell her no?" she asked, her red-tipped nails tapping her hip.

"Ah . . ." Neve plastered a smile on her face. "Have at it. I'm probably hungrier than I think."

Aneila smiled, looking pleased with herself. *Cut from the same cloth,* Neve thought. *Steamrollers in human suits.*

Biting back a sigh, Neve reached for the peach tea

she'd gotten from the fridge. "So how has your family been?"

"Well enough." A pleased smile curved Aneila's lips. "Did Granny tell you the news?"

"Ah . . . well. There's probably a lot of news I've missed."

"True." Aneila pursed her lips. "Okay, short version . . . Kiara is going to college in Kentucky—planning on being a doctor. Jazzy married her boyfriend, DeVantrè. He's off serving overseas now and she's living on base and she's going to make me an auntie—*and* Granny will be Great-Granny soon."

"Oh!" Neve clapped her hand over her mouth in surprise. "I bet Ella Sue is ecstatic!"

"Yes," said a satisfied voice behind them.

Both Aneila and Neve spun to find Ella Sue standing in the doorway. Aneila grinned. "Hey, Granny."

"Are you spoiling all my gossip, girl?" Ella Sue shook her head, not waiting for an answer. She came inside, studied the plate Aneila had in her hands, and then looked at Neve. "You *are* going to eat, young lady?"

"Of course," Neve said. Now she'd *have* to. "So. Great-grandma and one of your granddaughters is going to be a doctor, huh?"

"Oh, yes." Ella Sue smiled and gestured toward the plate.

Aneila gave Neve a sympathetic smile as she put it down. "You know better than to think you can win when it comes to food," she said, winking.

Ella Sue pretended not to hear. "Aneila seems to be settling in rather well, don't you think?"

"Ah . . . yes?"

That was the right answer, wasn't it? Hoping she wouldn't have to say anything else, Neve picked up a piece of summer squash and took a bite.

Ella Sue looked at her granddaughter and smiled. "She's going to do just fine here when she takes over for me in a year or two." Now she looked at Neve. Softly, she said, "I'm retiring."

Neve choked. Slamming a fist against her chest, she tried to dislodge the squash but it wouldn't come up.

"Well, heavens, child!"

She hit her chest again, panic setting in as the bite refused to go down, and then, abruptly, a pair of arms came around her. That was when the panic *really* set in, but as she was hauled back against a hard chest, a fist against her diaphragm, her lungs struggling for air, she couldn't even move. Her arms were trapped against her sides.

No, no, no!

And then, she felt pressure, hard and fast. Something came flying out of her throat, and she was released.

"Well, sis. It looks like you never did learn to chew your food."

Blood roared in her ears. Adrenaline drained out of her. Barely, just barely, Neve managed to keep from sinking in a puddle to the floor as the relief crashed into her.

It's okay. It's okay—

Slowly, she lifted her head and looked up at her big brother.

"Well, hi there, Brannon," she managed to wheeze out.

Fuck a duck.

Brannon stared at his younger sister.

Two things were glaringly clear—both Moira and Ian had been right on target.

Ian had said she was right beautiful—and she was.

Neve had always been pretty, but she'd gone from pretty to nearly breathtaking in the past few years.

And Moira had said Neve looked like she wasn't eating—again—and acting like she was expecting the ghost of old Paddy McKay to jump out from behind a corner and grab her.

Both of them had been too right.

And now, as she stared at him like she wasn't sure of her welcome, he found himself wondering just how much of what Ella Sue had said last night had also been right.

He'd adored Neve. His little sister had been part hellion, part angel, and all-around precocious. Even after Mom and Dad had died, she'd still seemed to be like that.

But everything had gotten harder.

She'd try to slip into his room at night, afraid to be alone—

Did you make time for her?

A thirteen-year-old kid didn't want to wake up and find his eight-year-old sister sneaking into his bedroom at night. And logically, the eight-year-old probably shouldn't want to.

But that eight-year-old had lost too much.

And when people had suggested things that might have helped . . . counseling, therapy . . .

Not us, Brannon thought bitterly. The McKays didn't do that shit.

"Hey, Neve," he said softly, lashing down the bitterness that began to bubble and brew inside him.

Son of a fucking bitch.

Just how badly *had* he and Moira screwed up?

That smile on her face didn't fool him at all, not when her eyes looked so bruised.

"Goodness, child."

Ella Sue bustled over to fuss, but Neve waved her off. "I'm fine. Just feel like an idiot."

The older woman gave her some space, but Brannon wasn't as nice. He moved in and caught his sister's face in his hands, and forced her to look at him. She plastered a wide, bright smile on her mouth as the bright color slowly drained away. The color was probably from nearly choking. The overbright glitter in her eyes could have something to do with what Ella Sue had just announced.

"Did you hear what Ella Sue said?"

He pressed a kiss to her forehead, lingered for a moment. He'd thought he'd be angry, thought he'd feel . . . fuck, a lot of things when she finally did come home.

But all he wanted to do was hug her, so that was what he did.

After a while, her arms came around him and she squeezed him back.

Then, after a few seconds, she said, "Ah . . . Brannon . . . I . . . um, I can't breathe . . ."

He let her go, grinned at her sheepishly.

"Did you hear what Ella Sue said?" she asked again, her voice plaintive.

He nodded, flicked the older woman a look. "Yeah. She told us a couple of weeks ago about her retirement."

"Talk her out of it, Bran." She caught his wrist as he would have turned away.

"Talk her out of it?" He grinned at her and then shook his head. "Ella Sue's made up her mind. You know what that means."

Then he gave Ella Sue a wink, who gave him a stern look but he ignored it. "Besides, unlike you and Moira, I know Ella Sue well enough to know that she'll end up spending half her time here eventually anyway. She loves us too much to ever really leave us."

Ella Sue sniffed. "Boy, you come around here so rarely, I hardly see you."

"Yep. That's why you're down at Treasure Island twice a week." He moved over and caught Ella Sue around the waist, hugged her. She hugged him back and, for a minute, he breathed in the scents of orange, spice, and baking bread. She was the closest thing to a mother that any of them had had since their own mother had died. But she'd earned this, and then some.

As he pulled back she glanced at him, and this time, her face wasn't wearing a smile. She looked grim and serious and her gaze slid past him, oh so fast, in Neve's direction.

She'd seen it, too.

He gave her a tiny nod.

Something wasn't right.

The question was when would Neve open up and talk.

She'd been gone a long time, and the distance between them hadn't just been physical. It had been much, much deeper.

"Come on."

Ella Sue had left them alone nearly a half hour ago and, although Brannon had kept the discussion light and easy, Neve knew him too well to think it would stay that way.

She should have made a break for it sooner, but it had been so . . . so nice, she decided. Just so nice to sit there and stare out over the gardens while her brother drank coffee and read the comics and snorted over the paper. It hadn't been that much different from when she'd left years ago.

But she knew better.

It was a lot different.

She was a lot different.

Everything was different.

Now, as his chair scraped back over the Italian marble, she looked up at him and tried to smile. "Pardon?"

"Come on. We're not going to hang around here half the day. You're back home. Let's go into town. We can walk around and maybe eat supper at the pub."

"Ah . . ." The pub.

Where she'd see Ian.

Brannon watched with a bland face. "Treasure Island . . . remember the old bar? It's mine now."

"Yeah. I was . . . um, I had a drink there last night."

"You should have had something to eat, too. The kitchen's amazing. Come on."

He stood there and just waited.

She couldn't outwait him—she'd never been able to. So now she either had to tell him she really didn't *want* to go to his pub, or she could just go. If she told him she didn't want to, she'd have to explain why, and she wasn't doing that.

Tired already, she braced her elbows on the edge of the table and said, "I don't suppose it's going to make any difference to you if I tell you that I'm not really up for going into town, that I don't really feel like hanging out until dinner and eating . . ." Then, she looked up. It took an effort to keep the relieved smile off her face, but she did it. "Ella Sue is making me supper here. She told me earlier. I can't back out. Telling Ella Sue no . . ." She didn't even have to feign the grimace.

Brannon even echoed her grimace. "That won't go over well."

Even as those words left his mouth, Ella Sue came bustling in. "I've already called your sister, sugar. She's not working late tonight." Her dark eyes met Brannon's and she gave him a serene smile. "Brannon, be here by six thirty."

He opened his mouth, then closed it. Then he just smiled. "Of course, Ella Sue."

As she went about clearing up the table, she asked, "What are you going to do today, Neve?"

"I—"

Smoothly, Brannon cut her off. "She's coming into town with me. I want to show her the pub, some of the other things that have changed. The bookstore."

"In other words, you want to show off," Ella Sue said, shaking her head. Then she patted Neve's back, unaware of the daggers Neve was shooting over the table at her brother. "That sounds like a good idea, though. Neve, I already had Mason bring your bag in. You only have the one . . . was there anything being sent in?"

"Mason . . . ?" she asked. She was losing ground here. It was like it was crumbling to nothing under her feet.

"Oh." Ella Sue turned back to her, frowning. "He's dating Aneila. He started working here about six months ago—helps with the maintenance around the house, the landscaping, a little bit of everything, really. He's already off to deal with something in the back of the estate. You'll meet him soon enough, though."

"Lovely." Neve dropped her head into her hands. "Just lovely."

"Nice car."

Neve looked up at Brannon as he stood there staring at the piece of shit Ford she'd picked up used when she'd hit the United States a few months earlier. "Thanks. It's a classic."

"What happened to the Koenigsegg?" he asked, his voice bland.

"The Egg?" She wondered what he'd say if she told him the truth, but decided not to bother. "I got bored with it. It's in storage, but just haven't gotten around to getting it out." Shrugging like it was no big deal, she walked past the Contour with its mismatched passenger door and studied the rest of the cars parked in the massive garage. Part of her wanted to stroke a hand down the smooth, gleaming paint of the classic 1968 Mustang Shelby, then move on to the absolutely beautiful black sports car that had to belong to her brother. The rest of her stood there, half appalled. After the way she'd spent the past couple of years . . . she thought of the faces she'd spent the past months looking at. How many of those lives could be changed—*forever*—with all the money put into these cars?

"Want to drive it?" Brannon dangled a set of keys in front of her face as she stared at the black car in front of her. She was close enough to see what it was.

A fucking Bugatti.

Trust Brannon to own one of those pieces of art.

"No," she said softly. "You can drive."

She went to open the door. His hand caught her arm and she looked up at him.

"Okay," he said, his voice slow and controlled. "I was going to be nice and give it some time, but fuck that."

She stiffened her spine.

"Maybe Moira and Ella Sue are too nice to call you on it." He paused. "I'm not. So here's the deal. You're either going to get into the car and take a drive with me while we talk—and you tell me what in the hell is going on—or I'll just take myself back on up to the house and spend the rest of the day digging it up on my own."

She closed her eyes.

She felt a tug on her hair.

The familiar gesture sent a rush of tears to her eyes,

and she opened them to find him studying her with his blue-green gaze—so very like Dad's. Then, to her surprise, he hooked an arm around her neck and tugged her up against him.

"What's it going to be, Nevie?"

If he hadn't said that, she would have slugged him in the stomach. Curling her hands into fists, she twisted away from him and walked away a few steps. Surrounding by the brilliant lights of the expansive garage, by what added up to millions of dollars' worth of cars, and under the weight of her brother's stare, she stood there.

"You're such an asshole," she said softly.

"Yeah, well . . . maybe it runs in the family. We don't hear from you for years and then you show up looking like you've been living out of a box . . ."

She tensed.

We don't hear from you in years. She turned and looked at him. "What do you mean, you haven't heard from me in years?"

"Pretty much exactly what you think I mean." Brannon looked at her like she'd lost her mind. "You all but fell off the face of the earth once you left, Neve. I get that you were upset and hurt—fuck, we all acted like assholes that last day and maybe . . ." He stopped and stared up at the ceiling. "Look, you had it rough and I don't know . . . I don't know, maybe Moira and I should have done more to make sure you were okay after the accident but—"

"Brannon!" Her shout echoed around the garage.

He stopped, glaring at her.

"I wrote you," she whispered.

He slashed a hand through the hair. "Get off it, Neve. We messed up those last few years and I don't even want to talk about it. I want to start things over, but first you need to tell me what's wrong."

"*I wrote you!*" she said it again, her voice rising. "You *and* Moira. Once or twice a fucking *month*. I *called*."

She thought of the days she'd spent in the hospital, the calls the nurses had made the first few days. Then, when she'd told them to stop bothering. Even when she'd stopped trying to call regularly, she'd still written. It had taken forever to actually work up the nerve to write down what had happened, but after a while it had become cathartic and she'd poured her heart and soul out in those letters.

But not a one of them had . . .

But they were *marked*.

Spinning on her heel, she stormed over to the car. It was probably locked, but—

She frowned when it opened up on its own, then she popped the trunk. The backpack wasn't in the trunk. Fine. She'd just go get it from her room.

Brannon caught her arm before she hit the door and she jerked away. "Let me go."

She had to get her backpack. Had to get the letters and ask why.

But the backpack wasn't in her room.

"Neve, damn it, we're going to talk," Brannon said, although *he* was practically running to keep up with her.

"I need Ella Sue," she said.

Her backpack was missing.

A bewildered Mason had come back to the house when Ella Sue called him on her cell phone and asked him about the backpack.

Neve wanted to think he was lying.

The long, gangly kid had stood there in front of Ella Sue with what amounted to terror in his eyes as the diminutive black woman stared up at him, and finally, she nodded at him and he left, dashing out of the back door like his ass was on fire.

Ella Sue came to sit on the island in front of her. "Is there any place else you could have left it?"

Brannon was still standing in the entryway to the kitchen, watching her. Neve kept her back to him. She didn't want to look at him, hear his accusing voice, or see the doubt in his eyes.

"No," she said, shaking her head. "I put it in there when I left Gideon's place this morning. It never left the trunk."

"You spent the night with Gideon."

She glanced over at Brannon now. His voice, so carefully blank, jabbed a hot needle into her side. "He let me crash in his guest room. It was late and I needed some rest."

Brannon opened his mouth, but Ella Sue hushed him. "Maybe you left it at his place by mistake," Ella Sue said. "Whatever is inside it, if he has it, you know it's in good hands."

"That's the problem," she muttered. Gideon *didn't* have it. She knew it. But she pulled out the cheap throw-away phone and the card he'd given her, punched in his number.

He answered after three rings, his voice brusque and distracted.

"Hey, Gideon. It's Neve." After a moment, she added, "McKay."

There was a pause and then he chuckled. "As if I know any other. How did the reunion go?"

Her laugh sounded strained even to her own ears. "About as well as we can hope, I guess. Hey, listen . . . did you see my backpack this morning?"

"Yeah. You put it in the trunk with your suitcase, crammed it in on the side."

She closed her eyes. "You're positive."

"Yeah. I saw you do it with my own two eyes, Nevie."

Bracing her elbow on the table, she dropped her forehead into her hand. *Shit.* Out loud, she just said, "Thanks."

"What's wrong?" Gideon's voice was matter of fact and blunt. Not consoling like Ella Sue's and not pushy like Brannon's. Something about it just soothed her.

For some reason, she found herself saying what she hadn't been able to say. "Somebody stole it out of my trunk this morning. I think it probably happened when I went to the museum."

Ella Sue's soft gasp made her squirm with embarrassment.

Brannon's muttered curse had her ducking her head even lower.

"It's missing?"

"Yes." Squeezing her eyes closed, she gave him an abbreviated version of what had happened—leaving out just why she had to get the backpack, what was inside it—just explaining that it was missing.

"Is there anything of value in it?" Gideon asked after she'd finished.

She stuck a finger in the hole of her jeans, worrying the hole there. "Some things that were important to me, yeah—that can't be replaced, but you can't put a price tag on them. Personal stuff. But I had my passport in there. Some emergency cash. Two different prescription meds. That's it."

"How much cash?"

"Only about two hundred dollars. I kept most of my money on me."

"Well . . ." Over the line, she heard Gideon blow out a harsh breath. "It's unlikely we'd get the money back. The passport and the medications are a problem—I assume they were your prescriptions?"

"Yes." She couldn't bite back the snap in her voice any more than she could keep from flinching at the accusation she only imagined she heard.

"It's okay, Neve. We need to file a report—those are the kind of things that can bite you and you'll need the report when you take care of the passport. You have to report that it was stolen right away. I can come over there or send an officer, or you can come to town—"

She slid off the stool. "I'll come to town."

She had to get away from here now anyway.

Had to breathe.

She wasn't going to do this—not again.

There were fights you could win, fights you might lose but they were worth fighting anyway, and then there were the ones that just weren't worth it.

Neve had pegged the fight with her brother as not worth it.

She had to get to town.

When Brannon told her he'd drive her, her instinct was to tell him to kiss her ass and then find the keys to the POS—*piece of shit*. She'd dubbed it that from day one, but she now used it with some affection. The POS had gotten her from Point A in New York City all the way down here without much trouble at all. It didn't guzzle gas and, even though it was uglier than sin, considering the neighborhoods she'd stuck to, it had blended in rather well.

But she wasn't going to argue with her brother over riding the twenty-five minutes into town just so she could avoid being with him in the close confines of his Bugatti.

Now, arms crossed, legs crossed, and her entire body angled toward the door, she gnawed nervously on her thumbnail and tried not to think about the backpack.

Nobody in town would know the significance of the backpack. Chances were that some kid had grabbed it, figured it had money or something easy to sell, and when he—or she—saw he was wrong, it would get dumped. Maybe she'd get it back, but it was unlikely.

Still, the thought of all those letters . . .

"So what's the deal with this backpack?"

It was the first time he'd spoken since they'd climbed into the car. Shooting him a look, Neve shrugged. "You heard me talking to Gideon. I had some medicine in it, my passport, money. Somebody stole it. I'd like it back."

The soft sound of his sigh drifted around the car. She squirmed and tried not to think about how well the leather seat cupped her or how rich the leather smelled or how the car purred like a rich, throaty beast on the prowl.

"You've always been able to make people believe just about anything you want, Neve. But it's not as easy with me or Moira. Let's try that again . . . with the truth," Brannon said.

"That was the truth." She gave him a cool look. "I had my passport in it. Money. My medication. There were also personal things in it that I don't really feel like discussing with you."

Because you're not going to believe me. Despair swamped her at the thought. He wouldn't—maybe he shouldn't. He wasn't wrong. She'd always been so good at manipulating people as a kid. That had changed, years ago, but she couldn't expect them to believe that, not without explaining everything to them. And the thought of doing that left her feeling exposed and bare, like she was parading naked in front of a classroom.

A few more miles passed in silence. She caught sight of the familiar sign, WELCOME TO MCKAY'S TREA-

SURE . . . AT THE HEART OF IT ALL. Neve had to fight to keep the sigh of relief trapped inside.

Brannon said softly, "You're in trouble."

Her heart lurched, then slammed hard against her ribs. In her lap, her hands twisted, then curled into fists. Licking her lips, she struggled to find words to explain. How had he figured out—

"I don't know what's going on, but you wouldn't have come home like this unless you were in trouble," he said after another moment, shaking his head. "I'd . . ."

He stopped, abruptly whipping the car into a parking slot, too sharp, too sudden, narrowly missing the curb. There, he shifted into park and just sat there, drumming a fist on the steering wheel. "Family is supposed to mean more than this . . . be better than this. I'd always hoped we could fix . . . whatever in the hell this is," he said quietly. "I want to fix it. But that ain't gonna happen unless you talk to us, Neve. Unless you decide you want us to be your family again."

She closed her eyes, the pain stabbing at her heart. Then, because she had to keep it together, she opened the door. Before climbing out, she said softly, "I never wanted us to stop being a family, Brannon."

She shut the door and started up the sidewalk.

The police station was just ahead.

She needed to talk to Gideon.

She also needed to make a call.

Pulling out her phone, she punched in a number. When a groggy voice answered, she said, "Hey . . . it's me. I know I probably woke you up. But I'm here. I'm safe."

CHAPTER FIVE

It had been a miserable night.

Ian had climbed out of his bed two hours before he needed to and had spent the first twenty minutes in the shower. It was his second cold shower in under eight hours and he couldn't be sure he wouldn't need another one before the day was over.

When the cold rush of water didn't do anything to help his situation, he'd taken his frustrations out with a hard run. It had been creeping up on ninety degrees by the time he was done, and this time when he'd crawled into the cool shower it had been because he'd thought he was going to die of bloody heatstroke.

It hadn't happened.

Too fucking bad, because now he had to deal with a blithering idiot who likely couldn't find his own prick without a torch and turn-by-turn directions.

"This isn't my order," he said again, putting the print-out of his order down on the bar. Hands braced on the surface, he met the deliveryman's eyes. He kept his voice low and tight, because yelling wouldn't do him a bit of good—and it would do his growing headache quite a bit of harm. He eyed the kegs of rat piss some local brewery was trying to pass off as a craft beer and shook his head. "I'm not keeping that. Take it back and find out what happened to the rest of my order."

The deliveryman scratched his head and leaned over, studied the invoice. He tapped the name of the craft beer that Ian *had* ordered. "We're running low on this one, buddy. I'll see what I can do, but . . ."

"You do that, mate." Ian bared his teeth in a smile. "In the meantime, I'll make some calls and see who else might be able to get that order filled. But don't bring that shite into my pub again."

"You sure you don't want to talk to the manager?"

Ian crossed his arms over his chest. "I *am* the manager."

"I thought it was that McKay dude."

That McKay dude chose that minute to drop onto a bar stool a few feet down. Ian gave him a dark look.

Brannon raised his brows and looked over at the delivery guy before looking away. Then he did a double take, staring at the name of the rat piss—*correction,* beer. He shifted his gaze back to Ian and said slowly, "Tell me you didn't order that."

"I didn't order that."

"Scared me, man." Then he came off the stool and ducked behind the bar, grabbing a glass and a bottle from the shelf. "What do you want with the McKay dude . . ." He looked at the name tag sewn onto the man's shirt. "Sean?"

"There's some confusion." Sean frowned.

Ian rolled his eyes. "Aye, that's some bloody confusion, alright," he muttered.

Now Sean smiled. "Yeah. I just want to make sure we get it straightened out. Mr. McKay likes to support local businesses, I'm told."

"I only support them when I like the product or I think I can sell it," Brannon said. "Ian says he didn't order that. I know I can't sell it. Take it back."

"Uh . . ."

Brannon splashed some scotch into a glass and returned the bottle back to the shelf before turning back to Sean. "You wanted to speak to the McKay dude. That's me. Although all you really need to hear is what the manager said." He jerked a thumb at Ian.

Ian smiled now. "Get that shite out of here and get the order straightened out."

Once Sean was on his confused way, Ian looked at Brannon and studied his scotch. "Hitting the bottle already?"

"Fuck off."

Ian raised his brow. Then he grabbed the order printout and made a mental note of the number. He'd straighten the mess out himself. Somehow, he suspected the rat-piss brewery had been behind the confusion. Another delivery came in and he dealt with that, and then shrieks from the kitchen caught his attention and he found one of the servers swaying and green. He swore and guided her over to a chair before trying to figure out the problem—her falling and taking a hit to her skull wasn't going to help.

The problem was Ernesto, one of the employees who helped with the prep in the kitchen. He stood at the sink, trying to staunch the blood flow.

"Bad one," Ian said, grabbing a hand towel and closing his hand around Ernesto's wrist. He applied pressure there and covered the hand with a towel. "We need to get you to the hospital. You need stitches—"

"Mr. Campbell, sir, it's no necessary," Ernesto said, his English coming out halting. "*Yo no*—I don't want to—"

"I don't give a bloody fuck what you want. You're gushing blood all over my kitchen. You—"

"Ian."

At the sound of Brannon's voice, he rolled his eyes.

Brannon moved in, grimacing at the sight of the blood that had already soaked through the towel. "Ernesto, your job won't go anywhere, okay?" the other man said, keeping his voice low. "You got hurt at work—the pub will cover the bills and you'll still have a job waiting for you."

Ian shifted his gaze from Ernesto to Brannon, then back, watched as something that might have been fear slowly bled out of Ernesto's eyes, replaced by relief. He didn't say anything, though, just gave a nod.

"Okay," Brannon said. "Let's get as much pressure on this as we can, and then we'll get you out of here."

"Forty stitches."

Ian put a bag in front of a harried-looking police officer and accepted the cash before looking at Brannon.

"Forty?"

Brannon grimaced. "Can't believe the idiot was going to try to get by *not* going to the hospital. The one on his middle finger almost down to the bone."

"Where the hell was his head?"

Brannon shrugged. "He told the doctor he got distracted, doesn't remember by what. The knife slipped and . . . there ya go. He needs a few days because the hand will hurt like a bitch, but next week we can probably bring him in and have him help seat people or something. He's pretty adamant about not taking more than a few days off."

Ian shook his head. "Sometimes this country of yours . . ." He stopped and sighed. "The man would have stood there bleeding half to death before he went to the hospital, scared you'd fire him if he missed a few days."

"*I* wouldn't." Brannon scraped his nails down his cheek, over the light stubble already darkening his face. "But it happens. People are assholes. Plenty of corporations are assholes."

"Corporations aren't people," Ian pointed out.

Brannon flashed him a smile. "Well, some try to act like they are." Then he shrugged. "But he's got a job. He'll have a job unless he does something stupid to *not* have one."

"That's because the McKay family wants to get nominated for sainthood," Ian said soberly.

Brannon picked up a wadded straw wrapper and threw it at him. "Suck my dick."

"I know you get lonely, Brannon, but you'll have to find somebody else to help you with that." Ian grinned at him and moved away to take a couple of drink orders. That turned into food orders, and he spent the next five minutes explaining the menu to a couple of college coeds.

As he was just repeating what was already on the menu, he suspected he was just doing it because they wanted to hear him talk. He was used to it. He had no desire to hear himself talk, but he'd always loved Yank accents himself, so while he didn't find his own voice appealing, he understood why there was an appeal.

Another woman came in, a businesswoman he saw once or twice a month—she was a slick piece of work in her sharp little suits and her horn-rimmed glasses and a practiced, perfect smile. "Evening, Miss Collette. What can I get for you?"

She let her eyes wander over him, as she tended to do, and then she held out a hand for a menu. "I'll see what catches my eye. I'll take a glass of Chardonnay for now."

He gave her a menu, got her the wine. As he put it down, she reached up and trailed a finger across his hand.

"How have you been, Ian?" she asked, her voice softer now, lower.

"Well enough. You?"

She stared into his eyes, a slow, familiar smile curling her lips upward. "Lonely. Thought maybe you were the same."

There were times when he was just that, and times when both he and Collette had used each other to scratch that itch. Off and on throughout the day, he'd found himself thinking of the past night and a vicious hunger would grab him, by the throat and the balls. He could spend the night with Collette in his bed—or he could make the drive to her place nearly an hour away. Collette was a pharmaceutical rep, which was how she ended up in Treasure every few weeks. He knew for a fact a night with her would leave him tired and satisfied in the morning—at least on the physical level.

But instead of finding the idea appealing, it left a hollow ache in his chest and he found himself thinking of a slim, pretty redhead. Insanity. That's what it was. How long had they talked? They hadn't, not really.

Ian gave Collette an easy smile. "As I said, I'm well enough right now. Let me know when you're ready to order, Collette."

He moved down the bar back to Brannon and felt the intensity of her glare cutting into him with every step.

"The she-lion looks like she wants to rip your heart out," Brannon said, a half-empty glass of sweet tea in front of him. He'd unearthed a set of blueprints from the bag he carried everywhere with him and Ian craned his head, tried to see if he could make heads or tails of it.

No.

He still couldn't make sense of it.

Then he flicked a look at Brannon. "She doesn't want my heart, never did."

"She wants your dick." Brannon shrugged. "Usually you don't complain."

Ian slid him a glance. "Who said I complained?"

"She only comes in here when she plans on spending the night or dragging you back to her lair. If you were taking her up on it, man, she wouldn't look at you like she wanted to cut your dick off and feed it to you."

Ian had little doubt of his words, even though he hadn't spared Collette a second look.

He grimaced at the imagery and then braced his hands on the bar. "Is it my heart she wants or my dick?"

"She collects both." Brannon grinned. "Or tries. I was one of her notches until you came along. You saved me from that look you're now getting, I expect."

Ian frowned. He hadn't known that—wasn't sure how he felt about the fact that he'd been sleeping with the woman his best friend had been sleeping with. Brannon just looked amused. Shaking his head, Ian shrugged. "Well, she says she's lonely. You're welcome to see if she wants company."

"Please. I escaped with my life. I'm not going down that road again." Brannon looked up from his plans. "Her Chardonnay needs a refill."

"You're an arse."

He braced himself for an unpleasant scene, but when he moved back to Collette, she was icily polite, placing an order for grilled tilapia with sautéed vegetables— *light* oil, please—and no rice. She ordered her second glass of Chardonnay and dismissed him.

Ouch. Amused at the circumstances, he spent another twenty minutes working the bar, building Guinnesses for a small group of students from a nearby college town.

He made a mental bet with himself that at least one of them would spit it out, and not one of them would finish it.

"The redhead."

"What?" he asked distractedly. He was already looking around—for a *particular* redhead. His hands started to itch. He wanted to smooth his hands down that slim back, grab the taut curve of her ass, and pull her up against him. Taste her—

"She'll be the one to spit it out." Brannon grinned at him.

The two of them had been friends too long.

"Reading my mind again, are you?" Ian asked, before glancing back at the clutch of college kids. The redhead was a small wisp of a girl, probably didn't even stand five feet. She stared at the Guinness with a mix of curiosity and trepidation. Still, something about her made him think she was the stubborn sort. He looked at the rest of the group and his eyes lingered on the biggest, loudest of the lot. "No. It's going to be him," he said, nodding. "Bragging like a peacock. He's going to toss it back like a shot of whiskey and nearly choke on it."

"Ten bucks says you're wrong."

Ian almost said no. He'd never been one for throwing money away, but then he looked back at the braggart, gave him another study. "I'll take that bet."

He waited until after he'd passed a handful of napkins to the group before he collected his money. "If you'd watched them for more than a minute, you wouldn't have thrown your money away, Bran." He tucked the bill away, grinning at the way the kids laughed at their friend.

Brannon snorted. Abruptly he looked up. "Did Neve have a backpack with her?"

Just the sound of her name was enough to cause his brain to malfunction, the synapses misfiring while he conjured up images of her. No, more like hallucinations. Hallucinations realistic enough that he could feel her hands on him, taste her under his mouth.

He shifted his gaze to Brannon's as he tried to push those images away. "A backpack?" Fuck, yeah, she'd had a backpack. One that had been decidedly void of a single bloody condom. If she'd had one, then at least he could have felt her under him that one single time.

Brannon stared at him oddly. Then he grimaced. "If you're thinking about my sister naked or in any other fashion, I'm going to hurt you."

"At some point, it may be best for you to just hit me, then, and get it over with," Ian suggested. "I won't touch her, but it might take a bit of time for me to stop thinking about seeing her naked."

Brannon ran his tongue along his teeth, clearly pondering the idea. "How much time?"

Ian patted his pockets and made a show of looking around. "Where's my phone?"

"Why?"

"I need a calendar. I want to know what date the end of never falls on."

"Fuck." Brannon said it miserably and tipped his head back, staring up at the ceiling.

"Tell me about it. You're not the one who's resigned himself to blue balls over it."

Brannon shoved the heel of his hand against his eye. "I never said you couldn't . . ." Then he snarled and turned away, storming into the back of the pub.

Ian signaled to Chap. Chap headed over. "Yeah, boss?"

"Can you handle the bar for a bit?"

Chap shrugged and took over behind the bar while Ian headed off after Brannon. He found his friend in the office that had formerly been his. Now it was Ian's. "I already told you I wasn't going to—"

"Look, if you want to go out with her and she's interested, I'm not going to say you can't, okay? Neve's a grown-up." Brannon stood with his hands jammed in his pockets. "This bullshit about being loyal or whatever . . . it's just that. Bullshit. She's my sister and . . . hell."

He reached up and pinched the bridge of his nose, squeezing tight before he turned and faced Ian's gaze. "We didn't do a good enough job with her. Ella Sue said something to that effect last night and I didn't want to hear it, but I'm starting to think . . ."

"As you said, she's a grown-up." Ian folded his arms over his chest. "Whatever happened when she was a child—"

"She was in the car with them," Brannon said quietly. "She saw them die, was trapped in the car for more than an hour before anybody found them. She watched my mother bleed to death—Dad practically had the top of his head taken off the way the car flipped and hit that tree. She was trapped, alone in the car, Ian. She was only eight."

Horror and pity welled up in Ian, so thick and strong that he couldn't think of anything to say.

Turning away, he moved to his desk and braced his hands on it, staring down at the brutally neat surface.

All day, he'd been haunted by images of her from the past night, her mouth swollen from his, her eyes fogged with heat.

Now he saw another image—that of a terrified young child, experiencing an indescribable accident. He knew how she'd looked as a child. After all, he'd spent many an hour at McKay's Ferry, where she'd grown up. Pictures of the lovely child she'd been were everywhere. No, he could see that lovely, frail child trapped and sobbing.

"What happened?"

"We don't know. Neve doesn't even remember that night." Brannon dropped into a chair. "We thought . . . we thought if she didn't remember, she'd do better. People talked about counseling, but we were afraid if there was counseling, she'd remember. We didn't want her to remember. There were nightmares at first. Bad ones. She'd wake up screaming. She'd climb into bed with me—fuck, I hated it. I was thirteen. I didn't want my eight-year-old sister climbing into my bed. I put up with it at first, but then I started yelling at her. She stopped doing it, and we found out later she'd been in the family room with the TV on, holding on to Mom and Dad's pillows. She'd stay down there. Ella Sue came in around five and she'd take Neve to bed, stay with her until she could sleep. Neve fell asleep in school a lot, started to fall behind . . ."

He stopped for a minute, sighed. Then he looked at Ian. "She got sick about six months after Mom and Dad died, just a bad cold, but Ella Sue told Moira to give her Benadryl at night. Neve was always smart. She figured out real fast that she fell asleep with it, and she talked us into giving her the Benadryl every night. Every fucking night. It was the only way she could sleep without the nightmares. At least that's what we figured she was doing. She stopped asking for it when she was older, but when she left, we found bottles of it in her room. She'd started buying it herself, took enough that she could get a few hours of sleep. If she woke up with nightmares after that, she'd just stay in her room. Never told us."

Brannon got up and started to pace. "She started

getting in trouble in middle school. Kids called her a freak—she didn't always manage to stay awake, cut school sometimes. Moira would yell, scold her . . . Neve would promise to do better, and she would for a few weeks, sometimes a month, and it would start all over again. Ella Sue tried to reprimand her sometimes, but Neve would just start crying and Ella Sue could never hold up against Neve crying." Brannon stopped, looking at something only he could see. "None of us could. She didn't cry for months after they died. We went out to see them on Mom's birthday, though, and that was when she started to cry—she threw herself at the grave."

Brannon's jaw flexed.

Ian closed his eyes.

"They're buried in the family vault at the cemetery— she pushed her arms through the iron bars . . . we had to call the groundskeeper to open the damn doors. She wouldn't let go. She cried . . . for hours. Made herself sick." He shook his head. "Anytime she started crying after that, we just remembered that day. We forgot how to say no."

He swore then, hard, ugly, and low. "Son of a *bitch*," he finished. He moved across the floor and jerked up the window, all but tearing at it as he fought to get it up. Brannon shoved his head outside like he'd die if he didn't get air.

"Bran . . ."

"What in the fuck did we do?"

"You did the best you could," Ian said quietly.

"And what good does that do for a little girl who conned her brother and sister into drugging her just so she could get a few hours of sleep?" Brannon demanded. "What good does that do for the kid who cried herself sick, clinging to her parents' tomb?"

"You were thirteen when they died." Ian didn't know

what to say here, what he *could* say. "Moira was the oldest of you, but fuck, she was all of eighteen, had barely started university, hadn't she? And she took over the business for your father on top of that. You were still a child, Bran and Moira . . . God love her, she wasn't ready to take over and be a mum." He stopped and then asked, roughly, "Why didn't they name somebody a guardian?"

Brannon turned and looked at him. Then he shook his head. "They did. But he'd ended up dying himself just a few weeks before—a heart attack. I know Mom and Dad had spent a lot of nights talking about what they'd do with me and Neve . . . they thought they had time."

Blowing out a sigh, Brannon said quietly, "Things were bad the year she left. I think she was trying to settle down. Her grades came up—a *lot*. She'd aced her SATs—had scholarship offers from six or seven colleges. She wanted to go to NYU, though Moira kept trying to talk her out of it. Neve wasn't going for it. Moira said she belonged here and Neve laughed. Then she said something about the board meetings and the business— if she belonged here, then we'd let her in on the business more. We both laughed at her. It just got worse from there. She kept her grades up, did better at school . . . got in less trouble, but there were . . . other problems."

He headed to the door and opened it. "Neve wasn't the only one who messed up. Maybe she didn't reach out, but then again, we didn't do much, either. And we were supposed to be the older ones—more mature. So if you're that attracted to Neve and you're avoiding it out of some misplaced loyalty to me, then you're being an idiot." Brannon went to shut the door, then he scowled and looked back. "And you didn't answer me about the backpack."

Ian scratched at his chin through his beard. "Aye. She

had a backpack. Didn't let it out of her sight even once. Didn't want to let it go, truth be told."

"Fuck." Brannon looked at the floor for a long, long moment and then he strode away.

"Is that it?" Neve accepted Gideon's card with the report number written neatly across the top.

"Yep." He leaned against his desk. "Officially. Unofficially . . ."

Neve looked away.

"*Unofficially*," he continued, "how about you tell me what's going on? What's with the backpack? What's up between you and Brannon? You and Moira? What are these problems you mentioned?"

"So you have hours?" she quipped. Rising from the chair where she'd been sitting, she moved to the window and stared outside. Brannon's Bugatti hadn't moved. That car of his was hard to miss. Her gut clenched just thinking about climbing back in it with him, dealing with the car ride home.

He hadn't believed her about the backpack. Not that she'd even mentioned what was in it.

What did it matter? A bunch of letters. So she'd poured her heart and soul out. So she'd found some . . . sense of self as she wrote them. Whether or not she had the letters didn't change that simple fact, and whether or not she had them didn't change the fact that she'd come home.

She was going to fix things with her family—or try anyway.

Looking back at Gideon, she took a slow, steadying breath, and then she nodded. "Okay. But this stays between us for now. I have to tell Bran and Moira some of it—I don't know what I'll tell them. But just don't . . . whatever I tell you, keep it to yourself, okay?"

* * *

It was almost impossible to sum up the entirety of the past ten years of her life in anything remotely short and sweet. Actually, there was nothing *sweet* about it, although the two years in New York hadn't completely sucked. College at NYU had been fun—sort of. She'd had to bust her ass, and for a while, she'd had to hire a tutor, not that she'd mentioned that to anybody—not then, or now.

There had been a few modeling contracts, and a few of them had been *sweet,* but she glossed over them. When Gideon probed more—asking about the jobs and why she'd hadn't pursued it—Neve just shrugged it away. She could have told him she'd had a serious chance there, that there had even been times when she'd been forced to turn jobs down, because always at the back of her mind had been the knowledge that she was at NYU for one reason—to prove herself. She hadn't planned on letting anything get in the way of that.

Then something, no, some*body* had.

William Clyde. William, with his so sexy British accent, clear blue eyes, and blond hair that he wore just a little too long, had knocked her off her feet.

He'd started showing up to meet her at the end of her classes or to take her to lunch. She had to admit, she'd kind of loved the envious looks from some of her friends on campus when they caught sight of him, or when he introduced himself and paused to take a hand, press a kiss to the back of it.

This elegant man was *hers.*

He would take her out to all the posh New York City restaurants that Moira would mention that she had frequented while meeting this guy from the board or discussing a buyout from a company. Always business, her big sister. She might be doing business at the best French restaurant in New York, but Neve had a sexy Englishman buying her dessert and hand-feeding it to her at the same damn place.

They'd been going out for nearly three months the first time she slept with him. It had been her first time and she'd cried through it, but he'd held her afterward and told her how much he loved her, how much he treasured her—she was *his* and he'd never let her go.

Never.

"I moved to London with him," she said softly, skirting around the intimate details, moving back to the window so she didn't have to look at Gideon now. "I figured I could go to school anywhere, and he had friends in the fashion industry—that was how we'd met anyway. And I did land some jobs there, good ones. Bigger contracts, even a couple of national ones. For a while, things were nothing but a blur of classes and jobs and . . . him. When I wasn't working or going to school, we traveled. I got to do all the things I'd always wanted. Things that . . ."

She stopped, swallowing the words down now.

She'd hurled the ugly accusations at Moira and Brannon that day and she'd hated herself for a long time. She was done blaming other people. "Anyway. I'd wanted to see the world. William made sure I did. I was so completely under his spell," she murmured. "I never even saw it. Not until it was too late."

"What do you mean?"

She looked back at Gideon, saw that he had settled in his chair at some point since she'd started to talk. She had no idea how much time had passed. Her throat was dry. A look out the window showed that all the cars—save for Brannon's Bugatti—were gone, and new ones had taken up the spaces in front of the pub just down Magnolia. "The only jobs I took were his. I'd changed my major to suit him. I'd planned on majoring in business. How could I actually figure out how to fit into the McKay family without knowing how business shit worked?"

"Neve, you *are* a McKay—you already fit in," Gideon said softly.

She just stared at him for a long time and then looked away. "I ended up pursuing a degree in fine arts. Never graduated but I can tell you all about paintings and artists that bore the shit out of me. It made him happy, though, seeing me learn all these things he thought a *refined lady* should know. And as long as I made William happy, I'd have somebody who loved me."

With her back to Gideon, she didn't see the way he closed his eyes, couldn't see the way his hands tightened into fists under the table.

"I sent a Christmas card home. I was twenty-one. I hadn't spent a Christmas at home in three years. . . . I sent a card to you, and one to Brannon and Moira." She flicked him a look, a faint smile on her face. "I had Hannah Parker figure out where you were. I called her off and on for a while."

"I got that card," he said quietly. It was one of the very few times he'd heard from her. "I wrote you back."

She blinked, startled. "I never got anything." Then she looked down. "But that doesn't surprise me. I wouldn't have even known there was a wedding going on if the invitation hadn't been sent via special courier. The courier ended up finding me while I was out shopping. I never did anything but shop. The job contracts had stopped coming. That summer, we'd gone to Italy and I didn't get registered for the upcoming school year . . . William acted like it wasn't a problem—maybe I should just plan on learning the *other things* I'd need to know." She paused and then muttered disgustedly.

"What other things? *Shopping*? That was all I did. Twice a week, I'd go out, go shopping—I owned more clothes than I'd ever wear and I only went out just to *get* out. . . . William seemed to think it was cute and he liked it when I'd show off the clothes. Like I was a fucking doll. I'd go out of the house with his driver. who would walk me into the store and wait for me . . . and that was where the courier found me. In a damn store."

A watery laugh escaped her and she looked at him. "Do you know what he said?"

Gideon just waited.

The anger, the horror, all of it was just as fresh now as it had been then.

"This guy tells me he's been trying to speak with me for nearly a week. Whether or not I wanted to accept the letter, could I at least have the courtesy to sign that I'd refused delivery?" Closing her eyes, she forced herself to take a breath, then another.

That night was the first time William ever struck her. She'd demanded to know why she hadn't been told her sister had written to her, and he'd just backhanded her.

The next day while he was at work, she'd left. She'd just packed up her belongings and left.

Her first stop had been to file a police report. The officer had stared at her with such skepticism—then he asked if she was *sure* she wanted to do that.

William, after all, was quite the name in London, famous and well respected. He was a barrister and handled contracts for one of the most high-end fashion designers in the world. He often spoke out for human rights and was on the board of several well-known charitable organizations.

Surely he'd never strike a woman.

It took him less than a day to find the hotel where

she'd registered. She'd refused to answer the door, but the next day, she was asked to leave.

He'd been waiting for her outside and he'd begged, pleaded with her to forgive him.

He just didn't understand why she'd consider leaving, going back to a family who'd ignored her for the past few years, people who had never once bothered to call, people who didn't even bother to send a Christmas card or a birthday card.

He'd struck at every vulnerability she had.

Why would you run back simply to attend a wedding? She only wants you there because it's proper.

I'm the one who's been here for you . . . I'm the one who loves you . . . I'm the only one who loves you.

"I stayed."

Gideon was two steps from flipping over his desk, two steps from punching his fist through something.

This wasn't the first time he'd listened to an abused woman tell her story. He heard it—too often—even here in this small town. Too many victims were never able to leave. Either they had no place to go or they felt like they had no place to go. The system too often worked against them, and in many cases it did just as much to protect an abuser as it did to protect the victim. *Well, he has rights.* Shit like that sometimes made him sick to even carry a badge.

But this was deeply personal. He'd known Neve for too long. Had sometimes held her when he'd find her crying, tears she rarely gave in to around anybody else. He'd been her self-appointed guardian since he was nineteen.

Gideon had been the one to find the car that night. He'd been on his motorcycle, speeding away from the

McKay estate after yet another stolen night out in the pool house with Moira.

Although that night had been different.

That night, he'd made her his, just as she made him hers. It had been their first night together and he'd been satiated and all but glowing with the love he had for Moira McKay.

Knowing he wouldn't sleep for a while, he'd pulled his bike over by the roadside and pulled out the cigarettes Moira hated. Because she hated them, he only smoked them at night, after he'd left her, knowing there would be time for the smell to fade before he saw her again.

As he stood there blowing smoke rings into the air, he'd heard the sound. Faint and soft in the velvety darkness, he almost hadn't heard it at all.

But it had come again.

Broken and soft, like a kitten's mewling.

He'd wheeled his bike around, pointing the single headlight toward the trees across the road from him, and he'd seen the car. Dread had crushed him from the very first moment, because he'd recognized the car, even upside down and mangled.

Somebody had driven by in that moment, and he'd almost gotten run down by the sheriff who practically lived to throw his ass in jail. Only the sheer terror in his voice had made Sheriff Jacobs listen to him.

The man's fondness for donuts had allowed Gideon to reach the car well ahead of him. He'd gone to his knees to approach that mewling sound ripping at his heart. Then he'd seen her, curled up in a ball on the far side of the car by her mother's body. Covered in blood. Her mother's blood.

He'd never forget the way she'd clung to him as he

pulled her out of the wreckage, and he knew he'd never forget how she looked now.

She'd been in trouble, all this time.

And not a fucking one of them had known.

"When did you leave?"

She was quiet for a long while and he started to think she was done talking. But finally, she turned from the window and came to sit down, her face pale, tired, and strained. She looked weary—the kind of weariness that came from carrying the weight of the world for far too long.

"Four years ago . . . three months. Six days." She paused, and he had a feeling she was mentally calculating it even down to the hour. "After that first time, he didn't raise a hand to me again for more than a year, and that was after I'd gotten home from meeting Brannon for lunch. He just . . . showed up. Brannon, I mean. He showed up at the door and I knew if I just shooed him away, he'd come back. If he came back when William was there, he'd . . ."

"He'd know," Gideon finished for her when her voice trailed away. "Brannon would have known, and your brother would have killed the son of a bitch."

Neve just looked away.

"Damn it, Neve, why didn't you tell him then? He would have gotten you away!" Fury ripped through the professional distance he'd been trying to maintain. "If you realized that Brannon would care enough to kill the son of a bitch, then why didn't you . . ."

He made himself stop when he saw the bruised look in her eyes.

"I can't give you a reason. I barely even knew myself at that point." Her voice was flat. "I can't even explain it *now*. Except . . . there was too much of *him* inside me. Part of me believed everything William had been feeding into my head over the past couple of years. My only value was to *him*. He was the only one who was there for me. . . . I didn't have anybody else. It didn't matter that Brannon was there *then*. Nobody else had been there for years. They didn't answer the few letters I sent—the birthday cards, nothing. And"—she blew out a rough, unsteady sigh—"I was afraid. William told me that if I left, he'd find me. I was his, after all. He'd always find me."

The words were haunted. Her hands were fisted in her lap, so tight her knuckles pressed white against her skin. He heard her swallow in the silence and dread gripped him as she continued. "He was home before I was. I'd left Brannon at the restaurant. Picked a fight with him when he started pushing about why I hadn't come home, when I'd *bother* to come home . . . It was getting late and I'd been waiting for something to chase him off with. That was the perfect reason. I threw one of my finest tantrums and raced off, left him there alone. And when I got home . . . William was there."

She reached up, touched her cheek, trailing her fingers down it. Gideon could see the echo of memory in her eyes. Unable to sit still, he rose and moved to her, crouching down in front of her. He reached up, touched her cheek, angled her head to the side. There was no scar there but she tried to twist away. He didn't let her. Instead, he continued his visual search. When he saw nothing, he pushed his fingers into her hair—there.

A long, thin line along the right side of her head, just above her ear.

"What happened?"

"He knocked me into a table." Her voice was tight, but steady. "I don't remember what else, but . . ." She sucked in a breath. "I couldn't see well when I woke up— my vision was blurred and . . . my clothes were torn off. I hurt everywhere. I got dressed as best as I could, grabbed my purse, and snuck out the back door. The servants were all over—they called him at the drop of a hat. I called for a taxi but when the driver got there, I didn't know what to tell him, where to go . . . he ended up taking me to the hospital."

"Remember his name? If I'm ever in London, I want to buy him a drink."

Neve smiled tiredly. "He died of a heart attack last year. But . . . yeah. He . . . um." She rubbed the heel of her hand over her heart. "He was there waiting when they released me and he asked me what I was going to do. I didn't know what he was talking about, told him to leave me alone. He took my hand, stopped me from leaving. Then he said something that probably saved my life. He said that maybe if somebody hadn't left his mother alone, maybe she'd still be alive. Then he took me to a shelter for women and children, told me that if I let them, they could help me."

Neve went quiet, thinking about Ned Satterfield. She'd gone to the shelter, told herself she'd stay a night. Just a night. She didn't belong there, in a *shelter* of all places.

But in those faces, she saw an echo of her own. At least, the faces of those who'd *look* at anybody.

She'd become a woman who couldn't stand to meet the eyes of another.

She had allowed William to *make* her into that woman.

It sickened her, shamed her, humiliated her.

She could have curled into a ball and just died, she was so ashamed.

Sometimes she still felt like that terrified, miserable excuse for a human.

She might have even stayed that way—if William hadn't discovered where she was and forced her to act.

In the end, it had been William's own arrogance, his own certainty that he could outmaneuver her that had pushed her to stand. "He threatened to have the shelter's funding messed with." She shrugged. "I . . . I still don't know how the funding for things works in the UK, but he kept saying that if I didn't leave with him he'd have the place shut down. He knew people, after all." A tight smile curled her lips. With her arms wrapped around herself to buffer a chill only she could feel, Neve said softly, "*I* know people, too. He thought I was some weak little nobody. But I'm a McKay, damn it."

Feeling Gideon watching her, she looked up and caught the glint of pride in his eyes. It made her blush. Jerking her gaze away, she swiped her damp hands down her jeans. "I called the family law firm. They've got contacts all over the place—I mean, we've got businesses, or at least partnerships, scattered from here to kingdom come. Short of contacting the Lord Almighty, I figured one of the lawyers would have an idea of what to do."

"Wait a minute." Tension underscored his voice. "You contacted one of the lawyers. Who was it?"

She didn't let herself flinch as she responded. "Amy Jo McCarty."

She watched as he rubbed his forehead, knowing a memory had surfaced. "You dated her for a little while when Moira and you were fighting."

"I dated her to make Moira jealous," he pointed out.

"Moira knew that. She laughed about it. Said Amy Jo had a laugh like a hyena and would drive you nuts."

"She was right," Gideon muttered. His eyes narrowed on her. "She's like a hyena in court, too. All sharp and predatory. And if your sister learns you contacted *her* while you were in trouble, but didn't call home? She'll have poor Amy Jo begging for mercy."

"Then don't *tell* her," Neve retorted.

"Fuck," he half snarled, standing up to pace. He stopped at the window, hands braced on his hips. "So what happened?"

"I don't know the specifics, but they had a barrister they knew in London step in, plus I made a donation to the shelter. The next time he came to the door, the head of the shelter laughed at him. I was in the doorway—I heard her." Neve swallowed, recalling the look of sheer fury she'd seen on his face as he left. "He . . . left."

"What happened after that?"

She closed her eyes. "Lots of things." The scars under her shirt itched, burned, although she knew that was all in her head. They'd long since healed. Physically, at least. "I ended up getting an apartment close by. Started to volunteer there. I felt safe there. Or safer. They—the shelter—tried to get me to press charges. I wouldn't. I was too afraid. But I didn't go back to him. Wouldn't. I started writing home a lot. Told Moira and Brannon what had happened—I kept waiting for them to show up. I wanted . . ." She stopped, waited for her voice to steady. "I kept hoping somebody would rescue me. Save me."

Taut, uneasy moments passed and she spoke again just to break that silence, just to fill the empty, aching void that seemed to echo what she felt inside. "William was always there, every time I turned around it seemed. I finally did try to get a restraining order—his name, his family—everybody laughed at me. But then, one day, he came into a store where I'd gone. I was just grabbing something for my head—I had headaches all the time. He'd waited until I was in the back, tried to force me out the rear exit, covering my mouth, dragging me out even as I was fighting him. There were cameras. And a couple of guys were unloading a delivery truck—they chased him off. I got the restraining order and he left me alone for a while. I decided I'd leave London." She smiled a little. "I moved north, went to Scotland for a while. Stayed in this pretty little village—Carrbridge. It was near the Cairngorms and I could see the mountains." Wistfully, she sighed. "It was so beautiful . . . and peaceful. I worked in a pub in a ski town a few miles away. I was there for almost a year before . . ."

"He found you."

Flatly, she said, "He never lost me." She had to finish the next part quickly, get it done in a rush or she wouldn't do it at all. Closing her hands into fists, she turned and met Gideon's eyes. "I went home one night after work—it was late. I always worked until midnight or so. The pub owner would have his son walk me out, even offered to drive me home instead of having me drive myself. They . . . they worried. Sometimes I wish I would have listened. William was in my room. He'd convinced the lady who'd owned the cottage where I was staying that he was my husband, that we'd separated after a fight, but he was sorry, was going to make it up to me. She let him in, went back to her house across the road. Her son lived with her—a big, burly guy—he always freaked me out. He watched me all the time. But when I screamed . . . I screamed and he broke down the door. He grabbed William and threw him into a wall so hard, William had a concussion from how hard he was hit. Maybe if William hadn't lied, if he hadn't cut me—"

The moment she said it, she wished she could have taken it back.

But the words hung there and she froze, her hands curled into fists, nails biting into her palms, while Gideon's gaze bore into the top of her bowed head.

"Cut you." The words were soft. She heard the anger beneath the softness, though, and she had a bad, bad feeling that he might not keep this conversation quiet. *Fuck*—

Haltingly, she nodded. The slim scars under her shirt burned hotter now, but she felt cold all over. Cold, sick, humiliated. "Yeah. It . . . he did it to scare me. That's all he wanted to do. He'd hit me hard enough to knock me down—then he dragged me to the bed."

Memory flashed. The green silk, wrapping around her wrists, her arms jerked overhead. "He . . . um. He tied my hands, gagged me. The gag was loose, though. He cut my shirt off—cut me. I'd rubbed the gag off and screamed—I barely remember what happened. Angus was there before I could even blink and there were police everywhere and my landlady was there, wringing her hands and crying about it—he was my husband and what was going on . . ." She laughed a little, the sound watery, drawing a narrow look from Gideon. "Angus pats his mother on the back. He's this big giant and she's like a china doll and he hugs her and tells her never to let a person in without talking to the tenant again. Turns out he was a private consultant for security out of Glasgow. He'd done a background check on me the day I moved in—knew all about William. He'd been heading to bed when his mother mentioned that she might need a new tenant, because my husband had come to fetch me. He was already across the road when he heard me scream."

She looked up. "And yes, I remember his last name if you're ever in Carrbridge. I just called him a little while ago—he made me promise to call him every week or so to let him know I'm safe, otherwise he said he'd have my ass."

It felt . . . *good* to get that out there, she realized. Unbelievably good. Freeing, she realized. Some of the weight she'd carried dropped from her shoulders and she thought she'd wilt from the relaxation that flooded through her. Slumping back against the seat, she settled into the surprisingly comfortable cushions and closed her eyes.

"If you want to wait until another time to finish . . ."

Neve opened one eye, stared at Gideon for a moment, then closed it. "There's not much left. I pressed charges—finally. William was sentenced, actually had to do time, but he was let out early for *good behavior*," she said mockingly. "I stayed in Carrbridge for a while—I felt safe there. But once I heard he was getting out, I thought I'd leave, go back to New York City. I had friends there and he didn't have his family name to fall back on. But after a while, he showed up. And I left. I went to Boston. Was there for four months . . . I'd been volunteering at a women's shelter and somebody called me, told me a guy was there asking questions. I never went back. Every damn place I went, I'd either see him, or he'd call, or I'd be informed somebody had been asking about me—or I'd just get a feeling . . ."

"How long has he been after you?"

"Nearly a year." She opened both eyes now and sat up slowly, staring at him. "I don't stay in hotels—I either go to cities where I had friends from New York or people I knew through what little modeling I did. Or . . . where there are shelters where you can stay. I work there, donate money . . ." She shrugged. "It's not ideal, but it makes it harder for him to track me down."

"Why didn't you come home?"

"I didn't feel like they wanted me," she said starkly. "I wrote them. So many times. Once I got stateside, I was writing every week, and the letters just came back—*return to sender*—every damn time. I figured they'd been doing the same thing all along, but . . ."

Gideon started to shake his head, slowly.

She rose from the seat, the hurt hitting her hard.

She was *tired* of people not believing her. It hadn't stopped when she'd left the UK, either. One of the reasons she'd preferred to stay at women's shelters was because *they* did believe her—when a box of roses would arrive for her at a friend's house, none of them had understood why she would freak out, why she'd get scared. Two of the friends she *had* told about William hadn't believed the man who'd been such a *stud*—so *amazing* and so *romantic*—could be such a monster. *Did you do something? Did you cheat?* Cops wouldn't take her seriously because she hadn't *seen* him.

She was *tired* of not being believed.

Her hand had already closed around the doorknob before Gideon managed to slam his hand against the door. "Hey, hey—where are you going?" he asked softly.

"I'm *tired* of people not believing me," she said, her voice trembling. It echoed how she felt inside. She felt like *she* was trembling—all over, inside, outside. "I'm *tired* of it. I get it—I was trouble when I was a kid. I lied. I stole shit. I got in trouble and I made trouble and I had fun with it. But I was a *fucking* kid. Do people not have a chance to—"

"Neve." Gideon cupped his hand over her shoulder. "I never said I didn't believe you."

Gideon *did* believe her.

If she said she'd been writing home, then she'd been writing home.

Where the letters had been going was a mystery that would have to be solved at a later time.

She stopped mid-sentence, watching him through narrow, distrustful eyes.

"I believe you," he said again. "It never made sense

to me that you'd go that long without writing *anybody*. It just didn't. We'll try to figure that out later—because I also don't see your brother and sister just sending the letters back." She opened her mouth but he shook his head. "They waited. Neve, they had gifts waiting for you at Christmas. Every year. They waited. I know, I saw it."

Her face crumpled and he braced himself for the tears. Tears were like a raging storm with her. She held them back, fought them like a soldier at war, but when she lost the battle—

But she closed her eyes, sucked in a deep breath.

Then another.

He watched as her face went blank, as her brow smoothed. When she looked back at him, the tears were gone and her eyes were clear. For some reason, that bothered him even more than it would have if she'd given in to the raging sea of misery he knew lay inside.

"Neve . . ." He brushed her hair back.

"The letters were in my backpack, Gideon. Those were the personal items I mentioned." She looked away now, her green eyes falling to the floor. "I . . . I'm a mess inside, probably have been all my life. I started to figure it out when I was at the shelter the first time. I figured the only way to fix myself was to start by fixing all the problems I'd caused and that had to happen by fixing things with Brannon and Moira—I started by just apologizing, but then . . . I started to write about . . . everything. It was like . . . I had to. Shit, it's probably best that the letters came back. Nobody needed to read that shit. But I had to write them."

Thirty minutes later, Neve stood in front of the pub.

She wanted to go in there about as much as she wanted to face Brannon, but she'd stopped running away from her problems. It seemed like every problem she'd ever faced in her adult life had started because she'd run from the problems here at home.

Gideon stood at her side and his expression was as troubled now as it had been when she finished telling him.

"I'll have to tell my people to watch for him, you know," he said softly.

Neve sighed. "Yeah."

"I can't control their curiosity. I can tell them not to be concerned with it, just to keep an eye out, but you know how this place is. Sooner or later, somebody will figure out why we're keeping an eye out, what he did. And word will get out."

The idea of that made her feel, once again, like she had that day in the shelter, like curling up in a ball, hiding away. Forever. Squaring her shoulders, she told herself what she did every damn day when she looked in the mirror. *You didn't do anything.*

Sometimes, it took on a double meaning—no, she hadn't *done* anything. Not when he hit her. Not when he slowly took control of her life. But she hadn't asked to be abused. She hadn't made him hurt her. He was the one who'd done that, and she'd been the one to walk away.

She'd done nothing wrong.

Nodding, she said quietly, "I know. It won't be the first time. I'll . . ."—she took a deep breath and then forced herself to smile—"I'll deal."

Then she rose up on her toes and pressed a kiss to his cheek. "I'll be okay, Gideon. And . . . thank you."

"You're welcome." He passed a hand down her hair. "I'm here, whenever you need me."

She nodded and then headed for the door. She didn't even make it five feet before she turned back.

Because it was Gideon, she was able to ask.

"Hey, if you really mean that . . . there's a family dinner tonight." She winced and then asked, "I feel terrible putting you on the spot, but I'll probably tell them some of it. I could . . . um . . ."

"Just tell me what time, Trouble."

CHAPTER SIX

Ian told himself it was none of his business, none of his concern, the way the two of them looked at each other.

So the fuck what if Gideon Marshall was at least a good ten years older than Neve McKay—and so the fuck what if he looked too . . . brusque for her. Neve needed somebody who'd cuddle her a bit.

Especially after what he'd listened to earlier.

Even if she was somewhat spoiled. Wasn't like it didn't make sense, what with how her life had gone. Gideon Marshall wouldn't put up with it—Ian knew the man was patient, but he wouldn't be a fit for Neve. Ian could see *himself* being a fit, though.

What are you doing? The mental question had him wanting to shake himself, kick himself.

He'd already gone through this, decided that even if maybe he'd been off base, or at least hasty in his judgment, giving in to an attraction to Neve McKay was just a complication he didn't need.

And now he stood, ready to leap over the bar, storm outside, and wallop a bloody cop, all because he was talking to Neve. When she gave him a slow smile, Ian thought his head would explode off his shoulders. She hadn't given *him* that smile.

What the fuck was this?

"She'll be fucking him within a week, just to get out of speeding tickets." Joel Fletcher dumped the load of dishes he'd been carting into the kitchen on a stool and looked out the window, studying the quiet, intimate conversation between Neve and Gideon. "What do you think?"

Even if Ian's blood boiled at the thought of Neve naked with Gideon—or *anybody*—it boiled even hotter at the smug way Joel spoke of her. Ian had been ready to set him on his arse even before he came into work, thanks to his display from last night.

Slowly, methodically, Ian put down the glass he'd been drying, then the towel. He came out from behind the bar in silence. Grasping the tray of dishes, he shoved it at Joel. "Want to know what I think?" he asked, waiting until Joel had taken it. "I'm thinking you should be minding your own business, doing the fucking job you were hired to do—not worrying about anybody else."

Joel thumped the dishes back down, his eyes narrowed. "My *fookin'* job?" he said, a sneer on his face as he mocked Ian's thick accent. "Why don't you learn to speak English?"

Ian smiled at him. "English . . . is it?" Arms crossed over his chest, he leaned in. "Now do tell me, exactly what is it am I speaking, if not English?"

"Not English," Joel snapped.

Ian rolled his eyes. "You do realize that *English* originated in *England*, don't ya? The *English* speak it. So do Scots. What *you* speak is *American* English. It's not my fault you're too bloody stupid to understand *my* English, you blithering idiot."

Joel sputtered for a minute and finally said, "You're a *fooking* dumb ass."

"*I'm* the dumb ass? At least I understand that the

language you're speaking didn't originate here," Ian pointed out.

As Joel went red, Ian grabbed the dishes and shoved them at him. "Now do your *fucking* job," he took care to enunciate it the same way Joel probably would, once he was in the kitchen and doing what he was paid to do. "Or you can just take your sorry *ass* home."

Joel's lips peeled back and Ian braced himself.

"Easy there, guys."

Gideon shoved between them.

Ian hadn't even noticed he'd come in—nor had he noticed Neve, although he had now and, as though she'd reached out and touched him, he felt the brush of her gaze drift over him.

Ian moved back behind the bar, suddenly in need of the physical barrier. As Gideon rattled the dishes Joel still held, Ian studied her from his lashes. Neve busied herself with looking at anything *but* him.

Is that how it's going to be?

He should leave it at that.

If he was smart.

But Ian realized he was something of an idiot himself.

As Joel turned and stomped back to the kitchen, Ian braced his elbows on the bar and focused on Neve. "Are you looking for Brannon?"

Her gaze came to his and the cool expression there would have been as effective as an ice slap, if he hadn't felt her body up against his—first in reality, then in his memory, and then his dreams, all bloody night.

"If he's available," she said, her voice remote, polite.

When he'd met Moira, he'd decided he could see her as a queen—remote and set apart, ruler of her small bit of territory. McKay's Treasure, in its way, was just that.

And now he was staring at the princess. Gone a long

while, but she had a haughty edge to her. Haughty and cool. It hadn't been last night, but then again, he hadn't been an oaf until the very end.

Damn if it didn't make him want to take another taste of her. A bigger one . . . a longer one.

"If you want to have a seat, I'll find him."

"I'll stand, thanks."

This, he mused, *is going to be harder than I thought.*

But after one long, lingering look at Neve, he couldn't even bring himself to question it—she'd be worth it. He gave her a nod and called out to Chap.

As Chap came to take Ian's place behind the bar, he told himself he'd just go find Brannon. She looked like she'd already had a day. He didn't need to add to it now, did he?

But instead of heading directly to the back, he found himself going to her.

Her shoulders went back.

Her chin went up.

What he did want to do was take those shoulders in his hands, cover her unsmiling mouth with his own.

Fuck it all.

"About last night . . ."

Neve lifted her eyebrow.

Ian felt like a big, stupid oaf. A big, stupid, *besotted* oaf.

Setting his jaw, he took in a deep breath. "About last night," he said again. "I owe you an apology."

She flicked a hand dismissively and looked away, her gaze on anything and everything but him. Clearly she didn't see the *point* in looking at him. "I don't see why. I kissed you back."

"Oh. I'm not sorry about kissing you, and about you kissing me *back*—I'm not entirely sure who kissed who first. But there was a fair bit of mutual kissing going on.

And again, that's not what I'm apologizing for, Miss Neve."

Now she looked at him.

Ian let his gaze wander down to her mouth and he moved in closer, half expecting her to back up.

She looked like she wanted to, but to his surprise, she squared her shoulders and held her ground, staring at him, challenge written all over her face.

"No, you see, I'm sorry for how I reacted after I heard your name. I think . . ." He weighed his words. "I think I handled that poorly."

"Handled that poorly," she said, mimicking his brogue, and he had to say, she did a fair imitation. Then she sniffed and cut around him. "Don't worry, Ian. You're hardly the first guy who's had a weird reaction when he realized he'd tangled tongues with a woman as rich as Croesus. I've had people mocking me for being that *one percent* just as much as I've had people chasing after me and wanting something for it. It's nothing new."

Ian gaped at her back, stunned into silence. It lasted long enough that she'd managed to make it halfway through the bar before he caught up with her.

He took hold of her arm.

She tensed.

It was subtle and she hid it well, forcing herself to relax as she gave him yet another one of her haughty smiles. This time, though, instead of being torn between amusement and wanting to kiss the damn smirk off her mouth, Ian felt something else.

The slow stir of something dark and ugly.

She couldn't quite hide the shadow in her eyes, either. Not fast enough, at least. Others might not have seen it.

But Ian had seen such a sight before—he knew those shadows. After all, his grandmother had hidden them well, too.

He didn't immediately let go of her arm. Instead, he relaxed his grip and swept his thumb across her inner arm. "I hate to be the one to knock you off your high throne, Princess Neve," he said, keeping his tone light as he gave her a mock bow.

"It's *high horse,*" she said, rolling her eyes.

"Horse. Throne. What's it matter? You're up higher than all of us peasants." He watched as her pretty, pale green eyes narrowed and color washed into her cheeks. Fighting a grin, he continued, "I don't give a bloody damn about your money. It's just . . ."

Brannon appeared in the doorway, and Ian gave her an exasperated, pained smile, exaggerating it as her brother drew closer. "It's just somewhat awkward. You see, your brother's my best friend . . . and I don't fancy having him try to shove his fist down my throat if he found out I'd had my hands all over you."

Neve didn't entirely believe him.

Despite the daggers Brannon shot his way, despite the glimmer of amusement and the heat that lingered still in Ian's gaze, she didn't entirely believe him.

She wanted to, because the heat that lingered in his gaze echoed inside her. She could feel it licking through her, warming things that had gone cold during the long, tense minutes in Gideon's office. Minutes? No. She realized she'd spent nearly two hours in there, recounting so much of what had happened over the past ten years of her life.

"Ian, go flirt with somebody else," Brannon said.

Ian continued to hold her arm, staring at her, those pale gray eyes steady on her face.

"But I think I like flirting with your sister, Brannon. She's a pretty lass," Ian said.

Flirting? Was this what he called *flirting?* This was

all but *seduction*, even if they were in public and even if they were still clothed.

His voice stroked over her like a caress of silken velvet, dragging over sensitized nerves. Her heart skipped a beat and she curled her free hand into a fist, her nails biting into her palm. It was either that or reach for him, and nothing good would come of that.

And his thumb was still stroking over her arm. How long had it been since a man had been able to touch her without inspiring terror in her? She didn't think Gideon counted. Neither did Brannon. But every other man did. Even the casual brush of a stranger caused that knee-jerk instinct. It might be gone in a blink, but it was still *there*.

After living several years where just a casual question might inspire a backhand, for her to be able to have somebody touch her and just *feel* . . .

The heat spreading through her became too much for her to process, making her thoughts short-circuit.

Before it became too much, Neve broke the contact and stepped away.

"Is that what you're doing now?" she asked, holding Ian's gaze. It took more willpower than she thought she possessed, standing there and watching him. But at the same time, just standing there watching him as he watched her did something to her. She couldn't quite describe what it was, either. For so long there had been a deep, aching cold inside her. It had been there so long that she'd forgotten what it was like for her to *not* feel that cold.

Standing there so close to Ian Campbell, it was like that cold knot wanted to dissolve.

It *hurt*.

It was the deep, oddly welcome sort of pain of a long-injured limb coming back to life.

It was terrifying.

The smile tugging up the corners of his mouth called to her, made her want to smile back even as part of her was whispering, *Get away. Get away . . . be smart . . .*

The roaring of blood in her ears drowned out the noise coming from the late-afternoon crowd and she could have almost pretended it was just the two of them.

She had to clear her throat before she could speak. "For the record, if and when I decide to carry on a flirtation with a man, my brother doesn't have a say in it," she said, proud of how level her voice was. Something hot flared in Ian's gaze and she saw the smile forming. Memories flashed of how it had felt to be kissed by that beautiful mouth, to stroke her fingers down over his dark beard.

He held out a hand.

Curious, she went to shake it. "I think we've already done the . . ."

The word *introductions* froze in her throat as he bent his head and pressed a kiss to the back of her hand.

"Until next time, Miss Neve."

"Damn it, Ian," Brannon said.

"I didn't realize there was going to *be* a next time," she said at the same time.

"Well . . ." He continued to hold her hand for a moment. "It's a small town, isn't it? We're bound to see each other from time to time. I find myself hoping it will be sometime soon."

Then he let go and turned back to the bar.

She gave herself a minute to stare at him, to appreciate the view. She couldn't complain about the kilt, either, although she shifted her gaze to Brannon. "You know, guys don't wear kilts on a regular basis in Scotland."

Brannon looked over at her. "Know from experience?"

"I stayed there for a . . . while."

"When were you there?" His voice was neutral. "Last I heard, you were still in London with William What-the-Fuck."

"Clyde," she said quietly. "His name was William Clyde."

"I know what his fucking name was."

She turned to look at Brannon and saw the fury simmering in his eyes. He opened his mouth, then snapped it shut, turning on his heel and storming away.

She could feel people staring at her. Ten years ago, she would have fired something off at them, told them to mind their own business.

Five years ago, she would have ducked her head and scurried away, tried to hide away from the attention.

Now she just mentally braced herself and followed after him.

She hadn't planned on doing this until tonight.

But if she didn't do it now, she'd feel like she was running.

She found Brannon in an office. It was neat and organized—that told her right away that it either wasn't his or that he'd changed just as much over the past decade as she had.

"Why?" he asked.

He stood staring out the window as he spoke, and he didn't turn to face her as he said that one single word.

She leaned back against the door, taking in a deep breath. She really didn't want to handle this emotional storm again. Not twice in one day.

Brannon turned to look at her and she knew she'd have to.

"Tell me why you decided that schmuck was so important you'd blow off your family for him, Neve."

She considered and discarded a hundred different

things. What would he listen to? What was going to cut through that icy anger? He looked at her and expected to see the spoiled brat she'd been when she left, the spoiled brat she'd displayed for him the one time he'd come after her in London—and, oh, had she played that part well.

When none of the answers seemed to fit, she found herself reaching for the hem of her shirt instead.

There were only two scars, thin and narrow, almost surgically near. William had taken great care—and great glee—when he carved the *X* into her belly.

X marks the spot, you stupid bint . . . ever leave me again and I'll drive this knife inside you and watch you bleed.

She dragged it up. Mechanically chilled air blew over her bared torso as she stood there and lifted her gaze, met her brother's across the office.

For the longest time, he just stared.

She let the shirt go and then she started to talk.

Gideon calmly explained himself again.

He didn't know how many times he'd done this, but he knew he'd have to do it again.

"Mrs. Mouton. I realize you don't see what the problem is with your dog . . . relieving himself in public and, yes, it is a natural body function. But it goes against the town ordinances. You need to clean up after Samwise," he said, nodding to the watermelon-sized pup snarling at the matron's feet.

"It's just plain foolishness, Gideon Marshall. A dog will go where it wants to go!" She sniffed at him and then glared at the ticket. "I will *not* accept that ticket. If I don't accept it, you can't make me pay it."

"It doesn't—"

He went quiet, hearing the noise coming from inside the pub just a few feet down.

"Brannon!"

Neve's voice, familiar, was the only warning before Brannon came rushing out the door. One of the signs that Ian propped out on the sidewalk in the evenings was knocked over, and he almost sent Joel Fletcher flying. Brannon barely noticed.

Aw, hell.

"Damn it, Brannon, would you stop?" Neve shouted after him as she appeared in the doorway.

Ian was at her shoulder a moment later.

Deciding he had more important concerns, he shoved the ticket in his pocket. "It's your lucky day, Mrs. Mouton. One final warning, but I suggest you have Mr. Mouton help you find those little baggies I told you about."

He delivered the rest of the words over his shoulder as he launched himself forward, using his body as a barricade between Brannon McKay and the Bugatti.

"Why don't you take a minute to calm down there, Bran?" he said softly.

"Get out of my way, Gideon," Brannon said, his voice tight, barely above a whisper.

"Can't do that." He shook his head, studying Brannon's blue-green eyes, saw the hell there. He understood— he'd been dealing with the same emotions for the past few hours. "You really think she needs you disappearing on her now?"

Bran went still. "You knew."

He shot out his hands then, jerking Gideon up against him.

"You *knew*!" Brannon roared.

"You need to calm down!" Gideon said. "One final warning."

Brannon's only response was a snarled, "Fuck *you*!"

It took more effort—and muscle—than Gideon would have liked. Brannon was a big, and determined, son of a bitch and the two of them had spent more than a little time squaring off with a pair of boxing gloves. But Gideon hadn't spent four years walking the sands in Afghanistan just to have his ass handed to him by the richest, if somewhat pissed-off, boy in town.

It took a lot of sweat, and a lot of creative maneuvering, but he managed to get Brannon pinned. Breathing hard, he shoved his knee into Brannon's back. "Is this what she needs?"

"Get off me!" Brannon snarled, scrabbling against Gideon's hold, but Gideon had his arm, caught and twisted up, rendering him almost immobile.

"I will—when you decide to put your head in front of your gut." Dipping lower, he put his mouth close to Brannon's ear. "You think I don't want him dead, too? But look at her. She *needs* her family, man. She *needs* you . . . and she needs you here."

"You miserable piece of shit." Brannon launched into a litany of other insults, most of which Gideon had heard before. He ended with, "I ought to rip off that badge of yours and make you choke on it."

"Okay. You ready to talk now?"

Brannon took a deep breath and then his big body shuddered. "Fine."

Gideon eased slowly, braced—ready. "You know, if you take a swing at me, I'm not going to blame you—and I'll still arrest your ass."

As Brannon came to his feet, he curled a lip in Gideon's direction. "I'll wait until you're not wearing the badge." He paused and then turned his head, met Gideon's eyes dead-on. "If he comes after her, no force on this earth will get in my way—you'd better not try."

Gideon didn't reply.

He didn't see the point.

Ian knew his friend and he knew him well.

Brannon was in a mood fit to kill, and that wasn't just a figure of speech. Very little could set Brannon off like that.

Judging by the white set of Neve's face, he had a bad feeling in his gut that he wouldn't like it.

Neve stood off to the side, shaken and pale, and he was torn between going to her and seeing what was wrong with Brannon. When Gideon went to Brannon it made the decision for him, and he cut toward Neve, ignoring the growing crowd that had come out of the pub or gathered on the sidewalk.

Neve flinched when he went to touch her, so he lowered his hand.

"Are you alright?" he asked.

She glanced at him, looking dazed. "I'm fine." Her gaze barely lingered on him before she shifted her focus back to her brother.

Alright? *Fuck me. No, you sod, she's not alright.* Ian could see it, in the fine tremor in her shoulders and the rigid way she held herself. But he didn't know what to do or what to say.

Somebody came rushing toward her and that made it easy, though. This was something he could do. He recognized the woman and her dog, but couldn't remember the name. Even as she tried to rush toward Neve, he blocked her. "Neve needs some peace right yet, if you would," he said, using his body as a buffer between her and those who were trying to edge closer.

After a moment, he caught Neve's arm and urged her closer to Gideon and Brannon.

She didn't resist.

But she didn't look at him, either.

He would have even thought she was unaware of him, if he hadn't heard the faint *Thank you* a moment later.

What Neve wanted more than anything was to curl in on herself and get away from the stares. She'd almost asked Ian if they could disappear into the pub, but she'd still have to come out again, still have to see everybody.

Instead, she let herself stand close, close enough to feel his heat and his strength.

As a child, she'd *thrived* on attention—it wasn't so much that it had made her *happy*, but she'd been the baby of a loving, chaotic family and she'd just come to expect it. Then after the wreck and the deaths of her parents, her world had flipped on its end. Brannon and Moira had both been shoved into maturing practically overnight, Brannon forced to take care of himself while Moira tried to take on both the roles of business leader, as the head of the board in the McKay family business, and parent, caring for Neve. The attention had just . . . disappeared.

For a while, Neve had thought if she was *good*, that would make it all better. But no matter how *good* she was, nobody had time for her anymore. Ella Sue had doted on her, but Ella Sue wasn't there when the nightmares chased her screaming into the hall at two A.M., and Ella Sue wasn't there when she sat shivering on the floor outside the bedroom where her parents had once slept. Moira had locked the door and hidden the key so Neve could no longer go inside.

It was purely accidental, but Neve eventually realized that being *bad* got her more attention. She'd been tired after too many nights of just a couple of hours of sleep, and at breakfast one morning she'd knocked Moira's coffee over, covering Moira's college assignments, something she was showing somebody at McKay, *and* a paper Brannon had been working on. Both of them tore into her and she'd started to cry.

For the first time in weeks, they'd stopped what they were doing and hugged her, talked to her—Moira was late leaving and Brannon said he'd drive her to school.

Being *bad* got her more attention than being *good* ever did and Neve set out to be very, very bad. Or, at least, she made them think she was, because the older she got, the more it took to get them to talk to her. She hung out with the wrong kids, she got caught with kids who were smoking and drinking—it didn't matter that Neve was never found drinking or smoking. Just being *with* them was enough.

But a few years down the road, she figured out how unwelcome some of the attention was, especially once guys like Joel Fletcher began assuming she'd do plenty of things—just because Neve was, after all, nothing but trouble.

One night Joel had trapped her up against the brand-new car Brannon and Moira had given her—once she promised she'd get her act together and get through summer school Joel had damn near ripped her dress off and she'd decided maybe she was done being known as *Trouble*. She'd gotten away from him, and when he tried to grab her again, she'd picked up a tree branch and brained him with it. As he lay there bleeding, she told him if he ever touched her again, he'd be sorry for it.

That was the week after she turned sixteen. She decided being bad wasn't all it was cracked up to be, and she'd stopped seeking attention. The change didn't do much to impress her brother and sister—and, yes, that had added to the depression she'd been dealing with since the death of her parents, although Neve hadn't recognized it at the time. What she *had* figured out was one crucial thing—she wanted *out*. She wanted away from Treasure, away from her brother and sister, just . . . *out*.

She wasn't totally able to escape notice—a McKay couldn't live in McKay's Treasure and not have people know who you were. And you couldn't go by the nickname *Trouble* and not have people expect just that from you, either.

She coasted through the next few years, graduating a year late, thanks to being held back her freshman year, but she did it—she got out, and she actually aced her last two years of high school.

In New York, she'd thought maybe she didn't mind attention so much—after all, she'd been able to use her looks and what she realized now had been a natural ability to charm people to luck her way into capturing the eye of the right people in the fashion industry. It had been short-lived, though, thanks to the collision course fate had put her on with William.

Those years with William had been a brutal, ugly, humiliating lesson.

She was happiest now when she knew people *weren't* giving her the side eye.

Plenty of the people back in the pub and on the streets of Treasure were doing exactly that—staring at her and Brannon with speculation. She could almost hear their thoughts, too. *I wonder what Neve's gotten herself into now. With her, there's no telling . . .*

Ian was a solid presence at her side, and probably the only reason she *didn't* curl in on herself and slink away, try to hide.

A voice raised and she looked up, saw Brannon striding toward the car. She darted a quick look at Ian, managed a smile.

He didn't return it, just stroked a hand down her back.

She moved toward the car, but before she could open the door, Ian was there, beating her to that simple task, and she ducked inside without a word.

Brannon viciously jerked open the driver's side and climbed in.

Ian closed the door, and as the silence wrapped around, she cleared her throat.

"Brannon . . ."

"You don't want to talk to me right now," he said, his voice deceptively calm.

"Look, if you would calm down for a minute—"

She wanted to swallow the words the moment they left her mouth.

He threw the car into reverse so hard, the tires squealed. She caught sight of Ian's somber face before she looked back at Brannon.

Her brother looked grim, his jaw tight as he whipped the car out of the parking slot and slammed it into gear. But his voice was level—*calm*—as he said, "You want me to be calm?"

Panic chittered in her head, an insane little monster.

She flinched at the controlled violence she sensed inside him—and immediately hated herself. He swore and drove his fist against the dashboard. Something cracked.

"You want me to be *calm*," he said, his voice harsh—and it cracked. "I'm trying damn hard to be calm here, Neve. But it's a struggle. My baby sister was on the other side of the world, being abused—had some monster slice her up—and I never knew. But sure. I'll be calm."

She swiped her hands down the front of her jeans and looked out the window.

It probably wasn't the time to tell him that she'd been writing.

The mystery of the missing letters, the backpack—and just *why* all the letters had been sent back was something that would have to be covered at a time when she felt a little less fragile.

"I don't understand," he said quietly.

She closed her eyes.

"Why didn't you *just come home*?"

"I'm here now. Doesn't that count for anything?"

When he didn't say anything, she dared to open her eyes, chanced a look at him. He glanced her way at just that moment.

He reached over, the movement slow, tentative.

She held still.

His hand brushed her cheek. Then he nodded.

"You think that's going to work as an answer for Moira?"

"For now," she murmured. "It's going to have to."

Brannon blew out a deep, harsh breath and then returned his hands to the steering wheel. He gripped it tightly, squeezed it hard enough that she heard another crack. "Neve, I'm trying to level out here, but I'm giving you one warning—if that son of a bitch wants to find himself a walking, talking corpse, it's a done deal, the minute I find out he crossed even a foot over the town line—hell, the Mississippi state line."

William Clyde idled in his car at the stop sign just outside of the small town of McKay's Treasure.

If the investigator he'd hired had been competent, William could have saved time and been waiting here for Neve when she'd gotten to town. It should have been clear to any clod with a brain that she was heading here, but it had taken until she'd already reached the town before his man had confirmed it.

Incompetents and idiots—that's how to describe the Yanks he'd met.

Eyeing the town sign, he lifted a brow at the date noted on it.

FOUNDED 1852.

Perhaps in America that was considered impressive.

Did this town even have a dot on the map? He tried to understand the faint note of pride he'd always detected in Neve's voice when she'd talked about home as he drove down the main thoroughfare.

He'd yet to find a single reason.

The place might be quaint, if that was what appealed, but there were prettier villages in England. Someone crossed the road ahead of him, shirtless, carrying a bucket in one hand. The man glanced at him and nodded with a smile.

William just stared at him. The man's fat belly hung over the waist of ratty blue jeans and his skin was leathery and dark.

A pickup truck came rolling across the intersection as William slowed at a stop sign. The driver laid on the horn and William whipped his head just in time to see the driver waving at a passerby.

As he pulled through the intersection, somebody laid on their brakes. William shoved a hand out the window and flipped him off.

The driver stared at him and then shoved his head out the window and proceeded to bellow after William as he drove away.

Inbred idiots.

And he'd have to tolerate the lot of them for the time it took for him to deal with Neve.

For now, he needed to find a hotel.

He activated the GPS and then swore as the bloody thing told him the nearest acceptable hotel was *forty minutes away*. Forty minutes! Whipping his car into the parking lot of a store, he sat there, squeezing the steering wheel for a moment.

He picked up the green silk scarf from the passenger seat and rubbed it against his cheek, forcing himself to think.

He'd find a place here. That's all there was to it.

The sign at the front of the lot caught his eye. It displayed a fat little pig and below the porcine creature read the words:

PIGGLY WIGGLY.

It was a bloody grocery store.

"She should fall on her knees and thank me for saving her from this place," William said.

Despite the air-conditioning, he could feel the heat of the sun through the windows, and it just added to the overall insult of being here. He'd been patient, he thought. Patient, perhaps even forgiving, considering all the trouble she'd put him through.

Considering the utter *humiliation* she'd put him through.

But the longer this took, the less patient he would be.

He'd told her once he'd always find her.

It didn't matter if she tried to run from him now—or fifty years from now.

Neve McKay was his.

"What do you think that was about?"

Ian had no idea, but he was both concerned and fed up. He didn't know exactly what he was angry at, but there was definitely something, he knew that well enough.

That he had no target just yet wasn't a problem for him.

He brooded over it as he stood in the door of the pub, arms crossed over his chest. More than a little concern—for both of the McKays—brewed inside him. Neve had been afraid. Upset. Sad. He didn't know what bothered him the most, the misery or the fear.

Morgan Wade, one of his assistant managers, stood behind him, her tray propped on her hip and a puzzled frown on her face.

"It's *Neve*," a snide voice replied.

Both Ian and Morgan followed the sound of the voice. Ian had to fight to keep his face blank.

He hated that he'd taken an instant dislike to her when they'd met some years back but the fact of it was, Shayla Hardee made it hard to like her. She gossiped loudly, she shoved her oversized breasts against him every chance she had, and more than once, he'd had to avoid her bloody hands when she decided to see for herself if *Scotsmen really did wear anything under their kilts*.

She'd followed him into his office after the last time she'd done it, and he'd been of a mind to call the police and have her ass hauled off out of his pub.

He should have, too, because her husband walked in just as she decided to throw her arms around him and plant her mouth on his. It was like having an ashtray shoved into his mouth, too.

He'd immediately removed himself from that situation, and informed her just how unpleasant it had been while he was at it.

Shayla hadn't had much use for him ever since and he was pleased with that. He would have ignored her comment altogether if Morgan could have just done the same. "Yes. That *was* Neve. Thank you, Shayla, for pointing out the obvious." She gave the other woman a saccharine smile that had Shayla going red.

"I *meant* it could be *anything*. For all *we* know, Neve

went and got herself involved in . . . in . . ." She paused, pressing her lips together as she searched for something suitably outrageous. When she smiled at them, Ian couldn't help but notice she'd gotten lipstick on her teeth. "She probably got messed up with drug dealers or prostitutes while she was up in New York. You never know what kind of people they have up there."

"Drug dealers or prostitutes." Morgan stared at her. "In New York."

"Of *course*." Shayla flapped a hand. "Everybody knows that kind of trash is all *over* the place up there. We don't take with that kind of thing down here."

Morgan caught her tongue between her teeth and then she said, "Wow. I guess I mishcard what you and Rog did for your anniversary when y'all went to NOLA then."

Shayla turned pink, her mouth falling open.

Morgan cheerfully continued. "Yeah, I was talking to some of the girls at the salon when I was getting a manicure and I overheard that you and Rog ended up having a few too many and when you woke up, there was some chick asking where her money was. But, hey, I must have misheard. We don't take with that down here, right?"

Shayla threw her half-cmpty glass of wine in Morgan's face—or would have, but Morgan ducked.

It ended up all down the front of Ian's shirt.

He sighed, torn between laughing and kicking Shayla out of his pub—once and for all. Plucking his shirt from his chest, he looked down and then up. Shayla stood in front of him, her chest heaving, threatening the decency of the halter top she'd worn. "You *disgusting* little—"

"Enough," Ian said, cutting her off.

Behind him, Morgan's snicker choked off.

He might throttle her—after he kissed her.

"Shayla, I think it's best you leave," he suggested.

"—*vile bitch!*" she shouted.

"And that's it!" Ian caught her as she tried to lunge past him.

She swiped out, trying to claw at his eyes.

He caught her elbow and used his body to hustle her out of the pub. She shoved against him the whole way, kicking at his shins, shoving at him, and, once, slapping him. "Settle yourself down," he warned. "I'll call the police if I have to."

"Kiss my ass, you piece of shit. Let me *go* or I'll sue this joint and take Brannon McKay for all he's worth!" Shayla screeched.

"Yeah and I'd like to see *that* happen." He let her go.

She made another go for his eyes and he barely caught her.

That would have hurt—she had nails nearly an inch long. The glitter on them served as a warning.

"I'm not going to tell you again—if you don't leave—"

"Problem?"

At the sound of Gideon's voice, Ian heaved out a sigh of relief. "A bit, yeah. Mind helping me out here, Marshall? Mrs. Hardee is somewhat unhappy with us tonight."

"Unhappy . . . is that what you call it?"

After a few more minutes, Ian stood out on the sidewalk, hands braced on his hips while he watched Shayla turn her fury on Gideon. She was nose to nose with him and Ian thought the man might be a candidate for sainthood, considering the patience he displayed.

"I've a *damn right* to have a drink!" she shouted, jabbing a finger at him after Gideon had explained, yet again, that Ian couldn't be arrested for refusing her service—and, no, he hadn't manhandled her when he'd walked her outside.

Ian coughed loudly, ignoring the left side of his face where it still stung from her vicious, openhanded slap. She turned to snarl at him.

Ian pointed to the neat little custom brass sign affixed to the wall just outside the door.

To be honest, there was rarely a need to point the sign out. Most of the pub's patrons were looking for a fine meal, a fine drink, and fine service. Ian was proud to offer those very things.

But the sign was there for a reason.

LOUD OR DISORDERLY PATRONS WILL BE ASKED TO LEAVE. IF THEY DO NOT LEAVE, THEY WILL BE ESCORTED OUT.

"You were very loud," Ian said soberly.

She swiped out a hand and grabbed a glass from one of the tables placed on the wide sidewalk on the nicer evenings. Ian prepared to duck but Gideon caught her hand.

"Alright, Shayla. I gave you a chance to calm down."

She was spitting at him by the time he had her in the back of the car.

"Don't suppose you could *try* to make my job a little easier," Gideon said as Ian handed him a wet towel he'd had Morgan bring out. Gideon swiped it down his face and went to hand it back.

"Keep it. My compliments."

Gideon tossed it in the open window of his car and looked up as a patrol car came to a stop in front of the pub. A uniform climbed out and Gideon turned away without another word.

Fifteen minutes later, Gideon came inside and wedged himself into an empty seat few inches at the packed bar.

"You're busy."

Ian looked at the chief of police and then skimmed

his eyes over the buzzing crowd that was packed into his pub. He gave a slow, thoughtful nod. "Chief, your powers of observation stagger me. Truly, they do."

"Smart-ass." Gideon jerked his head.

Ian sighed and made his way down to the end of the bar. "As you said, I'm busy. We don't often see a crowd like this in the middle of the week."

"That's how a small town works. Something out of the ordinary happens, people come out of the woodwork to talk." Gideon shrugged. Then he braced his elbows on the bar. "Do me a favor—and be a friend. Go out to Ferry. Stay on Brannon's ass for a few hours, make sure he doesn't do anything stupid."

Ian narrowed his eyes. The busy bar fell to the back of his mind. Both of his assistant managers were here and so was Chap. Chap could handle the bar. Ian could leave—they'd hate him, but he could do it.

The question was . . . *why*?

"Define stupid."

"Anything that would make me have to lock his ass up," Gideon said grimly. "I think he'll cool down— probably already has—but just in case."

Ian had a thousand questions, but he just nodded. "I need some time to settle things here. Have I got it?"

"Probably." Then he paused. "They're having dinner out there—Ella Sue was making something nice for Neve coming home. I'll call her and smooth things over. Charm your way inside if you have to. Just keep an eye on him for a while."

Gideon turned and got lost in the crowd, leaving Ian behind to wonder just what it was he was supposed to keep Brannon from doing.

"Rich fuck."

Gideon tuned it out as he finished talking to Beau

Crawford back at the police station—poor Beau was now getting the sharp side of Shayla's tongue. Gideon could hear her through the phone. "Just call her husband," Gideon told Beau. "If he wants to act like she's tied a few on, I don't care. If she calms down, she can leave. If not, she's spending the rest of the night in her cell."

After Gideon hung up, he stood there, torn about whether or not he should be heading out to McKay's Ferry himself—he still had questions, he was still pissed, and Moira . . .

He cut the thought off. *Don't go there, son,* he warned himself. That ship had already sailed and there was nothing to be done about it.

"I'm telling you, the prick practically took my front end off and then he flipped *me* off." There was a pause, followed by, "Probably somebody Brannon knows, driving that Porsche or Jaguar or whatever foreign piece of shit it was. Only car worth driving is American. Everybody knows that."

Now Gideon looked up, immediately seeking out the speaker.

Clive Owings. He talked loud, he talked long, and he talked a lot of bullshit. He also didn't like anybody who had it better than he did, and, since he didn't much like investing effort in anything, plenty of people had it better.

"Who did you piss off this time, Clive?" he asked.

Clive spat out a nasty stream of tobacco into the street and then bared stained teeth at Gideon in a smile. "I didn't do nothing, Marshall. Was just going through the stop sign and some dickhead almost crashed into me, then flipped me off." He paused, then added, "Not from here. Had Indiana plates. Fancy car. Probably somebody heading out to the McKay's. Ain't none of them able to drive worth shit."

"Neither can you." That came from one of the men sitting in the seats lined up in front of the hardware store, and everybody—save for Clive—started to laugh.

"Kiss my ass," Clive said. But he just shrugged it off. "What's it to you, Marshall?"

"Oh, nothing." Gideon smiled and nodded at them before turning around. He had half a mind to head back into the pub, have a drink, but then discarded it.

He sure as hell wanted a drink, he wanted something strong, preferably two or three of them, but first, he had a date with the heavy bag in his garage. The bag and some hard, crashing music while he pounded out the frustrations of a miserable day.

He was halfway home, already feeling the satisfaction of slamming his fists into something, when his phone started to ring, and damn it all if it wasn't a McKay.

Sometimes, he'd swear they ran his life. Today of all days, he couldn't ignore the call. Not even if it had been Brannon and his fool hot head. But it wasn't Brannon, or even Neve, the woman he loved like a sister and who owned a piece of his heart.

No. It was Moira—the woman who owned the rest of that useless, miserable piece of flesh.

"Son of a *bitch*."

Moira McKay—formerly Moira Hurst—was the picture of elegance and poise, even in a tank top and a pair of knee-length capris that bore signs of a long day of hard work. And when she was angry, she managed to swear in a way that made Gideon smile, even as it made him want to cover that cupid's bow mouth and kiss her senseless.

He hadn't had that pleasure in a good long while, and for too many years, he'd had to watch her at the side of another man. A useless waste of a man, too. Charles Hurst wasn't good for much of anything, in Gideon's opinion, and he certainly hadn't been good enough for the likes of Moira. A mutual appreciation for history and curating just wasn't grounds for a relationship, if you asked him.

You needed heat.

You needed love.

He'd thought they'd had both, but Moira had left him anyway.

Of course, after less than three years of marriage, she'd separated from Charles. Not that the man was giving up.

"Why now?"

Her soft, tired sigh came to him across the parking lot and he gave up on what he'd hoped would be a few personal moments to soothe his battered heart.

Taking care to make noise as he moved away from the shaded spot where he'd parked his car, he softly said, "Moira."

She'd already disconnected when he answered even though it had been on the second ring, but that hadn't kept him from heading over here. Of course it hadn't. He might as well have a hook in his mouth.

Her head came up. A faint smile curled her lips, but it was gone just as fast, almost as if she hadn't realized she was smiling.

She cocked a brow at him. "Well, it's nice to know the law enforcement in this part of the country is still around when you need them."

He followed the line of her gaze. A mix of frustration and borderline anger moved through him, although he hid both. Voice neutral, he said, "You called me because your tire is flat?"

"I didn't call you."

He took out his phone and pulled up the call log.

She groaned and then rubbed her temple. "Sorry. I must have hit the autodial when I was packing up my things for the day." Then she gave him a cheery smile. "But the timing is lovely. Can you give me a hand?"

The anger, the irritation—all of it misplaced—drained away and he managed a smile. It wasn't her fault she hadn't loved him enough. It wasn't her fault he wasn't able to cut the ties that bound him to her and just leave. "Of course. Serve and protect—that's the job, right, Moira?"

"I doubt you signed on to spend your time changing tires . . ." A glint of amusement danced in her eyes as she grinned at him. "Chief."

Was it pathetic that he'd be willing to do just that if it meant he could be near her? Screw the anger he'd felt. It gave him a reason to move closer, hold out his hand for her keys, to stand close enough to smell her hair and catch the hint of honeysuckle on her skin—she'd always loved the smell of it.

Get a grip. Take care of the tire. Leave. Bracing himself to do just that, he moved around to study the tire. The smile on his face faded as he knelt down and got a good look at it.

"Moira, you had any trouble around here lately?" he asked softly, although he knew the answer. Or at least he knew better.

"What? No. Why?" The confusion in her voice was clear.

He reached out and touched the ugly slash in the rubber. "Your tire was slashed."

"My—*what*?"

He looked up at her, but his response was interrupted by a familiar voice, one that grated against Gideon's nerves like metal dragging down a chalkboard. "Moira, pet, what are you doing on the ground?"

She rolled her eyes to the sky, an irritated sigh escaping her. "I'm playing in the dirt, Charles. I had a long day and I'm bored so I thought I'd relax a little before I headed home."

Even though the cop in him was already working the puzzle, Gideon found himself smiling. "Want to go look for worms, Moira?"

She laughed softly.

Rising, he held out a hand. She accepted, and he couldn't help but notice the way her shoulders stiffened as Charles approached. Gideon held her gaze a long moment. "It has been a while since we've gone fishing, you know."

Something softened in her eyes. "Hasn't it?" Slowly, she tugged her hand away and then turned to look at Charles. "Somebody slashed my tire."

It was embarrassing, Moira couldn't help but think, how Gideon Marshall managed to make her feel like this, even though it had been years since she had broken up with him, years since she'd done something that had ripped the heart out of her.

Giddy, soft, excited, the same way she'd felt when he'd kissed her for the first time. They'd been fourteen, on the Ferris wheel at the Riverboat Festival.

Those had been good days. Mom and Dad had still been alive. She had just been . . . a kid. Able to just . . . *be*. Life had been simple then. She hadn't had to worry about . . . well, anything.

She had, though.

Far too much.

Just like she did now.

Sighing, she brushed back a stray lock of hair as Charles came up. As he always did, he stood too close, invading space that was no longer his to invade. They'd separated two years ago, but they'd been well into the plans for the museum by then and he was too damn good at his job. The divorce, so unbelievably civil, had been final for well over a year.

The divorce had been as void of passion as their marriage.

Passion—something that had been sadly lacking from her life for too long. Brushing the thought aside, she casually shifted away under the pretense of taking a better look at the tire.

Sure enough, now that she was looking, she could see it. The tire was slashed. "What the hell," she muttered.

"The timing is . . . concerning."

She sensed more than saw how Gideon's attention shifted to Charles, and her ex-husband was aware of it, too, although his pale blue eyes never left her face. Of course, he wouldn't pay any attention to Gideon.

Gideon was simply a public servant in Charles's eyes, unworthy of notice most of the time.

"You going to elaborate on that?" she asked when her ex didn't continue.

He pursed his lips as though he had to consider it.

But she knew Charles a little too well.

The man was brilliant, but he was a born manipulator, a fact she hadn't realized until it was too late. She cared about him, and she knew he cared about her, but everything was a game of chess to him.

Including her.

Under the weight of her stare, Charles finally sighed, one manicured hand coming up to smooth his tie down. "Moira, love, surely you noticed how upset she was."

"Who?" she said, confused.

His mouth flattened out and he looked away. "Neve."

A low, harsh noise came from beside her. Automatically, she lifted a hand and rested it on Gideon's arm. Her hand buzzed from that light contact and she had to resist the urge to jerk it back, resist the urge to rub her fingers together to get rid of that tingling sensation. Damn him for still being able to get to her like this. Damn him for never finding somebody. If he had, maybe she could have made a better go of it with Charles.

And that was the problem, really.

She'd never been able to give her heart to Charles because in her heart, she was still the girl she'd been all those years ago. The girl who'd been in love with the boy from the wrong side of the tracks—the trouble-maker, the one who everybody had said would come to no good.

Yet here he was, the chief of police, and he was fighting the same anger she was—anger, because somebody had insulted her baby sister.

"Just what does Neve have to do with my tire, Charles?" she asked, lowering her hand to her side once she was relatively sure that Gideon wasn't going to say anything—not yet, anyway. "Are you implying she slashed my tire? *Really?*"

"Of course not." He moved toward her.

She hesitated, unwilling to let him draw closer, but reluctant to let him pin her up against the car or between him and Gideon. Now, if it was Gideon and, oh, say Tom Hiddleston, she might not mind. A Gideon and Tom sandwich was perfect fantasy material. But Gideon and Charles would be better if they were kept far apart, so Moira remained where she was, although she did lift a hand, holding him at bay. "Then exactly what *are* you saying?"

"I'm not *saying* anything," he said, his clipped accent making the words harsher, more biting. There were times when that British accent had seemed so urbane, so sexy and seductive. But lately, it was just . . . cold. Charles reached up and, although he smiled at her, that was all she felt. Cold. It was hard to warm up to him, though, when every time she looked at him she remembered how she found him in bed with another woman.

"Moira, love . . ."

She tugged her chin out of his grasp when he tried to cup her face. "Just spill it, Charles, okay?"

"Very well." He tucked a strand of her hair back from her face. "Surely you noticed. Neve's in trouble. It seemed that she . . ." He paused and looked away. "I think she needs help. Of course, I never did get the chance to know her well since she hasn't come home and we only had that one brief encounter in London years ago, but . . ." He looked away. "I suspect some of the trouble she always seemed to find has followed her home."

Moira went to argue, but then she stopped. She couldn't argue. Not really.

The look she'd seen in Neve's eyes, how thin her little sister was . . . and the way she'd clutched at Moira, as though her world was falling apart. Something *was* wrong. Moira knew that in her gut. The thing was . . . she *knew* her sister.

Charles had only met her once, at a brief awkward dinner when they'd been in London on a trip a few months after their marriage. It had lasted a few short hours.

Neve hadn't come home for the wedding.

She hadn't called.

Moira shoved that hurt down. She had to. If she let

herself think about it, it was going to break her heart, all over again. Distraction was always key when it came to avoiding personal miseries, so she pinned her ex with a narrow look. "Since when are you an expert on all things Neve?"

"I'm hardly an expert, pet." He turned away, head bent. "But you know me. She just looked unhappy, and I don't have to know her to understand she's never been the easiest of souls."

The easiest of souls. Moira managed to keep that miserable laugh trapped in her throat.

And, yeah, she knew Charles. He seemed to see clear through to a person. It made him useful in his job—he was a curator, but he'd also proved to be very helpful when they'd been adding to their collection. When Moira tended to take people at their word, he'd always known when somebody just needed more coaxing, more time, more money . . . more charm. That sort of skill came from knowing people, understanding them. That he'd looked at Neve and seen the misery inside her shouldn't come as a surprise.

"I can't worry about this now," she said, shaking her head. "Whoever did this, I'm sure it had nothing to do with Neve."

She turned to look at Gideon.

If she hadn't known him as well as she did, she would have missed it.

But she did know him.

Moira knew Gideon, far better than she knew the man she'd just turned her back on, and the glint in his eyes had her narrowing her own.

"What?" she asked.

"Nothing." He pulled the radio from his collar and started talking into it. "We need to get a report done up."

"Gideon. I know that look."

He ignored her blithely as he circled the car. His shrewd eyes focused on the lazy, elegant spread of the museum behind her and then he just shook his head.

"Moira, you want to tell me just *why* you had to park in the *one* spot that's practically blind?"

"Ah . . ." She blinked and then looked around. Her car was tucked in the corner, where the shade fell over it during the worst of the day's heat. Of course, that meant the car was in an area where it was bordered by trees on two sides. "Well. It gets hot."

"It gets hot," he muttered. Gideon shook his head and scraped his nails over the light growth of stubble darkening his jaw. "And you see the tire that got slashed . . . right? It's out of view of the camera." He demonstrated, kneeling in the spot, tapping the area next to him.

With a groan, she hunkered down, close enough that the scent of him flooded her head and, although it had to be her imagination, she thought she could feel the heat of his thigh reaching out to warm hers as they knelt there. As he gestured over the top of the car, she peeked up obediently. "I get the point, Chief Marshall," she said sourly. "I can't see the cameras. If I can't see them, they aren't going to see me, either."

Patient blue eyes stared back at her.

That patience of his just pissed her off sometimes.

"What?" she half shouted.

"Get cameras—*and* security lights—that cover the area out here better," he said, shaking his head.

"We live in Treasure. It's practically Mayberry," she pointed out. "The most crime we have around here is shoplifting down at the gas station or the occasional game of mailbox baseball." She paused and then grimaced. "Unless Barney and Bertram start going at it. Are they together again?"

Gideon ran his tongue along the inside of his lower lip. "Yeah. They are."

Barney and Bertram were two of the stranger—and not always in the best way—characters in Treasure. A gay couple who had moved to town nearly fifteen years ago, they had a very on-and-off-again relationship. Bert was actually bisexual and, when he wasn't with Barney, he tended to hook up with any number of females, a fact that drove Barney crazy. That was mostly why he did it, a fact he'd admitted to. Whenever they got back together, things got busy for local law enforcement.

Their idea of foreplay involved a lot of . . . physicality. The rougher, the better. Without fail, when the cops arrived, the two of them would be both fighting and laughing, or . . . very much distracted.

And their odd idea of affection was only between the two of them. With anybody else, they were as peaceful and placid as a couple of old dogs sunning themselves on the porch. Moira had heard they'd met up on a boxing circuit in Atlanta years before. She didn't know if this really was their idea of foreplay, or what.

"Barney and Bert don't have anything to do with the tire, though," Gideon said, his aggravation bleeding through his calm words. "At least I don't think . . . unless you've been flirting with Bert. Barney gets testy about that."

"Oh, please. Bert's not my style." She rolled her eyes and rose, wincing at the pull in her thighs. "Even if the big protective teddy thing is kind of cute. But he can't ever be faithful."

Moira managed, barely, not to look at Charles. Her voice cooled slightly, though, as she finished. "That's sort of key for me."

As Charles's eyes zoomed in on her, she locked her gaze on Gideon.

"Not a bad key, in my opinion," Gideon mused. Then he stood up and pulled a notepad from his pocket. As Charles opened his mouth, he smoothly cut the other man off. "Now . . . let's see about taking care of that report."

CHAPTER SEVEN

The sight of the shining silver Porsche pulling in front of Ferry made Neve want to throw herself back into the bed, pull the covers up over her head. She didn't need to see the perfectly groomed dark head to know who it was.

That wasn't a car Moira would drive, and it sure as hell wasn't Brannon.

No, it had to be the one and only Charles Hurst.

How much?

Her lip curled and she threw her legs over the window seat where she'd been nestled, watching for her older sister to come home.

She needed to talk to Moira. She needed to get this over with.

But as she stood there, Charles flicked a glance up. He couldn't see her from here. Maybe it had been years since she'd been home, but Ferry was still *home* and she knew it like the back of her hand. This was her spot, had always been her spot. The slant of the sun and the angle of the windows made it impossible for anybody to see much beyond the sparkle of the light glinting off the glass.

But she felt like he was looking for her.

How much?

Aggravated all over again, she spun on her heel. As she passed by the door to her suite of rooms, she grabbed the shoes she kicked off there and then hit the back stairs. She wasn't going to hang around if he was going to be here.

Especially since she had a feeling he'd come to see her.

He definitely wasn't here to chat with Ella Sue.

Men like him didn't view women like Ella Sue as somebody *worth* talking to, which only meant he wasn't worth the space that took up the suits he wore.

She hit the kitchen just as he hit the doorbell.

His voice crackled through the speaker when Ella Sue elected to use the intercom system instead of going to greet him. "Ella Sue, please come open the door. It seems my key no longer works," he said.

"Mr. Charles . . . ?" Ella Sue winked at Neve.

Neve rolled her eyes.

"Is that you, Mr. Charles?" Ella Sue said, despite the fact that he'd bitten off a terse *yes*.

"Didn't I just say it was? Open the door."

"Just give me a moment, sir. I'm in the middle of preparing a salad for dinner and my hands are a mess." She disconnected the intercom and looked down at her clean hands for a moment before reaching for a knife. She glanced at Neve. "I do love a nice salad with dinner, don't you?"

Neve snorted. Then she grabbed a carrot from the bowl of vegetables. "What does he want?"

"Who knows?" Ella Sue expertly chopped up romaine lettuce. "Please tell me you're not lingering around. If it's just me, he'll leave soon enough. But if you're here, he'll find a reason to stay. None of us need that."

"Hmmm. Good point." She munched the rest of the carrot and then headed for the door.

"Don't go far." She wagged a knife at her. "Dinner is in less than two hours."

Neve hesitated and then nodded. "I won't. Thank you."

If she couldn't lose herself somewhere on the sprawling grounds, then she didn't deserve to call herself a McKay.

"Oh, don't thank me. I'm doing this so *I* don't have to put up with him. Heaven knows why your sister married him. I kept hoping he'd take himself back to England once they divorced, but no . . ." Ella Sue's voice faded away until she was muttering to herself.

Grinning, Neve slid out the back door.

She headed off down the path that led to the gardens, and from there, the river. Something told her Charles wasn't a nature boy.

Gideon Marshall owed him.

Ian stood in the kitchen, hands folded behind him as he smiled at Ella Sue and tried not to snarl at Charles Hurst.

"I'm intruding," he said, ignoring the smug British sod as Ella Sue poured peach tea into a glass for him.

He'd drink it—probably even most of it—because Ella Sue was one of the dearest ladies he'd ever met, and she'd watch him with amusement in her dark brown eyes the entire time.

He'd once told her it was a wonder people had any teeth left after drinking tea like this their whole lives. He would swear he could feel the cavities forming after his first sip.

She'd laughed at him and ever since he found himself

holding a glass of sweet tea any time he was in her presence.

"You know you're always welcome." Ella Sue smiled serenely and then looked over at Charles. "Charles, of course, you're welcome to have a seat, but I don't know what you want me to tell you. I hardly keep tabs on the comings and goings of the people who live here."

You lovely, beautiful liar, Ian thought, oddly delighted. He took a healthy swallow of the tea and even managed not to shudder as the sugar hit his system all at once.

"Can you ring Brannon for me then?" Charles gave her a tight smile, ignoring Ian. "I've tried, but he must be busy. Moira always told me he knew better than to ignore your calls."

"You give me more credit than I deserve." She gave him a smile that was loaded with as much sugar as the tea Ian was gamely trying to drink as she opened the oven.

Ian started to salivate. He'd discovered he had a weakness for Ella Sue's cooking. "Ella Sue, put me out of my misery—divorce that worthless sod you married and be my wife. I'll treat you like a queen."

"A hundred men have told me that." She shot him a look. "You might have been able to tempt me, Ian, if Brannon had brought you over here before I finally found one good man." She pulled out a deep dish of ribs.

Ian thought he'd embarrass himself if he had to stand there and breathe in that rich, savory scent too much longer—drool never did work well on him. Particularly with the beard. As Charles went to open his mouth, likely to start with his blathering again, Ian cut around the island, doing the one thing that would earn the ire of the woman who secretly ran McKay's Ferry. He acted like he'd swipe a taste from the pan.

She reached out and grabbed the wooden spoon that seemed to perpetually linger beside the stove—it was never used, never dirty—and brought it down on the back of his hand.

"Don't you dare, Ian Campbell," she said, shaking the spoon at him. "I've a mind to throw you both out of my kitchen now."

"I'm sorry, Ella Sue," he said with false meekness, turning to see Charles watching him with shrewd eyes.

"I'd be happy to get out of your way—clearly you're busy, Ella Sue," Charles said. "I simply need to speak with Brannon about . . . a personal matter."

Grabbing an apple out of the dish on the island, Ian lobbed it up into the air. Cheerfully, he said, "Oh, I'd advise against that, Charlie. Unless you want to run up against the wrong side of his fist."

For the first time since he'd come into the kitchen, Charles spoke to him. "I beg your pardon, Campbell?"

"Brannon's brassed off about something." He caught the apple out of the air a second time, lifted it to his lips, and took a bite. He took his time chewing, then swallowing. Then he grinned at Charles. "Don't know if you've seen Bran in a temper before but you might want to steer clear. He's looking for something to hurt and, if you get in his way, it just might be you."

He took another bite and then blew out a breath. "As much as I'm loathe to do it, I suspect it will be me he hurts. Being a friend, I'll make the sacrifice. Somebody has to take it and I love him like a brother. I suppose I should go and find him and we'll pound on each other."

Charles studied him for a moment. "You're going to go find him so the two of you can pound on each other."

"Well, better me than you." He gave Charles a long look. "I don't think your fancy suit would hold up."

"Indeed." Charles shifted his gaze to Ella Sue, opened

his mouth, and then abruptly just turned and walked away. Over his shoulder, he said, "Please have him call—sooner rather than later."

Once he'd disappeared down the hall, Ella Sue reached for a towel and wiped her hands off. The polite expression on her face didn't fade, but the ice thawed and she looked at Ian. "Just what is Brannon . . . brassed off about?"

Ian looked down, contemplating his apple.

"If you take one more bite of that apple, I'm going to smack you again," she warned, shaking her spoon.

"It's a good apple," he said, smiling.

She stared at him for a long moment and then sighed. "I bet you drove your poor mother to distraction, Ian."

"I did, yes." He took another bite, polishing the rest of the apple off. "As to Brannon, that's not something I can discuss with you—even if I knew. It's something personal and not my place."

"Why are you here?" she asked quietly.

He considered a dozen answers and decided to be honest. "It's entirely likely Brannon and I will have a row. Gideon wants me to keep an eye on him—make sure he doesn't do anything stupid. I'm supposed to charm my way into staying for supper. Is he here?"

Ella Sue pursed her lips and then nodded. "He and Neve got in an hour ago." Then she waved toward the back door. "Try the garden path, follow it down to the river."

"Thank you."

He went to head out the door and she called his name. "If you're supposed to charm me into letting you stay for supper, is that the best you could do?"

He flashed a wide grin. "Miss Ella Sue, could I please trouble you to let me stay for supper? I'm quite famished."

She just shook her head. "It won't be more than another hour. Don't be any longer."

Ella Sue waited until he was out of sight before she left the kitchen. And although she'd heard the control pad for the alarm chime when the front door was opened, she went to check.

Yes, that fool Charles was gone as well.

Satisfied, she made her way through the house to the west wing.

Personally, this wasn't her favorite part of the house, although she knew it as well as the back of her hand. She oversaw the cleaning and care of McKay's Ferry— it had been her duty, and her privilege, to care for this family for nearly forty years. She'd started out as a cook and then worked her way up until she ran the household.

She knew more about running the home than any of the children did—children. She sighed as she opened the door that led to the indoor shooting range. They weren't children anymore, as hard as it was to accept that. She loved them as if they were her own, though, and if there was a problem . . . well, she'd just have to see what it was.

She waited until Brannon had lowered the weapon. It looked big and mean and capable in his hands—and just then, he looked big and mean and capable, too. As he glanced up at her, there was a look in his eyes that chilled her to the bone.

Brannon had always been the . . . easiest of the three. Not that any of them could be called *easy*, no. But he'd laughed a little more often, forgiven a little sooner, and was the first to smooth things over.

But under that calm, easygoing manner lurked a temper. A fierce one. It took quite a bit to get it going, and after more than thirty years of taking care of him, she knew almost every trigger he had. She could even name them.

Moira . . . and Neve.

"I need to be alone right now, Ella Sue," he said, his voice calm. Too calm.

"Are you going to tell me what's bothering you?" she asked after she took a moment to weigh his words.

He reloaded the gun, and she again had to note how capable he looked, how easily he handled the task.

"You'll hear," he said after a moment. "Soon enough." Then he grimaced. "And you might want to be down here with me when it's all over."

"Hardly." She wrinkled her nose and studied the weapons that lined the walls. They were secure, yet still on display—beautifully violent, they ranged from modern guns to ancient pieces that never left their protective cases. Many had been carried by the McKays who had served in the military. One of them was a rifle of some sort from the first World War. Brannon had written a report on the man who'd carried that rifle in middle school—she remembered helping him with the spelling late one night while his parents had been out of town traveling.

"Twenty bucks says you're wrong," Brannon said softly, drawing her attention back to him.

She sniffed. "Fifty bucks says I'm not."

He lifted the gun back and met her eyes. "It's a bet. If you don't want to join me by the end of the week, I'll pay up." Then, with a reckless, somewhat wild grin, he added, "I'll even double the bet—and I'll handle the cooking Friday night."

"Sounds lovely. I'd love a steak, out by the pool."

"When I win," Brannon said darkly, "I want lasagna. And double Dutch chocolate cake."

She laughed and let herself out. Ella Sue didn't lose bets.

Ian Campbell eyed the long, slim redhead standing on the edge of the dock and felt his heart start to race.

Not the redhead he'd been looking for.

Logic told him to beat a fast retreat.

Lust—and longing—told him to stay right where he was. No, not *stay*—move *closer*.

A lot closer.

She turned her head and glanced at him after a moment, and if she was surprised by the sight of him, she didn't show it.

"If you're just going to stand there, tell me now. It's hard to brood when somebody's staring at you." She turned back to the river and, as he watched, she lifted her face, catching a slight breeze just in time for it to lift her hair back from her face.

He wanted to catch those curls in his hands, tangle them in his fists, then catch that mouth and taste it again—taste her.

"The prodigal daughter," he said, moving out of the shadows of the trees, taking the path that led to the dock. There was an old rowboat tied there, and as he moved closer, he could hear it knocking against the dock.

Thump. Thump. Thump.

For a few moments, that was the only sound.

Then he joined her on the dock and the roar and rush of his own blood threatened to drown out everything else.

Standing this close to her was enough to make the wiring in his brain short-circuit. That could explain why everything in him overheated, he supposed. Could maybe even explain why he had sudden, almost uncontrollable urges to pull her against him, to stroke his hands down her long limbs and press his lips to her mouth. He'd talk to her, he thought. He wanted to talk to her, to know her, all about her, and then he wanted her naked. Wanted her astride him—

"You're just going to keep staring at me, aren't you?" Her voice startled him out of his reverie.

The words escaped him before he even realized what he was going to say. "It's hard not to stare at you, Neve. You're the closest I've ever come to seeing an angel."

She gave an indelicate snort and turned her head to meet his eyes.

Neve hadn't had a reaction to a man in so long, she sometimes thought her body was broken. She sometimes thought *she* was broken—that William had ripped out the parts of her that made her *human*, made her feel and act like anything other than a victim.

She *could* react—or at least she knew she used to be able to.

There had been a few guys she'd dated before she met William. One of them had been a musician and she'd dated him for two reasons, and two reasons only.

The first reason: She thought it would piss Moira off.

The second: When he kissed her, he lit everything up inside her, as if he had some secret path to a light switch at her core and all it took was just his touch, his lips on hers, his hand on her hip—anything—to make her feel like she was going to combust inside her clothing.

Part of her sometimes wondered what might have happened between them.

But he'd overdosed one night—partying after a gig. She found out only because she had been looking for him the next night when they were supposed to meet up, and the drummer had seen her. After he told her, he'd offered to let her cry on his shoulder—and other places.

Donnie.

His name had been Donnie, and sometimes she thought they could have had something between them, two lost, pitiful souls. Two broken people. But they probably would have just made a bigger mess of each other than they already were.

A sad, tired laugh escaped her as she tilted her head back to the sky. She'd always thought the rush with Donnie was the edge of the forbidden—and that was why she hadn't responded to William the same way.

A few days ago, in the span of a few minutes—actually with one kiss, maybe even just a look—Ian Campbell had shown her just how very wrong she'd been.

And he'd just called her an angel? She couldn't help but laugh at the idea of it.

"Let me in on the joke?" he asked.

"You're one hell of a flirt, you know that?" She turned her head and looked at him, felt her heart thud hard against her ribs as their gazes locked. His lashes were a thick, heavy fringe, as black as the hair on his head and the neat beard on his face. She could remember the feel of that beard rubbing against her—her face, her neck—and her knees threatened to melt as the image of feeling it in other places tried to take over her mind.

"If you keep looking at me like that, we're going to be in the same situation we were in a few days ago," Ian said, his voice calm, logical.

And his eyes all but scorched her flesh.

"The same situation." She shrugged and went back to studying the river. "Just which one is that? The one where suddenly you give me the side eye because I'm Brannon's baby sister?"

"Ah, now, and here I was thinking you'd decided to

forgive me for that one." His voice was wry, the self-deprecating humor unmistakable.

Neve wouldn't let herself look at him.

Lifting one shoulder in a shrug, she said, "Well, I'm still Brannon's baby sister. Nothing else has changed, either. So whether it's the fact that I'm his sister or something else that got in your way . . ." She paused and finally let herself shift her gaze back to him. He was so damn pretty. It all but sucked the air out of her to just look at him. He was so . . . *male*. Big and broad and solid and everything about him called to her.

Why *now*? Despair threaded through her and for a bizarre moment, she wanted to scream—just *scream* because it wasn't fair, wasn't right that she'd finally met somebody who actually made her *feel* something and it couldn't have happened at a worse time.

But then again, when in her life had it ever been a *good* time?

His eyes narrowed on her face, and she realized something of what she was feeling must have been showing. She quickly smoothed her expression. In a bored tone, she said, "You might as well quit the flirting. We both know you changed your mind."

"And who said I changed your mind?" he asked, looking put out. He crossed his arms over his chest.

"You did." She gave a lazy shrug. "I saw it on your face, clear as day." The look on his face was a challenge, but she couldn't let herself meet it, even if she could find that part of herself that would *want* to.

Because she wasn't sure she trusted herself, she sat down on the dock and dangled her legs over the edge, staring down into the dark water. Under the trees, it was almost cool here. Almost. Not quite. "You've been here for a little while—a few months or more, at least, I'm going to assume. So you've probably heard a few rumors, and I can't say I blame you for deciding I'm more trouble than I'm worth."

Boards creaked under him as he sat down next to her.

From the corner of her eye, she could see the way faded denim stretched over hard thighs, denim so worn it was going white at the seams. His T-shirt bore the logo for Manchester United and it was almost as faded as the denim. It would be soft against his skin, she thought. And under it, his skin would be incredibly hard and warm.

She wanted to curl her hands into his shirt, straddle his thighs, and rub herself against him. And she wanted to yell at him for making her think she could maybe have the small promise of oblivion with him.

You've lost your mind.

All this time with a nonexistent libido and now it was going haywire on her. To make matters worse, it wasn't even lust driving her now. She'd known that from the sucker punch of pain that had hit her when the heat in Ian's eyes had cooled, the moment he'd realized who she was.

"I've never been one to put much stock in rumors, Neve McKay," he said softly.

"Really." Turning her head, she studied him. "So the hot-to-cold act was all because you figured out I'm Brannon's little sister? Then why are you running warm again? I'm still his sister."

A pained look crossed his face. "You aren't one for the easy way, are you?"

"Are you kidding?" She laughed bitterly. "I *love* the easy way. But the easy way *hates* me. I figured that out ages ago. Besides, life isn't easy."

Ian leaned forward, elbows braced on his knees. "Brannon, he's one of my best friends. Has been since university. We met in London and it was like we'd known each other our whole lives." His voice was distant now as he gazed into the water. "Like a brother, he is."

Now he looked up and met her gaze. "I take issue when people hurt those I care about," he said. "And . . ."

She stiffened. Curling her hands around the boards, she focused on the far side of the bank. "Well, I'll give you points for the loyalty you show your friends then." She forced her fingers to unclench from the boards and went to stand.

"It's not just that." He caught her wrist before she could rise.

It was instinct that had her jerking back, instinct that had her pulse stopping than accelerating in fear.

It didn't go unnoticed by Ian, either, damn him.

Although he said nothing, he let go.

She managed to rise to her feet in a slow, unhurried motion. "Look, it doesn't matter. You're Brannon's friend and it's not a secret that I've got some fences to mend when it comes to my family." She gave him an easy smile and an easy shrug before she turned and headed down the dock. "But it's probably wiser all around if you just stop this . . . whatever this is. The hot-and-cold thing gets old and I—"

The words froze in her throat as she turned and found him just a foot away.

Whoa. He was quiet. Big. Sexy. Quiet.

And he watched her with eyes that saw a lot deeper than she liked.

"The problem with stopping the hot-and-cold thing is that there is no cold." He lifted a hand and caught one of her curls, twining it around his finger. His gaze, dark and seductive, richer than melted chocolate, held hers. "I look at you and feel nothing but fire in me, Neve. I think you know it, too. Now if it was just fire, then it wouldn't be such a problem. Fire is all well and good, but it's easy . . . and sometimes over in a flash. But this . . ." He moved a hand between them. "I don't think it's just fire. You feel it, too. That's why you're so nervous. That's why you're so afraid."

Her heart knocked up against her ribs.

"Well. Aren't *you* arrogant?" she said, surprising herself with how steady her voice sounded.

"Is it arrogance when we both know I'm right?"

He took another step, taking away a few of those precious inches between them, twining a bit more of her hair around his finger. She had to tilt her head back now to hold his gaze.

"I made a misstep when I let things I didn't understand influence any decision I made," he murmured, his eyes falling from hers now.

He was rubbing her hair, his thumb stroking back and forth over the curl he was toying with.

She could just barely see it but the action was oddly mesmerizing.

"There are, after all, two sides to every story, aren't there?"

Now his gaze lifted back to hers.

Swallowing, Neve tried for a snide tone as she asked, "Oh, is this where you ask me to explain *my* side of what happened?"

"No. This is where I kiss you."

If he'd given her any more warning, she might have been able to . . . to . . .

Oh, hell. Neve couldn't have done anything. Anything but grab at his shoulders and hold on tight.

She made his heart ache.

She made something inside him sing—made him feel alive in a way he couldn't even understand.

And when he kissed her, she made him think of honey and fire and the very devil.

Sweetness, heat, and all the temptation in the world, wrapped up in one intoxicating package.

As her mouth opened under his, he slid his hand around her waist, rested it at the small of her back. Rested it right there, although what he wanted to do was haul her against him and take her down to the boards under their feet. He didn't because he'd seen it. Oh, he'd had his suspicions, but that minute flinch she hadn't been able to hide earlier had confirmed what his gut already knew.

Somebody had hurt her. Ian knew it as well as he knew his own name.

And Marshall wanted him to talk Brannon down?

No, Ian wanted to hunt down whoever it was and bloody the bastard himself.

But for now . . .

Ian pulled her more securely against him, shuddering as the slight curves of her breasts went flat against his chest. She was long and slim and the thought of having her under him was enough to make his brain melt.

When she slid her hands under his shirt, he pulled his mouth away from hers.

"I want to see you naked," he said, pressing his mouth to her neck. "I want to see you in my bed. I want to see you smile, and make you laugh, and hold you while I do it. If you're not sure you're ready for that, then you need to pull back. Now."

She stilled and then lifted her head. "We're not having sex."

"Not here? Or not ever?" If she said not ever, he thought he might cry. Just go to his knees and sob.

She blinked, looking startled. Then she frowned.

"Here. We can't have sex here. And I still haven't decided if I even want to sleep with you."

"Well, then." He cupped her chin in his hand and lifted her face to his. *That's definitely not a* not ever, he thought, immensely satisfied. "I'll just have to work on convincing you that you really do want to sleep with me, then won't I? After all, you wanted to a few days ago."

He flicked his tongue against her lips, but she didn't open for him.

Her hands curled into his shirt and she averted her head. "A few days ago, I was looking for a way to not think. You were just going to be a distraction, Ian."

"I can still distract you." He slid his hand under her shirt and splayed it wide, stroking his thumb against the silken skin. "Neve, really, I think you spend too much time thinking as it is. Turn your brain off for a bit. Just feel . . ."

He raked his teeth down her throat. He loved the way that made her shiver. Sliding his hand down along the front of her chest, he cupped her breast through the faded red cotton. She jolted and he stilled. "Want me to stop?"

A shaky sigh escaped her. "I'm still deciding."

He trailed a line of kisses down her neck. "Well, you keep thinking then. Let me know when you've made your decision. While you think, though, you should be more comfortable . . ."

Her eyes flew wide and she clutched at his shoulders as he swept her up, then took her to her back. She fisted her hands in his shirt. "Lying on my back on a wooden deck is supposed to be more comfortable?"

"You looked like you wanted to get off your feet for a spell." He smiled as he leaned down and pressed a kiss to the middle of her chest, through the cotton of her shirt. Her heart bumped hard against her ribs—he felt it and he reached for the small buttons that held her top closed. "You look hot, too."

Now she snorted. "You must have been every mother's nightmare with lines like that." She reached up and caught his hand, stilling him before he'd finished with all those tiny little buttons.

Good enough for now, he decided. "I'm just trying to make you comfortable," he said, keeping his voice easy. And he liked seeing her smile, even if the shadows of fear and distrust hadn't entirely faded from her eyes. They would. He'd see to it. But for now . . . he'd settle for seeing the pleasure roll across her pretty face again. Her shirt gaped to just below her bra and he braced himself on his elbow as he stared down at her.

A ragged breath escaped him.

"That's a pretty sight, Neve," he murmured. Pretty, though, that didn't describe her. She was as pale as moonlight, and the black silk of her bra made her skin gleam like a pearl. He dipped his head and pressed a kiss to the soft swell of one breast, toying with the front clasp.

When he freed it, she just lay there, although she still held her hand protectively over the buttons that kept the bottom half of her shirt closed. "Are you still deciding?" he asked, as he levered his weight up over her.

Her eyes had gone dark, as dark as the mossy green that gathered under the trees here at the river. Her mouth was damp and she stared at him, half blind. "Deciding?"

He took that as a yes, so he lowered his head and caught one tight nipple between his teeth.

She closed one hand over the back of his head, rasping out his name.

"Let me know when you want me to stop," he said. He'd have to. He wouldn't make love to her the first time here on a wooden dock where the boards would bruise her, but he wasn't ready to stop yet.

And when she gripped the back of his head with her other hand, he thought maybe she wasn't ready for him to stop yet, either.

Now that she'd let go of her shirt, he dealt with the rest of her buttons and then caught her around the waist, twisting and rolling until she straddled him.

She moaned and arched, rubbing herself against him, and Ian thought he might come like that, just from the feel of her and the scalding heat of her as she moved against him. Curving one hand over her side, he rubbed the underside of her breast, stroked a path down the flat plane of her belly.

There was a faint line there—so faint, his brain didn't process it at first. Truly, he was focused on the ache in his cock, on the warmth of the woman moving against him—and on the fact that he'd decided they wouldn't have sex here, not to mention that she was still *deciding* . . .

His thumb brushed another one of those lines and some of the fog cleared from his mind just as she sank her teeth into his lip.

Groaning, he shifted his grip to her hip while he fisted the other hand in the heavy weight of her hair. "Are you still deciding? If you've made up your mind, I'm thinking I could have us at my place right quick— and I have condoms there this time."

She stilled against him and then sighed, her breath like a soft caress against his lips. "You make me lose my head."

"Mine's about ready to come clean off." He rocked up against her, leaving no doubt about what he meant.

She blushed and he rolled, spilling her onto her back,

careful to keep his weight off her. "Since you're still thinking . . ." He kissed his way down her neck.

She shivered. "Your beard tickles."

"That's what all the ladies say," he murmured.

She tugged on his ear. "That makes me want to decide *no*."

"Ladies? What ladies? . . . I've never touched another," he said, flashing her a wicked smile.

"You're a charming son of a bitch, aren't you?"

"I can do more than charm you, Neve." He slid his mouth down to the curve of her breast, moving slowly, feeling the shiver that raced through her as his beard teased her even before he closed his mouth over her nipple.

She whimpered.

Sliding his hand down, he cupped her between her legs.

She bucked against him.

He sucked her nipple deep into his mouth and rubbed against her, falling into the rhythm that had brought her to climax in the darkness of his gardens. "I want to hear you call out my name this time. Come for me, Neve . . ."

She did, and the sound of it rose into the air, echoing around them.

He sprawled between her legs, his cock miserably uncomfortable under the jeans he wore, the echo of her voice as she came already burned into his memory. "If you haven't decided yet, let me know."

To his delight, she laughed.

"If I say no, will you do that again?"

He pressed a kiss to her torso. "I'd be delighted . . ." Then he flicked her a look. "Or I could . . ."

Her breath trapped inside her lungs at the look in

his eyes. When he started to move lower, the only thing Neve could think was, *oh, shit.*

But then his lips brushed bare skin, the bare skin of her abdomen, and she realized her shirt was hanging open.

Oh. Shit!

She tensed up.

His mouth brushed the scars just as he noticed the tension in her body and Ian flicked a look up at her. Then he stopped, his brows dropping low as he pushed his weight up onto his elbows.

She tried to scramble back, but his hands caught her hips and held her still.

"What the bloody *fuck*?"

"Let me go." Panic and shame crowded inside her, and if he didn't let her go, she didn't know what she'd do—

But he did, and she awkwardly got to her feet, spinning away. She caught the edges of her shirt and tried to button it but her fingers wouldn't cooperate.

"Damn it." The words came out in a choked whisper. "Here."

She froze as he reached up and caught her hands. He kissed first one, then the other, before lowering them and took over the task of buttoning her shirt. She focused on the faded yellow script that stretched across his chest. "You're into soccer."

"Only you Americans call it soccer. It's football, that's what it is." His voice was gentle and that made her shake that much harder.

It also made it that much harder to pull away from him when he reached up and cupped her cheek, lifting her chin until their eyes met.

She waited for him to ask. She'd handled more than

her share of intrusive questions, and now that the shock of it was fading, she found herself reaching for anger. Anger was better. Anger was *always* better. It had taken her too long to find her mad, but once she had, it had kept her going.

But all he did was rub his thumb across her lips.

Then he stepped back.

She turned away, took a few steps on legs that were still stiff.

"Neve."

She went still.

"You can take your time deciding, but just know . . . I've already made my decision. I'm a patient man."

She curled her hands into fists. "What's that supposed to mean?"

"Just what you'd imagine it means." His hand settled on her spine. "I wanted you from the moment I laid eyes on you. That hasn't changed. I'll just keep waiting until you're done thinking."

She turned now, shrugging his hand away and glaring at him. "What is this? Are you offering me a pity fuck now?"

His lids drooped. "You think *pity* did this?"

She tensed as he caught her hand and then had to swallow as he brought it to the ridge in his pants. He was swollen and thick, hard under her touch, and, instinctively, she tightened her hand, or as much as she could with him confined behind the thick material of his jeans.

"Pity's got nothing to do with what I feel right now," he said, bringing up his arms and hooking them over her shoulders. The heavy weight of them held her in place, but his embrace was loose, loose enough that she could duck away, twist out of his arms. All she wanted to do was move closer and press herself against him— forget the past few minutes had even happened.

But he let her go and backed up.

"I think we both know that you'll end up in my bed." His voice was calm and level, although his eyes were burning hot. "When you do, just know the reason will be because we both want it."

"Again, you're arrogant." Her voice was raspy now. The anger had faded and the fear was gone. She felt . . . drained. Drained and confused. The one thing she *wasn't* confused about was that he was right. She did want him.

He shrugged. "If it's true . . ."

She turned around and headed back up the path.

She hadn't quite reached the tree line when he called out, "I'm joining you for dinner tonight. I'd say it was because I want to charm Ella Sue into marrying me so she'll cook for me every day for the rest of my life but . . ."

She went still as his voice drew nearer.

"I can't lie to you."

His voice was harder now and the brogue was thicker—the words came out *I cannae lie t' ya,* and she could almost feel the heat rolling from him. Slowly, she turned her head and stared at him from a distance of just a few feet.

"Marshall sent me out here—wanted me to make sure your brother didn't go and do something rash." A reckless smile lit his face. It should have made him look that much more charming—just a sexy, roguish bastard who could talk a woman out of her panties in no time flat.

But the glint in his eyes would chill a man's blood.

"All I want to do is hunt your brother down and see if he wants to join me. The man who put those marks on you, Neve . . . if I ever get my hands on him, he'll be begging for mercy by the time I'm done."

CHAPTER EIGHT

Ian waited until she was lost in the woods, waited until even the sound of her was gone before he turned and drove his fist into the trunk of the tree nearest him.

Pain shot up his arm and his fist started to throb.

It did nothing to ease the fury. The sight of the blood coming from his split knuckles only made him want to see *more* blood.

He'd thought she'd been hurt.

Hurt, yes.

But somebody had fucking terrified her.

It sickened him, infuriated him, and made him want to break things. At the same time, he wanted to cuddle her up close, although she wouldn't stand for that.

She'd gotten herself away.

It was written all over her face, in the proud way she held herself, in the way she tried to hide a fear that had to be etched on her soul.

Closing his eyes, he tipped his head back to the sky. He had the answer to his question now, although he wasn't any happier for it. He'd wanted to know just what had gotten under Brannon's skin.

He knew now. Not all of it, no. But enough.

And Gideon Marshall thought *Ian* was the one to help watch Brannon?

What a laugh that idea was.

He had no clue what he was asking.

None at all.

He'd tell Brannon later. They'd share a pint and have a laugh over it. Assuming they didn't both end up in jail. One thing was certain, though, Brannon would find out who it was. And once Brannon knew, Ian would damn well find out himself.

For now, though, he needed to get back to the house.

He wasn't hungry anymore, although he imagined once he sat down, he'd find his appetite. But he wouldn't be able to leave until he'd seen Neve again.

He'd put the shadows back in her eyes.

He'd try to take them away if he could.

That man was dangerous.

Neve tried to tell herself on the walk back to the house that the only thing she needed to do, as far as Ian Campbell was concerned, was stay far away.

She wasn't going to take her advice, though. Not at all.

That knowledge filled her with more than a little trepidation, but she was smart enough to know that the fears weren't grounded in anything resembling logic.

He took her breath away and he was sexy and he made her feel like she was in over her head, but those were the only things he had in common with William.

Even from the beginning, William hadn't let her be who she was, and now, with the experience of years behind her, she could see how easily he had manipulated her. Just as she could see that if she'd pulled away from Ian, he would have let her do just that. He might have quietly worked on wearing her down, but if she'd given him a firm no, he'd have taken it.

That was what made him really dangerous.

Not the fact that he turned her into a molten mass of need when he kissed her.

But that she knew she wouldn't be able to say no and she just might lose herself in him, right when she had finally figured out who she was—or who she needed to be.

Dangerous, she thought again.

By the time she'd reached the house, she was composed—mostly—and thought maybe she could handle looking at him across the table. It might not even be that bad. It would give her more time to compose herself and ready herself before she had to tell Moira.

More time to get her head and her emotions under control.

Going through this so many times in one day was leaving her feeling raw, and she thought she just might try to wheedle Brannon into giving her another day.

That was until she opened the door and found herself in the middle of World War III.

"—what you think. She didn't have shit to do with it and if you don't get out of here, I'm going to *throw* you out!"

Brannon's voice, big as life, boomed through the opened door.

Moira stood with her hips against the counter, her hand pressed to her temple.

A few feet away, Ella Sue stood watch and her face was a smooth, expressionless mask, but her eyes rested on one man with acute dislike—something that was so unlike Ella Sue that Neve found herself staring. Ella Sue didn't do that. Oh, she disliked plenty of people and those close to her would know—and hear the sharp edge of her tongue—but unless you were one of those people, you'd rarely see such obvious signs of her dislike.

Brannon said again, "Did you not *hear* me, Hurst? I want you out of my house."

"I thought you would be the rational one of the lot, Brannon," Charles said, his voice smooth. He flicked a look at Moira. "I tried to discuss this with Moira and she wouldn't listen. Don't you care that—"

They all seemed to notice her at the same time.

Gideon's mouth thinned down. Both Moira and Gideon set their jaws, but while Brannon started to swear under his breath, Moira shifted her attention to Charles and said in an icy voice, "We will discuss this later. Charles, you should go. We had a family dinner planned and you're interrupting."

The warm presence at her back had Neve shifting her attention over her shoulder, but only for a minute. She moved deeper into the kitchen, letting Ian come in.

"Family?" Charles smiled tightly. "Since when is the help at the local bar *family*?"

"Oh, since I started romancing Miss Ella Sue," Ian said easily. Seemingly unaware of the tension in the air, he crossed to the island and reached out, grabbing something from the tray Ella Sue had waiting there. "I intend to woo her away from her man, you see, and make her fall madly in love with me. I've already discussed wedding plans with Brannon."

Neve wondered if he was obtuse, but then he turned and she caught the glint in his eyes. It was almost as hard as the one in Brannon's.

She was tempted to just leave—go to her bedroom or take the car—but as gazes continued to flick to her, she found herself getting angry. *Fuck this*, she thought.

"So just what didn't I do?" she asked quietly.

"Neve, sweetie," Moira said, smiling gently.

"Don't." She looked at Moira, surprising herself by the soft, steely tone to her voice. "I'm neither a child nor an idiot teenager. If I'm being accused of something—and I'm pretty sure I am—I think I've got a right to know."

Moira stared at her, but remained silent.

Neve shifted her attention to Brannon, but he was glaring at Charles.

"Moira's tire was slashed at the museum."

Neve jerked her head around to stare at Ella Sue. "What?"

Ella Sue's lip curled as she raked Charles with a disgusted look. "And that fool there thinks *you* had something to do with it."

"Ella Sue!" Moira gave her a sharp look.

Ella Sue wheeled on her. "Don't you speak to me in that tone, Moira. Neve's not wrong. If she's being accused, she's got a right to know." She looked back at Neve. "So. Neve. Were you running around slashing tires?"

"Sure." She gave Charles a thin smile. "I did it between talking to the chief of police and my brother earlier. I had a busy afternoon."

"I knew you didn't have anything to do with it, Neve," Moira said, and the words were weary. "That's why I didn't even want him bothering you . . . What?"

Neve hadn't even thought of it.

Not until she saw the way Brannon's eyes skipped away from hers and slid to Gideon's.

Now, though, she couldn't stop thinking of it.

Closing her eyes, she turned away.

She might have even headed out the door if it hadn't been for one thing.

Or rather . . . one person.

Ian Campbell.

He'd somehow circled back around and stood leaning between her and the door, one tennis-shoe-clad foot hooked over the other. Gray eyes rested on hers and then he moved in, murmured, "Don't give that sorry piece of shite the satisfaction. Unless you went and slashed her fucking tire, you aren't responsible . . . and you know it."

The hard, direct words cut through the noise in her head and she stared at him. Something warm and steady moved through her and it gave her the strength to turn back to face the room.

Neve met Moira's gaze.

"We need to talk."

A heavy sigh came from Charles. "I knew it. Neve, whatever trouble you've brought with you—"

Gideon lunged after Brannon and caught him around the waist, but he barely stopped him in time. Brannon's fingers brushed against the lapels of Charles's suit jacket, and the only thing that kept Brannon from dragging him in was Charles jerking back at the last moment.

"Get out," Brannon snarled, struggling to break away from Gideon. "Get out now—Gideon, you bastard, get off me and get him out of here. I want him out of my house—*now*. Arrest his ass if he won't leave."

"You aren't sole owner," Charles said, but he eyed Brannon with a wary gaze.

"You have sixty seconds, Charles," Moira said, drawing Charles's gaze to her, "to get out that front door. Otherwise, it won't be an issue of Gideon arresting you." She gave him a tight smile. "After all, we are outside the town limits."

She drew her keys from her pocket and flashed them. "Sixty seconds, Charles, or I push the panic button. The sheriff's department will be here in roughly five minutes and I'll have you arrested for trespassing."

"Moira—"

"Forty-five." Her eyes flashed. "And if you push me, we'll be discussing your continued employment at the museum."

Neve counted five seconds before Charles turned. He left, his stiff-legged stride taking him down to the front door. Gideon let Brannon go. "Keep your hot-headed ass in here," he warned. "I'm going to make sure the up-tight prick leaves."

As all eyes shifted toward Neve, she had to fight the urge to fall back against the door.

Ian stood between her and the door, she remembered, the thought coming to her in an almost absent manner. She'd be falling back against him.

That idea really, really didn't bother her.

"Neve."

She blinked, looking across the room to meet Moira's gaze.

It was, as always, calm and placid, like a lake, undisturbed by even a single ripple.

"I think I want a drink." Neve moved over toward the fridge. "You might want to have one yourself."

"I don't want a drink," Moira snapped, and the sharpness of her tone had Neve pausing to look back.

Moira sucked in a breath. "I apologize. I just . . . please. Tell me what's going on."

"Here." Ella Sue lifted a bottle of wine that had been left open to breathe on the counter. She poured Neve a glass and turned it over. "Whatever it is, Neve, please . . . you know we love you . . . don't you? We'll always love you."

You can't escape me, Neve. . . . I'll always find you. She took a small sip of the wine to brace herself and then put it down.

She reached for the hem of her shirt and turned, baring the scar she'd already shown Brannon.

The muscles in his jaw were tight, bunching and clenching as he stood there. After a few seconds, he looked away.

The others just stared—including Ian. She hadn't even thought to tell him to go.

After a moment, she dropped her shirt.

That shattered the spell. Ella Sue turned away, lifting one hand to her mouth. Moira rushed forward but when she would have caught Neve's shirt, Neve lifted a hand. "Don't," she said, her voice flat.

"Who did that? What the *hell*, Neve?"

She tossed back the rest of her wine. Then, softly, she said, "The man I moved to London with. William."

She recited it as if by rote—the same way she'd go through her sodding grocery list. Ian stood near the door, thinking he should leave, yet oddly unable to make himself.

There were things she wasn't telling them, too—he could see that in her eyes—and it infuriated him just as much as the things she *did* say, but what was he to do?

What he wanted to do was hold her. Pick her up, carry her out of here, and hold her, because this was hurting her and it just wasn't acceptable. But he couldn't do that. He knew he couldn't. So he stood there, in silence, as it hurt her, and he let the rage grow inside him.

Nobody spoke.

He thought he might have stopped breathing there for a spell—that might explain why his chest felt tight.

"And that's it. He's in the United States. I know he is. For all I know, he's the one who slashed Moira's tire, although the thought of William Clyde getting on his knees to do something so . . . mundane . . . just doesn't fit." She shrugged.

Ian jerked his head up. "What did you say his name was?"

"William." Neve glanced at him, a soft flush on her cheeks, as though she'd half forgotten he was there. Now her gaze bounced away.

"His last name." Shoving away from the wall, he moved closer. "His last name. Clyde?"

"Yeah." Now she eyed him nervously. "Why?"

"And he was a barrister? From London?" Something hot and vicious and raw twisted in his gut as he stared at her. *Let me be wrong . . . can I be wrong on this?*

"Yeah." She swallowed and backed up a pace.

Ian realized he was crowding her and he made himself stop. "William—is that his first name or his middle, do you know?"

"Ian, back off," Brannon said, his voice low.

"It . . ." Neve licked her lips. "It was his middle name. How did you know that? His first name was Samuel."

"Samuel."

They said it at the same time.

Ian turned just as Brannon went to grab his arm.

"You know him," Neve said softly.

"Aye. Yeah," he muttered, shaking his head. Then he looked up at Brannon. "And you do, too. Sam Clyde, Bran. That piece of shite who tried to get me thrown out of university. Remember him now?"

Brannon stared at him for a long moment and then, as though it was just too hard to hold in place, his hand slid slackly away from Ian's shoulder. "Sam," he said, his voice thick.

"What are you two talking about?" Neve asked, her voice tight.

Ian thought he might be sick. There he'd been, wanting

to take her away from this pain, to hurt the man who'd caused it . . . and now . . .

Was it because of us?

Ian looked at Brannon, but Brannon had turned away, his hands over his face, shoulders slumped.

"It's been years," he finally said when it was clear Brannon was in no hurry to talk. "Brannon and me, we'd gone out to this pub. We didn't normally go there, but we'd heard there would be music, thought we'd try it. Turned out the music was bad and most of the people in there were more interested in looking important. So we left. We heard a scream."

He stopped then, looking away.

Brannon finally turned back. Ian thought he looked like he'd aged ten years in those few brief moments. "We'd cut through the back," Brannon said. "We didn't see anybody, almost just left, but then we . . . well, we didn't. There was a car on the far side of the lot. This sick fuck had one of the servers from the pub—I grabbed him, beat the shit out of him. Ian calls the cops, gets the girl out of the car. We give our reports . . . then nothing. The girl doesn't want to testify. She doesn't want to talk to us. That's fine, we get that. But I'd recognized him. I knew him. He went to school with us—we both had a couple of classes with him."

"Evil piece of shit," Ian said. He'd moved away from Neve, staring out the window over the landscaped yards. He wasn't seeing the flowers or the topiary or the lush green lawns, though. He saw pale flesh, bruised by vicious hands. "Turns out he had a name for himself—not that many people talked. Money made plenty of people forget. His father, uptight prick, came to my door, knocking. Said he could set me up in grand style if I'd just forget the misunderstanding I'd seen. I told him to fuck himself. The next time I saw Sam, I called him out—he was talking to this pretty thing—I don't even remember her name. She was in a class with us, wasn't she?"

"Yeah," Brannon said. "I want a fucking drink. And her name was Alice. She left school a few months later."

"I humiliated her, calling him out like that. Told everybody in the pub he was a rapist, a piece of shite—nothing but scum. People looked at her . . ." He stopped, shook his head. "Nothing to do for it now, is there? He came at me and I put him on the floor. A few days later, I'm asked to step out of a class. So is Brannon."

"His dad tried to get us thrown out of school." Brannon snorted as he poured himself a glass of whiskey from a decanter on a table next to the couch. "It took him a while to figure out that I wasn't going anywhere. Neither was Ian. We made that son of a bitch's life hell."

There was a soft noise.

"Brannon," Ian said quietly.

But Neve was already out the door.

"Neve!" Brannon was on his feet like a shot.

"Leave her alone."

Moira shoved in front of him, torn between rage and misery and guilt.

Because he was there—and useful—when Brannon tried to go around her, she shifted and put herself back in his path and shoved him, putting her temper and strength into it.

It wasn't a lot, but it caught his attention.

"Moira, damn it!"

"Do you think she wants to talk to you now?"

"I have to—"

"You can't fix this," she said softly. "Nobody can. I never had to deal with anybody who laid hands on me, but now . . ." She had to stop because the rage inside her threatened to take control and she never let anything control her. "It seems like maybe the son of a bitch did it because she's your baby sister. That just makes it worse. And we can't fix that."

"I have to . . ." Brannon stopped abruptly and just stood there, a look on his face that tore at her. He looked lost and frustrated and furious—the same way she felt.

Moving in, she hugged him. He caught her up against him, squeezing tight enough that her ribs ached, but she didn't care.

Ella Sue moved in. "Moira."

Looking at the woman who'd been like a mother to her for twenty years, she saw an echo of everything she felt written across Ella Sue's lovely, timeless face.

"Go up to her," Ella Sue said softly. "This isn't a time for her to be alone."

"But . . ."

"She needs somebody. Look . . . she came home for a reason. She needs to heal and she needs her family. Right now, she needs somebody more than ever." Ella Sue caught her hand and squeezed. "Who better than her sister?"

A sister who'd been there when she really needed her would probably be a better fit, Moira thought bitterly.

But she nodded. After all, she was the only sister Neve had.

Silence echoed behind her, seemed to follow her as she made her way through the house.

Nobody responded when she knocked on Neve's door, but she knew her sister was in there. She almost turned away.

She needs somebody.

She opened the door.

If she hadn't done her best to learn how to control her

temper for the past two decades, the sight in front of her would have had her screaming in outrage.

Neve glanced at her and then away, carrying the load of clothes in her arms to the bed.

"Leaving already?" Moira asked.

"No." Neve shrugged. Her arms were slender—almost too thin—but Moira couldn't overlook the muscle there.

Her sister had somehow become terribly strong in the past few years.

"Most of these clothes either don't fit or don't suit me anymore. I'm going to donate them. I need to buy some new stuff, but for now, I just want these out of here." She paused as she put her load down, stroked a hand across a red silk tank.

"That was one of your favorites," Moira said. She'd kept the damn clothes because she'd been convinced her sister would come back.

Neve shrugged. "It's just a shirt."

"Neve . . ."

Now she looked up, her pale green eyes vivid, the tears she'd been fighting welling up. "I don't want to talk about this."

"It's not . . ." Moira stopped, floundering.

"It's not what?" Neve stalked back over to the closet and disappeared inside. A moment later, she appeared with more clothes. "Not my fault?"

"No. It's not."

Neve stopped in the middle of the floor, all but quivering as she stood there. Tremors wracked her body and, abruptly, she flung down her armful of clothes. "You think I don't know that?" she shouted. "I *know*! I did the counseling and I read the pamphlets and I wrote my damn feelings down and I get up in the morning and remind myself of that *all the time*. And I *still* wonder why I stayed . . . but I never wondered why I *fell* for him."

She turned and went to move but the clothes tangled around her feet. Sighing, she knelt down, gathering them up.

Moira crossed the floor, kneeling down. She picked up a skinny-strapped black dress, something so short she never would have let Neve out of the house in it. She tossed it over her arm and added another black dress, then another.

"I never wondered . . . looking back, I knew it was a mistake, and I knew it was wrong, but it made sense," Neve said, her voice soft. "He made me feel . . . like I mattered. He was older and experienced, and he seemed like he'd seen and done everything. He just . . . took me over. And I let him. I didn't want to fight it. Not until it was too late. And now . . ."

"He used you." Moira stood, her arms full of clothes. She hugged them instead of her sister.

Neve stood up and met her eyes. "Yeah. It shouldn't matter, should it? He still hit me. He still hurt me. He'd still be doing it if I hadn't left . . . and now I feel like I'm back there all over again. It wasn't ever even about me."

Neve turned around, dumping the clothes on the bed. "Think Ella Sue can dig up a couple of boxes before she leaves?"

"Fuck the boxes." Moira caught her sister's arm, turning her around. "You were the one he hurt and it's your life he's still trying to mess up. I'd say it's very much about you."

Neve opened her mouth, then closed it. She went to pull away, but as she averted her face, Moira saw the tears she was still fighting.

She needs her sister.

Although the gulf of years separating them still felt

as wide as ever, she moved in and caught Neve around the waist, hugging her.

Neve didn't move—not for the longest time, and then, she started to sob.

"He never even loved me."

The words came into the quiet a long time later. Moira didn't know how much time had passed. They were curled up on the floor, Neve with her head pillowed on Moira's lap. Moira stroked Neve's hair back.

"That shouldn't even be a question. He used his fists on you. That's not love."

"That's not always true," Neve said, sighing. "Abusers can very well love . . . it's a twisted, dangerous kind of love, Moira. And the abuse is that much more subtle for it. It's the kind of stuff that leads to obsession. But he didn't love me. That was why I stayed for as long as I did—I thought he loved me. But it wasn't ever about that."

Moira didn't know what to say to that—she couldn't comprehend being with a man who'd hurt her. *Staying* with a man who'd hurt her. She wouldn't have thought Neve would, either. But she knew her sister—she'd once been incredibly strong-willed. Somehow, William Clyde, Sam Clyde, whoever he was, had damaged her enough to make her do just that. *Walk a mile in her shoes,* she thought. "In the end, it doesn't matter what it was about, I don't think," she finally said. "Right now, it's a kick in the gut. But what matters is that he's still the man who hurt you. One who might try to hurt you again."

"Yeah." Neve sighed, the sound shuddering out of her. "I just . . ."

The words trailed off.

"What, baby?"

Neve sat up, drawing long, denim-clad legs to her chest. "I was so happy with him. At first. I had this great guy . . . and yeah, it was all a lie. But there he was. I thought I'd finally have somebody who *wanted* me. Who *needed* me."

The words—the sheer loneliness in them—hit Moira hard.

"Nevie . . ."

Neve shook her head. "It doesn't matter."

"It does."

When Neve tried to stand up, Moira reached out. "Do you honestly think we didn't need you? Didn't want you?"

A sad smile curved her lips. "I was a pain in the ass, Moira. There were times when *I* didn't want me." Then she shrugged. "But it doesn't matter anyway."

She got to her feet, stretching her arms over her head.

Moira did the same, although her spine ached and every muscle in her body protested. "It matters," she said. "We should have done better—*I* should have done better. You needed me and I was too caught up in everything else to even realize how much I was messing up. You and Brannon were the two who needed me the most and I let you both down."

Neve looked away. "We all messed up. I'm . . . tired," she said after a moment. "I'm tired of looking back and wondering and questioning and wishing. I just want to forget half of my life and start over, if I can."

Then she looked back at her sister. "Brannon and I weren't the only ones who needed you, though. Gideon did, too."

The simply spoken words hit her like a fist and Moira opened her mouth only to realize she had absolutely nothing to say.

"I don't think the two of you ever got over it, either."
Neve turned toward her bed. "I guess I'll just fold these
for now. Thanks for . . . well, you know."

Moira opened her mouth to respond, but then she just
stood and moved to the bed. When she started to fold
the clothes, Neve looked at her.

"It's been years," Moira said, forcing her voice to be
level. "I figure we've got time to make up for. Even if
we're doing it over a pile of clothes that are . . ."—she
held up something insanely fuchsia and insanely floral—
"sadly outdated."

"That was yours," Neve said. "I just . . . borrowed
it."

Brannon and Ian had a method of communication that
seemed to involve odd looks, low grunts or mutters, and
lots of whiskey.

Gideon didn't bother asking for translations.

The two were close—they might as well have been
born in the same nursery. The fact that an ocean had
separated them for the first eighteen years of their lives
didn't matter much. They were as close as two friends
could get.

While they continued their indeterminate conversation, Gideon moved through the house, feeling at loose
ends.

Ella Sue had made coffee and then gone home.

He drank half the pot and then made himself walk
away. He would probably be up half the night anyway,
but at least now he'd know it was his own fault and not
the coffee.

As the clock crept up on ten, he found himself at the
foot of the steps.

It had been silent ever since Moira had followed Neve,
and now, like a string was tugging on him, Gideon was

drawn up the elegant staircase off to the west wing, where the family's bedrooms were.

Neve's had never been moved.

They'd never changed a single thing, a fact that surprised him not at all.

They'd just been waiting for her.

What infuriated him was that they'd *just* waited—that *he* had just waited. He should have known Neve wouldn't just . . . disappear like that. Hot as that temper was, she'd loved her family and she would have come home. Because nobody had pushed, look at what had happened.

The door was closed and he turned the handle gently, watching as a wedge of light from the hallway spilled inside.

The first thing he saw was the miniature tower city constructed of a tower of clothes neatly stacked on the floor in front of Neve's bed.

The second thing . . . the two women curled up on the bed.

Although Neve was the taller of the two, she lay curled up on her side, Moira at her back with a protective arm resting over her.

And her eyes were open. As Neve slept, her sister kept watch.

She met his gaze and, after a moment, her lashes swept down. He went to back away, but she eased off the massive bed, padding across the floor toward the open door.

He really should have just left.

She closed the door behind her and turned toward him.

Her face was flushed from sleep. She'd taken off her shoes and, at some point, she'd also lost the closely fitted, dressy little jacket she'd been wearing when he found her at the museum.

She looked mussed and sleepy and so completely beautiful.

She still turned his brain to mush and the love he had for her felt like it would explode out of him.

But he'd lived with this for years and he was able to give her a polite nod. "How is she?"

Moira sighed and slumped back against the wall. "I don't even know how to answer that. She's upset. She's angry." She lapsed into silence and then she added, "*I'm* angry. I want to kill him, Gideon."

"He won't hurt her again, Moira."

"He never should have hurt her to begin with." She curled her hands into fists, her gray-green eyes staring off down the hall. Her voice was muted and quiet as she added, "She wanted somebody to *need* her, Gideon. How badly did I mess up if I chased my baby sister into the arms of someone who'd hurt her just because she wanted to feel *needed*?"

Gideon had rules he tried to live by—as a cop, as a man.

And there were rules he had to live by to stay sane around Moira.

Number one—don't touch.

But he couldn't not touch her now.

He kept it light, casual, just a brush of his fingers down her arm. The contact brought her eyes to his. "You didn't drive her to him. You aren't responsible—neither is Neve. The only one responsible for this is the man who hurt her."

It didn't do anything to lessen the shadows in her eyes, but he hadn't expected it to.

After a moment, he just nodded. "You get some sleep, Moira."

She reached out and caught his arm.

The contact went through him like electricity, setting

his system to blaze, and he couldn't stop the way his muscles bunched, the way his heart rate rocketed up.

The one thing he could stop was the need to grab her and back her up against the wall, to pull her mouth to his and have her—taste her again—feel her once more. But it was easier if she wasn't touching him. Holding himself still, he watched as she moved closer. "Thank you," she said, her hand still on his arm.

"You don't need to thank me for anything, Moira."

"Yeah, I do. You're always there, Gideon." Her gaze slid across his face and heat blistered him as it landed briefly on his mouth. The hunger snarled, growling like a caged wolf.

I don't think the two of you ever got over it, either.

Gideon's eyes were glittering.

The hard lines of his face were harsh and he looked flushed.

But his voice was calm, completely level as he said, "I'm just doing my job, Moira. Besides, Neve's a friend—like a sister to me."

"Right." Her smile wobbled, almost fell under the intensity of his eyes. Yes, he'd always adored Neve and it was clear *that* hadn't changed. He still had the same easy affection for Neve.

For her?

Not so much.

He gave her another polite smile. He might as well have tipped an imaginary hat and said, *Afternoon, ma'am*. As he went to pull away, she moved in. "Gideon . . ."

He automatically dipped his head. He was so much taller than she was. She could remember how he used to tease her about propping her up on a stool when he kissed her . . . then he'd just pick her up and do it.

Now, his head just barely in reach, she rose on her toes and pressed her lips to his cheek. He froze. The stubble on his jawline scraped against her lips. Off balance, she rested a hand on his shirt, curling her fingers into it.

And under her hand, she felt his heart.

It lunged like a racehorse.

"Gideon . . ."

She rubbed her mouth across his cheek, just a fraction of an inch.

Two seconds later, she had her back plastered against the wall and his hand cupped her face. He lightly squeezed her jaw and her mouth fell open. Just as his mouth came down on hers, she had time for one vague thought.

Oh, hell.

And then she locked her arms around his neck and clung tight.

The taste of her, the feel of her after so long hit him like napalm.

No drug could ever touch the effect that Moira McKay had on his system.

She opened for him and he thrust his tongue inside, shuddering at the taste of her.

Still so sweet. But darker . . . headier, even. He wanted to go to his knees and kiss every inch of her flesh, learn what other difference there was. But that would require he move.

Her hands were fisted in his hair and he really didn't want to stop kissing her, either. He improvised and boosted her up closer, guiding her legs until she hooked them over his hips, and then he rocked against her, driving against the heat between her thighs.

Her body trembled in response.

He could have her . . .

Tearing his mouth away, he kissed a burning line down her neck as she pushed a hand inside the collar of his shirt.

Bedroom.

His brain was already processing the logistics of it. Her bedroom was too far away. Another room, then. He could have her, strip her naked . . . love her . . .

The thought echoed in his mind even as she caught his earlobe and bit down.

Love her . . .

Although the need to feel her naked underneath him still rode him hard, Gideon found himself going cold.

Slowly, he untangled himself from the limbs she'd twined around him.

"Gideon?" she whispered.

"We're not doing this," he said softly, easing her down to the floor.

"We're . . . what aren't we doing?"

He moved away and shoved a shaking hand through his hair. His radio chirped and he scowled, turning it off. He was off duty, but out of habit, he kept the damn thing on. Still gripping it in his hand, he turned to face her. "This," he said. "We're not doing this."

She just watched him with bruised eyes.

If somebody had told him he'd walk away from a chance at one more night—even one more time—with Moira McKay, he would have told that son of a bitch he was crazy.

But that was before he held her again. Before he realized he'd have to do it all over again, pick his heart up off the floor. He still didn't have all the pieces.

Damn if he'd let her kick him all over again.

"I'll be a lot of things for you, Moira," he said, clipping the radio back on. "I'll be a friend if you need one, and if you have problems, I'll do my damnedest to fix them. But this . . . I can't be . . . this for you. I'm sorry. I never should have kissed you."

Then he turned and walked away.

CHAPTER NINE

Ever since he'd put his hands on Neve McKay, Ian's nights had been haunted by dreams of her. Dreams that made him wake up sweaty and aching, dreams that sometimes sent him into the shower, standing under an icy stream until he thought he'd freeze himself to death.

Nothing had cooled that heat.

But no hot and sweet dream haunted him tonight.

When he came awake, panting for breath, it wasn't a hot sweat that slicked his flesh, but an icy one.

A dull headache throbbed at the base of his head and he thought he just might be sick.

He'd been at that pub in London all over again, but Brannon hadn't been with him.

He'd been alone and he'd heard the screams.

He'd run after the source of them and he'd found them.

It was no girl from the pub, but Neve. And Sam Clyde was bent over her, laughing in that taunting, cruel way of his as he cut into her soft flesh. "See how soft she is, Ian? See how easy it is to make her bleed?"

The words had been directed at Ian.

Because Neve had lain lifeless on the busted and broken pavement.

Now, standing under a brutally hot shower, he tried to scrub the memory of it out of him. It felt like it was imprinted on his skin and nothing would make him clean.

Clyde had gone after her because of what they'd done.

Ian didn't need any kind of proof to see that connection.

Hands braced on the tile wall, he fought to clear the rage from his mind.

He wanted that sod dead.

Wanted it almost as much as he wanted his next breath.

Wanted it almost as much as he wanted to feel Neve against him.

Brannon didn't sleep worth shit.

He woke up with a stream of thoughts already burning through his mind, and they were all tied into one thing.

Neve.

Neve . . . and what he'd done.

When the phone rang, he wasn't surprised to see his older sister's number. He wasn't surprised, but he didn't really want to talk to her, either.

When he ignored the first call, she sent him a text.

Answer the damn phone or I'll just show up there.

Two seconds later came another text.

Jackass.

So when she called again, he answered, still brooding over everything that had happened last night.

"What?" he asked, not bothering to be polite. Moira wouldn't expect it anyway.

This was his fault.

"It's my fault."

He scowled at the phone. "What?"

"What do you mean, *what*? Neve . . ." Moira's voice trailed off. "I did a lousy job with her, Brannon. I didn't give her anything she needed—things she wanted maybe, but what she needed?"

"It's not your fault," he said, a leaden weight in his gut. There was no mistaking it in his mind. *He* was responsible. Now that Ian had brought him to mind, Brannon couldn't get the smug face of Sam Clyde out of his head.

He'd run into the son of a bitch the last time he'd been in London. Not long before he'd had lunch with Neve. That smug look on his face . . .

Shaking his head, he pushed that aside. "It's not your fault, Moira."

"Yes, it is." Her voice was rough. "You know what she told me last night? She just wanted to be needed. I never made her feel needed, Brannon. She ended up with some sadistic piece of shit because I didn't take good enough care of her."

"Fuck." Brannon wanted to hit something.

What had they been talking about in there? He'd wanted to go up there, bang on her damn door until she opened, tell her how sorry he was, do what he could to fix this—but how did you fix the unfixable?

He didn't even know how to talk to her now. A gulf of years and angry words separated them. "Look, it's not your fault. He wouldn't have gone after her if it wasn't for me. Me and Ian."

Moira's softly drawn breath had shame skittering down his spine.

And then she said, "We can't do this. Listen to us— we're blaming ourselves. How much time has she wasted blaming herself? He's the one who did it. We can feel guilty and we've got plenty we did wrong, but what we need to do is find a way to help her."

Easier said than done. But he tried to force his thoughts away from the mental ass-kicking he'd been giving himself, tried to focus on the here and now. When it came time to deal with Sam—and it would, he knew—then he'd deal with him, piece by piece if he had to.

But for now . . .

"So how do we help her?" he asked, as he strode from his bathroom into the brightly lit bedroom. Two years ago, this area had been closed-up, dusty, and not habitable for anything but the mice that had been chewing up the walls. The building, just down from the pub, had once been beautiful, but the previous owners hadn't been able to take care of it and then they'd refused to sell it.

"I don't know," Moira said, her voice distant.

Sitting on the edge of the bed, Brannon stared off into the distance, not seeing the rehabbed condo he'd worked on for close to a year. He didn't see the custom flooring or the exposed brick walls he'd paid an arm and a leg to have cleaned.

He didn't see any of the condo that had been custom-designed to suit him. It was exactly as he'd wanted it.

Brannon McKay usually got what he wanted, but just then he didn't know how to make it happen.

He needed to make things better for his sister, but how did he do that?

"What has she been doing the past few years?" he asked softly.

"I honestly don't know. Why?"

"Just wondering," he murmured. "Look, we'll figure this out. We'll . . . we'll take care of her."

"I don't think she needs to be taken care of anymore, Bran," Moira said softly. "She took care of herself for a good long while. I think she just needs . . . us."

"Yeah." He sighed and shoved a hand back through his wet hair. "I'll be back out to Ferry sometime soon."

"I'll see you then. Bran? I love you."

"Love you, too," he murmured, disconnecting the call. He tossed the cell down on the bed and still, his mind worked.

Life was nothing but a series of puzzles and what he needed to do was figure out the right sort of solution for this puzzle. No, he couldn't fix what had happened and he couldn't undo what had happened to Neve.

She'd come home to heal—that was what Ella Sue thought, and Ella Sue was right. That was just the way things worked. The sun came up in the morning, the sun set in the evening, and Ella Sue was always right. But Neve wasn't going to heal sitting around the house and hiding.

So maybe he had an idea for her.

Digging up some boxers, he dropped the towel. As he did so, he glanced over to the bank of windows, more out of habit than anything else. His heart gave one hard, brutal beat against the wall of his chest and then it started to race. Hannah Parker sat on the narrow balcony just outside her apartment. And she was staring right at him.

Their gazes locked.

She lifted a brow as she sipped from her coffee cup.

The bold stare made it almost impossible for him to look away. Hannah just didn't look away, didn't back away, didn't back down.

She was a pain in the ass and he wished she didn't get under his skin.

Holding her gaze, he pulled the boxers on. She continued to watch. His skin continued to burn and heat drained from his head, straight down. He doubted she could see that clearly from across the street, but he turned anyway.

The last thing he needed to do was let her know she'd just given him the hard-on from hell.

It was almost cute, Hannah thought, the way he turned tail and ran. Except he didn't really *run*.

He strolled.

And it wasn't like he made it clear she'd embarrassed him or anything, either.

He just . . . Pursing her lips, she stared into her coffee as she pondered their non-interaction.

It had been going on for forever.

He'd wake up and she'd catch a glimpse of that beyond fantastic body.

Then he'd see her and, like it was the first time it had happened, he'd look surprised, then aggravated.

All the man had to do was close the damn curtains.

He never did.

She was glad, but at the same time, it was frustrating, because every time it happened, it made her want to do stupid things. Like catch him on the street when she saw him walking, ask him to join her for a cup of coffee, a drink at Treasure Island—or just for the rest of her life.

Stupid, stupid, stupid.

Hannah closed her eyes and rested her head against the back of her chair. If she was smart, she'd quit thinking about him like that. But she wasn't smart, clearly, because she'd been crazy about him for as long as she'd known him and he was as oblivious to her now as he'd always been.

Her brooding was cut short by the shrill ring of her phone, but one look at the number—or lack of—told her that she would have been happier brooding. She would have been happier in bed, or at work, or getting a root canal . . .

"Hello," she said wearily.

"You need to keep your nose out my fucking business, you crazy bitch!"

"Lloyd, nice to hear from you again," she drawled. She reached into her pocket and pulled out the small recorder she'd taken to carrying. She forgot it half the time, but today just wasn't Lloyd's lucky day. She hit record and angled the phone away enough that the microphone would pick up his rants.

"You stupid, fat, nosy feminazi. You are going to tell me where in the hell my wife is. You're going to stop with this shit you're feeding her!" His voice started to raise. "You're going to stop being a fucking *cunt* or I'm going to come up there one night and cut you up, you hear me?"

She cut him off. "What I'm going to do is turn this recording over to the cops, *Lloyd Thomas Hanson*. Then I'm going to call your P.O. and set up a meeting with him and play it for him. And the next time I see you—"

"You fucking *bitch*—"

She hung up. Her hands were shaking, but she refused to acknowledge it.

The pig was a coward, nothing but a coward. She wasn't going to waste her time being afraid of him.

However, he'd just added an annoyance to her day. Now she had to see a cop before she went into work.

In under fifteen minutes, Brannon had left his place and was on the road, the top of the car down, wind whipping his hair back from his face, and the music blasting.

The brutal music and the fast drive didn't do anything for his temper.

In his mind, he had a half-dozen arguments laid out

for what he wanted to ask Neve, and he was prepared to abandon all of them if he had even one hint that he was off base.

Because that bruised look in her eyes had his heart tripping, he made a side stop to the bakery.

Neve had always had an awful sweet tooth. It was pitiful, he guessed. Here he was, offering the equivalent of a week's worth of sugar in an effort to do anything to bring a smile to her face.

He grabbed himself a coffee and something slathered in chocolate and filled with cream, putting the box on the floorboard. The coffee he wedged between his thighs, and once he was on the road, he managed to dig out his donut, shoving the bag into the side pocket so the wind didn't snatch it.

He managed to clear his mind for a few minutes, thanks to the sugar rush and the beautiful stretch of road between town and the home where he'd grown up. It probably made him a shallow, materialistic son of a bitch, but there wasn't much in life that gave him the kind of thrill he got speeding down this stretch of road, the Bugatti clinging to the pavement, hugging each curve.

He might have even managed to arrive with something like a smile if it hadn't been for the sudden glare lights, the peal siren that all but blasted out his ears and the honking of a horn.

"Son of a *bitch*!" he snarled, looking over to see Gideon glaring at him from the lane next to him. The *wrong* lane. Gideon pointed at the side of the road and Brannon shot a look at the speedometer.

"Fuck."

With a groan, he pulled over and managed to cram the rest of the donut down his throat as he waited for Gideon.

"You stupid asshole, you were pushing ninety," Gideon snapped. "It's fifty-five miles an hour here. How many tickets do I have to write you?"

Instead of answering right away, Brannon lifted his coffee and took a sip. It had cooled to the point where it only burned his tongue instead of scorching off the skin. As he pondered Gideon's question, he caught sight of the other man coming up behind them.

The face was familiar, but it took a few minutes to place him. Griffin Parker. Hannah's cousin, if he remembered right. He'd moved here from Tuscaloosa and he was watching every second with a wide grin.

"I think the count is up to three this year," Brannon said once he'd thought it through. "That's down from last year."

Gideon didn't look amused. "If you keep this up," he said slowly, "I'm going to throw your ass in jail just for the hell of it."

Brannon opened his mouth, a hundred smart-ass remarks on his tongue. But he caught sight of the temper—real temper—in Gideon's eyes. Anybody who hadn't been a friend wouldn't have seen it. But then again, anybody who hadn't been a friend wouldn't have had Gideon all but snarling and swearing at him, either.

"I'll get the ticket paid," he said. "I always do."

"That's not the fucking point." Gideon dragged a hand through his hair. "Has it ever occurred to you that someday you might cause a wreck? Or that you might actually wreck one of these candy cars you love so much and kill yourself?"

For a split second, the *candy car* comment made Brannon just stare. He'd had this thing custom-built. He had his hands all over it and it could do things that police cruisers could only dream of.

As though Gideon read every thought, he leaned in.

"The car cost more than my house," he said bluntly, "and I don't fucking care. The tickets you rack up could probably fund some kid's college. And you never miss the money. I don't care. You're breaking the law, you don't give a shit, and more, you don't even seem to give a fuck that you could end up dead one of these days. Maybe you don't recall, but this is the same stretch of road where I had to pull your baby sister from the twisted mess that was left of your parents' car. Maybe that doesn't concern you."

Now the full force of the fury in Gideon's voice punched through. "Well, *I* care. I buried enough friends when I served my time in the army. And I sure as hell don't want to be the one telling Moira that your stupidity got you killed."

Gideon's temper tugged at Brannon's. But he wasn't stupid. Gideon was right on more than one front. Brannon definitely had been breaking the law, paying the tickets or not, and, no, he didn't usually give a shit. He drove fast. He was careful.

But . . . his gut twisted. Okay, yeah.

"I'm sorry," he said finally.

Gideon didn't respond, and Brannon looked up at the other man.

Gideon watched him, no expression on his face. "This doesn't happen again," Gideon said flatly. "Next time, I arrest your ass—and trust me, I'll find a reason and then I'm going to have your damn license suspended for as long as I can. With as many tickets as you've gotten, it should be a piece of cake."

"I get the point," Brannon said.

Five minutes later, with a shiny new ticket as a memento, he pulled back on the road and kept to the speed limit the entire time.

Somehow it just didn't feel the same, driving at fifty-five, but he'd have to deal.

When her brother first banged on the door, Neve was able to shove her head under the pillow. She was tired. If she ignored him, he'd probably go away.

She had a crying jag hangover and she didn't want to talk to anybody, think about anybody or anything.

She just wanted to sleep.

The pounding grew louder.

She scrunched up her eyes and added a second pillow.

After about sixty seconds, she heard his voice, louder, clearer. Groaning, she wrapped the blanket more firmly around her. It didn't help. Brannon yanked one pillow away and then a tug-of-war ensued for the second.

She finally relented and let him have it but as he tossed it away, she just buried herself deeper in her blankets. "Go away, Brannon."

"Why?" His voice was easy. He might as well have been discussing the weather. "So you can stay in here and hide and pretend the rest of the world doesn't exist?"

She didn't answer. She was kind of hoping to do just that. She'd woken up when Moira slid out of bed, although she hadn't let her sister know. She'd become a very, very light sleeper over the past few years and even when she wasn't waking up, thinking that William had found her, she still found herself twisting and turning, unable to get more than a few hours of sleep here and there.

She'd come to grips with what had happened—she really had.

Now she felt like she had to face it all over again.

"Is hiding from me going to make you feel better?" Brannon said softly.

Under the security of her blankets, she closed her eyes.

"I'm not hiding from you," she said. Sighing, she threw the blankets back and sat up, staring at him.

He looked at her, bitterness in his eyes. "If you were, I wouldn't blame you."

The words made the ache in her chest expand.

Closing her eyes, she rested her chin on her knees. "I'm trying this new thing where I blame the people who actually are responsible, Brannon."

"So you're not staying in that bed to hide away from me?"

"Didn't I just say that?" If she sounded a little bitchy, then so what.

A moment of silence passed before he said, "Then maybe you're just hiding there away from the rest of the world. Will it make your problems go away, Neve?"

"Did you go back to school and major in psych, Bran?" Lifting her head, she narrowed her eyes at him. "If not? Then save me the armchair psychology."

He shrugged. "It's not armchair psychology. I'm just remembering the girl who used to kick her problems in the teeth. Matter of fact, I remember a time when you even punched a problem so hard, you knocked one of *her* teeth out . . . and you knocked some punk kid's balls up into his throat." He leaned forward, his voice softer as he said, "Maybe it's time you find that part of yourself again, Neve."

"I don't think she exists anymore, Bran." She rolled her head back, staring up at the ceiling, at the insanely glittery light fixture over her bed. "If she existed . . ."

"She does."

Neve closed her eyes.

"She's still you—you're still her. It was that part of

you that gave you the courage to leave," Brannon said softly.

"Courage?" She laughed sourly. "That wasn't *courage*. I just didn't want to die."

Even as she said it, she wanted to take it back. Brannon flinched. Averting his face, he stared at the far wall.

"Look, Brannon." She flung an arm over her face so she didn't have to see the look she'd put on his face. "I'm tired."

Something rattled. "So am I, but I got up. Look . . . I've got donuts."

For some reason, the silly bribe, straight out of her childhood made her smile a little. He held a box in front of him now, something he must have stashed out of sight. He lifted the top and held out a big, fat donut, smeared with icing and liberally covered with rainbow sprinkles.

"I'm not ten years old anymore."

He shrugged. "Then I'll eat it."

"You're so juvenile." She sat up and held out a hand. "Gimme the damn donut."

He grinned and passed it over. "I've got something I want you to help me with."

She paused, the donut halfway to her mouth. She almost dropped it, then she thought about shoving it back at him. But some voice inside her insisted, *eat the damn donut*. She tore a bite out of it, chewed it, staring at Brannon. "I don't need you taking care of me."

"No. You *did* . . . and nobody was around when you needed us." He shrugged. "That's over and done and that's not what I'm doing. I've got a project. And I want somebody to help me out. Might as well be you."

"That's such a charming offer." She took another bite

of the donut, her belly growling demandingly. "Exactly what's this project?"

He gave her a secretive grin. "Now, for that, you have to get dressed and come to town. You need to see it to really get the full picture, sis."

CHAPTER TEN

The small town had perhaps a few small comforts, and they were small, but William was willing to give credit where credit was due. The bed-and-breakfast was small but charming, and the owner was, thankfully, English. Now a widow, she'd met and married her husband when he'd been stationed in Germany and she'd come back to the United States with him. When he'd died, she hadn't wanted to leave their children.

He learned all of this as she fed him a late supper—not part of the typical service, but it was lovely, she'd told him, to have a fellow country man stay at the inn.

So he'd enjoyed an excellent meal, an excellent pot of tea, and retired to his room to continue thinking about just how he would approach things with Neve.

The night had passed easily enough. He'd learned how to sleep in the worst of conditions—and how to wake at the drop of a hat—but the bed had been surprisingly comfortable and now, refreshed and rejuvenated, he stood on the small balcony overlooking the river and considered his options.

She would have told them by now, he decided. The green scarf all but burned a hole through the pocket of his sports coat and he reached for it, stroking it.

Would that miserable sod Brannon have remembered him? He'd stopped using his middle name once he'd opened his own practice, so it was possible Brannon wouldn't connect those dots. Still, he rather desperately wanted those dots connected—and when they did, he wouldn't mind seeing the look on Brannon's face.

Amused at the idea, he smiled through his breakfast, despite the fact that the eggs weren't to his liking and the tea hadn't quite hit the spot this time. She'd do better tonight. If not, he'd have a word with her. He believed in flawless service.

On his way out the door, he caught sight of her in her garden, although she wasn't working. She was speaking with the neighbor. When she waved a hand in his direction, he pretended not to see. He wasn't here to chat or make friends. His lip curled at the very idea of it.

Slipping into the car, he squinted out at the vivid bright sunlight. The sun already seared his retinas. Did the bloody thing never stop shining? The humid, muggy air promised a return of the previous day's heat as well. He pulled his sunglasses on and sat there, pondering his options.

He needed to see what his Neve was up to.

The full picture included industrial plastic wrap, scaffolding, ladders, and men who alternately shouted insults and traded laughter. One man was in the middle of a particularly inventive insult when a big hand smacked him across the side of his head.

"There's lady in the house, man. Watch your tongue," Ian Campbell said as he moved from behind whatever wooden structure the men were working.

Neve lifted an eyebrow, amusement threading through her, but it died as all eyes shifted toward her.

Tucking her hands into the back of her pockets, she

had to fight the urge to look down, look away, hunch her shoulders. For a moment, she had the utterly humiliating urge to dart behind her big brother and that absolutely *infuriated* her.

You used to kick your problems in the teeth.

Yeah. She'd done just that. Mentally squaring her shoulders, she let her gaze slide around the room, pausing a moment as she found herself looking at Ian Campbell. Damn. That was a man who could make a woman's brain melt. Along with other parts.

The corner of his mouth curled up in a smile and he dipped his head at her before he turned around and shouted, "Get to work, the lot of you. Maybe your bosses don't mind if you sit on your arses, but Brannon won't leave me be until this place is running and I'd just as soon be left alone to my pub."

"*My* pub," Brannon corrected as grumbling and voices filled the void.

Ian snorted. "You're done bored with it, aren't you? That's why you turned the day-to-day running of it over to me and started spending most of your time on this place. Of course, you keep dragging me over here because you can't decide what kind of lace doilies you want."

"It's not my fault you have better taste in lace doilies than I do," Brannon replied, unperturbed.

Ian's teeth flashed white against the neatly trimmed beard and then he looked at Neve. "Your brother there, he loves to start things up—he builds things and starts things, but once they take off, he leaves them alone. It's an odd habit. He's already half bored with this. Fortunately, he's mature enough to see it through."

"I'm not bored with the place." Brannon's voice took on an odd edge, odd enough that Neve slid him a look. His eyes were almost carefully blank. "I just have other things going on and I want somebody on hand to keep an eye on shit. You're right here, so why not you? You're a workaholic anyway."

"Keep telling yourself that." Ian kicked some plastic sheeting out of the way and gestured to them. "It's a bit quieter in the back."

"What are you going to do here?" Neve followed them, looking at everything around. Better to do that than look at Ian. Those muscles of his looked even more impressive today. The faded T-shirt was thin, soft from probably a thousand washings, and she had no trouble picturing the hard muscle underneath. The faded, threadbare jeans weren't any different and she jerked her eyes away when she realized she was staring at his ass.

What was *wrong* with her?

It was impossible not to notice how damned beautiful he was, but she shouldn't have so much trouble just putting Ian and his hard muscles and that amazing voice out of her mind.

She'd had a hard time not staring at him the other times she'd seen him. Had a hard time not staring at his hands as he pulled drinks, or not listening to his laughter as he flirted with the ladies.

"You're not wearing your kilt," she said. The words popped out of her without her even knowing she was going to say them. Each time she'd seen him in the pub, he'd been wearing what she guessed was the standard uniform for the people who worked there: a green shirt, paired with either jeans or a kilt. It amused her, considering how few men wore kilts in Scotland. There, kilts were formal wear. A guy didn't walking around wearing them every day.

Today he wore battered jeans and an equally battered black T-shirt.

"No." He glanced down at his dusty clothes with a

shrug. Then he smiled at her. "But I can go change . . . if you like."

"Ah . . ." Her heart fluttered. "No. No need to do it on my account."

"Stop flirting, Ian," Brannon said, his voice grouchy.

She slid him a look and saw that Brannon was frowning at her.

Ian had a different look altogether on his face and that sent a rush of heat through her.

"But she's such a pretty thing, Brannon." He winked at her and then slanted a look at her brother.

"If you don't—"

"Neve, you look like you could use a cup of coffee," Ian said, cutting her brother off. "They make a decent cup at the pub. Would you like Brannon to get you one?"

Brannon narrowed his eyes on the other man. She'd heard the weariness coming into her brother's voice, already knew he was kicking himself and that made her want to kick *herself*. But at the same time, she wanted a few minutes away from the guilt that all but choked the air around them.

She wanted a few minutes of the distraction that was Ian Campbell.

"Brannon, I could use some coffee. Black."

Brannon just studied Ian for another moment, then looked at her.

Without another word, he pushed past them.

Ian leaned back against what looked like a roughed-out version of a counter. He ran his tongue along the inside of his lower lip and she felt another tug down in her belly. Trying to ignore it, she lifted her chin and stared right back at him.

There were shadows under Ian's eyes and she thought maybe he looked tired. Feeling more than a little bitchy, she decided to point it out.

He shrugged, looking unperturbed. "I didn't sleep well. Kept thinking about . . ." Blowing out a breath, he slanted a look at her and asked, "Do you hate me?"

Neve blinked, caught off guard. "What?"

"Sam Clyde, what he did, it was because Bran and I humiliated him. We hurt him, good and proper, both of us. When he thought his money would smooth it all over and it didn't, that just made it worse. This was his revenge. If you hate me, I can't say I'd blame you."

If you hate me . . .

He said it so sincerely, but the words felt . . . *wrong.* So very wrong. "I don't hate you," she said quietly.

Silence fell between them, awkward and uncomfortable. When Ian finally spoke, he caught her off guard yet again.

"He's turning the place into a winery."

And yet again, she was confused. "What?"

Ian waved a hand around, a gesture that clearly encompassed the entire building. "It's going to be a place for people to try the wines from the winery he's been working on. Your brother can't seem to not be doing something."

She reached up and rubbed her ear. "Brannon wants to start a winery?"

"No." Ian said it slowly, his voice patient. "He doesn't *want* to. He's done it. It's not half bad, although I'll take a pint, or scotch, any day. It's something he started working on not long after he got out of university, I think."

He shrugged and went quiet.

Neve appreciated it, using that time to process what he'd just told her.

"Since you don't hate me, does that mean . . ." He paused, as if searching for the word. Finally, he said, "I can't sleep for want of you. I close my eyes and see you. Am I wasting my time?"

Neve turned away. "You're all about throwing me off balance, aren't you?" she asked faintly. "Look, I . . . William is responsible for what he did. I'm making myself accept that. I still blame me . . . sometimes . . . but I know that's wrong. I'm not going to blame you or Brannon, either."

She turned back, but not to look at him. She focused on the building around them instead. "So. A winery. That's . . . a big deal."

A winery.

The museum.

Big things—Brannon and Moira had all been doing big things.

A knot settled in her throat and she looked away. What did she have to show for the past ten years of her life?

"I can understand why he keeps hovering, seeing the look on your face now."

Ian's voice was closer now.

Slowly, she looked up.

His misty gray eyes were slightly narrowed and she didn't like the thorough way he watched her.

She suspected there was no way to hide from that gaze. Some people just saw past the barriers.

Now a faint smile curled his lips. "If it pisses you off, then you should probably stop letting them see you look so broken."

"Go fuck yourself," she said slowly.

He dipped his head.

Neve froze as his breath drifted over her skin. Goose bumps rose in the wake and her blood started to swim as she caught his scent. He smelled of sawdust and musk and something smoky. It was heady, intoxicating. Her heart jumped up to slam away in her throat and it took a moment to even focus on his words.

"But that's so boring, Neve." He straightened and then moved away. "You're not even close to broken. If you were, you never would have left that sad sack of shite. But you did."

Closing one hand into a fist, she met his eyes when he turned to look at her.

"This really isn't any of your concern."

"Well, that could depend on how you look at it."

"Oh, really," she said. Feeling exposed under his penetrating glance, she crossed her arms over her middle. "Do tell."

"It's your private business, of that there's no question." Ian studied her and then once more, closed the distance between them. "Your private business. But then there's this thing . . ."

His voice trailed off.

"What thing?"

"You know, if you'd told me you hated me, I wouldn't dare do this. But you didn't, so . . ."

She didn't even have time to brace herself before he kissed her.

With hard, rough hands, he cupped her face and tipped her head back.

Her heart banged hard against her ribs as he slid his tongue along her lower lip, teased the entrance to her mouth, but when she opened for him, he broke the kiss.

"That's the thing, Neve. I want you. I want you naked and in my bed, so that means I can't help but think about it." He swiped his thumb across her lower lip.

The sensation sent a shiver through her and heat chased back the chill.

But then he lowered his hands and turned away. "I can't help but think about it—and knowing that the fucker who did this to you likely did it because of your connection to Brannon eats at me, Neve. It's like a fire in my gut."

"I . . ." She stopped and forced herself to breathe. The ache in her chest spread as she watched him scrub his hands up and down his face. "I don't even know what to say to you."

He glanced back at her, his eyes unreadable. "You didn't pull away when I touched you."

"Was I supposed to?"

"Maybe." He lifted one heavy shoulder in a shrug. "Knowing what you know now—why shouldn't you pull away?"

"You didn't do anything." Cold, she wrapped her arms around herself. Unable to stand there, she started to pace. "You didn't do it. Brannon didn't." She stopped in the middle of the floor as she forced the rest of it out. "I didn't."

"You blame yourself."

Slowly, she looked up at him. "Are you a mind reader?"

"No." He blew out a harsh breath. "I just know that look on your face. I saw it on a face of my gran. My grandfather . . . he would hurt her. A lot. But she didn't leave him. She just killed herself instead."

Still haunted by what Ian had told her, it took a great deal of willpower for Neve to focus on Brannon as he walked her through the place, but she finally succeeded. To her surprise, the blueprints he showed her actually made sense to her—in a way. She could see some sort of roughed-out idea of what this place might look like and it delighted her.

"I have to admit I'm impressed." Neve studied the blueprints and eyed the mock-ups or whatever Brannon had called them.

He talked to her the same way he'd talk to a nervous horse. She found herself scowling at the image it brought to mind—Brannon handling her with kid gloves for fear of frightening her. It just pissed her off even more. She tried not to think about it, but abruptly, she put down the dregs of the coffee she'd been nursing and turned away from him, walking across the room that would eventually be an office.

"What's the point of all this, Brannon?"

"I already told you. I need help with it." He straightened up, that easy smile fixed firmly back in place.

"Why? Do you think I need somebody to hand me something so I feel like I'm needed?" The pathetic truth was that she *did* need something.

Something flashed in his eyes, but was hidden a moment later.

It snapped the threads of her temper. "Stop it!"

He frowned. "Stop what?"

"Stop treating me like I'm fragile." She swiped her hands down her jeans, and realized she was sweating. She *was* fragile. She felt that way. But how could she get past that if everybody treated her like some delicate piece of glass? "I fucked up but I survived it. If he comes looking—"

"I'll kill him," Brannon yelled, his voice echoing.

The clattering of hammers went silent.

He swore and stormed over to the frame that would eventually hold the door. "Clear out! Now!"

The next few minutes were filled with sounds of low voices, toolboxes slamming, and heavy boots thudding as everybody hit the door. From where she stood, Neve couldn't see them but she had no doubt people were leaving.

"Well." Crossing her arms over her chest, she angled a look at her brother. He was bent over the board that had been placed over two sawhorses. His shoulders were rounded, spine stiff with tension. "It looks like your temper is still the same."

Brannon was laid-back for the most part, but once you set him off, it was wise to stay out of the line of fire.

"Fuck, Neve. What am I supposed to do?"

"Let me breathe."

He straightened and turned to look at her.

She was still surprised the words had slid out and had to fumble with what to say next. "Brannon . . . I . . . look, I spent the past couple of years questioning everything I did, afraid to let myself get close to anybody . . . just alone. And afraid. I'm tired of being afraid, but if you want me to find that part of me that wasn't afraid to kick people in the teeth . . ." She stopped and swallowed. Did that girl still exist? She just didn't know. She'd been as lonely then. She'd wanted—*needed* somebody to just tell her it would be okay. She hadn't been *okay* in years. "I have to breathe. I have to work things out."

"I'm not trying to smother you, sis," he said, his voice tired now. She suspected he hadn't slept worth shit. He looked away, his jaw clenching as he stared outside. "But I can't be okay with this. I—I just can't."

"I'm not *okay* with it, either. But it's done. There's no changing it. Now I just have to go on." She crossed the floor and reached out to catch his hand. "I'd rather not have my big brother in jail."

A faint smile appeared on his face, gone almost as soon as it formed.

"As long as he stays out of our town, there's nothing to worry about." He reached up and tugged her toward him, hugging her tight. "You're not alone here. I wish . . ."

He didn't finish. She felt him shake his head. "That doesn't matter. You're here now. That matters."

"I love you, Brannon."

"Yeah. I love you, too, Neve."

Pulling away, she looked around. "This will be pretty cool when you're done. You don't need me for anything."

A pained look crossed his face. "But that's just the point. I don't *want* to finish it up."

"You started it." She scowled at him.

"Yeah." He shrugged now. "That's the fun part for me. I . . ." He trailed off and looked away. "Being around here, having to deal with all the day-to-day decisions isn't what I wanted to mess with. I want to be out at the winery, working there, handling that part."

He paused, then added, "Come on, Neve. Help me out."

CHAPTER ELEVEN

That lovely shade of red, William would know it anywhere.

At end of the block, he studied her. She stood in front of a shop, her arms wrapped around her, her expression thoughtful and the breeze turned her hair into a banner, whipping it around her face.

Gone were the lovely designer clothes he'd bought her. She wore threadbare jeans and a simple silk top. The top was sufficient, but the pants were a disgrace. Her shoes were a pair of black flats.

Still, despite the plain clothing, Neve McKay looked lovely. She always looked lovely. Once he had her back where she belonged, he'd see to it that she was dressed as was fitting for a woman of her station.

He moved closer, need pulsing inside him. It wouldn't take much. All he had to do was get her alone for a few minutes. A quick look around had him thinking hard and fast. It wasn't a bustling sort of town, that was certain. A few moments and he could bring her around.

She lifted a hand, brushing her hair back, and he could see the long, pale line of her neck. His own hands itched and he thought of that first night, when he'd wrapped the pretty green silk around her elegant neck and made her his.

His mouth watering, he took another step.

He'd talk to her. There was no reason for this utter nonsense to continue. She'd had her fun. Now it was time for it to end, for her to come home where she belonged. He might even be lenient.

The words were already forming on his tongue and he was already envisioning the look on her face, how her eyes would widen and the hesitant gasp she'd make.

When the man moved up to stand behind her, a vicious wash of red came across William's vision.

"He talked you into it, didn't he?"

Neve jumped at the sound of Ian's voice. She'd been about ready to leave, uneasy—there was an odd, rippling sensation crawling down her spine, like the weight of a hundred thousand gazes on her. Or one very evil one.

Standing in front of the bookstore, she looked into the glass and saw Ian in the reflection. "I remember this bookstore." She smiled. "Old Mrs. Stafford. My mom and dad would bring me here and I'd leave with an entire stack of books."

"You're a reader then," he said as he came to stand at her shoulder.

The uneasiness inside her gut faded, as if it had never been. "I used to be." Neve tried to think of the last time she'd read a book, the last time she'd had the time . . . or the presence of mind to focus on a book. "Lately, not so much."

"You should get back to it." He flicked at the ends of her hair. "What's your poison, my darling Neve? Do you want a swashbuckling pirate? Or do you prefer a mystery? Some epic tale where good and evil battle at the world's edge?"

"How about all of the above?" She shrugged. "It's been so long, I don't know the last time I even read a book."

"We should rectify that." He rested a hand on her waist.

Her heart skittered up into dangerous territory and she wondered what he'd do if she turned to face him, lean against him, press her mouth to his.

"You didn't answer me, you know."

Her gaze flew to his.

"Didn't answer what?" she asked, her voice trembling.

He turned, slowly. It seemed they were talking about something much more intimate than whether or not she was going to take on the job Brannon wanted to thrust upon her.

His dark eyes scorched her skin and she wanted to move closer, let him scorch her. She was tired of being cold, tired of being lonely.

Ian's thumb slid under the hem of her white silk shirt, rubbed over her skin. "I just asked if he talked you into it. Did he?"

Oh. That. She made a face at him even as she had to handle how her heart continued to race. "It's not that he talked me into it. It's that I need to do something more than just sit home. All the hard stuff is done. If all he needs is somebody to pick out paint chips and decide what kind of floor to lay down . . . I can handle that." She grinned. "If I mess it up, it's his own damn fault. I've already decided to veto the lace doilies."

"There is a God," Ian said, returning her grin. It faded, though, and he reached up, cupping her cheek.

That simple gesture made her heart melt.

"He's not going to be satisfied with you throwing me doilies out the window, though. He's looking for a way to keep you here." His thumb brushed against her cheek and Neve could have sworn the entire world seemed to fall away. "They missed you."

They missed me. Chilled now, she moved back. Ian's hand fell away. She turned back to the window of the bookstore, thinking of long, empty years, how long she'd gone with little more than a phone call, thought of the letters—

Her backpack. Anger gnawed at her, how the loss of that one simple item was indescribable.

They wrote me. They'd told her they had and she believed them, but despite that, there was a tiny knot of hurt still lodged in her heart. Keenly aware of Ian's gaze, she made herself focus. "I'm not leaving." She turned and studied the town, the busy main strip, the café across the street and the new restaurant next door. "This is home. I never should have left."

"Why did you?"

"Haven't you heard?" She cocked a brow at him.

"Not much." He shrugged and her mouth went dry as the movement stretched his T-shirt over that amazing body. "People talk, but people don't often know shite. I want to hear why you left—from *you.*"

"That's a long story." Crossing her arms over her chest, she took a step away from him. A police cruiser came by and she nodded at Gideon as he glanced her way. He turned in by the courthouse, just down the block and her gut twisted. She'd told Moira and Brannon what she thought they needed to know. But Gideon needed to know all of it—if she could handle telling him.

"Is there something between you?"

"What?" Confused by the edge she heard in his voice, she looked up at Ian.

"Marshall. You're staring rather hard at his car."

Laughter burst out of her. Some of the tension pent

up inside her drained away, carried away by the fit of giggles. "Me . . ." Another snort of laughter kept her from getting it out. Finally, she was able to say it with just a few chuckles. "Me and Gideon? Are you serious?"

"If that's your reaction, I guess the answer is no." He took another step closer.

The air around her got hotter, tighter. Swallowing the laughter that still bubbled in her throat, she met Ian's eyes. Wow. He had incredibly beautiful eyes. In that moment, they seemed to burn hot and the heat she'd felt between them earlier rekindled.

She barely knew this man—had met him just a couple of times, but he tugged reactions out of her that she wasn't sure she could handle.

"Look," she said, fumbling for the words. She started to knot her fingers together. As soon as she realized what she was doing, she stopped and shoved them into her back pockets. How many times had she done that in the past? When William yelled at her, what had she done but stood there and twisted her hands and wished she had the courage to just stand *up* to him. To *leave*.

"Aye," Ian said, drawing her back to the present. His voice was low and rough. "I'm looking at you."

It came out as *Aye, 'm lookin a ya* and the words rolled over her like silken velvet. She wanted to roll herself up in that voice, wrap it around herself. And run away. Both. At the very same time.

Blood rushed to her face. "You're one huge walking orgasm," she blurted out.

Ian blinked.

And then, to her surprise, a grin tugged up the corners of his lips. "I must say, that's the first time I've ever been accused of that." He stroked a hand down his beard and the grin went from being pensive to pleased. "I can't say I mind."

Groaning, Neve pressed one hand to her brow.

"Yeah, well, *that* surprises me not at all." She blew out a breath again, humiliation churning inside her. She couldn't believe she'd said that. Okay, so yes, she'd been *thinking* it. She'd stopped blurting out what she thought ages ago, though.

"William," she whispered. It hit her like a weight in the chest and she blew out a slow, careful breath. He'd all but beaten the impulsiveness out of her. Not through force, but with cutting insults and cold gestures.

A hand brushed across her cheek.

Instinctively, she flinched.

"You keep going away."

Never looked back up at him.

The intensity of his eyes lingered on her face.

"I can't help it. Some things . . . pull at me."

Ian reached up and cupped her cheek.

She found herself turning her face into his hand and it *felt so good*. The strength of a man's hand, gentle on her skin—she'd forgotten how that could feel. It felt *good*. "That's when you just have to pull back harder." Then he dipped his head and said, "And if that doesn't do it, you can always just beat the bloody hell out of it . . . or him."

The bruised look on her face was ripping the guts right out of him. Ian didn't know what he was going to do if he kept having to see it—the need to do something violent and bloody rode him hard, but the problem? The man who'd put that look on her face wasn't around for him to tear apart.

But Ian needed to see her smile again.

So he shifted his grip to her chin and tilted her head back. "So, when you get that chance, you be sure to let me know, because I think I'd love to have a chance to . . . hold him for you."

He made sure to keep the pause there lengthy and deliberate.

It worked, too, because Neve's pretty green eyes slid up to his and a smile bowed her lips. Oh, but he wanted to taste that mouth again. Wanted it more than he thought he'd ever wanted anything.

"You just want to hold him for me?"

"It seems like the thing for a gentleman to do." He lowered his hand and took a step back. If he didn't move back, he'd very well be moving forward in just a moment. The scent of her skin was going to drive him mad.

"You very much come off as a gentleman." She glanced away as she said it.

"Oh, I am. Very much so. And as a gentleman, it strikes me that you probably haven't had much of a chance to see how much things have changed since you've been gone. Why don't we go have lunch . . . I'll catch you up on some of the things Brannon's been up to."

She went to say *no*. He could even see her lips forming the *N*.

And he cursed himself for having no patience as he closed that distance between them back up. "Do you really just want to go back home? Stay locked inside Ferry the rest of the day?"

Neve narrowed her eyes.

And then, to his utter shock, she made a face. "Well, maybe I could use some lunch."

"This place has always had the best burgers."

Ian studied her over the massive sandwich she held, reaching out to steal one of her onion rings. "I'm sorry to hear that."

"Oh?" She wiped her mouth with the napkin and leaned back, the warm summer sunshine beating down on her back. They could have sat under the awning but it was crowded at the diner and Ian had asked if she'd mind taking one of the tables farther out.

"Yes." He crunched down on the onion ring and winked at her. "Here I was thinking that the best burgers were at my place."

"Nope." She shook her head. It hit her then, how relaxed she felt, how easy it was to sit there and be with him. "But you've got the best fish and chips."

"Nice to know I'm doing that much right," he said wryly. His lips curved in a smile.

At the sight of it, Neve found herself thinking about that night. When he'd kissed her, the feel of his beard, the way his hands had glided over her skin, rough in all the best ways.

A rough sigh came from the man across the table and Neve flicked her eyes up to his.

The heat there devastated her.

Neve lowered her eyes back to the table.

Since she wasn't looking at him, she wasn't prepared when his fingers brushed over the back of her hand. Such a simple touch. How could it possible affect her like this?

"The look on your face is going to undo me."

She swallowed and dragged her eyes back up to his.

"I want to touch you."

"You are." She managed to smile at him although it was strained. She didn't want to *smile*. She wanted to climb across the table and get in his lap, cuddle up, and rub against him like a cat. Then she wanted to curl around him and feel him inside her.

Sex hadn't ever felt so necessary, so vital.

She *needed* him.

"Neve. I already need a few minutes before I can stand without making a spectacle of myself. Either stop looking at me or we'll be sitting here for an age."

She laughed nervously. "What else am I supposed to look at?"

"Well." He blew out a breath and tipped his head back, staring up at the sky that stretched out over them like a bright blue bowl. "I can't really say. Because even if you're not looking at me, I'm looking at you. I need to think about something boring. Be boring, will you, Neve?"

"Be boring?" She pressed her lips together to stifle a laugh. "Just how am I supposed to do that?"

"I don't know." He glanced back at her, the thick fringe of his lashes shielding his eyes. "I can hear the smile in your voice and even that makes me want to kiss you."

Something giddy and warm unfurled inside her and she found herself overcome by the need to move closer to him. To curl up in his lap and wrap her arms around him. Kiss him, maybe. Or just hold him.

Her voice was breathless when she asked him, "Should I just stop talking?"

She'd have to stop breathing before he thought he could handle being this close and not wanting her. No. *He* would have to stop breathing.

As she continued to watch him, the remnants of her laughter still gleaming in her eyes, Ian felt his heart do a slow roll in his chest. He'd been an idiot. Thinking that he could actually *not* give into the emotions twisting through him when he looked at her, when he thought about her.

He'd never been one to believe in love at first sight— had never even wanted to look for love himself.

Mum had been a single parent after the sad, pathetic bastard who'd fathered him took off when he'd learned he'd be a father. After she'd died, he'd spent the last few years before university with his grandparents and hadn't they been a shining example of love? The old man had beat his grandmother, and often.

Love, in Ian's opinion, wasn't something to be sought. It was a pain in the backside.

Yet sitting there with Neve, he couldn't deny the odd way his heart ached, or the fact that each morning, he woke up thinking about her. They barely knew each other, true, but some part of him felt like he'd known her for always—that he'd been *waiting* for her for always.

"Talk," he said softly. "Talk with me, laugh with me."

The humor in her eyes faded away, replaced by an emotion that made his chest ache.

Leaning forward, he caught her fingers and lifted them to his lips, kissing the tips. "What are you doing to me, Neve McKay?"

Her tongue slid out and she wet her lips. Easing closer, he reached up and traced the lower curve of her mouth with his thumb.

Her lashes fluttered down low and he had to fight the urge to replace his thumb with his mouth.

This wasn't the place.

And despite the fact that he wanted her like he wanted his next breath, he didn't want to rush this.

Couldn't rush it—he had a feeling this could be the most important thing in his life and he had to be patient.

Because he was aware if this continued, he'd end up in the exact same position he'd described to her, he steered the conversation into what he hoped was fairly neutral territory—he asked about her time in Scotland.

They finished up their meal as she told him about

Carrbridge and he smiled when she mentioned the quaint bridge, but as they started to walk down the street that led to the river, his mood turned grim.

"Aviemore?" he murmured. "Aye. I know it."

"Been there?"

He shrugged. "I lived there for a few years."

"Did you?" Her head swung toward his, eyes curious.

He wanted to shrug it off, but after all she'd shared, how could he say nothing.

Spotting a bench, he sat, tugging her down to sit with him.

Somebody jogged by and he studied them for a moment and then looked back at Neve. "Some of you are mad, running in this heat."

She lifted a brow. "It gets a lot worse here."

Ian rolled his eyes. Then, leaning forward, he braced his elbows on his knees. Gaze locked on the lazy waters of the Mississippi, he said, "We lived in Braemar. Me and my mum. Beautiful village, up in the Cairngorms. So cold at times, you'd think your lungs would freeze right through, but you've never seen a place so lovely. Then Mum died when I was thirteen. Cancer. It happened fast. I had to go live with her parents in Aviemore. My gran . . . she was a kind lady. But scared. If my grandfather wasn't there, things weren't so bad, see? She liked to fuss over me and we'd play cards and talk, or she'd read and I'd watch the telly. But once it was time for him to be getting on home, well, things would change. He was a bastard, that one. A cruel one, too. If the meal wasn't on the table by five, then Gran would catch the wrong side of his fist. Only happened twice and once was because she had to take me to see the doctor. I'd fallen, broken my arm. Not that he cared." He shrugged, staring off into the distance, but it wasn't the grass or the lazy waters of the river he saw. It was his gran's face. "He was a drunk, too. A mean one. If she didn't move fast enough or if she did, he'd take it out on her. As I got older, I'd pick a fight with him just to spare her, but she hated that. I hated him. The day before I turned eighteen, I came home and found . . ." He sucked in his breath and stared up at the sky through the branches overhead. "She'd left a letter. Saying she loved me, truly. But now that I was a man, I didn't need her and she couldn't do it anymore. She was on her bed, like she was just sleeping. And she was smiling."

"Ian . . ."

When she touched his arm, he caught her hand. Turning his head, he met her gaze. "I knew somebody had hurt you. Not that first night, perhaps, but definitely the next day when you came back to the pub. I knew it. Something about the way your eyes looked. You had the same fear in your eyes. I want to break him, Neve."

She went to look away but he stopped her, reaching up to lay a hand on her cheek.

"Don't look away," he murmured.

Her throat worked as she swallowed and he rubbed a thumb over her lower lip.

"When I close my eyes, I remember how you taste."

A soft breath escaped her.

Her eyes met his and when he leaned in, she didn't pull away.

"But even though I remember your taste, I need more."

Then stop talking and kiss me!

Neve wished she had the nerve to tell him that. Instead, she reached up and pressed her fingertips to his lower lip. His mouth was so much softer than it appeared, his beard scratchy soft against her palm.

Curious, she stroked her fingers across it, then up to rest on his cheek, echoing the way he touched her.

When he slid his hand around to hook over the back of her neck, she didn't even think of pulling away.

But he didn't draw her closer, either.

Groaning in frustration, she moved in. She didn't have a chance to process the widening of the smile on his lips. Nor did she care, because in the next breath, that mouth was on hers and heat, hunger, need swamped her.

She'd never known anything like this.

His tongue slid along her lower lip, teasing and stroked and taunted, before slipping inside. She caught the tip and bit down, felt him shake.

He pulled her onto his lap and she tensed for a moment, but just a moment, then curled into him. He curved one arm around her lower back, the other rested on her legs. Twisting her upper body, she wrapped her arms around his neck.

Ian growled deep in his throat.

Neve plunged her hands into his hair and wiggled, struggling to get closer.

His teeth nipped her lower lip.

She bit his tongue.

A siren wailed.

She jumped.

She would have leaped off his lap if he hadn't tightened his arms.

"Damn Marshall," he muttered.

Blood rushed to her face as she dared to glance over her shoulder. Gideon was eyeing them from the street and if she wasn't mistaken, there was an amused look on his face.

Cringing in embarrassment, she pressed her face against Ian's neck.

"Oh, right, just sit there and smile at me, you sodding prick," Ian said.

A laugh escaped her.

Ian stroked a hand up her back. "I expect you think we should *thank* him."

"*Thank* him?"

She dared to lift her head, meeting his eyes. But she didn't look anywhere else. Gideon's car was still there. She could hear the motor.

"Well, yeah. If he hadn't shown up, I might now be trying to get you naked." He slid one hand to her waist and slid it up. "I can't say I've ever wanted to have public sex, but you tempt me. Not to have public sex, mind you, but just to have sex—with you—here. Screw that it's public."

She snorted, the strangled laugh that escaped her both nervous and embarrassed. "Sure. I'll thank him. As soon as I think I can look at him without wanting to hide."

Ian pressed his cheek to hers and she felt his beard rub against her, a soft caress. "Don't be wanting to hide, Neve. You think I'm embarrassed because you want me? I'd be tempted to brag about it, but my mum taught me better."

The slow, soothing stroke of his hand up and down her back helped drain the tension and after a moment, she looked up. "I don't see how this can be real," she said softly, meeting his dark, warm eyes. "How can I feel like this with you? I don't even know you."

"Do you want to?"

"Yes." There was no question about that. None at all.

"Sometimes people just fit, Neve." He pressed a soft kiss to her brow and then settled her back on the bench.

She could still feel Gideon there, making a show of *not* watching them as he sat in his car. But he was very

aware of them, and now she couldn't help but be aware
of him, too. Ian moved a few feet away, his hands in his
back pockets as he stared out over the river. "I think we
could maybe be a fit," he said. "I think we *are* a fit, Neve.
We'll just . . . give it time."

"Okay." She licked her lips and almost shuddered as
she caught the taste of him there. "I think I can handle
that."

He turned back to her, his eyes gleaming. "Right,
then. Have lunch with me."

"But we just had lunch."

"Well, that's the thing about lunch, darling Neve."
Holding her gaze with his, he strolled back to her and
hunkered down on his knees. "You eat it every day. Just
like breakfast and dinner."

As he waited for her answer, he took her hand and
nibbled at her knuckles. "Well," she said, sort of breathless. "If you're not already tired of me . . ."

"I could see you every day for a thousand years and
not be tired of you."

CHAPTER TWELVE

"Unless the building is on fire"—Ian took a moment to check the air—"and it isn't, then leave me alone for a night, would ya, Morgan?"

She laughed. "No. The building isn't on fire. "But, boss, you want to come down anyway."

"No. I don't." Ian was sprawled comfortably in front of the telly, watching *Doctor Who* and munching on popcorn. He had a blissful, wonderful day away from the pub. Workaholic that he was—and he was fine with it—he only had a day and a half off each week. Brannon had told him he ought to take the weekends off, seeing as how he managed the place and would probably own it outright in a few years, but Ian liked working. He was happy with it. But he also enjoyed the one day a week he was off. Or the one day he was *supposed* to be off. He rarely managed to go that one day without being called in to handle some such mess or another. But today, he'd made it all the way until eight in the evening. He'd damn well avoid—

"Fine." Morgan sighed theatrically before she added, "I'll just let Neve McKay sit at the bar by her lonesome then. Although it looks like Griffin—"

He shot up off the couch and didn't even think to

disconnect the call until he heard Morgan's laughter when he was in the bathroom, a minute later, hurriedly straightening his hair.

It was less than ten minutes before he was locking up his flat and less than twelve before he was striding into the pub, through the front door this time. After all, it was his day off, wasn't it?

And there she was, sitting at the bar, giving Griffin Parker a smile. Griffin, daft idiot that he was, likely couldn't tell that it was a half-hearted attempt at best. When Ian moved closer, Neve glanced up and the smile changed, bloomed into the one he knew was a *real* one and it lit him up inside, made him feel like he could climb mountains and jump over skyscrapers.

Griffin glanced over, following her gaze, and spotted him.

Ian saw the way the other man sort of rolled his eyes and then he gave a good-natured grimace.

"Mind if I join you?" he asked.

Griffin glanced down at his mostly eaten meal and then said, "How about you just take my seat? Bar's crowded. I'm about done."

A moment later, as Morgan cleared away Griffin's plate, Ian snuck a chip from Neve's plate. "Trying out my fish and chips, are you?"

"Well, somebody told me they were the best in town." That shy, nervous sort of smile curled her lips.

"You should have called me, told me you were coming in. I'd have met you here."

One smooth shoulder, bared by a skinny-strapped top, lifted. His mouth watered as he thought about pressing his lips to that elegant slope. "It was a last-minute sort of thing. You always seem to be here anyway . . ." Even as the words left her lips, she started to blush.

Ian could have pounded his bloody chest, he was so

delighted. "So . . ." He leaned in, one arm draped over the back of her seat. "Coming to see me, were you?"

That mouth of his was so damned beautiful, it all but made her forget her name. Right now, it was curled in a pleased grin and she was torn between blushing and laughing. Turning her attention to her plate, she grabbed a fry and popped it into her mouth. She washed it down with her watered-down Coke. In a deliberately lofty voice, she said, "I'll have you know, I wanted some food. Ella Sue is so determined to fatten me up, but she's hovering and it's driving me crazy. She was making pot roast and I was more in the mood for fish and chips."

"And you weren't even thinking of seeing me, not at all?" he murmured.

She swallowed. Turning her head, she met his eyes. He'd moved in so close, all she'd have to do was lean in the smallest bit and her mouth would touch his.

"Not at all?"

A smile trembled on her lips. "Well, seeing you is a bonus."

"You wound me, Neve."

Laughing, she turned back to her food. "With your ego, Ian, I think it would take a great deal more than that to wound you." Keeping her voice deliberately casual, she asked, "So I guess it's your day off, huh?"

"Yes." He stole another fry and she smacked his hand. "Oi!"

"Order your own."

"Will you keep me company if I do?" He gave a heavy sigh as he studied her half-empty plate. "I hate to eat alone, love. I truly do."

"I'm sure." Then, because she had come to see him and

they both knew it, she said, "I guess I can hang around a while."

"You're too kind to me."

"Spiders."

Neve slid him a look. "Seriously?"

"On my honor." Ian placed a hand on his chest as though swearing an oath. "And I blame J. K. Rowling. It's all her fault—and Hagrid's. That damn giant spider of his. I never liked them much, especially after reading *The Lord of the Rings,* but then I read about the monster he raised as a pet and . . ."

Ian shuddered dramatically.

Neve laughed. This crazy game he'd started—*what about . . . what are you . . .* was revealing all sorts of unusual things. He hated chocolate, he secretly loved Celine Dion—*and* country music—and although he forbade her from telling, he shuddered every time Ella Sue poured him a glass of her sweet tea.

Now she knew he disliked closed-in spaces and he hated spiders.

"What about you?"

She looked away. "It would be easier to talk about the things I'm *not* afraid of."

"But that's cheating," Ian chided, his voice light and teasing.

A smile tugged at her lips. He already knew the big fears. She supposed she didn't have to go into those. "Um . . . well. I hate shots. I gave Moira a bloody nose once, trying to get away from her and the nurses before they could give me my vaccinations."

Ian came to a stop, gaping at her. "You what?"

She blushed, furiously embarrassed. "You heard me. I hate shots. They terrify me." She jerked a shoulder in an awkward shrug. "I haven't had one since . . . hell. I don't even know. I get the flu vaccine now, but only because they came out with that nasal mist. Back in high school, I even passed out once."

Ian rubbed his ear. "I'm sorry, I'm still hung up on the *bloody nose* bit."

Neve rolled her eyes.

"I'm serious," he said, shaking his head. "Your sister, she can be rather intimidating. That you bloodied her nose . . . well, that's rather shocking."

With a sound that was part laughter, part derisive snort, she started to walk again, tugging on his hand. She moved her gaze to the river, the moon shining down on it and splintering into a thousand shards of silvery-white.

"I've missed this."

The night air was soft, wrapping around them like a muggy blanket. Sweat beaded on the back of her neck, but it didn't bother her.

Ian just looked at her, waiting.

"Home," she said simply. "New York . . . well, I loved it there. London—it would be hard to say if I enjoyed it or not, since I never really had a chance to experience it on my own. I loved Scotland, though. But no place every really felt like home."

"That's because no place else was home for you." He squeezed her hand.

Nerves fluttered inside her. She told herself not to ask, but she couldn't stop herself. "Is . . . is Scotland still home for you?"

"In some ways, yes. Braemar, in a way, will always be home. But there are shadows there," Ian told her. He came to a halt, still holding her hand.

She turned to face him, but he was gazing out over the river. "Braemar was home because it was where

Mum raised me. I was happy there. But when she died, a part of me died, too. You can probably understand that, I think. It . . . it was fast and ugly, she hurt so much. I barely recognized her in the end. Those memories tarnish the memories of home. Aviemore . . ." He jerked a shoulder in a shrug. "As much as I loved my gran, that place was never home. I moved to Glasgow after university, lived there until Brannon talked me into coming here, but it wasn't home."

"Where is home?"

Finally, he turned his head and smiled at her. "It's here. I miss Scotland, but I can go back in the summer and last year, I went back at Christmas. I can always go back and visit, but when it's done, I'm ready to come back here. I think I've found my home, Neve."

Those words made one of the knots in her chest loosen. It didn't unfurl completely, but she thought maybe it was starting to.

Lost in the shadows, William watched.

When Neve had driven into town that evening, anticipation had spread through him.

He knew Campbell's schedule. Not only had he been watching, but he'd made a couple of careful questions, had even made a few calls—asking when he might be able to find the manager in. Oh, he took caution there. *I've a business matter to discuss with the manager— which days is he available? Should I set up a meeting or just drop in . . . of course, of course. Thank you so much.*

Thursdays were the only days he wasn't in the pub, so naturally, when the Thursday rolled around and he saw Neve approach, he'd been excited. He'd even considered going in after her, but decided against it. Brannon lived in town as well and William had prowled around enough to know that there was a back entrance. Both of those sods could and did use the back entrance.

It was a good thing he'd exercised caution because no sooner had he made the decision not to go in after Neve did he see Campbell come striding down the walk of the building next door.

And into the pub he'd gone.

Now the two of them were making fools of themselves, Neve plastered against Campbell. Blood roared in William's ears as he saw Campbell's hands settle on Neve's bottom. In response, she wiggled even closer.

She'd never reacted to him quite like that.

In the beginning, there had been some shy, almost hesitant responses, but as years passed, it had been like he'd been touching a doll. A beautiful, living doll. *His* fucking doll.

"Whore," he whispered.

Neither of them heard.

He clenched his hands into fists and thought about going after her right there, grabbing her away from Campbell.

But memory stopped him.

Pride kept him from remembering it accurately— kept him from remembering how Campbell had thrashed him rather soundly. But his body *did* remember.

So he stood there—and he hated.

"I see you're avoiding going off the beaten path these days."

Neve blushed as Gideon stopped by the table.

Ian leaned back in his chair and grinned up at Gideon. "Well, now. I wouldn't say that. We've just chosen to find a bench a little more . . . out of the way."

Gideon lifted a brow.

Neve kicked Ian under the table.

They hadn't done anything of the sort, although *now* she wondered if there were more private . . . benches close by.

It might not do much good, though.

Ian had played the perfect gentleman, right up until the time it took for him to walk her back to her car and at that point, he proceeded to kiss her until she was panting for breath and her knees threatened to collapse on her.

She thought maybe he was trying to drive her out of her mind.

Further evidence came when a hand came to rest on her knee under the table. His thumb began to trace a pattern that sent a shiver through her.

"I'd keep that to yourself if I was you," Gideon advised. "Somebody mentioned they'd seen the two of you out in a lip-lock yesterday in front of Brannon and he looked like he'd swallowed a bug."

"He's a big boy, Brannon." Ian said as his fingers slid a little higher on her thigh. "He'll handle it."

Gideon just shook his head, amused. "You two behave." Then he made a quick stop by the counter to grab his lunch and was gone.

"You just like getting a reaction out of people," Neve said, shaking her head.

Ian smiled. "I'd like to get certain reactions out of you."

He squeezed her knee and just like that, his hands were gone. "I was thinking, maybe we could try something besides lunch soon."

Wary, she eyed him. "Oh?"

"A movie, maybe. We could drive over the bridge to Louisiana one weekend . . . grab a movie."

A real date. She grabbed her drink and took a healthy swallow, trying to give herself time to think. But then she remembered what he'd told her. *You think too much.*

Just as she was looking up, something across the street caught her eye.

She froze, the cup falling from numb hands.

She barely noticed as it started to tip over. Ian caught it, but she was leaning forward. Was that—

A car drove by, cutting off her view.

No. The man turned his head, called to somebody down the road.

"Neve."

Ian's voice was soft, gentle.

She turned her head and met his eyes.

"Are you okay?"

"I'm fine," she said. She had to clear her throat, though, and then she said it again, more to herself than anything. "I'm fine."

Still, that uneasiness wouldn't go away.

"Would you like a bit of lunch?"

William barely spared the plump English innkeeper a glance as he strode across the foyer.

They'd been at the diner *again*, Neve and Campbell.

They were together almost every bloody day.

She was hardly ever alone and when she was, it was for just a moment and even when she *was* alone, there were people around.

Each day, he watched, waited for a chance to speak with her. He'd tried calling, but the phone would just ring endlessly. Once, to see what she'd do, he'd tried calling her as she sat with that arrogant sod.

Just as he'd given up waiting for her to answer, she'd glanced down and reached for her purse, pulling out a phone.

He'd held his breath—

And the rings continued as she answered a phone that clearly had a different number, a warm smile on her face as she greeted her caller.

She'd gotten a new phone.

"I've got some fresh soup and bread—"

"No, thank you," he said, shooting a narrow look at his hostess.

"Is . . ."

He turned his head and stared at her, briefly wondering what she'd said her name was, but then he dismissed it. It didn't matter what her name was. She was providing a service and he expected courtesy and efficiency. He did *not* expect conversation, nor did he desire it.

"Well, then." She gave him a tight smile and nodded. "If you're in the mood for tea later this afternoon, just let me know."

She disappeared into the house, the line of her shoulders rigid.

William ignored her, moving straight to his room. Fury was a burning lance in his gut but he closed the door calmly.

Neve was making a fool of herself—and him. She was his, yet every day for nearly a week, he'd watched her sharing a meal with another man. *Laughing* and *smiling* at that man, as though William wasn't even a passing thought in her head anymore.

It wasn't to be tolerated.

Moving to the window, he stared out over the tree-lined street, considering his options.

He'd waited for a chance for them to speak privately and that had yet to happen. He'd tried calling her and the stupid bint had changed her number.

Something, William mused, had to be done.

CHAPTER THIRTEEN

"You should go."

"Right, I should do that." Instead of doing anything of the sort, Ian pressed his mouth to Neve's neck.

Her soft, shaky sigh was the reason behind that gesture, just as it had been the reason he'd done it the first time, five minutes earlier. Her fingers twisted in the front of his black shirt and the sun beating down on him had sweat forming under the dark material, but really, what did he care if he had a heatstroke? He figured it would be Brannon's fault. Brannon was the sod who'd insisted that if Ian wouldn't wear the McKay colors he'd had to make do with the *unobstrusive* black and khaki. Like Ian was going to wear the plaid of the McKays. He was a fucking Campbell.

Neve whispered his name and he skimmed his lips up her neck to kiss her again.

She kissed him back and he toyed with the hem of her shirt.

"Ian!"

He recognized the voice. Decided he'd just as soon ignore it.

But Neve pushed her hands between them.

Couldn't ignore that.

As her brother came striding up, she blushed a lovely shade of pink and he caught her hand, lifting it to his lips.

"Can't you find some other place to paw my sister?" Brannon snapped.

"I could." Ian winked at her. "Want to come up to my place?"

Neve choked out a nervous laugh and Ian had to dodge away as Brannon made a swipe for him.

"Don't hurt me," Ian warned, trying not to laugh. "You'll have to handle the deliveries if you do. Chap hates the delivery driver that comes today."

Brannon gave him a snarling sort of glare and Ian chanced one last quick kiss for Neve, then dodged around the car, jogging up to the pub.

Neve watched him go, her heart racing while a grin lingered on her lips.

"This is apparently a regular thing for you."

She turned her head to see Brannon studying her. "What?"

"This . . ." He waved a hand between her and the pub. "You two."

"We . . ." Um. She cleared her throat. "Well, we're just having lunch."

He stared at her hard, but didn't push. Instead, he changed the subject. "We need to go over some of the plans—the tile I wanted for the main room apparently isn't going to work. They did a recall. You got time?"

She made a face. "I guess I'll have to make time."

As they started up the sidewalk, Brannon jammed his hands into his pockets. "So what's with you and Ian?"

She stopped dead in her tracks. "Me and Ian?"

"Yeah." He stared at her hard. "You know, the big guy who had his hands all over you. In the middle of the street."

She narrowed her eyes. "We weren't in the middle of the street. We were by the car. But next time, we can try kissing in the middle of the street. For comparison."

Brannon went to say something and then apparently thought better of it. They started to walk again, but before they reached the building, he asked, "Have you heard anything from . . ."

Ice suddenly replaced the heat in her veins. "No." Her voice trembled and she hated it. Clearing her voice, she said it again. "No."

"Will you?"

She reached out to push the door open but paused to look back at him. She wanted to lie, wished she could. But all she could offer was the truth. "I don't know."

"What do you think?"

Troubled, she looked away. "I think . . . yes. I think sooner or later, William will come looking for me. I embarrassed him, Bran. He won't tolerate that."

"Running late, boss!" Chap grinned at him from behind the bar, his lean, dark face amused.

"I'm *one* minute behind," he pointed out.

"Considering that you're usually here about twenty minutes *early*, that makes you *twenty-one* minutes behind." Morgan grinned at him from where she stood, wiping down menus. She wagged her brows at him. "And how is Neve today?"

"Sod off, all of you," he suggested.

Chap laughed.

Morgan, though, followed after him as he headed to his office. "Is . . . um . . . well, is Neve doing okay?"

He glanced at her, frowning.

"What do you mean?"

Morgan shrugged. "I used to hang out with her some in school. Not a lot, but some. We used to get in a lot of trouble. Mostly because of who we were with. The few times I've seen her here, she just doesn't seem like herself. I've wondered."

Ian took his time answering. He liked Morgan quite a bit, really. But he didn't join in on gossip. "I think you'd need to talk to Neve about that." After a moment, he added, "I don't think a lot of people have spared much time to visit with her. She'd probably enjoy it."

Morgan gave him a weak smile. "We didn't exactly spend much time talking. We were mostly just looking to . . . well, get out of school. Kill time. It's not like we were best friends or anything."

"I don't think you need to be best friends to drop in and tell somebody hello." But he left it at that.

And when Morgan left, he dropped down behind the desk and gave himself a few more minutes to relive the pleasure of yet another afternoon with Neve, the woman who was slowly turning him inside out.

Now if he could just figure out how to have her join him for something *other* than lunch.

"I'm sorry. We're not open yet."

Walt Stephenson bit back on the frustration he felt and pasted an affable smile on his face.

Considering the fact that they had one giant-ass sign out front announcing just *when* the museum would open, he didn't see why he needed to be pointing this out, but the man in the three-piece suit apparently either couldn't or chose not to read said sign.

"Yes, thank you."

Walt's belly growled, reminding him that it had been going on six hours since he'd sat down to the monster breakfast his wife of twenty years still insisted on cooking every day. He'd been on his way outside to eat the sack lunch she'd prepared from last night's leftovers and he wanted to get off his feet awhile. Moira McKay looked like a little bit of fluff, but she worked his damn rear end off.

But the man wasn't moving. Scratching at his neck, Walt tried again. "Seeing as how we're not open yet, is there something I can do for you?" He paused a moment and then asked, "Are you lost?"

"Hardly."

A lash of disdain worked its way into that single word and Walt slowly straightened, but the man smiled then and it warmed his face considerably. "I'm looking for Ms. McKay—Moira McKay. She's in charge here, yes?"

"That'd be right." Walt plucked at his left brow, an old, absent gesture. "But she's not here. She had meetings today. You should call next time before you come out. She's only here a few days a week."

"Hmm. What about the younger McKay . . . Neve? It's important that I speak to one of them. Or perhaps Mr. McKay?"

"None of them are here." Tapping his bagged lunch against his thigh, Walt continued. "I run things when Moira isn't here. And then there's Mr. Hurst. He could talk to you, if it's urgent business about the museum."

"No." Angling his head, the man studied Walt.

It gave him the feeling that he was a bug on a slide, the way this guy kept eyeing him. *Want me to do a trick or what?* He managed to keep his expression polite and his irritation under wraps, but he was getting annoyed.

"Then perhaps you could come back later. Or leave a message."

"It is urgent," he said. "And personal. Perhaps you could tell me where I could find the McKays? They live in town, correct?"

Walt took a step forward, forcing the other man to

either back up or hold his position and stare up at Walt's thick, sun-reddened neck.

The man backed up.

Walt had assumed he would. He was a big guy. Most people didn't want him in their personal space. "You'd have to get that information elsewhere, Mister . . . ?"

"Of course. I'm sorry to intrude."

Walt stood exactly where he was until the man climbed into his car, a dark blue sedan—the pricey kind. It started with a low purr and once the man had driven away, Walt reached for the bandanna he carried. Swiping it over his forehead, he shoved it back into his pocket and started to brood.

He had every intention of telling Moira about the pushy bastard.

But then he got the call from his daughter.

His wife—sweet, sweet Meg—was in the hospital. They thought she'd had a heart attack.

He completely forgot all about the arrogant schmuck who'd delayed his lunch.

"Yes, yes . . . look, you handle it. You've been to every meeting and you know what's going on, what we expect if they actually want us to fund them."

Neve stood in the doorway, listening to Moira as she talked.

When she caught sight of the annoyance on her sister's face, she leaned against the arched entry and waited.

"I'm sorry, but it will have to suffice, Angie. My top man at the museum needs some personal time off and we can't go off schedule now, which means I need to be out there."

Moira saw Neve and gave her a distracted smile as she wrapped up the conversation.

As Moira put the phone down, Neve edged a few feet into the office. It had been their mother's office once, but clearly Moira had put her stamp on it. The blue walls were the same, and the colors of the rug, warm and thick beneath their feet, were faded but still beautiful. It had belonged to their great-grandmother, something she'd picked up on a yearly trip to Europe decades ago.

But many other things were different. The lush green drapes that blocked much of the sun's light, the deep cherry furniture replacing the pale, blond oak their mother had been fond of.

"Working?" she asked as Moira dropped down into the chair behind the massive desk. Somehow, she still managed to make the move look elegant and graceful.

Of course, Moira McKay could make *anything* look elegant and graceful.

"Nonstop." Moira rested her head on the back of the chair for a moment. "You remember Walt Stephenson?"

Neve squinted. "Barely. He worked on some projects with Dad, didn't he?"

"Yep. He's been helping me with the museum, but his wife had a heart attack."

"Oh, no!" Meg, Neve remembered. Meg had often been there in the days after the funeral, dropping in to check on them, offering to watch her if Ella Sue needed to run errands. She was a sweet, sweet lady.

"She'll be fine. Walt held on like he was drowning when I stopped in to check, but they think she's out of danger." Moira popped open one eye. "He's this big, gruff, grouchy son of a bitch, but his wife turns him into a teddy bear. He all but cried when the doctors came to get him."

She sat up straighter, then flipping through a thick stack of folders on her desk. "I'm going to have to juggle my schedule so I can get out there more than once or twice a week. I was supposed to go to Sydney for a few days for meetings, but that will have to wait."

"Sydney?"

"Australia." Moira shot her a grin. "One of the patents Dad held—there's a medical group there who is interested in it."

"Are we . . ." Neve stopped and looked away. "Is McKay thinking of selling it?"

"It's *we*, Neve," Moira said quietly. "*We*."

Neve slanted a look at her sister. "I don't quite feel like *we* is a thing yet, Moira. I want it to be, but . . ."

"It's always been *we*."

When Neve didn't respond, Moira sighed. "Anyway, yes, we are thinking of selling—or possibly a merger between our medical arm and their company. They have some interesting ideas on making some sort of gadget— or improving something—for clinics and smaller hospitals. It has something to do with MRIs, I think." Moira pursed her lips, pausing over a folder. "Yeah. MRIs. It would help a lot of people and they've got a good brain behind the project. I just wanted to get a better feel of who we'd be working with. But I'll have to reschedule. I can't leave with Walt not being there and I can't let the museum fall behind schedule. We're set to open in a month."

"Well, I'd offer to help, but I don't know what to do." Neve moved to the window and rocked back on her heels as she stared out over the garden.

"Didn't Brannon dump enough on you?"

Neve lifted a brow.

Moira smiled blandly. "He's the king of starters. Staying power, though . . ."

Neve almost choked. "Eesh, Moira! Imagery!"

"Heh. I told him that once and he turned as red as his hair." Impishly, Moira added, "So be sure to work it into a conversation if you can."

Neve rolled her eyes and plucked at a loose thread on her jeans. "I'll do what I can. Anyway, yeah. I'm working on picking out the furniture and all that for inside the winery."

"It's a big deal, Nevie. That winery is his baby." She rolled her eyes. "Give him some time and he'll drag you down there. You'll learn more about wine and soil than you *ever* wanted to know. Anyway, how is it going? Making a lot of headway?"

"It's going." Neve shrugged. "How much headway I'm making . . . well. I don't even know why Bran asked me to help with this."

"You're helping with the design part, Neve. You always had a good eye for that. It's not like he asked for you to come up with the blueprints." She grinned. "I offered a few suggestions there and he bit my head off. You should be flattered . . . Brannon asked you to help dress his baby." She sighed and looked down at everything spread out in front of her.

Neve watched as her sister wrinkled her nose and pushed at one piece of paper with a look of acute dislike.

"What's up?"

"Meeting. Roberts. Some state senator.. He's hobnobbing and in the baby-kissing stage. His people keep nagging me about letting him do an event at the museum." She slid Neve a look. "That museum is *my* baby. I don't want some two-faced politician coming in and throwing mud on my baby."

"Tell him to fuck off." Neve shrugged.

"But it would be good publicity for the place. Which is why I keep putting off making a decision." Moira made a face. Then she lifted a brow, pinning Neve with a hard look. "Sooooo . . ."

At that tone, Neve flicked her sister a cautious glance. "So, what?"

"You've been seeing a lot of Ian lately. You two having lunch again?"

"It's lunch." Defensively, Neve crossed her arms across her chest. "We eat it daily, so why not eat it together?"

"Hey, no reason that I can think of." Moira jabbed the pen in Neve's direction. "Trust me, there are much worse people to . . . have lunch with around here."

Blood rushed up to her cheeks, but Neve couldn't quite wipe the smile off her face.

"Geez, between you and Brannon today." She crossed her arms across her middle. But she couldn't even really say she was upset by their nosiness. She almost even *enjoyed* it. "So, he . . . Ian, I mean. He said something about maybe a movie. Or go over into Louisiana or something for the day. Kind of a date, I guess. A real one."

Moira lifted a brow. "Honey, the two of you have already *been* on several real dates, if you don't mind my saying so."

"That's just lunch," she said, fighting the urge to squirm.

"Okay." A look of mild interest on her face, Moira straightened in the chair and pinned a look on Neve. "So during these . . . lunches . . . he's kept his hands completely to himself? Conversation never veers into the personal territory? Everything feels completely friendly? Like it would if you were . . . I don't know . . . having lunch with Gideon?"

Neve glared at her.

Moira grinned in return. "See? Dates." As Neve

started to rub the heel of her hand over her chest, Moira chuckled. "Honey, relax. That's one hell of a man to have all but falling over his feet to get you to notice him."

One hell of a man.

A day later, Neve reminded herself of her sister's words as she caught sight of Ian, already sitting in what was rapidly becoming *their* spot. He saw her and rose, the smile on his face setting her heart to racing.

Yeah, Gideon smiling at her wouldn't cause that.

And she had to admit, she knew none of her other *friends* would cause this reaction, either.

"I've been thinking," Ian said as he pulled out her chair.

"Yeah?"

He waited.

"So what are you thinking about?" she asked, sitting down and scooting in.

"Well, right now I'm thinking your brother and you don't have much in common." Ian's cheeks creased with his grin. "Because he wouldn't have let that *I've been thinking* comment go without commenting on it."

"I did comment." She tried not to let herself drool as he tugged out his seat and sat back down. "I said *yeah*."

"Not much of a comment." Ian picked up the tall glass, condensation already forming drops on the red plastic. "*But* . . . as I was saying, I've been thinking. We should go on a date."

Neve had been ready to give him the smart-ass comment he'd clearly expected, but the words trapped in her throat.

"We . . . um . . . well, didn't we discuss this? The movie . . . or whatever?" Panic started to chitter in her mind. What if she'd misunderstood him? What if Moira had been wrong? What if these lunches hadn't been dates or what if—

"We talked about it. But you never gave much of an answer and I'm thinking maybe I didn't make myself clear. I want to do that. I'd like to take you out. On a date." His fingers brushed against hers and she automatically turned over her hand, gripping his. "In a way, we've already been on *six* dates now, if you consider lunch."

The band around her chest loosened and she started to breathe.

"Dinner," Ian said, his voice soft and coaxing. "We'll go out for dinner, take a ride. We can see a movie if you want, or if you don't, we can just ride around and talk."

His lids drooped and the temperature spiked—it was already a sweltering ninety degrees and she wouldn't have been surprised if she'd spontaneously combusted. "And I could kiss you again."

"You have to take me out to kiss me?"

"No." He stroked his thumb across her knuckles and lifted her hand. As he pressed a kiss to the back, he met her eyes. "But I want to take you out. And I want to kiss you. Two birds . . . one stone."

She practically wilted in the seat. *I want to kiss you . . . yes, please!*

"I guess a date isn't totally unreasonable." She focused on him, staring at him hard as she pushed past all the noise building up in her head. So much going on up there, it was a wonder she had room for *her* thoughts.

"It's been a very, very long time since I've gone on a *date*." She thought back and realized it had been close to five years, although were they really dates? Those frozen, stilted dinners with William where he'd been more focused on parading her about instead of spending time with her?

Ian's warm, low laugh had her pulse bumping up. "I'll do my best to make sure our date is a memorable one."

Hair. Check.

Nails. Check.

Makeup. Raid Moira's bathroom . . . check.

It took twice as long as it would have taken ten years earlier. Even five years ago. Apparently primping isn't like riding a bike.

But as the minute hand hovered at five 'til seven, Neve stood in front of the floor-length mirror in her bathroom and gave herself a critical study. Considering she still needed to put another ten pounds or so back on and considering she'd ended up having Ella Sue give her a quick haircut to deal with the dead ends and considering she'd spent nearly forty-five minutes fixing the natural disasters that were her hands, Neve thought she looked pretty good.

The dress was cut in a retro style with wide shoulder straps and a sweetheart neckline that nipped in at the waist before flaring out wide in a circle skirt. The black petticoat underneath rustled as she walked and she'd found black and green underwear that matched the dress and petticoat. Just in case she decided . . . *no, not thinking about that*, she told herself.

A few years ago, she would have had a few dozen pieces of jewelry to select from, but the things that had been so easy before felt impossible now and she stood in front of the lovely cabinet that held the jewelry she'd left behind, unsure what to wear.

Hesitant, she touched her fingers to the pearl necklace there. Brannon and Moira had given it to her when she'd graduated, but she'd left it behind in a fit of pique. She was glad now, because it either would have been sold or she might have been forced to leave it with William when she ran.

She'd gotten rid of almost everything she'd taken with her.

Now, she took it out and wrapped the short, simple strand around her neck, keeping her gaze downcast as she finished the task. Once it was done, she turned to look.

"Oh, my."

She jumped at the sound of Moira's voice.

"I'm sorry."

Meeting her sister's gaze in the mirror, Neve forced a smile. "It's okay." Looking back at her reflection, she squared her shoulders. "How do I look?"

"Lovely." Moira moved closer. "The necklace . . ."

Neve reached up and touched it, her gaze falling away. "That day . . ."

"Don't, Nevie." Moira slid an arm around her waist. "I . . ." She stopped and lifted her face to the ceiling, blinking hard and fast. "At some point, we'll have to talk about it all, I know that. But I'm still spinning over everything you went through and I think it would be better to wait until we're all steadier. But I'm sorry. Brannon and I . . . we tried, but I'm starting to realize we made some serious mistakes. If we'd put you in therapy, or maybe just talked to you more . . ."

A knot settled in Neve's throat. "It's not your fault."

"Yes, it is. Some of it, at least." Moira looked back at her. "Can we . . ."

Neve reached out and caught her sister's hand. "It's done. It's over. If you made mistakes, then so did I." Squeezing Moira's fingers, she made herself smile. "What I want is to stop looking back. Can we do that?"

"We can do that." Moira's eyes glittered overbright.

"So. Ian, huh? That accent makes my girl parts all tingly."

Neve's mouth dropped open. And then she started to laugh.

"Oof."

Ian Campbell wasn't a man to be struck speechless, but that was about all he could manage when he first looked up and saw Neve descending the stairs, dressed in some green confection that made her skin glow and set her hair on fire.

"You'll have to do better than that," Ella Sue said in a low voice as she walked past him.

Ian cleared his throat. "Neve."

She lifted a brow. "Ian."

Lovely. He remembered her name—and he still knew his name, because that was his name she'd just said and he'd recognized the sound of it on her lips. Now he wanted to hear the sound of it as she moaned it, preferably as she lay underneath him after he'd stripped that shimmery green silk away—

Her heels clicked on the floor and he gave himself a mental kick in the arse.

"You look . . ." The spit in his mouth had dried up on him. He cleared his throat again. "Lovely. You look lovely."

And he sounded like an oaf. A stupid oaf.

She smiled. "Thank you."

"Neve, I think this is the first time I've seen that charmer struck speechless," Ella Sue said, laughter in her voice.

Ian could almost feel the blood rushing up to stain his cheeks red. He couldn't think of a time when he'd been more thankful for the fact that he had a beard. It hid a fair amount of his face. And he hid the rest of it by grabbing Neve's hand and bending over it, pressing his lips to the back of it in a light kiss. "Well, if a man's to be struck speechless over anything," he murmured. "Why shouldn't it be because of a beautiful woman?"

"Oh, that was smooth."

Moira's voice drifted down from the second-floor balcony and he straightened, looking past Neve to see the eldest McKay watching him. She was grinning, practically *laughing* at him. He could see it. And if she'd been much closer, he just might have kissed her, because that amusement helped drag his head back down to earth. "Good evening, Moira. And how are you doing, if I may ask?"

"Oh, ask away." She lifted one shoulder in a shrug. "I don't have a sexy Scot here to romance me, but I'm not doing too bad, overall."

He wagged his eyebrows at her. "I'm free tomorrow."

"I'll keep that in mind," Moira said dryly. "You all have a good night. I've got a hot date with an inventory spreadsheet and my museum plans. Oh . . . and a bottle of muscadine fresh from Brannon's winery."

"How you drink that sugar is a mystery." Ian gave a mock shudder. Feeling steadier, he looked back at Neve. And felt that sucker punch all over again. He swallowed the knot that seemed to take up the whole of his throat and managed to smile. "Are you ready?"

"Yes." She took a purse from the table nearby. "Let's go before Ella Sue decides to try and give me a curfew."

"I heard that," the older woman said from across the brightly lit foyer.

Neve's laugh echoed off the walls and brought a smile to Ian's face.

The sound of her laugh . . . he thought he could get used to hearing it. Yes. Yes, he thought he could.

* * *

"Um." Neve blinked at the bike. Then she looked down at her skirt. "This might be a problem."

"No, it won't." Ian climbed and gestured behind him. Then he grinned. "Well, you might flash some leg. I don't mind if you do. But other than that . . . ?"

"Won't it get in the way?" she asked doubtfully, moving closer.

"It's a petticoat you've got on under there, right?" He shrugged. "You'll just hitch up your skirts some as you get on and then tuck it around you. But if you want to change or maybe take a car from the garage?" A wicked gleam lit his eyes. "I've always wanted to take one of Brannon's toys out for a spin."

Neve rolled her eyes. "He'd have my ass." That alone was enough to make her consider it, but in the end, she gave in to temptation. The temptation of riding so close to Ian. "Let's see if I can manage this first."

It wasn't hard, though, she realized.

Managing Ian though? He *was* hard.

Everywhere.

She swallowed at the feel of his muscled thighs pressed against her nearly naked ones after he helped tuck the skirt down around her. He ended up taking some of the skirt and sitting on it, trapping her behind him. They tucked the rest of the material between their respective legs and he said, "See? Easy."

Easy . . . ?

She leaned in, pressing her legs to his to help keep the dress down and he started the bike. This was a lot of things but *easy* wasn't one of them.

A low moan rose in her throat as he pulled away from the house.

"What was that?"

"Nothing," she said, raising her voice.

Nothing . . . nothing at all. Just me trying to keep from turning into a pitiful mess of hormones.

"Gideon taught me to fish here."

"Did he now?" They'd decided against a movie—the closest theater was a thirty-minute drive away, so after dinner, Ian had driven Neve to the river. He'd turned the bike off and put it on its stand, but she made no move to climb off and he was quite fine as he was, the warmth of her snug against his back, her breath teasing his neck. He slid a hand back, rested on her thigh.

Through the silk of her dress, he could feel the warm, elegant length of her thigh.

He wanted to touch.

So fucking bad.

All throughout dinner, throughout the leisurely drive through town.

Now . . .

She gave a shaky sigh and relaxed against his back, her brow pressing to the back of his neck.

He spread his fingers wide and caught the fussy, flouncy silk of her dress and eased it higher. "I've driven myself half mad, thinking about touching you again, Miss Neve. Touching you . . . tasting you."

She had one hand on his waist and at his words, she tightened her fingers. "Is that a fact?"

"That's a fact." He turned his head, angling his body just slightly.

She met him more than halfway, one palm coming up to cup his cheek.

The soft night air wrapped around them, the breeze coming off the river blowing her hair so that it teased his cheek. He wanted to tangle his hands in it, feel the strands slipping across his chest, his belly.

In the dim light, he could see her eyes, misty and pale, soft and green, as she slid a look down to his mouth.

A groan ripped out of him.

She sighed, the sound low and soft.

Turn around, you fool. Just drive on back to the house with her. Thank her for a lovely time and beg her to go out with you again. Soon.

It wasn't a bad plan, even the begging. He could see himself on his knees in front of her for a great many things, her attention just one of them. But as he went to turn back around, she increased the pressure on his cheek and then leaned in.

His heart lunged against his rib cage, beating like a caged beast as Neve brushed her lips across his. It was a sweet kiss. Soft, simple, and sweet, and he could have been quite happy with just that—even though his cock pulsed and throbbed, already demanding more.

But Neve licked at the entrance to his mouth and he could practically hear one tiny crack, then another and another—he thought it was the steely wall of his control that he'd wrapped around himself all night. And it was shattering, crumbling to nothing under Neve's light, almost delicate kiss.

When she slid her hand back to his neck and tightened her fingers, he covered her palm with his, twisting more to meet her kiss. She sucked his tongue into her mouth and he thought maybe he'd just died. Died and gone to heaven.

Or maybe this was hell . . . and all of this was punishment, a tempting sweet pleasure that would be yanked away—

Neve whimpered and lifted up slightly, straining to get closer.

Fuck this.

Ian pulled away and then half turned, scooping her onto his lap. Her startled gasp was smothered against his mouth as he cupped her chin and once more, had himself a taste of Neve McKay.

Sweet.

That's what she was.

Sweet and sinful and seductive . . . and shy. He could feel it, taste it in the hesitant way she slowly relaxed against him. Shy, but not scared. He'd cut off his arm before he let himself scare her and he'd hold himself to that promise, too.

Silk slithered and whispered as she twisted around until she was straddling him, her knees gripping at his hips as she rocked against him. It sent him straight into glory, he knew it did. Ian cupped her bottom and tugged her closer as he moved.

A harsh choked noise left her lips and she tore away, her head falling back. She stared blindly up at the sky as she rocked against him again. He traced his fingers across the slope of her breasts, framed so prettily by the bodice of the dress she wore. "I do love this dress, Neve," he murmured.

She said nothing.

Pressing a kiss to the corner of her mouth, he asked softly, "Should I stop?"

"What's the other option?"

The smile on her face wobbled a little, but the look in her eyes was steady as she slid her hands down his chest.

"Ah, Neve. I thought you'd never ask."

The other option was . . . *bliss.*

Neve clutched at Ian as he skimmed his fingers up her back, the calluses rough along her skin. When he caught the zipper and gave it a light tug, almost as if asking permission, she eased forward against his chest, hoping he'd follow the cue.

She was lousy at this.

Ian certainly wasn't. His lips brushed over her brow as he tugged the zipper down, only partway and she felt blood rising to stain her cheeks when he eased her back, his gaze slipping from her face to move down.

She'd stood naked in front of more than a few people during her abbreviated modeling career, but there was something entirely different about the way *he* looked at her.

He dipped his head and she shivered as he trailed his lips down her throat. "I want to see you naked in my bed, Neve," he murmured. "I want that very much."

The words, whispered against her skin, sent a shiver racing through her. She curled her hands around the back of his head, holding him tight when he caught a patch of skin between his teeth and sucked.

She sat astride him on the bike and almost every time she breathed, she felt the pulse of his cock against her. He braced an arm behind her and arched her back, his mouth still brushing over her skin. "I . . ." she swallowed. "I don't think I want to wait that long."

Ian stilled.

He lifted his head and stared at her, his pale eyes glinting, shadows thrown across his face. They were in the darkest part of the small, pitted excuse of a parking lot. It wasn't even a lot, just a square of gravel. This spot by the river wasn't unknown, but people didn't often head out this way, miles past town and too out of the way for much of anything other than fishing.

Only the faint silvery light from the moon filtering through the trees provided any light and she could see the way his lips parted, his teeth white against the darkness of his beard. "Wait how long?"

"To get to your bed." She'd been caught in a fog of need ever since he'd looked up at her, a slightly stunned look on his face. Although if she was honest, she'd admit to herself that she'd felt caught by *him* pretty much since that first night.

When she was with Ian, fear didn't guide her actions and she loved it.

When she was with Ian, she felt like . . . *herself.* She felt like herself in a way that she hadn't in far too long, maybe forever.

Sliding her hand up, she pressed it against his cheek, feeling the soft, neat growth of his beard against her palm and the warmth of his skin higher up where her fingers brushed his temple. "I've never had sex on a motorcycle, but I've heard it's possible."

A wicked grin curled his lips and he straightened, tugging her up close against him. Her dress drooped, the straps slipping down her shoulders and now she was keenly aware of the hardness of his chest. "Aye, it's possible." Then he gave her an innocent smile. "Not that I know from experience."

She wrinkled her nose. "Have you had sex on this bike?"

"Nooo." He drew it out, then leaned in and nipped her lip. "But I'd be happy to remedy that, if you like."

Throat tight, she turned her face to his. She hoped he recognized her kiss for what it was because she'd gotten really, really bad at asking for anything.

His mouth opened under hers and she sensed the difference. He'd held himself back before and now . . . she trembled under the intensity of the kiss, a kiss that stole her breath away and made her wonder if she knew anything at all about kissing.

No man had ever kissed her like this.

His hands cradled her face, held like she was

something treasured and adored, while his tongue rubbed against hers in a taunting, sinuous play. His touch was careful—his kiss was carnal—and the contrast between the two had her mind spinning and whirling.

When he skipped his fingers down to toy with the straps, she tore her mouth away, sucking in desperate breaths of air.

"Should I stop?"

"Hell, no."

He chuckled and eased the straps the rest of the way down, even as he cast a look around. "I've never been here. How likely is it that somebody will pass by, Neve?"

"Not." She struggled to think as his hands closed over her rib cage, his thumbs stroking the undersides of her breasts. "Never was a busy place. Well . . ." She swallowed. "Then."

He cupped her chin and tilted her head back. The smile on his face was pure, unadulterated heat and she could feel an answer licking up her core. "And you don't want me to stop?"

"I don't think so."

He didn't question that and she was glad.

She was even gladder when his mouth came to hers and he started to kiss her, more of those deep, drugging kisses that stole the strength of her limbs and turned everything inside her to molten lava. One hand moved at her back but she didn't realize what he'd been doing until she felt his hands on her naked breasts. Instinctively, she tensed.

"You're lovely, sweet Neve," he murmured, his mouth easing away from hers. "I want to look at you. D'you mind?"

She nervously shook her head and held herself rigid as he eased her back.

"Now that's pretty," he muttered, his gaze rapt on her.

Instinctively, she glanced down. Dazed, mystifying heat swamped her as she saw his hands, so dark compared to her skin, plump up her breasts. Still rigid with tension, she tried to relax. She'd never much liked it when William had touched her breasts, even before he'd shown his true colors—then fumbling tugs had gone to hard tweaks and cruel pulls.

Ian circled her right nipple with his thumb.

She shivered.

He echoed the action on the other side and then eased her back, still watching her as he slid one arm behind her, arching her back. Her breasts lifted to him and she froze as his dark head bent over her. Then she cried out. His mouth was hot and wet, his tongue teasing the peak until it throbbed in time with her heart. There was a tickling sensation from his beard that added to the tangle of pleasure.

He shifted his attention to her other breast and she clutched at him, instinctively started to rock against him—or tried to. She had no leverage and frustrated, she wiggled, straining to get closer.

"What is it?" Ian muttered, lifting his head and staring at her. His mouth was wet.

"I want . . ." She groaned and sat up straighter, gripping his shoulders as she tightened her hips. "Please. I don't . . ."

She looked so frustrated and flushed—so fucking fantastic he thought he'd never again be able to ride his bike without getting a bloody hard-on. As she fumbled with the words, he caught one thigh and then guided her leg farther around him. "Put your foot down. There's a peg."

She did so, first the right then the left and he had to wonder what the hell he had been thinking. She moved against him. Through his trousers and whatever skimpy thing she wore under the so-sexy dress, he could feel her and she was wet and he wanted to feel more of her.

Swearing, he caught the material of her dress and shoved it up. Ruffled flounces and silk bunched around his wrists as he closed his hands around her rump. Soft, sleek curves and warm skin, covered by a bit of something lacy. That was all that separated them.

It was too much. "I need you naked and these are in the way, love."

She groaned and then went to push away before stopping. "I don't want to stop touching you long enough to take the damn panties off."

"Well, then." He caught the material at the sides, fisted both hands in the silk, and ripped.

Her startled gasp sounded terribly loud and he held still. "Should I not have done that?"

Neve responded by wiggling her hips and moving closer. "Please tell me you have condoms."

He let his mouth fall open. "But I thought . . ."

She stared at him. Her lashes fluttered and then she sucked in a breath. "But . . ."

He bit her lower lip playfully. "I've condoms, alright. Brought them with me on a hope and a prayer, but I have them. I was just teasing you, love."

"I'll hurt you." She jabbed him in the ribs. "You do that to me again and I'll hurt . . . oh."

He pressed a kiss to her collarbone, her skin so smooth and soft and warm. "I'm sorry . . . should I beg forgiveness?" He didn't want for her to answer as he tugged the material of her panties away with one hand. With the other, he found paradise.

She was slick and wet and hot.

"I can go down on my knees," he whispered against her lips. Then, as her head fell back on a moan, he pushed two fingers inside her. "And beg you. Shall I do that, Neve?"

He pumped his fingers in, once, twice, drawing the slickness of her hunger out. He rubbed his thumb around the swollen bud of her clitoris. "You're not answering me."

"I want you inside me," she said, the words tight, almost choked. "Not on your knees."

"But if I'm on my knees . . ." He twisted his wrist.

"Ian!"

She bucked against him and he braced his legs as she pumped against his hand, her climax breaking over her. His hunger snarled, raged. "Perhaps I'll beg ya later."

Neve blinked at him sleepily and he was about ready to beg himself—for mercy, for control. Instead, he fumbled a rubber out of his pocket and fought with the packet, with the flounces of her skirt, and the trembling of his own fingers as he sheathed himself.

"You're certain of this?" he whispered against her mouth.

She bit his lower lip.

When he pressed against her, Neve tensed.

She couldn't stop it.

It had been too long since she'd had sex and that hadn't been pleasant.

"Easy, love," Ian said, his voice a steadying presence as his hands gripped her hips.

She rolled against him and gasped as the action worked him deeper inside.

"*Ian . . .*"

He groaned and she felt the heavy ridge of his cock jerk inside her. Instinctively, she tightened around him. The fingers on her hips gripped her harder and he swore.

"Don't . . ." A long shudder wracked his body and he stopped for a few seconds.

She could hear him sucking in air and then he spoke again, his breath coming in hard, ragged pants. "Don't do that. You're killin' me . . ."

His brogue thickened and she barely understood him. Barely understood anything save for the need to have more. Curling an arm around his neck, she moved closer, her dress smashed between them.

Ian's body tensed and she cried as he drove up into her, hard and fast.

Immediately, he froze. "Did I hurt ya?"

"No. Please . . ." She moved against him, but it wasn't enough. Wasn't *enough*—

He drove into her again and she cried out. "Please!"

"Please what?" He fisted a hand in her hair, forcing her to meet his eyes in the dark night.

"More." She gulped in air, all thoughts of shyness gone. "I want more."

"Fuck *me*."

The hard, driving rhythm stole the air out of her lungs, stole the scream from her lips and left her clutching at him, breathless. One big hand caught her hip and drew her closer and the angle had her crying out. "Please, please, please . . ."

She didn't even know she was talking.

She sank her nails into his arms without realizing she'd broken the skin.

And all the while, Ian drove up into her.

When the orgasm rushed up on her, she thought it just might swallow her whole. She tried to say his name, and couldn't. But she heard him say hers, a low, ragged groan against her ear.

It was a pleasure so complete, it left her completely shattered.

* * *

The throbbing in his left hand pulled him back to earth.

Slowly, William lowered his head to stare down and he realized he'd wrapped the silk scarf so tightly around his hand, he'd cut off the blood supply.

Ian.

Rage tore vicious bites out of him as he tried to pierce the darkness to see the man's face.

It wasn't necessary, though.

He already knew who it was out there. *Fucking his woman.* "Mine," he whispered, the word all but soundless in the night, lost in the sounds caused by the night creatures—and the fucking whore William had chased halfway across the world.

That was Ian Campbell, a man who'd humiliated him. And Ian had his hands all over Neve.

William clutched the scarf tighter, imagined wrapping it around her lily white throat . . . and pulling.

Brannon wanted to feel accomplished, and maybe he would. Later.

For now, he needed to hit something and he needed to do it hard and fast.

He had a message from Ella Sue and it made him want to hit something.

Let me know when you want that lasagna.

But the idea that Ella Sue now understood his fury was enough to twist his guts into hard, ugly knots. This kind of cruelty wasn't supposed to touch his world, his life. That monster had come into his life.

Back at his loft, he hit the heavy punching bag he had set up in the small home gym. It took thirty minutes of pounding before he felt like he'd shed even a fraction of the fury.

He'd kept his mood under control.

Ever since Neve had told them.

But earlier that afternoon, he'd received the report. No, he hadn't been content to just go by what Neve had told him; he'd respect her privacy and keep what he'd learned to himself, but he'd damn well know what he was dealing with.

Neve had put the son of a bitch in jail and while pride burst inside him, it was mixed with fear. The sick son of a bitch had tried to break her but she hadn't let him. Still, while he hadn't connected *William* Clyde with that bastard from university, he hadn't forgotten what Sam was like.

Both Brannon and Sam—William—had been born into money, but there were oceans of difference between them.

His parents had made sure he knew early on that the world didn't owe him jackshit—but he *did* have responsibilities. The McKay name came with power, and his dad had used the old adage, "With great power comes great responsibility."

The McKays took pride in their history, in their family name, and they worked damn hard.

But William . . . Well, William was the sort of man who believed the world *did* owe him. He thought the whole world had been handed to him. Not on a silver platter, but a platinum one. What wasn't given was simply to be taken and money could cover all sins.

He'd used his money and the family name to hurt Neve. Brannon thought maybe he could tear the coward apart with his own hands.

In his mind, it wasn't a heavy bag he was pounding on, but William. He drove his fists into it, listening to the rattle of the chain. Those *clinks* and *clangs* became

a man's pitiful cries and the leather of the bag trans-
formed into the broken, bloody body of the man who'd
hurt his baby sister.

It still wasn't enough.

The river of rage was so deep, so all-consuming, he
couldn't see past it, couldn't think past it. He wanted to
find Neve, make her tell him where Sam was. She wasn't
home. Moira had gleefully told him she was out on a
date with Ian.

Ian. His best friend was dating his baby sister.

Brannon slammed one foot into the heavy bag—one
final driving kick—just as somebody knocked on his
door.

He stopped, bent over at the waist as he panted for
air. Blood thrummed in his ears and his heart had found
a rhythm that was something close to *oh, fuck*.

It got even worse when he opened the door and saw
who was waiting on the other side.

Hannah Parker had been a thorn in his side almost
since the day he'd come home from London.

He'd seen her in Treasure Island, back when it had
still been a dive, back before he'd first started contemplating the idea of buying the place and doing something
more with it.

She'd been bent over a pint of Harp and laughing with
a guy she'd dumped a few months later. He'd known
who she was, just from the sound of her laughter—rich
and full and throaty—the same laugh she'd had when
she'd been one of Neve's few friends.

She'd glanced up at him and he felt the impact of it
straight down to his balls. Brannon had wanted, even
then, to kiss her until neither of them could think
straight.

It wouldn't have taken much. He couldn't think

straight now; just looking at her turned him stupid. And
that made him surly.

"What?"

My, my, my . . .

There had never been a man more beautiful than
Brannon McKay, not in her opinion.

He might not be the angelic sort of pretty made famous in some of the big museums and he might not be
Hollywood handsome, but he was still the most beautiful man she'd ever seen.

His red hair was darker with sweat and curling around
his face, while his blue-green eyes shone with sparks of
temper. He was shirtless, his chest rising and falling in
hard, heavy pants.

The temper in his eyes was nothing new. He seemed
to live in a constant state of temper, as far as she was
concerned. She didn't know why he was considered to
be the more laid-back of the family. She'd always loved
Neve the most, but then again, she was probably preju-
diced. Neve had saved her tail once or twice—or a dozen
times—back in high school and she adored her.

Unconsciously, she touched her tongue to her lower
lip as a bead of sweat rolled down his temple to his jawline before following the line of his neck on down his
chest.

And whoa. What a chest.

Thanks to his lack of modesty—and curtains—she'd
seen him bare chested—and bare assed and bare everything more than a few times, but it had never been up
close.

Damn if she hadn't been missing out.

"You just going to stare at me like always or did you
want something?" he demanded in typical Brannon
fashion.

She blinked and fought the blush that threatened to turn her as red as a rose. She'd thank the heat, and the fact that she'd been out running.

She'd been trying to burn off her temper—and her worry. Joanie Hanson had called to say she was going back to that prick, Lloyd.

The run hadn't done a thing to level out the anger or the fear, so now she was hot, sweaty, and agitated.

Her agitation was sliding into something else altogether as she stared at Brannon. He was every bit as sweaty as she was, although it looked a lot better on him than it did on her.

Some of her temper bubbled out and she snapped at him. "Is there a reason you're always such an ass to me, Brannon McKay? Did I piss in your Cheerios or something?"

Brannon blinked. Then he straightened, crossing his arms over his chest. "Maybe I don't like being your morning entertainment."

"My . . ." Hannah narrowed her eyes. *You arrogant ass.* She curled her hand tighter around the item she'd found on the sidewalk—the item she'd found that belonged to him. She was tempted to throw it in his face, but at the last minute, she controlled that instinct. Brannon McKay might not be like the school bullies who'd haunted her life for too long, but he still had one thing in common with them—he wanted to get a reaction. She'd give him a reaction, all right.

Cocking her head to the side, she let a slow, wicked smile curve her lips. She held his green gaze with her own and then let her eyes run over his entirely too-delicious body. "Honey." She drew it out, drawling it with the sugared warmth only the ladies of the South can manage. That tone somehow managed to convey humor and insult all at once. Brannon's shoulders stiffened slightly as she took one step, then another, closing the distance between them. "I wouldn't call that entertainment. Scenery, maybe, but it takes more than a good-looking guy in the buff to . . . entertain me."

His lids flickered as she eased just a bit closer. The hot scent of him rose to tease her and when she breathed in, it all but flooded her senses. Was it her or did he seem to get even *hotter*? Maybe it was both of them. The temperature seemed to spike and Hannah was so hot, she thought she might combust.

"Now," she whispered, close enough that she could feel the caress of his breath teasing over her skin. "If you want to *entertain* me, I can give you a suggestion."

He dipped his head and she stared into his eyes.

Heat scorched her.

"Well?" She swayed closer as she spoke, close enough that words were all but murmured against his lips.

Taut silence slid between them and she sighed.

"Too bad." She eased back. "Here."

He didn't even look down. He just continued to stare at her.

Her nipples went tight, stabbing into the sturdy cloth of her sports bra—that damn thing was practically bulletproof, it was so thick, but it was no barrier to the erect pressure of her nipples.

"Oh for crying out loud," she muttered as he continued to watch her.

She edged sideways and leaned past him just enough to dump his wallet on the little table near the door. "You have a ni—"

The temptation of Hannah Parker was one he'd been able to resist, as long as she stayed away, as long as he was able to keep his vague memories of her from years ago firmly in the forefront of his mind.

She'd just shattered those memories. Gone was the painfully shy child who'd all but been Neve's shadow. Now, the predominant image he'd have of her in his head would always be how she'd looked as she backed away from that almost kiss—her face flushed from her run, her wavy hair escaping from her braid to frame her face in wisps and her porn-star mouth curved in a taunting smile. As if that wasn't bad enough, his peripheral vision had caught a view of her chest and that would haunt him—large nipples stabbing into her tank top and now he thought he just might die if he didn't peel her damp clothes away and lick the sweat from her, make her damp in other ways.

As she brushed against him to dump his wallet— where in the hell had she found it—on the table, Brannon's control snapped and he caged her up against the doorjamb, his mouth crushing against hers as he swallowed down whatever smart-ass comment she'd been about to make.

A small, startled noise caught in her throat and he held there, not ending the kiss, but not doing anything else—yet.

When her arms came up and curled around his neck, he hauled her against him.

Hannah had the body of a starlet from Hollywood's golden years: full hips, large, natural breasts that would fill his hands to overflowing, and long, lush legs. He slid his hands down to cup her ass and yank her closer.

She made an approving sound and arched to meet him.

Before sanity completely deserted him, he pulled them both inside, spinning and using her body to shut the door. She reached for him but he caught her hips and pushed back, nudging her back against the door. When he caught her tank, he looked up, stared into her eyes.

Her chest rose and fell in a ragged rhythm and he couldn't fucking wait to see get her naked.

When she didn't do anything to protest, he pulled her tank away and then wrestled the sports bra off, too. The damn thing was like a suit of armor, double-layered and sturdy, but when he peeled it away, he could practically feel his tongue gluing itself to the roof of his mouth. She was . . . Brannon groaned and went to his knees in front of her, tugging her down until she half straddled him. Her skin was a warm, soft tan—all over—and he had to wonder how she managed that lovely shade of gold.

Cupping her breasts in his hands, he stroked his thumbs around the nipples, slowly, working his way in.

Hannah shivered.

"I've probably fantasized about getting my hands on your tits about a hundred times now."

Her eyes went foggy.

When she went to lick her lips, he leaned in, doing it for her, licking at the seam of her mouth until she opened for him. She tasted salty and warm and she moaned into his mouth, the low, rough sound of need tripping down his spine like an audible caress.

Tearing his mouth from hers, he kissed a hot, hungry line up to her ear and rasped, "If you're going to call this quits, now's the time."

Her response was to bite his lower lip.

"Up," he ordered, wrapping his hands around her waist and urging her back to her feet. She wobbled and leaned back, resting her weight against the door as he rose.

Still staring at her, he reached out and snagged his wallet.

Luck was with him. He had one condom in there. There were more in his bedroom, too, which was good because he didn't think one taste would be enough.

Shoving the condom into one of the loose pockets of his gym shorts, he caught the waistband of her form-fitting capris.

Her eyes went wide as he dragged them down, but she didn't move.

Dropping the black cloth to the floor, he braced his hands over her head and stared down at her. Her body was a wet dream. Breasts rising and falling with each breath, she stared back at him boldly and when he lowered his eyes to study her, she did the same. He could feel the heat of her gaze roaming over him and it had his cock jerking, throbbing like a bad tooth.

She reached out and every muscle tightened in anticipation. Her fingers brushed down his neck, along the line of his right shoulder before moving down to his chest. Each gentle stroke sent a jolt of sensation ripping through him, arrowing straight down to his balls.

When she slid her hand down and cupped him through his shorts, he hissed out. Fisting his hands, he held himself locked in place as she started to stroke. The thin material of his shorts was suddenly a terrible thing and he wanted them gone, but if he moved, even a muscle, his control would snap and he'd put his hands on her and this crazy ride would be over before it started.

She stroked up, squeezed, stroked down. Stroke up, squeeze . . .

Brannon closed his eyes.

Stroke up, squeeze . . .

He panted and shoved himself into her hand. She made a low, hungry sound in her throat.

Brannon opened his eyes and stared at her.

But she wasn't looking at his face.

She was staring down, her gaze locked on the rhythm of her hand. When her tongue slid out, Brannon swore.

* * *

Hannah's mind was whirling.

She could count her lovers on one hand and still have fingers left over. The lovers who had made her feel like *this*? Count of zero.

When Brannon knocked her hands away, she blinked up at him, startled. "What . . . ?"

The question was smothered under his lips.

She heard foil tear.

Reaching up, she slid her hands up the ridged muscles of his sides and clutched at him.

He boosted her up, and automatically she curled her legs around his waist. That simple action forced her open and she whimpered as it brought her in full contact with the rigid length of his cock.

She caught her breath.

He knocked it right out of her as he drove in, one hard, deep surge that buried him inside her completely.

A strangled moan choked her.

He pulled out and then drove back in.

Scrabbling against him, she tried to ground herself.

Another deep, lunging thrust.

Hannah opened her mouth, tried to tell him to slow down, to . . . to . . . to *what*? Let her breathe? She didn't know and before she could figure that out, his mouth slanted down over hers and he pushed his tongue into her mouth, echoing the hard, stabbing motions of his cock.

Hannah lost it.

The world exploded and fell away and she couldn't do anything more than hang on to him. A gathering heat tightened deep down low inside her.

He caught her ass and tilted her hips, changing the angle—just the slightest shift, but it left her screaming. Or she *would* have screamed, if she'd had the breath.

It hit her hard and fast, the pleasure exploding out

from her core, but it didn't stop—it kept going and going, rippling through her with every thrust of his hips.

She whimpered his name as tiny black pinpricks swam before her eyes.

Vaguely, she heard him groan, felt the rhythmic pulsation of his cock.

His lips brushed across her cheek.

Hannah turned her face away, because she had the worst feeling she just might start to cry.

CHAPTER FOURTEEN

A couple of giggling teenagers probably would have attracted less attention, but fortunately for them, there was nobody around to notice as Ian and Neve half tumbled off his bike and all but supported each other on the way up to the door that led to his flat.

They didn't make it inside on the first try.

Ian pinned Neve to the door, his hands on her waist, his mouth on hers as he whispered, "I can't even walk through here now without seeing you, d'you know that? I see you, taste you, feel you . . ."

She whimpered as he kissed his way down her neck, his beard tickling and soft against her skin.

Through the silk of her dress, she felt his mouth, hot as a brand, just as devastating. He kept going, moving down and down, and then she gasped because he'd somehow caught the hem of her skirt and the petticoat, shoving them up and disappearing beneath them.

"Ian!" It came out a choked, strangled cry and when she would have spoken again, she only made a low moan, because he had speared his tongue through her damp curls and was licking her.

Dazed, she looked down.

was somehow twice as erotic, not to be able to see

him as he hid below the cover of her skirt and petticoat, his hands now gripping her hips and his mouth pressed against her aching core. He licked her again and a shudder left her shaking so hard, she would have fallen if he hadn't steadied her.

She reached down, blindly seeking the support of his shoulders. Her hands slipped off his shoulders twice before she found purchase and then she started to move against him.

He responded with a low, hungry growl.

She felt it vibrate all the way through her.

The climax was hard and fast and when it ended, Ian stood up.

She would have said something but he was already kissing her now. "Now," he muttered in one of the brief pauses.

"Now?" she asked, dazed.

He boosted her up and she forgot how to breathe as he drove inside her.

"I told myself," he panted against her mouth. "I told myself I'd have you here, like this . . . just like we would have been that night . . ."

Arms curled around his neck, she clung to him.

Her heart raced, keeping time with the driving, deep thrusts and when he drove her into a breath-stealing climax, she thought maybe, just maybe, this was the closest thing to bliss she'd ever known.

Something soft brushed her skin.

Light teased her eyes.

"Are you waking up there?"

Neve jolted upright, a gasp lodging in her throat.

She let it out in a wheeze when she found herself staring into Ian's eyes.

Ian.

She swallowed and looked around.

Ian's bedroom.

She closed her eyes and sucked in a deep breath.

She was with Ian in his bedroom. She'd spent the night with him.

"That look on your face, Neve. It's devastating me. Second thoughts already?"

She opened her eyes, a denial rushing to her lips only to stop when she saw the teasing smile on his lips.

"You're terrible," she said, reaching up to touch his mouth, his beard soft and silken against her palm. She'd gotten to experience firsthand just how fantastic that beard felt, rubbing against her belly, her thighs—so many parts of her, because it seemed Ian had been determined to brand her with his mouth.

"I'm a desperate man," he corrected. "I had heaven in my bed last night and I'd be nothing if I discovered she regretted it already."

"Heaven." She snorted. "You're the biggest flirt I think I've ever met."

He held out a cup of coffee. "Perhaps. But it's no less true. There are times when even I have no words but the truth to give."

She glanced at the coffee and accepted. "I . . . um. I guess that means you had a good night."

"No."

She bobbled the coffee and he steadied her hands.

"Nuh . . ." Swallowing, Neve searched his face. "No?"

"It wasn't *good*. I consider it a good night if I come home after a hard day's work and can put my feet up a bit. *Good* is a pale shadow of what last night was." He leaned in and pressed a kiss to the corner of her mouth. "Spectacular is a wee bit closer. Amazing. Earthshaking . . . life-changing."

She rolled her eyes and took a drink from the coffee

while blood rushed to stain her cheeks. "You have low standards if last night was life-changing."

"No."

The hardness in his tone had her looking up.

He took the coffee away and she scowled at him. He tumbled her back down on the bed. His weight pinned her down, but she didn't even have a chance to consider fear. With a featherlight touch, he skimmed his lips over her jawline, up to tease the soft skin behind her ear.

"You need to have a better opinion of yourself, Miss Neve," he said softly.

He lifted his head and peered down into her eyes and she felt her heart stutter to a stop. Ian cupped her cheek and ran his thumb over her lips. "Although I guess I'm not being clear. I think my life started to change the very moment I saw you staring at me down in my pub."

Neve had had her heart smashed on, ripped out, and thrown away. She'd had people talk about her, talk down to her, through her. She didn't think she'd ever had any-body talk to her as if she was something so . . . treasured.

"You break my heart when you look at me like that," Ian said.

He rubbed his lips over hers.

Unable to say anything, she curled her arms around his neck and tugged him closer.

That, at least, she was starting to understand. The rub of his body on hers, the feel of his strength as he surged inside her. "Make love to me," she whispered.

Ian could have said a hundred other things that had started to change, all starting the very moment he'd looked at her, but seeing the sparkle in her green eyes, the wet shine of tears, and hearing those words, there was no other thing he could do, other than give her what she wanted.

"You're wearing my shirt," he said, reaching up to flick open the buttons, one at a time, baring more and more of her lovely form. "I think I want it back."

She caught her lower lip between her teeth. "I like it, though."

"I still want it back." He stared at her, watching as her eyes widened. As her face flushed pink.

"I guess I'll have to let you have it, then." She sighed softly as he finished the last of the buttons and pushed open the lapels. One slim hand reached up and tugged. "Should I take it off?"

"Hmm. In a bit. Maybe. I'm considering letting you keep it, seeing as how you look so lovely in it." He settled back on his heels and stared at her. He hadn't been able to see her well last night at all, not even when they'd come home because he'd been too desperate to have her again.

But now, with morning sunlight coming in through the blinds, he could see all of her.

Stroking his hands down her torso, he forced himself not to stare at the X and its slightly uneven lines. So easily. Sam Clyde could have taken her from this life so easily and then Ian never would have had a chance to know her.

It made his hands shake with fury and with fear, and in an effort to keep from staring at it any longer, he stretched his weight out on top of hers and then rolled them so that he lay on his back.

"I'll let you keep the shirt," he said. "I've a trade in mind."

"A trade." Her eyes glittered down at him and his thoughts went all hazy and hot as Neve scraped her nails over his flat nipples. She sat astride him and through the shorts he'd pulled on when he woke up, he could feel how hot and ready she was for him.

"Yes." Catching her hips, he nudged her weight down until she straddled his thighs and then he caught her hand. "I want to feel your hands on me again."

She slid the tips of her fingers inside the waistband of his shorts. "This would be easier if you hadn't put clothes on."

"But then I wouldn't have the pleasure of having you pull them off."

She caught her lower lip between her teeth as she pushed his shorts down, lifting her weight up when he arched his hips. Her eyes met and held his as she wrapped her fingers around his cock. That . . . he shuddered. That was nice.

It went from nice to complete bliss when she dipped her head and pressed a kiss to his chest, her bare breasts rubbing across him.

He shuddered as she rose back up over him and held him steady, moving to take him inside.

She was silky and wet and . . .

Snarling, he rolled, pinning her beneath him once more as he remembered why he'd gotten dressed in the first place.

"Neve . . ."

She blinked up at him, startled.

"We used the last rubber last night."

"We . . . what? Oh."

"Yeah. Oh." He dropped his head to rest against her brow, keeping his weight on his elbows.

Heated seconds passed between them and the hunger didn't abate—not for him, at least. It might have had something to do with the way her nipples seemed to stab into him, hard little peaks of need. It might have something to do with the way she gripped his arms, her fingers kneading his muscles.

"I—"

"I'm on the pill."

They both spoke at once and he slowly lifted his head as the meaning behind her words sank in.

"Neve . . ." Shifting his weight, he reached up to cup her cheek.

"I'm on the pill," she said again. "I decided to go on it a few months ago. I . . . um. I was afraid he'd find me again and . . . and . . ."

"Shhh." Fury blistered in him, an ugly red film that enveloped his entire soul. He had to push it down and focus on her. "Neve, that's . . ."

"I won't get pregnant. So unless—I mean, if you want to—"

He pressed his mouth to hers to stop her from talking. "Want . . . that doesn't touch it. But Neve, are you sure?"

Her answer was to reach down and tug on his hips again.

Such a gentle gesture shouldn't turn him inside out, but it did. Everything about her seemed to turn him inside out.

He shifted again, reaching down to wrap his hand around his cock, steadying himself.

Neve brought one knee up, her skin sliding smooth as satin against him as she arched.

Heat.

Pure, liquid heat kissed the head of his cock as he pressed against her. She yielded to him with a soft sigh of a moan and he thought maybe, just maybe, he'd died and gone to heaven.

When he went to withdraw, she whimpered and caught him, tugging him back to her.

They kept up that slow dance, him retreating and her drawing him back in, and it was the sweetest, most erotic thing of his life.

She moaned out her climax as he lost the reins to his control and exploded inside her.

William sat in his chair just in front of the little café, staring across the street.

She'd gone inside with him.

William had been following them most of the night, keeping a safe distance, but really, how hard was it to follow a man on a motorcycle in a town this size? Not hard at all. When they'd pulled off at the river last night, he'd just driven past them, then turned around and killed the lights, parking some distance away so he could walk.

He'd waited until they had a safe distance ahead of him before he'd turned on his lights and followed them back into town. He'd wanted to know where she lived, but it must have been Campbell's place, because she'd nattered on enough about her house that he knew it couldn't be the simple building where the bastard had parked his bike.

And they were still inside.

William had taken his time—too much of it—and Neve had gone and forgotten herself. Giving her body to Campbell like some frowsy whore.

But she'd learn.

Once they went to leave, she'd understand that this—all of this—was done.

Hannah's whole body felt bruised.

But it was nothing compared to her heart.

She'd pretended to sleep when Brannon had pulled out of bed. How she wished she really *had* been asleep.

She heard him swear under his breath, and the disgust in his voice all but ripped her heart out.

He hadn't said it to be cruel. If he'd known she was awake, she knew he wouldn't have said anything.

But in those brief, unguarded moments, she'd realized she was wasting her time.

Hannah had loved Brannon McKay for years—too many years. She'd entertained a hundred foolish fantasies and now she knew, without a doubt, they were nothing *but* fantasies.

She needed to leave, but she couldn't get out of the damn bed and face him until she knew she wouldn't cry.

The ringing of the phone caught her attention and she held her breath, listening to the low rumble of his voice.

Moira.

Slowly, she eased herself upright and sat on the edge of the bed.

". . . seen her? No . . . no, she *what*?" Out in the living room, Brannon made a disgusted sound. "Listen, I'll call Ian and see if she . . . spent the night or something. Yeah, okay. *Okay,* Moira."

A few seconds passed and then Brannon muttered, "I'll see if she spent the night, then I'll kick his ass. Just on principle."

Hannah stood up. Spying her clothes on the small table near the door, she grabbed them and hurried her way into them. She'd just shoved her feet into her shoes when she felt him watching her.

He was on the phone.

His eyes burned in her, traced over her body even as his face took on a harder, focused look. "Ian. Is Neve there? She . . . Ian, I'm going to punch you." He paused, not saying anything for a moment as he moved into the bedroom. When he went to brush his fingers through her hair, Hannah moved around him. Too aware of his watchful stare, she strode into the living room.

"No, I'm not mad at you. I just feel like punching you. You had sex with my sister, I'm entitled."

Hannah made a face.

Closing a hand over the doorknob, she told herself to leave. Now. It was the best thing to do, really.

She sucked in a breath when a hand slammed down on the door just as she went to open it.

"Look, I'll call you later. But have Neve call home. Moira's worried. No. No . . . *bye,* Ian." The final words came out in a growl and Hannah gave the door a half desperate jerk.

It opened a fraction, but Brannon just leaned into it—leaned into her.

"I need to go," she said, keeping her tone disinterested, bored. "I've got to shower and start getting ready for work."

He buried his face in her hair. "What's wrong?"

What's wrong? She stifled a hysterical giggle. "Nothing's wrong," she said, lying through her teeth. She even managed a casual smile as she turned around and stared at him.

He opened his mouth to say something.

But nothing came out and she turned back to the door.

His hand fell away and she left, without either of them saying another word.

What good would words do, anyway?

It wouldn't change anything.

As she hurried home, she tried to silence the voice in her head.

But she still heard him.

Brannon, you stupid fuck . . . what did you do?

CHAPTER FIFTEEN

Neve didn't want to leave.

If she had her way, she would have stopped time and kept the two of them locked up in Ian's condo for the rest of her life.

But Ian had to work.

And Moira left her feeling more than a little guilty as she'd hung up the phone.

Brannon knew.

Moira now knew.

Who else knew?

"What are you thinking about?" Ian asked as they moved down the steps. He caught her hand, his thumb rubbing over the inside of her wrist.

She rolled her eyes. "Facing Moira. Brannon. It's stupid. I mean, I'm a grown woman, but . . ."

"Are you sorry?" Ian stopped right in front of the door that led out to the small garden behind his condo.

"No!" It came out of her in a rush and she winced as the word bounced off the high ceilings, echoing back to her. "Ah . . . no. It's not that. It's just . . ." She pursed her lips. "I haven't done this. Ever."

"Well . . ." He scratched his chin. "If it makes you feel better, you did it very, very well."

She shoved him lightly, trying not to laugh. "That . . . I mean. Arrghh . . ." She groaned and turned away, pacing up and down the mellow gold of the hardwood floods. "You're only the second guy I've slept with . . . and I went out with him for three months before we . . . um . . ."

She closed her eyes, the memories stabbing at her anew.

When Ian moved up behind her and closed his arms around her, she sank back against him. "Does it make you feel any better to know you're the first woman I've had spend the night at my place in . . . hell, forever? I think it's been more than ten years."

Slowly, she turned in his arms. "Are you saying you haven't . . ."

He laughed. "No." His cheeks went slightly pink over his beard and he glanced away. "Noooo, not that. I just . . ." He sighed and brushed a hand down her hair. "There's a woman. She comes into the pub every now and then. Lives about forty-five minutes away from here. And . . ."

He looked embarrassed now—*she* was embarrassed and not entirely certain she wanted to hear this. "If you're going to tell me you're seeing somebody else—"

Ian pressed his finger to her lips. "No. I'm not. I haven't been seriously involved with anybody in a long, long time, Neve. It's just that . . . we've gotten together a few times. Sometimes she'd come visit me . . . ah . . . here. But if we were having a night together, it was always at her place. She's asked about staying the night and I . . ." He shook his head. "I never wanted her to stay. We've . . . um. Well. Never wanted a woman in my bed with me all night long . . . until you."

Her breath caught. "Oh. Well."

"Yes." He rubbed his mouth against hers. "Oh. Well.

You're twisting me something awful, Neve. And I love it."

She reached for him but before she could do more than brush her fingertips against his arms, he pulled away. "Have to go, love," he said, backing up. "Otherwise, the only place we'd be going is back up to my flat."

A tug of longing gripped her. "Ah . . . I'm fine with that."

"I would be, too, but I can't be late for work. The boss is something of a dick about that."

"I thought you were the guy in charge at the pub." As they pushed through the door, she slanted a look up at him.

"I am. Which is how I know I'm a dick about promptness." He grinned down at her and then looked away.

Neve saw the expression on his face—the faint smile, his lips curling up just a little at the corner—and then saw it falter. Ice replaced the warmth in his eyes. "What the fuck?"

She looked over, confused.

The only thing she saw was the green.

Stumbling backward, Neve swung out a hand as her legs threatened to give away beneath her.

The pale, soft green fluttered in the wind and it blinded her to everything else.

"William," she whispered.

"Neve?"

Ian turned to her and caught her arms as she struggled to find the strength in her legs once more. "Neve!" He shook her slightly.

Dazed, she lifted her face to his. "He's here. William . . . he's here."

Brannon stood at his window, staring out.

Something wasn't right.

Oh, he'd heard Hannah's words, heard her say nothing was wrong, but he knew women. He had two sisters, had Ella Sue, had been in a few off-and-on relationships, not to mention all the women he'd worked with in his life.

He knew when *nothing* meant *everything* and he knew when *I'm fine* meant *I want to punch you.*

The look on her face had hovered on the fine line between misery and anger, hurt and . . .

Brannon closed his eyes. Humiliation.

Something he'd done . . .

"What did you do?" he muttered to himself, scrubbing the heels of his hands down his face, stubble rasping under his palms. "What did you . . ."

It hit him, then, memory, like a punch in the gut. He'd said those very words just a short time ago. While Hannah lay sprawled on her belly in his bed and he'd fought the urge to press his body to hers—*again*—lift her to her hands and knees and sink inside her. He'd made love to her four times—

"Sex," he muttered. "It was sex."

So, yeah. They'd had sex—the best sex of his life—four times last night and all he could think about was having her again. When that was the *last* thing he needed to be doing.

He'd steered clear of Hannah for a reason.

He'd always known he'd get in over his head with her.

And now, when the last thing he needed was a distraction, she was filling his thoughts. *One* night.

He opened his eyes and stared back out the window, all but willing her to come outside, to sit down on the balcony like she so often did.

A flicker of movement caught his eyes and he turned his head, saw the woman pass in front of a window. She was clad in a robe, her hair hanging in a damp, tangled skein down her back. As he watched, Hannah reached up and swiped at her face.

Was she—

She turned her head and through the glass, she met his eyes.

His heart ramped up, slamming hard against his ribs as she moved to the window. Brannon curled one hand into a fist. He'd call her. Or go over there.

She continued to stare at him.

And then, she jerked the curtains closed.

Brannon felt the rejection straight to his soul.

"Son of . . ."

He scowled as a familiar car, lights flashing, pulled up to the curb.

When Gideon Marshall climbed out, he almost turned away. But then he saw the other car—another cruiser.

Something held him there and the heart that had felt so hollow just moments ago started to race.

Neve—

He took off down the stairs, trying to find the rational voice that would tell him that he was panicking over nothing. The voice was silent though, and just a few minutes later, he understood why.

"You're sure it's the same scarf."

Gideon stared at her like she was a bug under a microscope. It was beyond unnerving. Not that she had many nerves *left* at this point.

William was in McKay's Treasure. He'd followed her straight here, to her home.

Swallowing the knot in her throat, she forced herself to speak. "Yes. It's the same one." She held out a hand and Gideon put it in the evidence bag. One of the uniformed officers had been the first to arrive, a man with familiar blue eyes. He seemed familiar, but she couldn't place him—his name tag read *Parker* and she'd briefly wondered if he was related to Hannah, an old friend from school.

Now, all she could think about was the scarf. She turned it over, studying it, her fingers trembling. "He had it personalized. See?"

The *N* and *M* were stylized, embroidered into the silk with silvery threads.

"Okay." Gideon took the scarf back and passed it off to Parker. The uniform had been studying Ian's bike—Ian's *trashed* bike. The damage was all superficial, but that wasn't the point. It was the outright ugliness of the act.

Neve tried really hard not to stare at the bike.

Not that it made any difference. She could still see the slashed tires, the ugly green that sprawled across the bike's gas tank. The word *whore* was emblazoned on her mind.

He had to have been watching her.

"What's going on?"

At the sound of her brother's voice, she groaned and lowered her head.

Fortunately, she was saved from answering when Brannon caught sight of Ian's bike. "Man, your bike. What the hell happened?"

"I think Sammy's hit town." Ian's voice was almost coldly polite.

Neve suppressed a shiver but not well enough. Ian moved up and stroked a hand up and down her spine. She could feel the warmth of his hand, but it did nothing to penetrate the chill.

The strained silence threatened to shatter her nerves. Curling her hands into fists, she focused on the small pain of her nails biting into her flesh. She looked up at the sound of boots crunching on the rock and rubble on the ground.

"Neve?" Brannon said softly.

She nodded jerkily toward the scarf Gideon had just passed over to Griffin. "The scarf." Her voice was terribly thin and she cleared her throat and tried again. "William gave me the scarf a few months after we'd started dating."

"We came down," Ian said, taking over when she couldn't find anything else to say. "Saw the bike. The scarf was tied to the handlebars. Like a soddin' flag."

"You haven't seen him," Gideon said.

"No." She said reaching up, worrying the necklace she wore with her fingertips. "Hell, no. If I'd seen him, I would have said something."

"Okay, then."

It all passed in a blur, Ian and Gideon speaking, Brannon standing there brooding. A few times, Gideon directed a question her way. She answered each one as best as she could, although she'd be hard-pressed to say just what the questions, or even her answers, were.

All the while, she stared at the scarf.

She was so pale.

Ian wanted to punch something. No. He wanted to grab that bit of green, hunt down William Clyde, and twist it around his pathetic neck. Then rip his balls off and feed them to him. The impotent fury had him closing his hands into tight, useless fists, the rage bubbling inside him.

When her eyes tracked back to the young officer—and the scarf—yet again, Ian moved in front of her, blocking her view. "You should sit," he said.

Neve lifted her pale face to his. The pretty green of her eyes had gone glassy and when he curled one hand around her elbow, she didn't resist. But when he tried to guide her to the narrow bit of porch, she broke away. "No. No, I can't sit. I need . . ." She sucked in a great breath of air as if she were starved for oxygen. "I need to walk."

She turned to Gideon. "Can I . . . are we done?"

Gideon studied her for a moment. "I need some time."

Ian was about ready to shove the scarf down Gideon's throat now. But before either he or Brannon had a chance to tell the cop to let Neve breathe, Gideon looked at him. "Why don't the two of you take a few minutes? I need to go over the scene again anyway."

Neve didn't say anything, just turned and blindly walked up the narrow alley that ran between the pub and the building where he lived, his flat on the second floor. Ian fell into step behind her with one last look at the men still gathered near the bike.

He should say something.

He opened his mouth, staring at the back of her head, but the words just wouldn't come.

Words were *easy* for him. He knew how to stroke and cuddle and comfort. He'd never been the sort of man to shy away from a woman's pain—or even her tears—but here, when it seemed to matter the most, Ian couldn't find a single thing to say.

Neve passed through the mouth of the alley without a single glance backward and began to pace on the sidewalk, oblivious to the curious glances coming from those in the area closest to them. Ian went to jam his hands into the pockets of his jeans only to scowl as he remembered he had to work—and he was wearing that idiot kilt.

Neve still wore her pretty dress from last night. Earlier, she'd looked all sexily mussed and it had tempted him to muss her up more, but now she looked forlorn and bedraggled and that just added fuel to the flames of his anger.

His hands felt too big and too empty and too useless. Folding his arms over his chest, he settled against the brick wall at his back and waited.

But he had no idea what he waited for.

When she passed by him for easily the tenth time in under five minutes, he reached out and caught her arm. Her gaze swept up to his and he still had no words.

So don't use them.

He tugged her closer, keeping his grip on her arm loose. When she didn't pull away, he caught her up against him. Her entire body trembled and Ian felt his heart twist in his chest.

He smoothed his hand up the long, delicate line of her spine as he pressed his chin to the top of her crown.

A harsh, shuddering breath escaped her lungs. "He's here," she said, the words harsh and jagged, as though they were bits and pieces of broken glass. "He's *here,* Ian."

"I know." Hooking one arm over her neck, he wrapped his other arm snug around her waist. "He won't hurt you, Neve. I'll cut off my arm before I let him near you again." He pressed a kiss to her brow. "But I'd really rather cut off *his* arms. Then his balls. Then his legs."

A weak, watery laugh escaped her, the sound perilously close to sobs.

"He won't hurt you," he whispered.

"How can you stop him? I can't live in your back pocket, Ian. I can't trap myself up in Ferry for the rest of my life. And he *won't stop*. He came all this way and he won't *stop*."

"Then we'll just have to make him stop." She felt terribly fragile against him, her hair silken, her slim form trembling.

"How?"

He just shook his head.

He hadn't quite gotten that far yet, but he hoped the plan, whatever it was, involved a lot of pain for the dickhead who'd dare to terrify his woman.

His woman.

Mine, Ian thought, acknowledging the truth of it. *Mine.* She'd felt like his almost from the start—just like he knew she already owned him.

They stood like that a few moments and perhaps it was just his wishful thinking, but he thought the tremors were easing, thought perhaps her breathing wasn't quite so ragged.

"Ian."

He looked up at the sound of his name, saw Brannon standing a few feet away.

There was a look on his face that made Ian think his old friend had been watching them for some time. Neve lifted her head and Ian tightened his arm when she would have pulled away. She resisted for less than a heartbeat and then sank back against him as if the very presence of his body made it easier for her to stand there.

"Aye?"

Brannon's gaze tracked back and forth between them, but the irritation he'd half expected to see on Brannon's face wasn't there. Brannon was no longer *irritated* by the idea that Ian and Neve had spent the night together. Sheer fury had replaced that weak emotion, and Ian had no doubt who the target of all the anger was.

"Can I talk to you for a minute?"

Ian sighed and this time, when Neve pulled back, he let her, giving her arm a lingering caress before he shoved off the wall.

"Are you . . ." He stopped before he could finish. He'd been ready to ask her if she was well, but how could she be *well*? Not even an hour ago, the two of them had been half drunk from the night they'd had and now . . . Fury ate at Ian. Their night together had been tarnished by this. Yet another thing that William would answer for. Touching Neve's cheek, he said softly, "I'll be right here."

She nodded and turned away.

When he looked back at Brannon, he saw fire burning in those green eyes.

Let's find him then, he thought, moving across the sidewalk. *You and me, Bran. Find him and deal with this.*

"Hey."

Neve jerked her head up at the sound of that voice, one that was vaguely familiar. Squinting against the bright light shining down around the woman in front of her, she tried to make the voice match the face.

"Hannah." The other woman smiled as she said it. "It's Hannah Parker."

For a few brief seconds, surprise and pleasure replaced the fear and uncertainty. "Wow," Neve said, shaking her head. "You look . . ."

Hannah shrugged. "Like shit. I didn't sleep much last night."

"That was so not what I was going to say." Neve managed a smile. "You look amazing. You lost weight."

"Yeah. Fifty-something pounds." She jerked her shoulder up again and settled against the wall next to Neve. "Normally, I'd be all over you, hugging you, fussing at you for not calling me as soon as you hit town, but . . ."

Hannah's blue eyes moved to the cop cars and then she looked back at Neve. "Not that it's not fantastic to see you and FYI, we *are* having dinner soon. For now, though, what the hell is going on?"

"Where do I start?" Neve asked, her voice shaking despite her best attempts to keep it level.

Hannah cocked her head, lips pursed in a thoughtful frown. "How about with you telling me your Prince Charming wasn't such a prince?"

Neve blinked.

Hannah waited.

"If you're talking about William . . ."

Hannah nodded, her gaze moving past her to linger on the two men still by the alley. "Definitely not talking about our local sexy Scotsman, although . . . *day-yum*, Nevie. He's yummy. I'll tell you what—perhaps that boy is no Prince Charming, but who the hell cares? Although I bet he could charm a nun out of her panties."

Neve blushed but couldn't stop from looking over at Ian. *Yummy* didn't touch him. "Ah . . . um . . ." She had to clear her throat.

Hannah laughed. "You're not a nun, are you, Nevie?"

"Hannah. Shut up. And by the way, if you're not a nun, I don't want to know."

"Relax." Hannah patted her knee. "A hundred women around here wish *they* weren't nuns, too."

Neve rolled her eyes. "Fine." It felt good to smile, even over something so silly. But her heart wrenched a little as she thought back over the night they'd had—a night that had been tarnished now. *William, why can't you just leave me* alone?

"So?" Hannah swayed closer, using her shoulder to bump Neve's.

"So what?" Neve asked, pretending ignorance.

"Prince Charming."

Neve grimaced. "No. He wasn't a prince." She almost

choked holding back the bitter laugh that tried to escape. *Prince Charming.* "How come you're so sure about that, though?"

"Instinct." Face almost carefully blank, Hannah stared out over the road, ignoring the speculative glances, the lingering looks that came their way. "I know his type, Neve."

"You never even met him."

Hannah turned her head and stared at Neve. Hard. "Didn't I?" She shrugged. "Granted, when my mom remarried . . . well, that guy might not have actually *been* William, but they were cut from the same cloth. He swept her up like she was Cinderella—the same way William did with you. Once she was so totally wrapped up in him, he cut the rest of her world away until *he* was all that was left. He became her world—*our* world."

Neve felt frozen. When Hannah slid her back down the wall to sit on the sidewalk, Neve echoed her actions but while her friend crossed her legs, Neve drew hers to her chest, huddling away from the world. Or trying to.

"I'm right, aren't I?"

"Yeah."

Hannah looked down. "I . . . I had a bad feeling about him from the beginning. You made him sound so wonderful, but I kept seeing my stepdad in my head." She gave Neve a wry smile. "I figured I was being stupid, but then you stopped calling. I hardly ever heard from you and it made me worry. I . . . shit. I should have tried harder."

"It's not your fault," Neve said softly. Resting her chin on her knees, she closed her eyes. "And it wouldn't have mattered. He'd pretty much cut me off from my family—they'd call and I'd never know. They'd write and the letters would end up who knows where? And my letters . . ."

She stopped.

"Your letters?"

Shoving upright, she wrapped her arms around her middle. "I wrote home. Not a lot, at first, but as time went by, I started writing. But I never heard anything from them and it turns out they never got any of the letters. How did he manage that, Hannah? It had to be him, *somehow*, but how was he doing it?"

"Crazy people tend to be very creative." With a slight wince, Hannah stood up.

"Are you okay?"

"Ah . . ." A vivid blush stained her cheeks pink and Hannah looked away. "I'm fine. Just tired."

"You're a lousy liar," Neve said.

"I'm not . . ."

She went quiet, her gaze locked on a point past Neve's shoulder. Neve looked behind her and saw Ian and Brannon moving toward them. "You still got a thing for my brother," she said, shaking her head.

"No." It came out cool and flat and when Neve looked at Hannah, the blush had faded. Hannah's expression was remote and she glanced at Brannon with little more than a nod before she looked at Ian. "Heya, Campbell."

"Heya back, Parker," Ian said with a quick smile.

Neither Brannon nor Hannah said a single word to the other.

"Gideon needs to speak with you some more," Brannon said quietly.

Neve nodded. "Yeah. I know. I . . ." She cleared her throat and glanced at Ian. "You need to get to work soon. I don't want to hold you up."

"You're not." Ian looked unaffected. "It shouldn't be much longer, then I'll run you home."

"I'll get her home."

Ian scowled at her brother.

Brannon just lifted a brow. "Your bike is trashed. It needs a new paint job and tires. Unless you were planning on giving her a piggyback ride?"

"I can drive the soddin' bike as soon as I get the tires dealt with." Ian's jaw was set.

Before Brannon could argue, Neve rested a hand on Ian's arm. "It's okay," she said softly. Then she looked at Brannon and nodded. She was too tired to listen to their friendly arguments. "Can we lend Ian a car or something, though? I can drive it back out here later."

She shifted her gaze back to Ian and cocked her head. "Maybe you can drive me home?"

"That means you going somewhere *alone*," Brannon said.

She closed her eyes. "Stop, Brannon."

"He's *here*," Brannon said. "He'll be watching for a chance to put his hands on you and I'm not letting it happen."

"And I'm not going back into a cage—I've *been* there. He put me in a cage." Fury and fear trembled inside her, a nasty little storm. But she had to do this, get these words out. "I spent *years* trapped, all because I let him trap me and I'm not *doing* it again."

"Use your brain, Neve!"

"Brannon, shut your mouth," Ian said, cutting between them.

"Don't tell me *you* are okay with the idea of her running around by herself!"

"I'm a grown woman!"

It was almost enough.

William smiled to himself. He held a book in front of him but it was just for show. Every few minutes, he'd turn the page, but his attention was on the tableau unfolding on the other side of the street.

"I'm a grown woman!"

Neve's shout carried, drawing attention toward her and William mentally shook his head. Making a spectacle of herself.

He could imagine what they were arguing about.

He hadn't expected Brannon to show up, not like this, and he idly toyed with the lovely scenario of killing those two. Ian and Brannon. Not Neve. Never Neve. She'd come home. He'd remind her of her place. He had no doubt it would take time and he expected he'd have a hard time forgiving her latest lapse. He might not even be able to, but he had no plans of letting her get away from him.

"More coffee?"

He jerked his gaze up, caught off guard by the interruption. With a terse *no*, he sent the girl on her way.

He needed to get out of here.

So far, they'd been too busy arguing—or pawing each other in Neve and Ian's case—to notice him, but he wasn't about to take the chance that any of them would see him.

Not yet.

The hair on the back of Gideon's neck stood on end.

He caught the seemingly casual glance from Ian and wondered if the other man felt it, too.

Neve and Brannon were too busy trying to go at each other's throats and when Neve took one step toward her brother, her face flushed, Gideon thought maybe he should put an end to this before she decided to get in touch with her childhood nickname.

He could see her punching her brother and thought it might even do her some good to vent some of the emotion he could sense surging inside her.

But not here.

Not now.

"Enough," he said. As he moved between them, he sent a casual look around. They did the same, although he wasn't doing it to make them aware of just how much attention they were attracting. He was looking. He even had a feeling he knew just *who* he was looking for.

Somebody was watching them. Watching the whole thing and Gideon would bet his left nut that it was William Clyde.

"Are you trying to provide free entertainment for the whole town?" he asked when Brannon went to snarl at him.

The town can go get fucked, Brannon's expression clearly said.

Slanting a look at Neve, Gideon waited.

"If you try to tell me that you honestly expect me to go into hiding—"

"I don't," he said, interrupting.

She blinked, caught off guard.

"You . . . what?"

That came from Brannon, and Gideon reached up, skimming the flat of his hand across his head before he looked back at the older McKay. "If she tries to hide, he'll just come after her," Gideon pointed out. "He's already demonstrated that."

Demonstrated a hell of a lot more, too. Keeping his frustration down, Gideon swept the surrounding area with another quick look but saw nothing out of place. People out for a late breakfast or early lunch cloistered around the small tables outside the diner. Several couples, a small family, a couple of lone diners, all of them focused on breakfast, coffee, paying their tabs.

The bookstore hadn't opened yet, although he could see the manager Vera puttering around inside, getting ready for the day.

The hardware store was busy, although more than a few loitered on the huge porch. Their attention was none too subtly focused on the cop cars—and Neve.

A perfectly normal morning.

But it wasn't.

"Look," he said, attention split between the McKays and everybody moving around them. He was here. William Clyde. Gideon could all but *feel* him. He needed to get Neve off the street, back home. Not that he planned on telling her that. Neve needed more careful handling than that. "Neve is right—she's a grown woman. She can't live her life trapped up in Ferry and only leaving when she has you or Moira there to hold her hand."

"Fine." Brannon bit the word off. "Ian can hold her fucking hand."

Gideon took a deep breath. "Brannon—"

"Chief."

"What?" Aggravation underscoring the word, he spun to glare at his man. Griffin stood there, a battered green bag hanging from one gloved hand.

"My backpack!" Neve shoved past the three men and Hannah, advancing on the man in uniform.

"It was on the ground in the alley," Griffin said. He glanced over at Gideon and the look was telling. And when Neve went to reach for it, he shifted out of her reach. "Chief."

What now?

Gideon joined Neve as Griffin turned over the backpack to her. It looked like something from an army surplus store, old and worn, fading at the seams. Neve clutched it to her chest like it was made of gold. But that lasted all of two seconds before she lowered it, a frown appearing on her face.

She unzipped it.

Griffin glanced at him again.

Gideon steeled himself and crowded in until he could see inside the bag.

But that wasn't really necessary.

It fell from Neve's hands, spilling its contents out on the sidewalk.

CHAPTER SIXTEEN

It had been a long time since Neve had been in *this* position.

Numb and hollowed-out, she sat in a hard, ladder-backed chair while Brannon braced his hands on Gideon's desk. "You're not talking to her until she has a fucking lawyer."

A lawyer.

Well, that was new.

All the times she'd been requested to come to the police department—*a few items are missing . . . the shop owner said Neve was in the store—now, Ms. McKay, we're not insinuating your sister stole anything, but some money is missing from the cash register*—but she'd never heard *that*.

Odd, really. As often as she'd been brought in here, by a scowling Moira or a disappointed Ella Sue, she'd never once heard the word *lawyer*. She wondered just what Ella Sue and Moira had done all those times. Not that she'd actually been the one to steal anything, but she'd played the distraction or looked the other way more than a few times with her so-called *friends*.

The only real friend she'd had in high school had

been Hannah and Hannah had always hurried home after school.

"If you'd just sit your ass down and take a few deep breaths, we'll talk about that," Gideon said.

"You." Brannon jabbed a finger toward Gideon. "You can shove the idea of talking up your ass until—"

"Boys."

Neve fought the urge to hunch her shoulders and cower into the chair at the sound of Moira's cool voice.

Brannon tossed a furious look over his shoulder. "Moira, have you gotten ahold of Danvers?"

"Yes." She sighed and glanced over at Neve, a tired smile on her lips. "But he's on a fishing trip with his son. He can get here if it's urgent, but it will take an hour at least."

"It's *not* urgent," Gideon said.

"Oh, go fuck yourself, Marshall!"

"Enough!"

Neve didn't know who was more surprised, her siblings or herself. Gideon, though, he looked like he was biting back a smile. As she stood, he sat down and damn if she wasn't right. He had a smile in his eyes.

"I don't see anything amusing about this." She glared a hole through him—or tried to.

"Oh, I'm not amused." Gideon raised his shoulders. "I'm just enjoying a nice, quick moment of *I knew it*."

"Knew what?" She wanted to curl back into the chair and hide away.

"I knew you were still in there, Trouble."

While she was processing that, he looked at Brannon. "I know it's hard for you to cool off once you get worked up, Bran, but yank your head out of your ass and listen to me—for two minutes."

"I'm not—"

"You are." Moira cut him off and grabbed his arm.

It was almost comical, watching her diminutive sister pull her much taller brother away from the desk. She shoved him toward a chair and it wasn't a surprise to anybody that he actually sat down.

"I know it isn't hers," Gideon said into the silence.

Neve closed her eyes and breathed out a sigh of relief, barely hearing Brannon's confused question over the pounding in her ears.

Their voices blurred into nothing but white noise as she forced herself to take a breath.

Then she opened her eyes and stared at Gideon. *Thank you.*

She didn't say it, but he seemed to hear the words nonetheless.

"If you *know* that, then why are we *here*?"

"Excuse me." Moira was coolly polite, her best *I'm in charge* smile firmly in place. "But you are forgetting I missed the earlier parts of this story, so if somebody could please enlighten me . . . ?"

Neve tried to find the words to explain. But while she was looking for them, Gideon was acting. He drew on a glove and then reached down next to the desk.

Neve stared at her familiar old bag, watching with a curious sense of detachment as Gideon dumped the contents out.

Moira sucked in a breath.

Neve braced herself.

"This is a bunch of bullshit." Moira, hands planted on her hips, stared at the items on the desk with a look of disgust. "Gideon, you *know* this is a bunch of bullshit."

"Oh, yeah." He nodded, picking up a pen to nudge the items around. He'd acted quickly out on the street, snatching gloves from his pockets and scooping everything back into the bag even as he told Neve she'd have to come to the station.

How many had seen, though?

How many had seen the hypodermic needle, the syringe? The unlabeled vials and the little white baggie.

She didn't need anybody to tell her what it was.

A few of the women she'd known during her terribly brief modeling career had been coke users. The powdery white substance had all but mocked her.

Trouble. You're nothing but trouble.

She'd come here expecting Gideon to question her, expecting Brannon and Moira's disappointment.

Swallowing, she forced herself to speak. "How . . ." She had to clear her throat before she could manage another word. "How do you know it's not mine?"

The three of them looked at her.

She met their gazes, Brannon's, Gideon's, finally Moira's. "How do you know?" she asked again. "Y'all haven't seen me in years. I could have picked up a lot of bad habits."

Gideon snorted. "Neve, your worst habit is finding yourself in a mess."

"Honey." Moira reached down, going to pick up something from the desk, but Gideon stopped her.

"Evidence," he said softly.

She rolled her eyes and then snatched a pencil from the cup on his desk, using it in much the same fashion Gideon had. "I'd believe you had sprouted horns and a tail before I'd believe you'd shoot up, Neve." She nudged the hypodermic out of the mess and slid Neve a look. "You can't even look at a needle without feeling like you're going to pass out."

"I can . . ." Her gaze dropped to the needle and blood started to roar in her ears. Black dots danced in front of her eyes and she turned away. "Well. Point made."

Abruptly, she laughed. "Thanks for that."

"For what?"

She looked back to watch as Moira settled her hips against Gideon's desk, her back to him as she studied her younger sister. Moira couldn't see the way Gideon's gaze slid to her, then away, then back again as if he just couldn't help a few lingering, longing glances.

He looked up then and saw Neve watching him. His lids drooped over his eyes and she averted her gaze, giving him the illusion of privacy, although both of them knew it was just that—an illusion. She understood how he felt, and she hurt for him.

Completely unaware, Moira lifted a perfectly plucked brow. "Thanks for remembering all the times we had to forcibly hold you down when you had to get shots? Remembering how you once gave me a bloody nose trying to get away from the needles?"

"I think I apologized for that," Neve said, embarrassed. She looked back at the needle and felt that familiar churning in her gut. She *hated* needles. Hated them.

"So it looks like we've got another thing to thank your ex-boyfriend for," Brannon said and the words were steely, cold. "Trying to set you up like this."

Neve frowned.

Gideon caught sight of it and lifted a brow.

She gave him a vague smile, her mind already churning, pushing around the new pieces to this very odd puzzle. "I guess my letters are gone," she said, a constriction settling deep inside her chest. "I . . . uh. Well. They're gone."

"What letters?" Moira asked.

Neve licked her lips and then glanced at Gideon. He rubbed his neck and gave her a short nod.

"I wrote you." She moved to the window and stared outside. The awning over the pub beckoned her and she thought about going down there, sitting at the bar and just watching Ian. The very idea heated her skin in ways she couldn't even begin to grasp. Just the thought of him settled her and *that* was unsettling. Instead of thinking about that, she pushed Ian out of her mind. "I wrote you both. Ella Sue, too . . . although I couldn't remember her address, so I just sent them to her at Ferry."

The strained silence behind her left her nerves humming and she felt like she could snap. As an ache settled behind her eyes, she turned to face her brother and sister.

"We . . ." Moira looked at Brannon and then back to her. "We never got any letters, Neve."

"I know." She shot Brannon a look, saw the dull red creeping up his cheeks. She was too tired to be irritated with him, though. "I also know you all wrote me . . . but I never got a single damn letter."

While Moira sagged against the desk, dazed, Neve shrugged. "I don't know what happened to the letters you sent me, although I imagine William had something to do with that. The ones I sent you? No idea. But once I got stateside, they started coming back to me. *Return to sender* was written across each one. They'd never even been opened."

"That doesn't make any sense," Moira said, shaking her head. She shoved off the desk and started to pace.

Neve could see her reflection in the window, a blur of constant motion and dark red hair. "Tell me about it."

But she might as well have not said anything.

"Gideon, why would somebody do that? Could it have been William?" She said his name like it tasted bad.

Gideon responded, but Neve didn't even process his words, staring out the window as she tried to puzzle it out in her head.

She could think of any number of reasons why William would have—and *had*—interfered with her contacting her family. What she didn't understand was how he'd managed to get in the way even after she left him, even after she left the country—and then Europe altogether.

While they talked behind her, she closed her eyes and fought the half-mad panic that kept trying to well up inside her.

He was close.

He'd been watching her.

Every other time this had happened, she'd taken off and disappeared. She knew it was still an option. She could run and she could, if she tried, find a way to *really* disappear. She had the money and she had the time.

But she was done running.

Fighting those urges wasn't easy.

This was home.

Courage had nothing do with it, because if she'd been courageous, she would have left him the very first time he'd raised a hand to her. She would have left him once she saw through his machinations—and she had. Twisting everything up on her so that she once more doubted herself, that she continued to doubt her family.

"Neve?"

Tired, she turned back to the room. "What?"

Moira hesitated, whatever question she'd had in mind seeming to freeze in her throat as the two sisters stared at each other.

"Are you . . ." Moira stopped and huffed out a breath. "I want to ask if you're okay, and that's stupid. How can you be okay? I want to do something."

"You already did." Chilled despite the heat that warmed the window at her back, Neve rubbed her hands down her arms. "All of you did. You trusted me."

Brannon made a disgusted noise under his breath. "It's got nothing to do with trust." He shook his head, his face dark with a scowl. "We know you."

"Do you?" She angled her head to the side. "I've been gone a long time and I was just a kid when I left. A kid who got into a whole hell of a lot of trouble, who *caused* a whole hell of a lot of trouble."

Brannon looked away.

"Neve."

The guilt in Brannon's eyes, echoes of regret and rage, tugged at her and added to the mess of emotions inside her. But they didn't *know* her—

"Neve." Gideon had crossed the room to stand in front of her and he reached out, caught her hand. "*I* know you." A faint smile curled his lips and she saw the truth there, plainly written in his eyes. Gideon *did* know her. The handful of years that stretched between them made little difference to him. "I didn't even have a second's doubt when I saw the drug paraphernalia. Your brother and sister? They didn't, either."

He squeezed her hand and then let go. "Now . . . we need to start thinking. Those things don't belong to you. We need to focus on other issues now."

He didn't elaborate, but she knew those things weren't things at all. It was a person.

William.

A set of keys dangled in front of him.

Turning his head, Ian met Neve's eyes.

Neve's *guarded* eyes.

He'd seen what was in her bag well enough. He had eyes. But he also had a brain. He'd seen the stunned surprise on Neve's face and more, he remembered.

She was terrified of needles.

Her bag had gone missing either the night she hit

town or the next day. Plenty of time for somebody to plant things in there that weren't hers. Plenty of time, although he couldn't quite figure out the *why*.

Reaching up, he took the keys, pretending to study them with disappointment. "It's not his Bugatti."

"Please." Some of the tension faded from her rigid form and she slid onto a stool in front of him. "As if he'd let *me* touch those keys—or that car."

"I drove it once." Ian braced his hands on the bar and leaned forward slightly, just enough that he could catch the scent of her over everything else. That scent had clung to his skin most of the night and he'd hated to wash it off.

Neve pursed her lips. "He let you drive the Bugatti?"

"Well, we had a wager. He lost. I won." Ian winked at her. "That was the prize."

"And if he'd won? What would he have gotten?"

"I don't know." Ian shrugged. It was mid-afternoon, past the lunch rush and well before the evening crowd and he wished he didn't have to be working the bar at the pub.

Neve seemed to be busy examining the surface of the bar and when she started to trace the grain of the glossy wood, he reached out and caught her hand. "I don't believe it."

She tensed.

Staring at the crown of her head, he willed her to look up at him.

After a few more moments, she did and he reached out, cupping her cheek in his hand.

He was more than aware that several people were watching them and he didn't care. What he cared about was bringing the smile back into her eyes. "I saw what was in the bag," he said, keeping his voice low. "And I don't believe it."

When she didn't respond, he traced his finger over the curve of her lower lip. "That shite, it wasn't yours."

"No." A heavy breath escaped from her and she slumped, almost as if she'd deflated, but he understood. She'd come in here, half afraid of the reception she'd receive. If he'd had his way, he would have tossed her over his shoulder and taken her back to his flat. If it was just the two of them, he could erase the shadows in her eyes.

That wasn't an option, though.

"How do you know?" she asked softly. "Was . . . did Brannon or Gideon call you?"

"No." With a snort, he pushed away from the bar just as one of the servers came up, already giving him the order. He started on a Guinness and dug out a bottle of Bud Light, popping the cap before turning the bottle over to be delivered. He checked the Guinness and went back to Neve. "I knew it just by the look on your face. You'd told me you had a fear of needles and I believed you so the drugs didn't make sense but I've gotten to know you and aside from that . . . all I had to do was see your face."

Another order came in; he took care of that and finished off the Guinness before returning to her.

"So, there you go. I don't believe it." He shrugged when she glanced up at him. Once more, he braced his hands on the bar's smooth surface. It was that or reach for her and he didn't really want to go pulling her over the bar.

"I was . . ." She broke off and then gave him a jerky shrug. "I was thinking I'd hang around. Eat some dinner. You can drive me home when you're done."

He had other ideas in mind that sounded preferable, but the bruised look in her eyes had him keeping quiet on those plans. "I think we can make that work."

He spun the keys and then leaned over, pressing a quick, hard kiss to her lips, ignoring her quick gasp. "Maybe you and I can talk about our plans, then."

"What plans?" Neve's brow furrowed as she stared at him.

"The plans I'm putting together for our next date." He slid a finger down the back of her hand, studying her from under his lashes. "I've got an urge to seduce you, Neve McKay."

CHAPTER SEVENTEEN

Ian studied her solemnly and then looked down. After another moment, he picked up a letter and added it to the board game in front of them.

Neve looked down and felt her face go red as she read the word *c-u-m*. "That doesn't count as a word. Well, not unless you're a thirteen-year-old boy."

Ian winked at her. "A thirteen-year-old boy lives in the heart of every man, love."

She rolled her eyes. "You're just trying to get cheap points now. I'm going to win and you know it."

"Well, if we'd played strip Scrabble, it wouldn't matter who won or lost. But we had to play it with our clothes . . . oi, that's not a word, either!" He glared at the board where she'd used a *d* to make out the word *v-a-d-e-r*.

"Sure it is. As in *Darth Vader*." She smugly tallied up the points. "If you can use dirty words, then I can use names."

"Dirty words, eh?"

She realized she'd somehow unconsciously challenged him. A few minutes later, he had the word *c-u-n-t* and she wrinkled her nose at him. "I don't like that word."

"I don't see why not." He shrugged, unabashed. "It's

short for cunnilingus, you know, and you *do* enjoy that. So if I were to say, Neve, I want to lick your cunt—"

She threw one of the little letters at him and he didn't dodge it in time. "Come now," he said, rubbing at the red mark on his cheek. "What if you'd hit me in me mouth? I wouldn't be able to put it to good use later."

"Are we going to play or are you just using this to try and embarrass me?"

Ian reached out and stroked his finger down her hand. "Why would it embarrass you to know that I plan on putting my hands all over you later, Neve?"

Her breath hitched when he caught her hand and lifted it to his lips, catching one finger in his mouth and sucking on it. Heat fluttered inside, then spread when he pulled that finger out and moved to the other. "It wouldn't embarrass me if you sat there and told me that you wanted to put your mouth on my cock. Or any other part of me."

Before she could formulate any sort of reply, he let her hand go and then braced his elbows on the coffee table. The lights were dim, the remnants of a pizza on the table next to them. "Right, then. Your turn, Neve."

Dazed, she looked down at her letters.

She had no idea what possessed her but she did it.

She reached out and took from the words already on the board, highly aware of Ian's bemused expression. As she spelled out the word *c-o-c-k*, she didn't dare look at him.

A moment later, the Scrabble board went flying and she was on her back on the couch, with Ian sprawled on top of her.

"I think you win that round," he said, his voice gruff.

Ian could, without a doubt, seduce her. Even with something as simple as dirty Scrabble and pizza by candlelight.

He could also destroy her.

Her hands gripped the edge of the table, and she sucked in a breath as he pushed her thighs wider and licked her.

The table was cool under her back—cool and slippery—and when she tried to arch closer, her shirt slid over the smooth surface. Ian's hands caught her hips and held her steady.

Those hands might be the only thing keeping her from flying into a thousand pieces as he started to toy with her clitoris, using his tongue in a rhythm that set her to gasping and whimpering all over again.

She came with hard, near savage intensity and when he levered his weight up over her, she stared at him, panting.

"That was dessert," he said.

"Dessert?" It took two tries to get the word out.

"Aye. It's time for the main course, though. I'm so hungry for you." Ian nuzzled her breasts through her T-shirt and she wished she'd thought to take it off. Clothes had never been so annoying as they were around him. If they could both just spend their time together naked . . .

The loud rasp of a zipper had her heart hammering harder against her ribs.

"We . . . um."

He came down over her and she used her hands as a buffer, holding him at bay as she looked around.

"Ian, we're on your table."

"I know." He rolled his eyes. "The next time I sit down here to eat, I'll end up with an erection and blue balls."

"But . . ."

His lips lightly pressed against the corner of her mouth. "Neve, can I tell you a fantasy of mine?"

He didn't wait for her to answer, just forged right on ahead. "I want to see you naked in every room of my house and have you on every flat surface that will hold our weight."

A laugh bubbled out of her, a mix of excitement and embarrassment. "The back of your couch wasn't flat."

"Well, then. I'll have to amend my fantasy."

He brushed against her and the discomfort she felt, the vague embarrassment, faded at the feel of his cock, so hard and thick, stroking against the folds of her sex.

"I . . ."

He sank inside her.

"I think I could get on board with this fantasy," she squeezed out as he withdrew and surged forward again.

"I knew you'd see it my way."

His mouth came down on hers and rational thought spun away, lost in a haze of bliss.

William idly stroked his thumb against his forefinger, a habit he seemed to have picked up almost overnight. The scarf.

He shouldn't have left the scarf.

As much as he would have liked to have watched the whole spectacle play itself out, he'd stayed in his chair, pretending to read the pitiful excuse this town had for a newspaper. He'd been surprised she'd reported it. First one, then a second, police car had arrived and they'd stayed there for close to an hour.

Neve had strode out from between the two buildings at one point. Anticipation had burned in him and he'd laid out enough money to cover the coffee he'd been drinking, but she hadn't left that spot.

No. Ian fucking Campbell had emerged from the alley behind her and the two of them had been all but joined at the hip.

Then there was the blonde—the women had spoken together for some time and he'd spun yet another scenario in his head. Perhaps she'd leave with the woman. If she left with the other woman, he could follow . . .

But she hadn't.

It had been almost a week since he'd left his message for her and he'd yet to see her more than a handful of times and not *once* had he been able to approach her.

When she'd hopped out of a flamboyant car that was the most atrocious shade of red, he'd felt the frustration course through him yet again. She paused to wave at the car behind her and William curled his lip at the sight of Brannon McKay.

Neve had then disappeared into a shop just down the walk. Renovations were going on inside and he knew he wouldn't have even a whisper of a hope of her being alone.

Men with tool belts came and went in an unending parade and more than once, Campbell had gone in there and the two of them would emerge.

They'd done that, just twenty short minutes ago.

He'd watched, expecting them to go into the pub.

But Campbell had dipped his head toward Neve's, perhaps to say something. She'd looked up at him, and then they'd kissed.

Neve hadn't even *pretended* reluctance when she let him lead her into the alley.

They were inside Campbell's flat. He'd followed and now William could hear them, low grunts and soft moans.

He reached up and traced his finger over the small, round sticker. It was discreet, but its message was clear.

There was an alarm system and he'd already seen how promptly calls to the police were handled. More than a few uniformed men tended to have their lunch in the pub. He doubted he could get in there and get out without being seen by the cops—pursued, even.

As a broken cry echoed through the door, William turned.

He'd go back to the diner.

Sooner or later, she'd slip up.

She always did.

Then she'd pay and if he was lucky, perhaps he could even get his hands on Campbell. Just the thought of him putting his hands on Neve made William's vision run red.

His.

She was his.

She'd learn how foolish it was to humiliate him like this, just as her brother had learned. Did Ian Campbell know?

Did the sod know that Neve was *his*?

He would, and so would Neve, once and for all.

Nobody humiliated him and just walked away from it.

It had taken time to figure out just how he'd handle it, but he'd done it. That meeting in New York, running into Neve McKay, although it hadn't been an accidental meeting as she'd always assumed.

No, he'd been watching and waiting for a chance. She thought she was so fucking powerful, all of them did. Fucking McKays with their money and their name. But he knew people, too. He had friends as well and he knew who to talk to, knew how to wait, so he'd done just that.

He'd watched, he'd listened, and when he heard about Neve, he'd known she'd be perfect. Ripe for the plucking.

He'd just planned to have a bit of sport with her, but she'd been so vulnerable. So needy. So *perfect*.

She was *his*. He'd have his chance at her soon. He'd just have to be patient again and watch, wait.

Neve would be his again and he'd teach her the same sort of lesson he was teaching Campbell and her prick of a brother. Nobody humiliated William Clyde. Nobody.

Somebody appeared at the table and he looked up.

The female gaze that pinned him was cool, assessing. William returned her stare with one of his own.

A slow smile stretched across her lips.

"I saw you." Shayla Hardee said the words coolly, calmly.

The man across from her put his coffee cup down on the table and leaned back, studying her with a faint, amused expression on his face. "You saw me . . . here? How observant of you."

"Very funny." She leaned in. The crowd around them had her lowering her voice. "I *saw* you . . . last week. Out behind the pub."

His lids flickered. He said nothing, but when he cocked his head, she smiled. "Joel Fletcher lives in one of the little apartments in the building behind the pub. It's on High Street. His apartment is in the back. We were . . . visiting."

"Visiting." He laughed shortly. "Is that what it's called these days?"

She ignored him, reaching out to rest a hand flat on the table. "She went into the police department, you know. I heard what happened, about the bag . . ." Shayla fluttered a hand vaguely. "Small towns, ya know. People talk."

"Indeed."

Unperturbed by his cool demeanor, Shayla leaned back over the table, elbows braced on the candy-apple red surface. Smiling, she added, "All that mess goes down behind the pub, nobody knows anything, saw anything . . . Ian's bike get trashed. Neve's got a back-pack back there filled up with drugs. That was stupid, you know. Neve's got this fear of needles that's . . . well. It's legendary. People might believe she'd *sell* them for the hell of it, but *use* them? Oh, hell, no."

"Is there a point to this?" He lifted his coffee cup and sipped, staring at her over the brim.

"You had a bag with you. I saw it."

Impatience started to leap inside her when his eyes remained cool and unreadable.

"What would you like?" he asked easily. "A medal?"

"Well." She lifted one shoulder in a shrug. "You're not too far off. Medals are, after all, usually gold."

She let those words sink in.

"Money." His lip curled as he said it, the word clearly distasteful. Still, in that crisp accent, he sounded so elegant, so refined. "You want me to pay you."

Shayla smiled. "That's the idea."

He studied her with narrow eyes and then leaned in. "There's a boat dock a few miles out of town. Landry's. You know it?"

"Who doesn't?" Shayla rolled her eyes.

"Be there tonight at ten. We'll discuss this more . . . openly."

"You better be ready to trade." As he stood up, she slumped more comfortably in the chair and lifted her hand to flag down the server. This called for French fries.

"I've been thinking."

Ian's chest was warm under her and she could feel his heart beating. It was a soothing, steady cadence and she thought maybe she could be happy to spend the rest of her life like this. Or the rest of the day, at least. Sooner or later, they'd need food.

Then she'd want sex again.

Then they could go back to lying like this.

But he'd said something. Popping one eye open, she studied the room. Soft light fell through the window, painting everything with warm, golden colors.

"Thinking. Why?"

Ian laughed softly. "Because sometimes it saves time and trouble."

"Sometimes thinking *causes* trouble." She shifted around and rolled onto her belly to stare at him. "Aren't you the one who tells me I think too much?"

That face.

Just looking at him like this was enough to make her feel all hot and raw inside. And *greedy*. Not just for sex, although she'd come to appreciate that act far more than she would have thought possible.

But she was greedy for *him*. For everything about him—she wanted more time, she wanted more laughs, she wanted more conversations late in the night while she lay in her bed back at Ferry and he lay in his here in town.

Why couldn't she have found *him* instead of William?

What would she be like if she hadn't been so . . .

". . . not a bad idea, is it?"

"Huh?" She blinked at him. Blushing, she sat up. "I'm sorry. My mind was wandering."

"Just what a man wants to hear when he's got a lovely woman in his bed." Ian glowered at her, but she saw the glint in his eyes.

"I was thinking about you, if that helps." She reached out and touched a finger to his lower lip. The softness of his beard and the warmth of him sent a shiver of pleasure up her spine.

"It helps." He caught her hand and pressed a kiss to her palm.

Then he sat up, levering his weight back against the headboard. "So . . ." He drew the word out pointedly, staring at her. "I was *thinking* that maybe you could bring some of your stuff here. That way, if you end up staying the night again, you have clothes."

Bring some of your stuff . . .

A wave of cold hit her. Air knocked out of her chest. *Just a few things, Neve darling. It would be so much better that way and really, I can't stay in your flat. There's hardly room for you.* William's voice, so gentle and persuasive, rose out of the depths of her memories to mock her.

"My . . ." She licked her lips. "My stuff?"

She didn't know *where* exactly it came from, or why it hit her like that, but suddenly, the lazy, easy warmth was gone. Even those thoughts of *staying like this forever* had faded.

Clambering out of the bed, she grabbed the shirt he'd left on the foot of the bed and jerked it on. "No."

He made no response and she turned around, jerked up her chin to glare at him. "Aren't you going to say anything?"

His eyes were closed.

While she stood there shaking on the inside, he sat in the bed, looking relaxed and he had his eyes closed like he wanted to grab another five minutes of sleep.

"What am I to say, Neve?" he asked softly. "If you're not ready for that, then you're not ready. I can't push you."

"But you are!"

"No." He opened his eyes and climbed out of the bed, staring at her from across the room. "I asked you. That's not pushing."

"But you asked me too soon! I barely know you!"

A muscle pulsed in his jaw, his eyes glinting.

Even saying that felt like a lie, but Neve didn't take it back. She *didn't* know him.

"What's this about, Neve?" Ian asked.

He could see her throat working as she swallowed but she didn't answer him. Sighing, he turned and grabbed the clothes he'd piled haphazardly on a chair near the door. He'd have time to shower, if he hurried, and get back down to the pub. He'd been an idiot, asking her so soon. Wasn't like he'd asked her to move in with him, but maybe he had pushed.

He'd *wanted* to. Did it amount to the same thing?

"I knew William for *months* before I slept with him. Dated him for *months* before I moved in with him. And that was *still* a disaster."

Temper snapped out of him and whirled to face her. "I'm nothing like him."

Neve blinked hard and he watched one hand curl into a fist, so tight her knuckles went bloodless.

"Neve—"

"I'm sorry." She spun on her heel and ducked into the other room.

Ian stood there, rubbing his hands up and down his face. *Calm down, lad. Just calm down . . .*

He gave himself thirty seconds before he went after her, using the time to pull something on over his naked arse. The door to the hall bath closed with a soft but firm click.

He'd bungled this. Rushed her. No, he didn't think he'd *pushed* but he had rushed and now he'd have to fix it.

He was gone over on her, near stupid with want and need, and lately, he was having thoughts of *forever*.

It wasn't something he'd ever entertained and it made him nervous.

But he could fix this.

The door opened and he looked up, saw Neve hesitate

there before she came out, an empty smile on her pretty face. "I need to get going," she said, the words too forced, too loud.

"Neve, wait. We should talk."

"We will." The smile she shot him then was almost blinding in its intensity and so blatantly fake, it ripped his heart right out. "I just remembered there are things I've got to get done before the weekend gets here. This job Brannon dumped on me, I swear, I'm so not prepared for it and I don't want to let him down."

She continued to babble as she hunted down her shoes and shoved her feet into them.

Ian folded his arms over his chest and let her keep right on.

When she paused for a breath, he said, "We're talking. Tonight."

"Of course."

She continued to talk, as though she feared silence would be an invitation for him to say something else she wouldn't want to hear. When at last she left, he walked to the window and made sure she got into the car. Only once she was driving down the street did he give into the anger.

He slammed a fist into the wall.

Skin split, but he barely noticed.

Sinking to the ground, he stared listlessly at nothing.

He'd fucked that up, good and proper.

She ran.

Neve had told herself she'd stop running from her problems, but she ran.

And what made it so much worse was the fact that she didn't even understand *why* she was running. She just knew she had to get away. For a brief, brief moment, she'd thought . . . *wow*.

But then panic had grabbed her and now it wouldn't let go. It tangled her in sticky threads, like a spiderweb and the more she struggled, the harder it was to get free.

Leave some things at Ian's. So simple . . . right?

But that made it seem more permanent and what if . . . what if . . .

Thoughts whirled in a useless tumble in her head as she drove home. She managed to pull into the garage, but only because she didn't want Ella Sue or anybody else to see her because she knew she was a few steps shy of falling apart.

She half screamed as she slammed the car into park and climbed out. She closed the door shut with all the force she could muster and that didn't do anything to help, so she kicked the tire.

And still, she felt trapped. Scared . . .

Stupid.

I'm nothing like him.

No. Ian was nothing like William. Had she made him think he was? A sob welled out of her and she clapped her hand over her mouth, struggling to hold it back.

How could she have done that?

Ian made her feel . . . *amazing.* She felt strong and beautiful and . . .

Loved.

"Oh, shit," she whispered.

Numb, she dropped to the hard concrete.

The brilliant lights of the huge garage shone down on her and her voice echoed back to her from the depths of the cavernous space. No wonder she couldn't understand how she felt.

But just as soon as that realization came over her, she pushed it away.

Too soon.

It was just . . .

"Too soon."

She left the garage, hurrying toward the house like hell itself chased after her.

She couldn't think about this now.

Couldn't think about the misery she'd caught in his eyes, for the briefest moment.

Moira had to fight the urge to hang up the phone.

Even as she resisted, though, she made the mental note to get a new one—Monday.

Maybe even today. A new phone, a new phone number and she'd kill the person who passed on her *personal* number to this asshole.

"Senator Roberts, what a surprise," she said.

She stood behind at the window that faced out over the museum but instead of the swell of pride she normally had, she just felt aggravation. She wanted to be out there working, checking on the exhibits, following up on the invites—yeah, she had a manager, and a good one.

Colleen Messer was a godsend and Moira didn't know what she'd do without the woman, but at the same time, Moira had to be involved in *everything*.

Instead, she was talking to the senator. She should have just told his aides and assistants and everybody else *flat-out no*. Maybe that wasn't something most people would think of doing, but hell, she could buy and sell the senator two times over—assuming she wanted a politician in her pocket, and she didn't.

But since she hadn't shut him down, he must have decided to try his hand at cajoling her himself.

She knew the man.

She should have expected this.

"Moira, darling. I hope I'm not disturbing you. I know how busy you must be," he said, his voice smooth and warm, open and inviting.

It was like an icepick in her ear, because it just sounded *fake*.

"The life of a businesswoman," she said glibly, refusing to lie to the man and tell him he *wasn't* disturbing her. "Always busy. Is there something I can do for you, sir? I've got a pretty cramped schedule today."

"Well, Moira, you see, we've been trying to pin you down for that party we'd like to have at that quaint little museum you've put together for your family," the senator said. "As you know, I grew up in Treasure myself, still have a family home there and everything. It would mean a great deal to me—and my constituents, I'm sure, to be able to have one of my fund-raisers there."

Moira gritted her teeth together as she stared out over her place.

Quaint?

It managed to combine the McKay family's Scottish roots with the elegance of the Old South. Every single thing had been carefully and painstakingly thought-out.

And he was calling it *quaint*?

Decision made, she said, "Did you have a particular time in mind?"

"Well, it's so late now, I've only got two dates that are open." He named one.

Moira resisted the urge to pump her fist in the air. "That will not work for me, I'm afraid. That's the grand opening for the museum and it's a town function. I can't change all the information that's already going out or disappoint all the people who've been looking forward to it—these, after all, are some of your constituents as well. You wouldn't want to tell them that we have to delay the opening because of a fund-raiser many of them can't even begin to consider affording."

"Hmmm. Of course, of course."

She smiled, satisfied that was off the plate.

"So the other date we were looking at is closer to the end of my campaign," Senator Roberts said and his voice took on a harder note. "I'm hoping you can accommodate me this time, Moira."

She lifted a brow. *Really.*

He named the date.

She lied through her teeth.

When he hung up the phone a few minutes later, using just a little too much force, she made a face.

Then she grabbed the phone.

No piece-of-shit politician was going to try and bully *her* into doing what he wanted.

Period.

"You're having a party."

Brannon closed his eyes.

"No. I'm not."

"Yes," Moira said slowly, her voice like steel. "You are. At my museum."

She named the date and Brannon blew out a breath before grabbing a pen. "Just why am I having a party?"

"Because you asked me about three days ago and I promised. You thought it would be a great way to have a community open-house sort of thing for your winery—and another draw for the museum. Since your in-town store isn't as big as the museum, this was a great fit. Really, Brannon, you're brilliant."

He rubbed the back of his neck and out of habit, glanced across the street to Hannah's. The balcony had been empty for going on a week. He never would have thought he'd miss a Peeping Tom—or Peeping *Hannah*—so much, but he did. He missed her.

Pushing her out of his head for a moment, he focused back on his sister. "Okay, again . . . why am I suddenly deciding to have this party?"

"Because Senator Roberts tried to steamroll me into hosting his fund-raiser here and I'm not going to be steamrolled by anybody."

"Of course not," Brannon said sourly. "You're just going to steamroll me."

Moira sounded like she wanted to argue and then abruptly, she laughed. "Okay, look. Brannon, do you really want that guy coming into our museum with his baby-kissing smile and pressing palms, and using *our* name on his campaign?"

"Nope." He didn't even have to think about that. "Fine. I guess I'm having a party."

There was a minute pause and then Moira said, "He . . . um. Well, he grumbled about how it would be a shame if things got held up with your place. Stay on top of things, Brannon."

He narrowed his eyes. "If that pompous piece of shit tries to bog things down for me, he's going to have more to handle than kissing babies and shaking hands, sis."

They disconnected and he took a minute to call his manager out at the winery. Tag would take care of notifying the rest of the group. And Brannon, slick, brilliant genius that he was, made sure to let them know he'd talked it over with Moira a few days ago, but just hadn't gotten around to making up his mind until today.

Tag, of course, thought it was a brilliant idea.

Brannon would pass the compliment on to the real genius.

Then he went back to brooding and staring out the window at the empty balcony.

How could he miss her this much?

Hannah's sly smile in the morning and her unabashed boldness had done something to him and he didn't know what.

But he knew what it was doing to him *now* to look up there and not *see* her.

It was pissing him off and he was tired of it.

So he was going to do something about it.

He locked up and headed out of town. He'd tried knocking on the door earlier, before his sister had called. Hannah wasn't home. He'd knocked a good five minutes before he gave up.

He'd decided—after the five wasted minutes at her door—to see if her car was parked around back. It wasn't and that just made him feel that much more idiotic.

But he knew where to find her.

He'd worked damn hard to avoid Hannah Parker, true, but he'd still learned things.

And Hannah spent a fair amount of time down at the houseboat her grandmother had left her when she'd passed away a few years ago, a sudden heart attack in the middle of the night.

He found her parked car and strode up the narrow strip that served to connect the dock to the houseboat. Music was blasting.

Again, his knock went unanswered, but he had no doubt she was here.

Undeterred by the lack of response, he eyed the distance between him and the boat. And then he jumped it. Clearing it easily, he started to search.

It didn't take long to find her.

And when he did, all of the oxygen squeezed out of his lungs.

Hannah sighed and stretched her arms high overhead. The brilliance of the sun shining down on her and the warmth of the late afternoon had her feeling lazy.

Lazy, and almost relaxed.

If she worked hard enough at keeping her mind empty, she could forget about the sneering looks she'd gotten in town that morning from Lloyd, and as long as she was careful, she could even pretend she wasn't thinking about Brannon every other hour.

That was an improvement, really.

She'd been thinking about him on the hour for most of the past week, telling herself she had to get over him, and her stupid, juvenile fantasy.

She'd spent the past week telling herself to get over him.

She'd spent the past week telling herself she'd tried.

But the truth was, she hadn't tried hard enough. Ever since he'd come home from England, she'd felt like she was waiting for him. She'd been young, yes, but even before he'd left Treasure, she'd felt something for him.

A girl's first crush, she'd wanted to believe.

But it was more and it always had been.

And it was just as useless as a girl's first crush, too.

Hannah was nothing if not pragmatic.

It was useless and now, on top of the memories of that night together, it *hurt*.

So she'd just stop.

It wouldn't be as easy as that, no, but she'd find a way to get over him.

Today, for the first time, she'd almost come to grips with the decision. Lying under the sun, feeling the heat of the day, she came to peace with the foolishness of what she felt. Maybe it even had something to do with what she'd seen in Joanie's eyes when she saw her with Lloyd. Oh, not that Brannon was anything like Lloyd— they were about as far apart as the North and South Poles.

But Lloyd had an unhealthy hold on his wife.

And Hannah had let herself develop an unhealthy fixation on Brannon, the man who only barely let himself realize she existed.

Yeah, it was time to let it go, move on.

Decision made, she pushed up onto her elbows. Opening her eyes, she went to squint up at the sun to try and guess the time.

Her heart froze in her chest.

It took a full thirty seconds before it started to beat again.

Brannon McKay stood on the deck of her houseboat and he was staring at her with an almost dazed expression on his face.

Fear made her voice sharp as she snapped, "What in the *hell* are you doing here?"

The sound of her voice seemed to rouse him and he blinked, looking like a man coming out of a fugue. With a curl of his lips, he shrugged. "Paybacks."

She gaped at him.

He didn't seem to notice. His gaze had slid down, running all over her and the heat in that look made the day seem cool by comparison. Snatching a towel up, she held it in front of her breasts.

"Okay, yeah. So I sunbathe naked. But that doesn't explain what you're doing here." She glared at him, fumbling the towel into place. It took more effort than it should because her hands were shaking.

"I wanted to talk to you. Heard the music." He slid his gaze back up to hers and took a step closer.

Hannah backed up.

Brannon cocked his head, studying her. "You didn't answer."

"I didn't hear you." Folding her arms over her chest, she turned away and moved to the music, hitting the power button.

It went abruptly silent.

Hannah fought the urge to hunch her shoulders. He was staring at her. She could *feel* the heat of his gaze, could *feel* him all but willing her to look at him. Her ice water sat on the towel she'd spread out and she moved back to it, bending over to pick it up.

"You know, if you're trying to distract me, that's an excellent way to do it."

A blush bloomed up her neck, the heat of it scalding her. In what she hoped was a casual move, she took a sip of her water as she turned to face him. The icy water eased her parched throat, but did nothing to cool the flames on her face—or in her belly. It licked at her, adding to the heat already building inside. Heat she'd ignore this time.

She was done with this.

Done hoping, done wishing, done waiting.

He didn't even realize.

You never told him.

No.

She hadn't. Gripping the glass, she focused on his face. "What do you want, Brannon?"

His lashes drooped and the heavy-lidded look on his face brought vivid memories swimming back.

"You're mad at me," he said bluntly. "And I think I know why."

She started to tap her foot, masking the nerves and misery she felt with impatience. When it came to hiding how she felt, Hannah was a pro. She'd learned the value of keeping her true emotions concealed and the lessons had been ugly, painful ones.

A scowl twisted his face. "You were awake."

She tightened her grip on the glass and propped her other hand on her hip. Hopefully that would keep him from noticing the shaking. "Don't worry, Brannon. I won't dirty your doorstep again."

"I . . . what?"

"Please." Unable to keep looking at him, she turned away. "I don't think you could have sounded any more disgusted if you'd found a dead rat in your underwear drawer."

Without waiting for a response, she strode toward the door.

When she went to shut it, he slammed a hand against it. "Just hold up there, Hannah."

She went to shove him back but decided not to bother. She'd never move him and she wasn't going to give up any more dignity than she had to. "Do you mind? I'd like to shower and get dressed."

"Don't let me stop you." He crowded her up against the wall of the narrow hallway, his big, muscled body blocking out everything else.

She swallowed as he fisted a hand in the towel she'd wrapped around herself. One tug, and it would be gone.

"You're sort of in the *way*," she pointed out. "I can't shower when you're pinning me up against the wall."

And I can't think when you're so close. Please . . . just go away.

"Am I in the way?"

She opened her mouth and Brannon braced himself for whatever smart-ass reply she'd come up with. He'd take her anger, because he'd earned it.

But no words came out and Brannon felt something hollow settle in his chest when she closed her eyes and dropped her head back to the wall behind her.

"Would you please leave me alone?" she asked and her voice was soft, trembling.

"I'm sorry." Brannon pressed his mouth to the corner

of hers as he spoke. "I . . . fuck, Hannah. If you think I was disgusted with *you*, then clearly you weren't paying attention."

He unclenched his fist from her towel, resisting the urge to tug it away. Her body . . . damn, he didn't know if he'd ever be able to sleep without seeing those powerhouse curves in his dream. And he wanted *more*. Skimming his hand down, he curved it over her hip and held her still as he leaned into her, slowly rolling his hips. "If that's the case, then pay attention *now*."

A low, shaky noise escaped her.

"Does this seem like I'm *disgusted*?"

She pushed her hands against his chest and something cold splashed on him.

Looking down, he saw the glass, a wet stain spilling across his chest. He took the glass from her and looked around. There was a narrow alcove with a table and he leaned over, dumped the glass there before focusing back on her.

Harsh breaths escaped her, forcing her breasts up and down and the towel started to slip.

She went to catch it but he got there first and her eyes widened on his as he peeled the towel away, baring the lush, ripe curves. Still watching her, he let the towel fall to the floor before he reached up and skimmed the back of his knuckles across one erect nipple. It drew even tighter and he dipped his head, catching the swollen peak in his mouth.

She whimpered and the sound jolted through him. Once more, she pressed her hands to his chest and he braced himself for her to push him back.

But she fisted her hands in his shirt and arched closer.

Control snapped and he grabbed her, boosting her up

and leaning into her, her weight supported by his body and the wall at her back.

"I want you," he growled against her mouth. "Say you want me."

Her nails bit into his skin through his shirt. Her sigh, soft and erratic, ghosted across his lips when he lifted his head to stare at her, waiting.

"Want . . ." She looked almost sad as smiled at him. "I guess that's one way to phrase it."

Before he could puzzle through that one, she tugged his mouth back to hers.

Mindless need replaced rational thought and Brannon gave into the driving urge to have her again.

She clutched at his shoulders, her long legs wrapped around his hips as she rocked against him.

He barely remembered fumbling his jeans open, barely remembered shoving them out of the way. They were an obstacle, something that stood between him and her and that was the only importance they had. His cock, exposed to the air, jerked viciously and he shifted her weight, hooking her legs behind the knees with his elbows to open her.

Hot silk, wet as rain, flowered open around him as he found her entrance.

Without thinking about anything but the need to *take*, Brannon surged forward, burying himself inside her.

She cried out and he caught the wavering clamor with his mouth, driving his tongue inside her mouth as he drove his cock into her slick, wet core.

Again, again, again . . .

She strained against him, twisting and rocking in an effort to take him faster, harder. He answered the unspoken plea with deep, driving strokes.

She came around him, hard and fast, and unable to

fight the pleasure, he shattered, erupting inside her with a furious snarl.

Wet trickled down her thighs as he lowered her feet to the ground.

Hannah's legs wobbled and she clutched at his shoulders, trying to steady herself.

He'd come inside her.

No rubber.

She mentally groaned, even as she thanked the irregular periods that had eventually forced her to start taking the pill. That much, at least, should be okay.

Brannon stroked his hand down her back, easing in closer, his breathing still heavy and fast.

When he went to kiss her again, she averted her face. Then, forcing herself to do what she should have done to begin with, she pushed him away.

He went reluctantly and she ducked out from between him and the wall.

Not bothering to grab the towel, she strode to the minuscule bathroom and grabbed her robe from the hook on the door. As she fumbled her way into it, she heard him coming up behind her.

She freed her hair, staring at the small couch in the little living room of the houseboat. "We didn't use a rubber."

Slowly, she turned and stared at him.

He'd tugged his jeans back up, but he hadn't zipped them or buttoned them and the thickness of his cock pressing against his underwear seemed to belie the past few, furious minutes.

He was still hard.

And she still wanted him, ached inside for him. Not just for the hard thrust of his cock, but for *him*. Everything about him.

"I . . ." His jaw went tight and he reached up, rubbing his hands up and down his face. "Son of a bitch. I'm sorry. I wasn't thinking."

She looked away. She hadn't been thinking, either.

"I'm on the pill." Turning away, she strode into the kitchen. She needed a drink. She *wanted* something strong—whiskey, preferably, the hot burn of it gliding down her throat and easing the edges of the misery. "So that's not a big concern there. I'm clean."

She grabbed a bottle of water from the fridge as she waited for him to answer.

"I . . ." He sighed.

Something cold gripped her and she turned, staring at him. "Brannon?"

"Shit, stop looking so panicked. This is the first time I've ever been with anybody without a rubber." He eyed the water bottle. "Got another one of those?"

Silently, she retrieved a bottle.

As he accepted it, he started to speak. "I can't say I've ever been checked for anything, but I don't have sex without a condom. Well. At least up until a few minutes ago."

"Good." She jerked a shroud of ice around her emotions, pushing past him.

"Would you . . . son of a bitch. I'll get checked. But you don't have to worry."

She wasn't *worried*.

She was *tired*. The emotions she'd kept hidden inside had snuck out past her guard and ambushed her, stripping away any and all defenses and at the worst possible time.

"Hannah."

He came up behind her and she closed her eyes as he curved an arm around her waist. "I'm sorry I hurt you. I just . . ."

She closed her eyes as he lowered his head to her shoulder. "I'm fine, Brannon," she lied.

He seemed to hear the falsehood.

"Then what's wrong? You haven't . . . how insane will you think I sound if I tell you I've kinda missed seeing you on your balcony?"

"What?" She gave a derisive snort as another crack formed in her heart. "You miss me playing Peeping Tom? Although, *FYI,* you could always just close your damn curtains."

"Then I wouldn't see you." His teeth scraped over her shoulder.

It sent a shiver down her spine. "I find it hard to believe that would bother you much. You go out of your way to avoid me."

"Because I didn't want . . . this."

She didn't think he meant to say that. Slowly, she turned and when she looked into his eyes, he averted his. "This," she echoed.

"I . . . look, Hannah. I've known you too long." Blood rushed up to stain his cheeks red as he turned his head and met her eyes once more. "In my head, I've had you about a hundred ways to Sunday and every time I see you, I want to try at least *one* of those ways out. But I . . ."

His words trailed off.

Feeling chilled, she pulled away from him. Moving to the small *L* of the counters, she leaned back. "You what?" she asked coolly.

"I'm not looking for any sort of relationship," he said, voice flat. "Sex is all well and good, but I don't want anything else. That's not . . . I just don't want it. Especially not now. I've got too much going on as it is and somehow, I get the feeling casual sex isn't really your speed."

Well. He summed that up pretty nicely, she thought dully. She couldn't fault him for being honest—or accurate. No. She didn't do casual sex.

This was what it felt like to have the deepest desires of the heart shattered.

It sucked.

She went to tell him to leave, but that wasn't what came out of her mouth.

"I've been in love with you since I was in high school."

Brannon's mouth fell open.

She should have been horrified, but all she felt was *numb*. It spread through her, turning everything inside her icy and cold.

"No, Brannon. Casual sex isn't my speed."

"Hannah, I . . ." He shook his head, looking completely lost.

"You don't need to say anything." Nodding her head to the door, she gave up on the dream. "You just need to leave."

"Hannah, wait . . ."

"No!" It ripped out of her and she shoved past him, intent on just one thing. Getting the hell away from him. She ducked into her room and slammed the door. Just before it closed, she saw him moving toward her. She flipped the lock and leaned back against it. "Go *away*, Brannon."

"Hannah, come on."

"Are you fucking *deaf*? I want you *gone*!" She clapped a hand over her mouth and slid down to the floor, her back still braced against the door. "Just leave . . ."

Dazed, Brannon sat in the car.

Sweat trickled down his face and it wasn't until it stung his eyes that he realized he was sitting in the car with the doors and windows closed, the trapped, over-heated air turning the small space into a suffocating sauna.

Swearing, he started the car and stabbed at the buttons, sending the windows gliding silently down.

In love with you . . .

Her words rang inside his head.

It was bullshit, of course. She couldn't be in love with him.

Still, he felt miserable and hollow, sitting there, parked in front of Hannah's houseboat while he knew she was inside, hurting.

Had she been crying?

He hadn't wanted to leave.

No, he didn't want any kind of relationship, but when she told him she loved him, her voice oddly flat and lacking the familiar sarcastic humor, all he'd wanted to do was hold her.

All she wanted was him gone. She'd made that clear.

Okay. Okay. He'd leave. For now. Leave, think. Let her calm down and then he'd come back.

They'd . . . talk.

Hopefully, he could get her to realize that she didn't really love him.

The idea settled inside him, uncomfortable and hollow, so he shoved it aside.

He'd go out to his place. He spent too little time there as it was.

CHAPTER EIGHTEEN

Shayla Hardee was a lot of things, but she wasn't stupid.

She'd been doing this a long, long time, after all. She'd started out small and worked her up. She'd made a few mistakes on the way—and a few of them had almost gotten her in trouble, but she'd lived and learned.

Along the way, she'd collected quite a few cards in her deck, including a cop, a news anchor over in Baton Rouge, more than a few businessmen throughout the state, a judge or two, and most recently, a damn state *senator.*

This latest one, though . . . oh, he was a feather in her cap.

She'd been trying for years to get this sort of mark. She checked the time as she killed the engine. She was early—very early. Roger was out of town. He told her he had a business thing to deal with, but she knew the truth. He had some stupid little trailer-trash whore about a half an hour away. Really, Shayla didn't care. She had her own fun, but she was careful when and where she took it.

She might take some of her fun tonight, even, after she dealt with business.

She got to the marina early and took her time setting up the cameras—there was the first one, set up in a fairly obvious manner. But the other one? That was the kicker and it took a few minutes.

The second one had to go in a place where it couldn't possibly be seen, but would still catch everything. She'd started doing this after one of her *clients*—really, that is how she saw them—had tried to get physical.

She was nervous.

This could be big—so big.

But that meant dangerous, too. The bigger the pig, the bigger the danger. But she'd stay in the light, by her car, keep her distance while they did business. If he tried to get too close or get her to walk anywhere with him? She had the sweet little handgun Roger had given her for Christmas. She was a damn good shot, too.

Minutes ticked by.

As the hour got later, Shayla's nerves got stronger and she checked her watch, checked the parking lot, listened hard. The narrow path that led her was so narrow and rutted with potholes big enough to bury a car, there was no way anybody could sneak up on her. He wasn't here.

What if he wasn't coming?

Swearing, she started to pace.

She'd been so certain.

Agitated, she checked the gravel road once more and then hurried over to the camera, giving it one final check.

Was that a car—

Something came around her throat.

"What—"

"Idiot." It was delivered in a cool, condescending voice. "You stupid cow, did you really think you could manipulate me so easily?"

He jerked harder. Shayla's feet left the ground and

terror had her reaching up, dragging her nails down the back of his hands, trying to claw her way free.

She couldn't breathe.

. . . couldn't . . . breathe . . .

He dropped her body to the ground, chest heaving as he struggled to slow his breathing. She was stronger than she'd looked. Stronger, and stupider.

Dead now.

He knelt by her side and touched her throat, just to be certain.

There was no pulse.

Her eyes were wide and fixed, staring up overhead.

He checked the camera she'd set up by her car. What had she planned to do? Immortalize her own stupidity?

Behind the mask he wore, he smiled.

In a way, she'd done just that.

They'd find her body. A murder in such a small town was rarely forgotten.

Her back braced against the tree, Hannah struggled not to make a sound.

He was moving through the trees now, quick and fast, and she was torn between taking off after him or rushing to Shayla's side. Okay, there was a third urge—the urge to tuck herself into a ball and hide, but she'd done that for too much of her life. She'd watched her mother get knocked around and she'd never done anything to help her.

But she could try to help Shayla.

Something too strong to be called frustration gnawed at her as she slipped around the tree, moving with care and watching the darkness around her, waiting for him to come back.

She clutched a heavy branch in one hand, the bark

all but cutting into her palm from how hard she gripped it. If she hadn't dropped and busted her phone, she could have already called for help.

But she was nearly a mile from the dock where she kept her houseboat.

Terror chittering inside, Hannah knelt by Shayla and had to swallow the urge to puke. She'd dealt with dead people before. She was a paramedic. It was almost a job requirement.

But she'd never *seen* anybody killed and her vision kept trying to gray out on her and her stomach was violently heaving.

Shayla's skin was still warm, her eyes wide open and staring.

With another look around, she bent over and straightened Shayla's neck. She'd try to resuscitate her for a minute, but if she didn't have any luck, she'd have to call for help. She fell into the rhythm and each second dragged by.

Nothing.

She bent over, blew another desperate breath into Shayla's mouth.

Breathe!

A branch cracked.

Jerking her head up, she stared into the darkness.

A shadow, darker than the rest.

Shit.

Jumping up, she grabbed the branch. Something clinked near her feet and she looked down.

Keys!

She swiped them and took off running, never more thankful for the running habit she'd developed back when she was struggling to lose weight in college.

She never ran fast, but the ground seemed to fly by

under her feet and she burst into the small parking lot just as she heard a low, ugly voice behind her.

He'd seen her.

She dove for Shayla's car. Phone. There'd be a phone—

Jerking on the handle, she shot one look back.

"Fuck the phone," she whispered. He was there, on the edge of the tree line and bearing down on her far faster than she could hope to move. Diving into the car, she fumbled the keys.

Darkness hid too much of him and she was too afraid to look at him as she threw the car into drive and punched the gas.

Shayla's sleek, sexy little Mustang convertible took off and she blasted by him just as he made a lunge for the car.

"Thank God." Hannah sucked in a gulp of air. "Thank God."

She started to shake but she fought the tremors back. She could go into shock later. Much later.

Darting a look down into the seat, she saw Shayla's phone. "Oh, thank God." She breathed out a sigh of relief and grabbed the phone. Chancing one look behind her, she whipped the wheel to the right.

She shot another look at the parking lot. It was empty, the brightly lit concrete square empty from the road to the river.

Daring to breathe out a tiny sigh of relief, she hit the screen. It was locked, but she had a similar model. Emergency calls.

Saying a prayer, Hannah dialied *9-1-1*.

When it started to ring, she almost began to cry.

"I need . . ." She gulped in. "This is Hannah Parker. I need to report a murder. Shayla—"

Somebody stumbled into the road and she jerked the wheel.

As she screamed, the call-taker calmly said, "Ma'am, please slow down . . ."

Too late.

The car hit the tree with a thunderous crash.

"I'm an idiot."

"You're not an idiot."

Neve glared balefully at her sister over a half-eaten slice of pizza. "I'm most definitely an idiot."

Moira swallowed the bite she'd just taken and then asked, "So are you ready to tell me what's wrong?"

"I just did." Dumping the slice on the plate, Neve put her food down and settled more comfortably into the couch. A movie played on the giant screen on the wall in front of them but she couldn't say what had happened. She was too busy brooding.

"Okay, not that I think you're an idiot, but how about you tell me what's up and then we discuss your idiot status."

"It's Ian . . ." Her voice tripped and then to her disgust, she started to cry.

"Hey, hey . . ."

Moira settled down next to her and she found herself wrapped in her sister's arms. It took forever and no time at all. When the storm ended, Moira murmured into her hair, "I think that was long overdue, sis."

Neve sniffled.

"Why don't you tell me what's going?"

"I'm an idiot."

"So you've said. But how about some details?"

Details? Squeezing her eyes shut, she pressed her face against Moira's shoulder. Then, slowly, she started to talk.

Moira listened without saying anything, but once she

finished, Moira brushed her hair back. "So, first thing . . . you're not an idiot. You went through hell and you panicked. Second thing, Ian's a great guy—and *he's* not an idiot. Chances are, he already knows all of this."

"I *was* stupid," Neve said, folding her arms across her belly and resting her head on the thickly padded back of the couch.

"Oh, stop. You're not an idiot." Moira turned to face her, crossing her legs. Clad in a cami and pajama bottoms, she still managed to look regal, like a queen. "You know what happened, I bet."

"I panicked." Swallowing, Neve looked away.

She'd freaked out over nothing.

Okay. Maybe it hadn't been *nothing*.

But she'd hurt Ian—she knew she had and for no good reason.

William had taken her over and she knew it. Looking back now, she could even see how clearly, how easily he'd manipulated her.

Ian, though, wasn't taking her over. He was filling her up. Filling up all those hollow and empty spaces and it felt *wonderful*.

She'd spent most of the day brooding over it and she needed to just call him. Or go see him.

She went to brush the idea aside.

"He works Fridays. He'll be there until two or three in the morning, I bet," Moira said.

For a moment, she just stared at her sister. No. She couldn't just up and go out there. It was already past ten.

But then . . .

She closed her eyes and saw his face in her mind.

Spinning away, she said, "I have to change."

Feeling a little lighter, Neve rushed through a shower and dressed in some of the new clothes she'd picked up a few days ago. Skinny skirt, a blue silk top with a draping neckline, heels.

She didn't let herself primp because she was already nervous. Besides, she looked good. One thing she knew how to do was turn herself out. Clothes were armor and she'd always armed herself well.

"Well, damn."

Coming up short in the doorway of the kitchen, Neve stared at Moira.

"What?" She shifted from one foot to the other.

"You look gorgeous." Moira held an unopened bottle of wine and a corkscrew. "So. Go get him."

"I don't know what to say," Neve said, moving to lean against the counter next to Moira.

"Oh, honey." Moira put down the wine bottle and hugged her sister. She gave her a quick hug and went back to opening the bottle. As she poured a glass, she continued to speak. "Look, this isn't the end of the world. You had a fight—they happen. Now you just have to talk to him."

Restless, Neve started to pace. "I don't . . . Moira, I don't know how to do relationships."

"Well, I'm with you there." Making a face, Moira lifted her wine and took a sip. "I'm not exactly a pro at them, as you well know. But I think the key here is just . . . let it happen."

"Let *what* happen?" Neve twisted her fingers together. "I . . . Moira, I feel crazy things for him and I barely know him."

"There's plenty of time for that. But Neve, sweetie, if you two could see the way you look together, the way you look *at* each other . . . you *fit*. I've never seen anybody fit together the way you two do." A faint smile curved her lips, sad and sweet. "Except maybe Mom and Dad."

"You and Gideon fit."

Moira closed her eyes. Then she took another drink of wine—a *huge* drink—tossing it back like it was whiskey. "We were young," she said softly. "We were very young and life was too complicated."

"It's always complicated." Neve almost let it go at that. "And you're not young now. And he still loves you."

Moira's response was the last thing Neve expected to hear. "I know." With a small shrug, Moira turned away.

"You know," Neve said slowly. "You still love him." This time, Moira said nothing, but Neve didn't let that deter her. "You know he still loves you and you still love him. What are you waiting for?"

"I hurt him," Moira said. "I did what was necessary—"

"It *wasn't* necessary but screw that. Forget about that. It's done. Worry about *now*." *Worry about now* . . . Neve drew in a breath. "And that's what I need to do."

"Sounds like good advice." Moira brooded into her wine. "So get out of here."

Neve moved to her sister and grabbed her in a tight hug as giddiness welled inside her.

"Hey," Moira said, laughing. "You're going to make me spill wine all over you."

"I'm going to stop this," she said, pulling back and staring at her sister. "I'm going to stop worrying about *everything*—sometimes I still feel like I'm trapped but it's my own fear doing it now, not William. I'm stopping this."

"Good."

Yeah . . . A smile bloomed across her face, a weight falling away. Yeah, it was good.

So William was lurking around somewhere. Maybe he was in town and maybe he wasn't, but she wasn't going to let him ruin any more of her life. She wasn't going to stay caged by fear and she wasn't going to let him control every action she did, even if it was just through the memories.

"I'm going to see Ian. I'm fixing this," she said. "And you should call Gideon."

"No, I . . ."

Narrowing her eyes, Neve grabbed Moira's phone from where she'd dropped it on the counter. As Moira tried to grab it, Neve backed away, pulling up Gideon's number. There was a picture of him, and Neve's heart twisted looking at it. "You still love him," she said. She dialed the number as Moira made another swipe for the phone. When Gideon came on the line, she said, "Moira needs to tell you something."

She didn't wait for his response, just passed the phone over. *Tell him,* she mouthed. Then she headed toward the door.

Moira sagged against the counter. "Gideon . . ."

She shot a look back over her shoulder, grinning at her sister as she went to open the door. "Hello, pet."

Oh, how he'd waited for this.

Neve stood in the doorway, staring at him as though she'd seen a ghost.

William relished every second of it, from the way her pupils dilated to the way her breathing began to race.

"Did you miss me, love?"

She clutched at the doorknob and he saw her muscles tighten. Throwing up a hand, he stopped her from slamming the door. Shoving his way inside, he reached out.

Neve backed away.

"Oh, don't do that," he said silkily. "I'm already cross with you."

"Get out." The words were steady and delivered in a steely voice.

"Come, Neve. We've so much to talk about."

"No."

Tensing, he turned his head and watched the other woman move into his line of sight. "You don't have *any-thing* to talk about."

The other woman was slim and slight, her features startling in their similarity to Neve's. She had a few lines around her eyes, though, and her voice was frosty.

"You must be Moira," he said.

"And you . . . I don't think I need an introduction." The smile Moira gave him was positively savage, like blood-drenched ice. "Now get the hell out of my house."

William studied her for a moment. That contemptuous look on her face made him want to strike it from her lovely face. But she wasn't who he'd come for. "I will. Now that I've got what I came for."

"If you think I'm leaving with you, you're out of your ever-loving mind."

He cut a look toward Neve. A ripple of surprise swept through him when she didn't back down.

No, she lifted her chin. Her mouth trembled and he could see the mad flutter of her pulse in her neck.

"Enough," he said.

"Are you *crazy*?" She backed away, stopping when she came up against the large island that dominated the brightly lit kitchen. "I'll come with you when *hell* freezes over."

"Darling." He sighed and smoothed a hand down his shirtfront. He really hadn't wanted it to come to this, but what was he to do? "You'll come *now*."

"Get out." Moira stepped in front of her sister and it was a comical sight. Neve was the taller of the two, her slender, elegant frame towering over the shorter woman, but Moira's protectiveness was undeniable.

Family was such a nuisance.

Although it could come in handy. "Neve," he said softly. "If you don't come with me now, it won't go well for you. Either of you."

"We're going in quiet," Gideon barked into his radio. "If I see a single light flashing or hear a fucking siren, I'm going to personally skin the son of a bitch responsible."

"Got it, Chief."

A moment later, another voice came over the radio. "Gideon, we'll get there. Just remember, this is my jurisdiction," Sheriff Tank Granger said, his voice firm. "I'm not letting some son of a bitch skate by on a technicality."

If Gideon accidentally killed the fucker, *technicalities* wouldn't be an issue.

He was there.

Gideon had been quietly searching for the man who'd laid his hands on Neve ever since she'd come home. But it had been a fruitless search and he had started calling any motel, hotel, or inn within an hour's drive. He hadn't seen William Clyde as the type to rough it.

He'd struck pay dirt—too late—when he'd run into Karen White, owner of Bygone Treasures, one of the few bed-and-breakfasts in town.

Too late. Too little, too late.

If Clyde hurt either of his ladies, there wouldn't be a hole dark enough or deep enough for him to hide in.

The miles sped by, his cruiser eating up the distance between the town and Ferry at a speed that would have made Brannon's driving look sedate. Dust flew up behind him as he whipped the car to the right at the intersection, finally on the road that led to McKay's Ferry—and his heart.

He'd get there.

Nothing would happen

Next to him, his phone remained on mute, playing out what was happening with Gideon a silent, helpless witness.

Neve's voice came through it, shaking, but strong. *"Get out of my house, William."*

There was a sharp cry in the next moment and Gideon tightened his hands on the steering wheel.

Ian climbed off his bike, staring up at the big house with trepidation. The nasty words painted on the fuel tank had been covered with a coat of primer, but he he hadn't decided on how he wanted the bike to look yet, so he was stuck with the dull gray. The whole ride out here, he'd wondered if he'd done the right thing, calling in his assistant manager to hold down the fort at the pub so he could come see Neve.

He almost knocked, but he was worried if he did, Neve might not answer.

He'd just let himself in.

They almost always kept the door off the kitchen open and more often than not, the family came and went through that door. So he'd just do that, too.

He hadn't managed to clear the corner of the sprawling home when he heard a roar coming up behind him.

Scowling, he turned his head.

His gut turned to shards of ice, deep and cutting, as he saw the line of police cars tearing up the drive toward him. Instinct screamed for him to take off, get inside that house and find Neve.

But he held still.

When Gideon came out of his car, all but exploding in a fury of motion and rage, Ian closed one hand into a fist.

Gideon saw him and beckoned him.

Ian looked back at the house and then shook his head, turning on his heel and taking off up the path that led to the house. He wouldn't get in the way. He'd do his best to *stay* out of the way.

But Neve was in there. Fuck them if they thought he'd just sit idly on by without knowing that she was safe.

The darkness, nearly complete, had him moving at a snail's pace up the cobbled pathway and he had to bite back a snarl of fury when hard hands grabbed him. He reacted out of habit, spinning to take the fucker down.

It didn't happen that way. Gideon wasn't quite as big as he was, but he was canny and quick, and the two of them had a brief tussle that ended with Ian being slammed against the wall.

"Stop," Gideon said, his voice a growling whisper. "Clyde's in there with Neve and Moira and if you get in my way, I'll see your ass in jail."

Mind-numbing panic and blood-boiling fury, they both blistered inside Ian, rising up in a storm that had him ready to explode. "I'll stay back." Abruptly, he shifted his weight and twisted, managed to break away from Gideon. Officers fanned out around him. He'd fight his way through every last one of them. But they might not have time. "I'll stay back. But I'm going up there."

Neve bit back a scream as Moira crumpled to the floor.

William had blood on his face and a fury unlike anything she'd ever witnessed lit his eyes.

He went to kick Moira as she rolled to her knees.

Neve leaped on him and her weight sent him staggering forward. "You bastard." Fear was an ugly red rose in her belly, but fury smashed it, choking it and strangling until it started to die. He'd hit her sister.

Fisting a hand in his hair, she jerked.

He'd hurt Moira.

His hands caught her hair and he yanked, trying to throw her off him but she'd wrapped her legs around him.

He reared back, driving her spine into the counter and she cried out as pain tore through her.

Then there was more pain and she heard a sickening wet *crack*.

Blood roared in her ears as he threw her off and she fell to the ground, clutching her left hand.

"I'll deal with you later," William said frostily.

Then he turned to Moira.

Moira had staggered her way upright, clutching at her side, and she stared at William, eyes gone to ice.

William started toward her.

Neve tried to fumble her way up, scrabbling at the surface of the island. Her hand brushed against something and she looked down. Time slowed as she curled her hand around the corkscrew, the sharp spiral still jutting out.

"Some man you are," Moira said, curling her lip. "You get your rocks off knocking women around?"

"I'll *get my rocks off,* as you crudely put it, when I shut you up, you frigid little bitch."

Neve slid off the island.

Her body didn't feel like her own.

The hand clutching the corkscrew could have belonged to a stranger.

And her voice, soft and strangely flat, sounded nothing like her as she said, "William."

He tossed her a dismissive look.

That look turned to shock as she swung up, burying the corkscrew in his neck.

He roared.

Neve jerked the utensil sideways as blood splashed out.

He gurgled.

And then, as she let go of the corkscrew, William Clyde slid to his knees, lifting a hand to his neck. Hot red blood spurted out.

The door crashed open.

Still feeling like she wasn't even part of herself, she lifted her head and watched as uniformed officers swarmed the room.

They went to block her view, but she stepped around them, going to her knees just at the edge of the ever-widening pool of blood.

William's eyes were closed.

"Neve . . ."

Warm arms caught her. "Ian . . ."

"Aye. I'm here, love. I'm here."

When he caught her up against him, she turned her face into his neck, closing her eyes against the river of red that soaked the floor of her family home.

CHAPTER NINETEEN

William was here.

Brannon fought the terror as he sped down the road.
He's dead. I think.

Moira's words circled through his head over and over
in an endless loop. His calm, cool, collected older sister
had spoken in a shaking voice and he could still hear the
panic that had underscored her voice.

Moira was *never* afraid. But she'd been petrified.

*William was here. He's dead. I think. Neve killed
him.*

His hands shook and he tightened them on the wheel.

If William Clyde *wasn't* dead, then Brannon would
rectify that.

He'd touched his sisters. The son of a bitch would die
for it.

Breathing through his teeth, fighting the urge to
pound something, he flicked a look at the clock.

When he looked up, he swore long and loud, slamming on the brakes with a force that all but shoved the
pedal through the floor of the car.

Joel Fletcher stumbled toward him.

"She's dead. I think . . . I think she's dead. I didn't . . ."

He sucked in a breath and then went to his knees on the shoulder as Brannon rolled down the window to tell him . . .

"Hannah," Joel croaked out.

Nothing else could have gotten through to him. Nothing but that single name. The words penetrated the fog of rage and fear and his aggravation stuttered, veered immediately into a whole new kind of terror.

Hannah. The woman he wanted more than he'd ever wanted anything—the woman he'd walked away from only hours before. *His* Hannah?

Throwing open the door, Brannan went to haul Joel back to his feet.

"She's dead. Hannah's dead . . ." The man wretched, then started to puke.

"Where's Hannah?" Brannon demanded in between spasms. Joel swayed and then lifted his head.

"Fletcher, talk!"

Something in his voice cut through and Joel raised a hand, waved toward the trees on the right side of the road. "She wrecked. I ran off the road and was walking . . . she . . . she almost hit me and crashed."

Brannon dropped Fletcher and turned, staring at the broken and busted greenery on the side of the road.

The red was buried in it, all but lost in the kudzu and grass.

That wasn't Hannah's car.

He started to breathe once more as he jogged over. Shayla. That was Shayla Hardee's car.

Okay, it was a bad wreck and as much as Shayla annoyed him, he hated to think of her being hurt. But it wasn't Hannah—

Long, golden hair shone through the window.

Brannon's world screeched to a grinding halt as his

gaze landed on the blooming red of blood that dripped down her still, lifeless face.

Gideon stood in the waiting room of the small county ER.

Small it might be, but the emergency department was state of the art. Gideon suspected there was a plaque somewhere with the McKay family name imprinted on it.

One of the women he loved was tucked away in one of the exam beds, with Ian Campbell at her side.

The other, Moira, sat on a chair a few feet away, her hands clenched into tight little fists while she stared stonily ahead.

He wanted to go to her.

But he couldn't.

Not yet.

"Dead," he said quietly after the deputy on the other end of the phone finished up a quick oral report. "You're telling me you found Shayla Hardee dead."

"Yeah." There was a pause and then Deputy Clayton Hodges said, "Hannah Parker was in her car when she wrecked. I know she runs out on the path by the river a lot. We're . . ." He hesitated and then continued. "We're thinking she saw something, maybe whoever hurt Shayla and was running away or found Shayla's keys or something. We don't have an official time of death, but Shayla's been dead a couple of hours. Dispatch had a call at approximately ten thirty-eight. The connection was touch and go, but the call taker says she thought it was Hannah. Hannah said something about somebody dead."

"She saw something."

"The sheriff was sending in someone to question her—"

"No point," Gideon said gruffly. "She's . . ." He closed his eyes and forced himself to steady out before he said it. "Hannah's in a coma. Doctors aren't sure if she'll wake up at this point or not."

"She'll wake up."

Hearing the low, determined voice, Gideon opened his eyes and stared at Griffin Parker.

The other man came out of his seat, glaring at Gideon, jaw tight and eyes resolute.

"Hey, Hodges. I'll get back to you. I'm going to keep a man on her door. We'll talk once you get up here."

He ended the call without waiting for a response.

Eyes on Griffin, he tucked his phone away. "Griffin—"

"She'll wake up!" Griffin said again.

The determination in the other man's voice had Gideon nodding. Sometimes, a man just had to believe.

"She'll wake up," Griffin said again, but his voice was softer, as if he had to convince himself now.

Gideon nodded. Reaching out, he rested a hand on Griffin's shoulder and squeezed. "Okay, then. I'm going to bet on you being right—and on Hannah. She's a tough woman, there's no doubt about that."

"Yeah." Griffin closed his eyes tight and sucked in a breath. "She's tough. And she will wake up."

"Chief."

They turned as one to look at the doctor, standing in the doorway of the waiting room, one hand on the wall. His face was grim, his eyes dark.

"No." Griffin's harsh voice drowned out the doctor's next words.

"She's still alive," Dr. Howard Briscoe reached up and tugged off his glasses, giving them a cursory wipe with a handkerchief he pulled from his pocket. He barely flicked a glance at anybody else, his gaze intent on Gideon and Griffin.

Too intent.

"What is it?"

The physician inclined his head and stepped back, holding up a badge to the electronic scanner near the door. It slid open with a hiss. "I think it's best if we speak . . . privately."

"Tests show swelling on the brain. Likely the cause of the coma. As she recovers . . ." Briscoe grimaced as he stood at the glass window, staring in at his patient. "It's entirely likely she'll wake up as the swelling goes down."

"But . . ."

"It's not much of a *but*." Briscoe nudged his glasses up his nose, the gesture an absent-minded one for a man who did the same thing a dozen times a day or more. Briscoe was a tall man, rail thin, his graying hair buzzed short. He was going bald, but he'd never been the vain type and didn't attempt to camouflage his slowly receding hairline. His eyes were hazel and studious, and still as grim as they'd been earlier.

"What is it?" Gideon asked when Briscoe tucked his hands into his pockets and continued to contemplate the silent form of Hannah Parker.

"We did some tests. Standard tests for all female patients."

He turned then, staring at Gideon, his gaze briefly flicking to Hannah's cousin, Officer Griffin Parker. Griff was her only living relative and he'd authorized Gideon's presence. Having a cop in the family made things easier sometimes.

Right now, Griffin watched on, eyes narrowed. He hadn't figured it out yet.

But Gideon had.

"Aw, hell," Gideon whispered. Turning away, he rubbed his hands up and down his face.

"Now wait a minute," Griffin broke in, his voice rough. "Are you telling me . . ." His gaze tripped over to his cousin, slid to her belly. There was no so sign of the baby growing there.

"She's pregnant," he said quietly.

Briscoe neither confirmed nor denied. After a moment, he said, "I've heard what happened—or what the police think happened. I know Shayla Hardee was murdered, that Hannah was in the area—or supposedly in the area. Is there . . ."

When he didn't continue, Gideon turned to him. "Is there what?"

Briscoe took a deep breath, as if bracing himself to speak. "Speculation is that she was there, saw what happened to Shayla—in the wrong place at the wrong time. But what if Shayla was the one at the wrong place at the wrong time?"

"What are you getting at, doctor?"

Briscoe scratched his chin. "Hannah is a runner. I see her down at the path along the river all the time when I'm out on my own run. Anybody who knows her is likely to know she'd be out there running. What if *she* was the target and Shayla was in the wrong place at the wrong time?"

"Doing my job now for me, doc?" Gideon scowled at the idea of what Briscoe was laying out. He didn't like the idea. At all.

"I'm just explaining that there are . . . interesting circumstances," Briscoe said, shrugging. "She's pregnant. Involved in something unusual and she's the only one who could shed light on what's going on."

Shit.

* * *

He looked like a maniac, busting through the doors—
and the truth of it was, if everybody in town wasn't
aware of who the wild-eyed man was, it was entirely
possible that the sober-eyed uniformed officer would
have been moving toward him with a weapon in hand.

As it was, Officer Griffin Parker caught sight of Brannon McKay and curled his lip.

He'd just wrapped his brain around the fact that his
cousin was in a coma and then he got slammed with the
new fact that she was pregnant and *now* he had accept
the possibility—slim as it was—that maybe *she* had
been the victim all along.

The last thing he needed to deal with was this prick.

It was respect for his boss and his badge that kept him
from turning away entirely.

But Chief Marshall had told him to keep an eye out
for McKay and to be honest, Griffin had his doubts
about whether or not the bastard would show up.

Looks like the chief called it again. Griffin tried not
to let his temper show as he cut McKay off. He didn't
want to be out here playing nice with some rich, entitled
prick. He wanted to be back there with his cousin. But
he was still on the clock and that meant the job came
first.

Marshall had given him fifteen minutes of personal
time to sit with Hannah and get his head on straight, and
by the time he came back out here, he had to admit—
yes, maybe he could see why the doctor and Marshall
were concerned. No, it *wasn't* likely that Hannah had
been the target, but yeah, everybody knew she was down
at the park all the time running. Nobody ever saw Shayla
down there. She was even known to say that she preferred to do her sweating *indoors, thank you very much,
where there are showers to be had when it's all done.*

People could tell the day and time by when her damn red car was parked outside the gym—Mondays, Wednesdays, and Fridays from eight to ten and Thursdays from one to three.

Fuck, Griffin hated himself, but he hoped she'd been the target and not his cousin.

Some weird shit was going on and somebody might be trying to hurt Hannah.

As Brannon McKay came striding toward him, he crossed his arms over his chest and pasted a bland smile on his face.

Nobody got back to talk to Hannah without the chief's okay.

Including Mr. Megabucks here.

As far as Griffin was concerned, Mr. Megabucks didn't ever need to talk to his cousin again. Unless it was over a child support hearing. Griffen already knew who the daddy was. Then he could bleed zeroes for being an asshole.

"Hey there, McKay." Griffin gave him an easy smile. Nobody had to know that he felt like punching the bastard. Griffin and Hannah were close. Maybe they didn't sit around and braid each other's hair but he knew his cousin and the woman was in love with this prick. Brannon McKay probably didn't love anything other than his cars and himself. Maybe his sisters. But Hannah hurt over him.

"Out of my way, Parker," McKay said, the words coming out in a low, nearly soundless whisper.

"Can't do that." He gave a mock grimace. "Hannah's condition is pretty serious." He paused and then added, "I assume you *are* here to see her. I think your sisters are down the other hallway—unless they've already come and gone?"

"Get out of my way," McKay said again.

Griffin just smiled. "Come on, now. Shouldn't you be sitting with Neve, patting her hand? She could have been killed tonight. Her and Moira both."

McKay just stared at him coldly.

"That's what I thought."

Unblinking green eyes simply held his and Griffin suspected this could continue indefinitely. He crossed his arms over his chest and settled himself more comfortably.

McKay did the same thing.

His suspicion on how long this might last wasn't tested, though.

The doors opened with a light *swish* behind him in the next moment and he heard a familiar voice. "Brannon. Had a feeling you'd show up."

The affable smile on Griffin Parker's face didn't fool Brannon at all. He had to admit, Gideon's timing was spot-on. If he hadn't shown up, Brannon might have done something stupid. Something like gotten into a fistfight with a cop. He thought he could probably take Parker. He was bigger, and he suspected he was stronger. He had a healthy respect for the skinny wiry type—he'd seen that sort lay a person out flat quicker than it seemed possible, but he'd tangled with his share of skinny wiry types, plus, he'd seen Griffin taking a go at both Gideon and Ian down at the gym.

It might have landed his ass in jail for a while, but Brannon would have had a chance to see Hannah with his own eyes and know she was alive, breathing.

Gideon had saved him from that particular complication and for a while yet, he could say he still hadn't seen the inside of a jail. As he cut around Griffin Parker, he gave Gideon a hard look. "I'm seeing her," he said flatly.

Gideon inclined his head. "Maybe in a bit. We need to talk first."

That wasn't a *no*. Running his tongue across his teeth, Brannon debated and then he gave a quick nod. "As long as you keep it short. I need to see her."

"You can't be alone," Gideon advised.

"Fine." As long as he got to see her. His gut had been in a tangle ever since he'd heard the news.

He'd gone to Neve first.

It had taken him too long to get to his sister, because he'd stood by helpless, as paramedics cut Hannah out of the mangled car, then loaded her into the ambulance. The doors had swung shut before he even had a chance to try and leap in.

So he'd had to follow, emergency flashers on. Heaven help the person who tried to pull him over or slow him down.

They hadn't let him into the emergency room and nobody had told him shit. He'd gone to see Neve and Moira, his older sister's words still playing in his head. *William was here* . . .

But for the first time in his life, he'd been torn between the love for his sisters and his need for Hannah. He'd clung to his siblings, breathed out silent prayers of relief over their safety.

And all the while, he'd worried over Hannah.

He'd had ten calls—most of them about the wreck, but three different people had told him a bunch of twisted-up shit—Shayla Hardee was dead, Joel Fletcher had made Hannah wreck and she'd been driving Shayla's car.

What in the hell was going on?

Not seeing Hannah was driving him nuts.

"Parker."

Gideon's brusque voice caught Brannon's attention

and he looked up just as Gideon gave his officer orders
to take over for Ruiz.

Ruiz—an image flashed through Brannon's mind.
Petite woman. Hispanic. Short cap of black hair, big dark
eyes that should have looked soft, but they were wicked
sharp and could go hard as nails in a blink. Maria Ruiz.
"You've got cops on Hannah's door," he said softly.

Gideon lifted a brow. "Yes, we do."

"Why?"

"That's my concern, Bran."

Brannon dragged his hands down his face. "Let me
see her," he said abruptly.

"We discussed this."

"For fuck's sake," he snarled, whirling on Gideon.
"Just walk me by her damn door. I need to see that
she's . . ." His breath caught in his chest. "I have to know
she's okay. That's she . . . she's . . ."

He couldn't even finish it.

He couldn't say the fear that had taken root inside
him when he'd heard that she'd been in an accident.

All of his fears, all of them, had happened in one
day.

Neve.

Moira.

Hannah.

"I'm fine." Neve sat on the edge of the bed, glaring at
the doctor who stood in the doorway. "I want to leave."

No, *want* didn't describe it.

She *had* to leave. Just *being* here was wearing her
composure thin and she could feel it shuddering under
the weight of the storm building inside her. She was
cold—*freezing*. Ice wrapped around her and she had the
bizarre image in mind of an icicle dome while a storm
raged inside.

"Ms. McKay, you had a rather traumatic experience. You were in shock when you came in."

You were in shock. The words bounced around in her head, refusing to connect, refusing to make sense. They were like raindrops pounding down on that barrier of ice.

And the ice was breaking.

"I was in shock," she said slowly, taking care with each word. She nodded. "Yeah. I guess I was in shock. My former boyfriend comes after me, forces his way into the house, hurts my sister, breaks two of my fingers and then hey . . . I shoved a corkscrew into his . . ."

Her breathing hitched.

She twisted her fingers in the sheet, fisting it and tugging on it, and she could feel another crack splinter through the ice blocking out her emotions.

Breathe, she told herself. *You have to breathe.*

"He's dead," she said when she thought she could speak. "William is dead."

Chunks of ice started to tremble and the ice barrier shuddered.

"Ms. McKay—"

"He's dead!" she shouted and then clapped a hand over her mouth. Moaning, she started to rock.

"Hey, hey . . ." Ian shouldered past the doctor and crouched on the floor in front of her.

He caught her shoulders and shook her lightly, forcing her to look at him. "Look at me," he said. He stroked his hand up her forearm. "Neve, look at me."

She did.

He rested a hand on her cheek. "It's alright. Neve, it's going to be alright."

She sucked in a breath. "Ian . . ."

"It's alright." He leaned in and pressed a quick, hard kiss to her lips.

She reached out and fisted her hand in his shirt.

Alright . . . it's alright. She hadn't been able to believe *anything* could be alright for so long. Because of William.

He was gone now.

Gone because . . . "I killed him," she whispered.

"You didn't have a choice." Ian brushed her hair back and rested a hand on her cheek.

"He's dead." She sucked in a breath and whispered it again, "He's dead . . . and I killed him."

The painful crack in her chest seemed to echo in the sob that tore out of her. Ian moved onto the bed and pulled her into his lap. She didn't see the fulminating look Ian shot the doctor over her head.

She closed her eyes and blood spread across her mind. William's blood. She could still feel it, hot on her hands, and she could still see it pulsing out of him in an arcing spray of red.

As the rest of the ice shattered and fell to pieces, Neve looked up at Ian. "I killed him. Shouldn't . . ." She swallowed. "Shouldn't I feel guilty?"

"That's just shite." Ian spoke against her temple, his brogue thickening, his voice so rough and low. And his arms around her were secure and strong. "You should feel what you feel—not what you *think* you should feel. He was a man who hurt you, love. He hurt you terribly and now he's gone. You don't have to feel guilty for that, or anything." He tugged lightly on her hair, drawing her gaze to him as he leaned back. "Well, except maybe not leaving me a piece of him."

For a moment, she just stared at him and then she started to giggle. Even to her own ears, the laughter seemed too close to hysteria. But she didn't care.

She'd take hysteria over the numbness.

Ian rocked her, one hand tangling in her hair.

"He can't hurt me anymore. It's . . ." She sucked in a breath. "He can't hurt me anymore. It's over."

It's over.

As Gideon Marshall pulled his cruiser up in front of the police department, Clive Owings studied the camera he'd found. There were days when he could scrounge around and not find much more than loose change and empty Coke cans. But then he'd hit pay dirt.

Once he'd stumbled across a billfold with nearly two hundred dollars cash—and a license, but he didn't see why he should be responsible for somebody else's carelessness. He'd dumped the license in the trash outside the pub and used the cash to buy himself the best damn dinner he could: steak and a baked potato and green beans, plus the best damn whiskey that putz Campbell could afford. It had been one hell of a night.

Another time, he'd come across a gold Rolex. It had taken a jaunt into Baton Rouge to find a man to buy it— idiots these days had no idea what it meant to *lose* something. You *lost* it, it just ain't yours anymore. Too many pawnshops asking nosy questions, so it wasn't like he got top dollar for the thing—it was worth more than the three hundred he'd gotten for it, but he'd gotten that three hundred with no questions asked.

Everything was a trade-off.

He didn't think he'd be able to do much with the camera. It wasn't a bad model and he'd bet his eyeteeth it was fairly new, but the scratches on it were problematic.

Still, he might be able to do something with it.

He popped out the SD card and carefully put it in his wallet and then fiddled around with the settings until he found out how to reformat it. He'd hoped he'd find something that would get him another decent meal. Half his money from the factory, it seemed like it went to child support.

Support, his ass.

That money didn't go to take care of his kids. His ex-wife Linda hadn't *needed* his money, not with her working for the only decent-sized law firm in the area. She was a paralegal, but she made good money and she could have taken care of those kids just fine. Especially since her parents had left her the house.

But she'd taken him to the cleaners and now the only money he could call *his* was the money he made on his little field trips. People were always losing shit.

And Clive was a finder.

Too bad he hadn't found much more than the camera today. He couldn't even try to sell it around here.

Absently, he looked up as Chief Gideon Marshall slammed the door to his cruiser shut and headed up the walk to the police department. Clive put the camera down, keeping it out of sight of the chief. He was one of the idiots who didn't get the *lost* thing, for sure.

Clive had found a cell phone once—it had been one of the first things he'd found and he figured out how easy it was, making money off those things. Granted, he hadn't earned the money because he sold the phone. Not after the pawnshop owner made sure to let Gideon know a phone belonging to one of the call-takers at the small dispatch center had been found—that asshole at the pawnshop had tried to get Clive arrested, all because he'd found something.

No, Clive had earned his money because he'd seen the pictures on said phone. Then he'd talked to the owner and . . . discussed a few things. He was entitled, he figured, to a finder's fee. And he'd be happy to destroy the copies he'd made if she'd just pay him two hundred, cash.

Not that he'd made any copies, but the stupid woman hadn't known that.

He'd take a look at the camera's SD card later, see if he could find anything useful on it. Who knows? It might make him more money than he thought. Cheered by the thought, he turned back to the other items he'd found out on the path that led out to the river.

Runners were always dropping shit.

CHAPTER TWENTY

"I'll get you home." Ian tucked Neve's hair back behind her ear. "You'll rest."

She caught his hand before he could shut the door. Apparently he did have a car—something other than the bike. She wished he'd brought the bike, though. She'd rather ride pressed up against him. Sitting there in the passenger seat of his Jeep, she felt cold.

And tired.

Tired . . . but oddly enough, she felt easier now than she had in a while.

William was *gone*.

"I was coming to see you," she said softly.

He leaned in, one arm braced on the car as he studied her. "Were you now?"

"Yeah." Licking her lips, she tightened her fingers on his hand. "I'd figured something out. And I had to apologize."

Ian sighed, looking away. "You don't owe me an apology, Neve. I *was* rushing things."

"No." She tugged on his hand until he looked back at her. "I think . . . I got scared, because you feel too right to me, Ian. I don't trust good things. I don't believe in good things. But . . . I . . . I believe in you."

"Neve." He bent in, ducking his head to avoid the top of the car.

He didn't kiss her though. He tangled a hand in her hair and pressed his brow to hers.

"I want to believe this isn't going to blow up on me," she said, forcing herself to go on. "Everything good that happens to me seems to not be so good after all. It started when my parents . . ."

He lifted his head and she looked away as she continued. "They were taking me out the night they died, you know. I'd gotten good grades and they always tried to treat each of us, by ourselves, from time to time. I'd gotten good grades and we were going to get tacos. They did. I still hate tacos."

Ian rubbed his thumb across her cheek.

"You feel so right to me—you feel . . . *good*," she said. Her heart slammed as he stared into her eyes and she managed a weak smile. "I panicked and I guess it's because *good* things never last. Not for me."

"I'll last."

Under the intense warmth of his gaze, she realized she was breathing fast. Hard and fast and her heart was racing. "I want to believe that."

"Then believe it." He pressed his thumb to her mouth when she tried to say something.

Yielding to the silent request that she listen, she waited.

"I can't promise that nothing bad will ever happen to me. Life can be a horrid bitch, Neve." He leaned in, replacing his thumb with his lips, a quick, hard kiss. "But I can promise I won't hurt you. I can promise I want nothing more than to see you smiling at me, day after day. I can promise that no woman has ever crawled inside me, gotten in my blood the way you have. I can promise you that for as long as you want me—and as long as life lets me—I'll be here."

"Talk about rushing it," she said weakly.

"I . . ." He blew out a breath. "I'm sorry. See, I told you I was rushing—"

It was her turn to silence him, pressing her finger to his mouth. His beard was silky soft and she scraped her nails lightly through it before sliding her hand around to cradle the back of his neck. "I can promise you the same things. Maybe we are rushing it, Ian. But I can't think of anybody who's ever made me happy—not like this. Not like I am with you."

His heart pounded.

His hands were shaking.

Without letting himself think it through, Ian tugged her out of the car. Oh, he wanted to get the hell out of here, but he couldn't think of anything he wanted more in that moment than to pull her up against him and hold on tight.

She came to him, wrapping her arms around him and burying her face against his neck.

He opened his mouth to speak, but couldn't find the words.

The only thing that came to him was her name.

"Neve."

She seemed to hear all the things he didn't know how to articulate, clutching him tighter and tighter.

"Take me home, Ian."

"Aye." He nodded and went to pull back. "I'll get you to Ferry, then."

"No." She made a face then and said, "Okay. We can go to Ferry for a little bit. I need to see Moira, talk to Brannon. But then I want to go back to your place. I just want to be with you right now."

"Well." He rubbed his cheek against hers. "I think I can do that easily enough."

He straightened, and she smiled at him before turning back to the car.

Abruptly she stopped and looked back at him. "You know, I was expecting a lot of things when I came back to Treasure, Ian. But I sure as hell wasn't expecting you. I half expected everybody I met to laugh at me. I was just Trouble, after all. That was what everybody called me."

He leaned in, caught her lower lip between his teeth. "Is that a fact?" Ian lifted his head and nudged her into the car. "Just goes to show how stupid some people are, Neve. Don't you know the best things in life are worth a little bit of trouble?"

Read on for an excerpt from the next book by
SHILOH WALKER

TROUBLE WITH TEMPTATION

Coming soon from St. Martin's Paperbacks

His eyes strayed to Hannah's and lingered and she felt her heart skip a few beats in that moment.

"Hell. That's romantic," Griffin said. Then he blew out a breath. His eyes narrowed on Brannon and he studied the other man for a long moment.

When he held out a hand, Hannah felt something in her chest knot up.

Watching the two men make some move toward friendship had her feeling all stupid and sappy and weepy.

She was going to claim pregnancy hormones.

She was almost a month along.

She could do that, right?

It took just a few more minutes for them to be alone and Hannah found herself more self-conscious than she could ever remember feeling. Of course, there was still plenty she didn't remember, so that wasn't saying much. Still, as Brannon finished locking up the door, she busied herself in the kitchen with stupid little things that didn't need doing—like washing her hands, again, and wiping down a counter that didn't need to be wiped down.

Her head was a muzzy, hazy mess and her body ached with fatigue. She was worn out.

Of course, that could have something to do with the fact that she was still struggling to recover from the crash, the coma . . . coming to grips with the baby, the amnesia. All of the above.

The reality of it all crashed into her and she turned, leaning back against the counter. Covering her belly with her hands, she lifted her gaze to Brannon's and just stared at him.

"I don't even know what's going on with my life right now," she said bluntly. "My head is spinning so fast, I don't know what to make of anything."

He came to her.

She held still as he cupped her face in long-fingered hands.

His touch made her want to shiver.

His touch made her want to sigh.

Then he brushed his lips across her forehead and she wanted to curl herself around him, cling tight and never, ever let him go.

"Six days ago, you were in a coma. A few weeks ago, you were in a wreck that could have killed you. I think you just need to tell your head to slow down so the rest of you can catch up."

She laughed and the half-manic edge in it had her cringing. "You think that will work?"

Instead of answering, Brannon brought her in closer. "Just slow down," he murmured against her brow. "Let yourself catch up."

"I think . . ." She held onto his waist. "I'll just stay right here."

"That sounds good."

Brannon closed his eyes and rested his head against the soft silk of her hair.

She relaxed against him and he was able to push the guilt away. She wanted him there. She'd said as much.

She seemed less . . . haunted.

Yeah.

That word fit.

She'd hidden it well, but during the day, as people came and went, she had been tense and on edge. But now as the quiet wrapped around the two of them, that tension began to drain away. Smoothing a hand up and down her back, he closed his eyes and turned his face into the softness of her hair.

How had he thought he didn't want this?

He must have been crazy. Or stupid. Or both.

Her lips brushed against his neck as she sighed and it sent a rush of heat through him, but he shoved it down. He thought maybe he'd ask her if she wanted him to spend the night. On the couch, that was all. But she might feel better if he was there, right? Yeah, maybe—

Her lips brushed against his neck again and he couldn't stop the low, unsteady breath that escaped him.

Hannah eased away, looking at him from under her lashes.

Her tongue slid out, wet her lips and he had to clench his jaw, remind himself of just how fragile she was right now—not just physically, either. He could still see fading bruises on her face, the fading pink marks on her hands from where she'd been cut when the car wrecked.

It got so much harder to remember that when she reached up and touched his mouth.

"I know we've kissed," she said, her voice low and husky. "Sometimes, I almost think I remember it. But then it's gone. And it's driving me crazy."

"Hannah . . ."

Her gaze dropped to his mouth, lingered there a moment and then she looked back at him.

Her eyes were huge and dark, a heat burning there that threatened to consume him—and damn if he'd mind.

"I want that memory back, Brannon. I want to know how you taste, how your mouth feels on mine. Will you kiss me?"

Well, hell. It would take a stronger man than him to walk away from that.

Cupping her face in his hands, he arched her head back. Their first kiss had been a mix of fury and frustrated passion. This one wouldn't be like that. He'd kiss her the way he should have kissed her to begin with.

Slowly, he lowered his head, brushing his mouth against hers, once, twice.

Her lips parted on a sigh.

But he didn't take that offering just yet.

Instead, he caught her lower lip between his and sucked lightly, listening as her breathing hitched. Her hands came up to grasp his waist and he moved in closer, letting his body rest against the powerhouse curves of hers.

She made a hungry noise in her throat and opened her mouth under his.

Still, he didn't deepen the kiss—much.

He traced the line of her lips with his tongue, learning the curves as if this was the first time he'd ever had the chance. For her, it was. Maybe it was for him, too. They'd start over. Completely over. And he'd make sure that this time she knew she mattered to him.

Hannah grew impatient and tried to take control of the kiss, her tongue coming out to curl and stroke against his. He eased back, whispering against her lips. "You wanted me to kiss you, baby."

"Then do it." She bit his lower lip.

That demanding nip set his blood to boiling but he kept an iron grip on his control, teasing the entrance of her mouth with quick, light strokes. She caught his tongue and sucked on him and the blood began to drain southward, his cock thickening.

Just a kiss, he told himself. *Just a kiss.*

Her hands slid down to grab his hips, pulling him more firmly against her and he had to keep reminding himself that this was *just* a kiss. Nothing more.

Her breathing sped up.

His heart pounded harder, faster.

The taste of her flooded him as he sought out the hidden depths of her mouth, learning her in a way he'd never taken the time to do before.

She began to move against him, her hips circling impatiently. But he was still in control. He thought. Right up until she slid a hand between them. A shudder wracked him as she stroked him through his jeans.

Aw, fuck . . .